BURNABLE
Book

BRUCE
HOLSINGER

HARPER

Harper
An imprint of HarperCollins*Publishers*
77–85 Fulham Palace Road,
Hammersmith, London W6 8JB

www.harpercollins.co.uk

This paperback edition 2014
1

A catalogue record for this book
is available from the British Library

ISBN: 978 0 00 749332 6

This novel is entirely a work of fiction. The names,
characters and incidents portrayed in it are the work of the
author's imagination. Any resemblance to actual persons, living
or dead, events or localities is entirely coincidental.

Set in Sabon by Palimpsest Book Production Limited,
Falkirk, Stirlingshire

Printed and bound in Great Britain by
Clays Ltd, St Ives plc

MIX
Paper from
responsible sources
FSC
www.fsc.org **FSC C007454**

*For my mother,
Sheila,
who taught me to write*

CAST OF CHARACTERS

ENGLISH ROYALS, MAGNATES, AND RELATIONS

Richard II, *King, son of Prince Edward (the Black Prince)*
John of Gaunt, *Duke of Lancaster, brother of Prince Edward*
Henry of Bolingbroke, *son and heir to John of Gaunt*
Joan, *Countess of Kent, mother of King Richard II*
Robert de Vere, *Earl of Oxford*
Stephen Weldon, *knight of Oxford's faction*
Katherine Swynford, *governess and consort to John of Gaunt, sister-in-law of Geoffrey Chaucer*
Robert Braybrooke, *Bishop of London*
William Wykeham, *Bishop of Winchester*
Michael de la Pole, *Baron de la Pole and Lord Chancellor of England*
Isabel Syward, *Prioress of St Leonard's Bromley*

OFFICERS OF THE CITY OF LONDON AND SERVANTS OF THE CROWN

Thomas Pinchbeak, *serjeant-at-law*

Ralph Strode, *common serjeant of London*
James Tewburn, *his clerk*
Thomas Tyle, *King's Coroner of London*
Nicholas Symkok, *clerk to the King's Coroner*
Richard Bickle, *goldsmith of London, beadle of Cheap Ward*
Thomas Tugg, *keeper of Newgate Prison*
Geoffrey Chaucer, *controller of the wool custom*
Philippa Chaucer, *his wife, sister of Katherine Swynford*

COMMON WOMEN OF LONDON AND SOUTHWARK

Eleanor/Edgar Rykener, *maudlyn of Gropecunt Lane*
Mary Potts, *maudlyn of Gropecunt Lane*
Agnes Fonteyn, *maudlyn of Gropecunt Lane*
Joan Rugg, *their bawd*
Bess Waller, *bawd of the Pricking Bishop; mother of Agnes
   and Millicent Fonteyn*
St Cath, *maudlyn of the Pricking Bishop*

TRADESMEN, FREEMEN OF LONDON AND SOUTHWARK, AND COMMONERS

John Gower *of Southwark, esquire and poet*
Will Cooper, *his servant*
Simon Gower, *his son, clerk to Sir John Hawkwood*
Mark Blythe, *mason of Southwark*
George Lawler, *spicerer of Cornhull*
Jane Lawler, *his wife*
Denise Haveryng, *widow of Cornhull*
Nathan Grimes, *master butcher of Cutter Lane, Southwark*
Tom Nayler, *his first apprentice*

Gerald Rykener, *his second apprentice and ward; brother of Eleanor/Edgar*

Millicent Fonteyn, *singlewoman of Cornhull; sister of Agnes Fonteyn*

Sam Varney, *gravedigger*

IN OXFORD

Peter de Quincey, *keeper of the books of Durham*

John Clanvowe, *knight of the King's Chamber*

John Purvey, *curate of Lutterworth, disciple of John Wycliffe*

IN FLORENCE

John Hawkwood, *mercenary knight, chief of the White Company*

Adam Scarlett, *his chief lieutenant*

Jacopo da Pietrasanta, *his chancellor*

Giovanni Desilio, *doctor of the Studium Generale, Siena*

King Edward III m. Philippa of Hainault
(1312–1377)   (c.1311–1369)

Edward Prince of Wales
'The Black Prince'
(1330–1376)
m.
Joan of Kent
Countess of Kent
(1328–)

Lionel of Antwerp
Duke of Clarence
(1338–1368)
m.
(1) Elizabeth de Burgh
(1332–1363)
(2) Violante Visconti
(1353–)

Edward of Lancaster
(1365–1372)

King Richard II
(1367–)
m.
Anne of Bohemia
(1366–)

Philippa
(1355–c.1380)
m.
Edmund
Mortimer
Earl of March
(c.1352–1381)

Philippa
(1360–1415)

Elizabeth
(1364–)

Henry Bolingbroke
(1367–)
m.
Mary de Bohun
(1368–)

Deceased:
John (by 1364)
Edward (1365)
John (1366)
Isabella (1368)

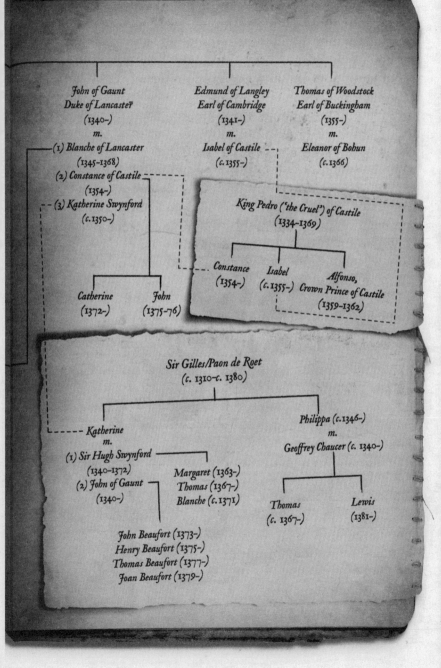

John of Gaunt
Duke of Lancaster
(1340–)
m.
(1) Blanche of Lancaster
(1345–1368)
(2) Constance of Castile
(1354–)
(3) Katherine Swynford
(c.1350–)

Edmund of Langley
Earl of Cambridge
(1341–)
m.
Isabel of Castile
(c.1355–)

Thomas of Woodstock
Earl of Buckingham
(1355–)
m.
Eleanor of Bohun
(c.1366)

King Pedro ('the Cruel') of Castile
(1334–1369)

Constance
(1354–)

Isabel
(c.1355–)

Alfonso,
Crown Prince of Castile
(1359–1362)

Catherine
(1372–)

John
(1375–76)

Sir Gilles/Paon de Roet
(c. 1310–c. 1380)

Philippa (c.1346–)
m.
Geoffrey Chaucer (c. 1340–)

Katherine
m.
(1) Sir Hugh Swynford
(1340–1372)
(2) John of Gaunt
(1340–)

Margaret (1363–)
Thomas (1367–)
Blanche (c.1371)

Thomas
(c. 1367–)

Lewis
(1381–)

John Beaufort (1373–)
Henry Beaufort (1375–)
Thomas Beaufort (1377–)
Joan Beaufort (1379–)

At Prince of Plums shall prelate oppose
A faun of three feathers with flaunting of fur,
Long castle will collar and cast out the core,
His reign to fall ruin, mors regis to roar.
    By bank of a bishop shall butchers abide,
To nest, by God's name, with knives in hand,
Then springen in service at spiritus sung.
    In palace of prelate with pearls all appointed,
By kingmaker's cunning a king to unking,
A magnate whose majesty mingles with mort.
    By Half-ten of Hawks might shender be shown.
On day of Saint Dunstan shall Death have his
    doom.

The thirteenth prophecy, from
Liber de Mortibus Regum Anglorum
('Book of the Deaths of English Kings')

Prologue

Moorfields, north of the walls

Under a clouded moon Agnes huddles in a sliver of utter darkness and watches him, this dark-cloaked man, as he questions the girl by the dying fire. At first he is kind seeming, almost gentle with her. They speak something like French: not the flavour of Stratford-at-Bowe nor of Paris, but a deep and throated tongue, tinged with the south. Olives and figs in his voice, the embrace of a warmer sea.

He repeats his last question.

The girl is silent.

He hits her.

She falls to the ground. He squats, fingers coiled through her lush hair.

'*Doovay leebro?*' he gently chants. '*Ileebro, mee ragazza. Ileebro.*' It could be a love song.

The girl shakes her head. This time he brings a fist, loosing a spray of blood and spittle from her lips. A sizzle on a smouldering log. Now he pulls her up, dangling her head before him, her body a broken doll in his hands. Another blow, and the girl's nose cracks.

1

'*Ileebro.*' Screaming at her now, shaking her small frame.

'*Nonloso!*' she cries. '*Nonloso, seenoray.*' She spits in his face.

He releases her and stands. Hands on his knees, he lets fly a string of words. Agnes can make nothing of them, but the girl shakes her head violently, her hands clasped in prayer.

'*No no no, seenoray, no no no.*' She screams, sobs, now whimpers as her softening cries fade into the silence of the moor.

When she is still he speaks again. '*Doovay leebro?*'

This time the girl hesitates. Moonlight catches the whites of her eyes, her gaze darting toward the dense foliage.

In the thick brush Agnes stiffens, ready to spring. The moment lengthens. Finally, in the clearing, the girl lowers her head. '*Nonloso.*' Her voice rings confident this time, unafraid.

The man raises a hand. In it he clutches a stick of some kind. No, a hammer. 'This is your last chance, my dear.'

Agnes's limbs go cold. *Perfect gentleman's English.* More than that, she knows this man's voice, has heard it close to her ear, though she can't summon the face. One of a thousand.

Now the girl throws back her head, lips parted to the dark sky, the dread ascending in a last flux of words: '*Though faun escape the falcon's claws and crochet cut its snare, when father, son, and ghost we sing, of city's blade beware!*'

English again, brushed with an accent, confusing the night with these strange portents hurled at the stars. She's taunting him, Agnes thinks. He hesitates, the hammer still in the air.

Finally it descends. There is a glint of iron, and a sound Agnes will never forget.

✤

For hours Agnes waits, as the moon leaves the sky, as the din of night creatures falls slowly into a bottomless silence. Now dawn, birdsong mingling with the distant shouts of

2

workingmen within the city walls. The priory rings Lauds, and light rises across the moor.

Time to move. She arms aside a span of branches, scoring her wrists on dense clusters of twigs and nubs. A tentative foot out among the primrose, a pale blanket of scent.

Her gaze glides over the clearing: the lean-to, the remnants of the fire, the body. Her killer has stripped the girl to the flesh. Not with unthinkable intent, but with a deliberation that makes clear his aim. He was searching her, picking at her, like a wolf at a fresh kill. No rings on the delicate fingers, no brooch at the slender neck, though a silver bracelet circles her wrist. With her right hand Agnes clumsily unclasps it, admiring the small pearl pendant, the delicate chain. She pockets it. The only other item of value is a damask dress, tossed over a rotten log. Too big and bulky to carry into the city, and too fine for Agnes to wear.

Her left arm, still pinned at her side, aches. The small bundle has been clutched too tightly to her breast, almost moulded to her body. A thousand thorns wake her limb as she examines what the doomed girl thrust wordlessly at her hours ago. A bright piece of cloth, tied in leather cord, wrapped around a rectangular object of some kind. She collapses on a high stone and rests the bundle on her knees. With one tug the cord comes free.

A book. She opens it, looking for pictures. None. She tosses the thin manuscript to the ground.

What she notices next is the cloth. A square of silk, the embroidery dense and loud, the whole of it still stiff with the volume's shape. She spreads the cloth to its full span. Here is a language she reads: of splits and underside couching, of pulled thread and chain stitch, an occulted story told in thread of azure, gold, and green. At the centre of the cloth appear symbols that speak of ranks far above hers. Here a boy, there a castle, there a king; here lions rampant, there lilies of France; here a sword, there a shield.

Agnes knows something of livery, suspects the import of what she holds. A woman has just died for it, a man has just killed. For what? She remembers the girl's last, haunting words.

> *Though faun escape the falcon's claws and crochet*
> *   cut its snare,*
> *When father, son, and ghost we sing, of city's blade*
> *   beware!*

The rhythm of a minstrel's verse, one she has never heard. Yet the rhyme will not leave her mind, and she mouths it as she thinks her way back through the walls. Which road is less likely to be watched, which gate's keepers less likely to bother with a tired whore, some random maudlyn dragging it into London at this hour?

Cripplegate. Agnes takes a final kneel next to the dead girl and whispers a prayer. She retrieves the book and wraps it once more in the cloth, hiding them both in her skirts.

Soon she has left the Moorfields and traced a route below the causeway, circling north of a city suddenly foreign to her, though she has spent nearly all her life between its many gates. She enters London dimly aware that she holds things of great value on her person and in her mind, though unsure what to do with any of them, nor what they mean, nor whom to trust.

A cloth, a book, a snatch of verse.

Which is worth dying for?

PART ONE

The Prince of Plums

*Day xv before the Kalends of April
to the Ides of April, 8 Richard II
(18 March–13 April 1385)*

ONE

Newgate, Ward of Farringdon

If you build your own life around the secret lives of others, if you erect your house on the corrupt foundations of theirs, you soon come to regard all useful knowledge as your due. Information becomes your entitlement. You pay handsomely for it; you use it selectively and well. If you are not exactly trusted in certain circles, you are respected, and your name carries a certain weight. You are rarely surprised, and never deceived.

Yet there may come a time when your knowledge will betray you. A time when you will find even the brightest certainties – of friendship, of family, even of faith – dimming into shadows of bewilderment. When the light fails and belief fades into nothingness, and the season of your darkest ignorance begins.

Mine fell in the eighth year of Richard's reign, over that span of weeks separating the sobriety of Lent from the revelry of St Dunstan's Day. London often treats the passing of winter into spring with cold indifference. That year was no different. February had been an unforgiving month, March worse, and as the city scraped along toward April the air seemed to grow only more bitter, the sky more grey, the rain more penetrating as it lifted every hint of warmth from surfaces of timber and stone.

So too with the jail at Newgate: a stink in the air, a coating on the tongue. I had come over the bridge that leaden morning to speak with Mark Blythe, jailed on the death of his apprentice. I had come, too, as a small favour to the prior of St Mary Overey, the Southwark parish that Blythe once served as head mason. For years I had let a house along the priory's south wall, and knew Blythe's family well.

We had been chewing for a while on the subject of the coming trial, and whether I might help him avoid it. No fire in the musty side-chamber. I was losing my patience, and more of my vision than usual. 'You have no choice, unless you want to hang, or worse,' I told him. 'And there is worse, Mark. I've seen it. I've smelled it.'

'It was an accident, Master Gower.'

'So you've said, Mark. How could you have known the axle would break?' Despite the prison chill a bead of moisture, thick as wheel oil, cleared a path down his cheek. Blythe had lost three fingers, two from his left hand as well as his right thumb, his body marked with the perils of his craft, and Newgate's heavy irons had scored his forearms. I softened my voice. 'But the axle did break. The stones, half a ton of them, did spill out and crush that boy's legs. Your apprentice did die, Mark. And the soundness of that cart was your responsibility.'

'Not's how I saw it, and as for the axle . . .' His voice trailed off.

I heard a sigh, realized it was my own. 'The problem, Mark, is that the law sees different kinds of accidents. You can't claim accidental injury when your own negligence – when your carelessness has been taken as the cause of death.'

8

Blythe's hands dropped to the table.

'Please don't make me tell your wife you've just put your life in the hands of a petty jury.'

His eyes widened. 'But you'd stand for me, wouldn't you then, Master Gower?'

'I'm not an advocate, Mark. What I have are connections. And money. I can put those at your service. But not before a jury.' Poor timing, I didn't say. Before the crackdown last year I could have bribed any jury in the realm.

His shoulders slumped. 'No trial, then. How quick to get me out?'

I hesitated. 'You'll be here until next delivery. June, I would think.'

'More time, sir? In *here*?' He shook his head. 'They'll send me down, sir, down to the Bocardo. They press them down there, it's said. Sticks them with nails like Jesu himself, do abominations each to the other. Don't want the Bocardo, Master Gower, not by the blood.'

My hands settled on Blythe's mangled fingers, stilling them against the wood. Mutilated, cracked, darkened with years of stonework, these fingers had shaped their share of useful beauty over the years: a lintel, a buttress, the pearled spans of a bishop's palace, the mortaring so precise you would never know from beyond a few feet that what you saw was not a single stone. 'Mark, I will do what I can to—'

'Have an end!'

I flinched at the yawn of old hinges and half-turned to the door. Tom Tugg, keeper of Newgate, a cock in the yard. He swung a ring of keys, each a gnarled foot of iron. 'Fees to be tallied and collected presently,' he crooned, and two turnkeys did their work. Blythe moaned, the irons biting his swollen wrists.

It took a moment, but finally Tugg saw my face. Even in the scant light of three candles I caught his gape.

'Whatsit – who let this *fiend* speak to my prisoner?' He spun on his men. 'Who put them in here?'

Your deputy. A small threat for a small thing. The turnkeys just shrugged.

'Take him back,' Tugg ordered, a spit of disgust. He looked at me, and got my heartiest smile. He licked his lips. 'Come along, then.'

I gave Blythe's broad back a pat before he was pulled in the opposite direction. Tugg led me along the passage to the outer gatehouse. A fight had broken out in the women's chamber, a crowd cheering the crunch of bone on the stone floor. At the gatehouse door Tugg turned on me. 'Well?' His chin was pocked, unshaved.

'I would like Blythe transferred to Ludgate until delivery.'

Tugg wrinkled his heavy brow. 'Ludgate, you say?' The new prison, recently completed at the western gate and now under the custody of the city chamber, housed those accused only of civil offences. So pleasant were its conditions that stories were circulating of inmates striking deals to remain jailed. 'You've got to understand my *situation* here, Gower,' he said with a slight twinge of his jaw. 'Newgate's abrim with spies.'

'So I've heard,' I said, prepared for this. 'Secret alliances with the Scots, French agents lurking behind every door.'

'Twenty of them at last count, held without surety.'

'All the more reason to move Mark Blythe, then, for he's no spy,' I said. 'Relieve the overcrowding, put a petty criminal out of your mind.' Almost there. 'You can say it was your idea, sound leader that you are.'

He blew out a breath. 'A pound, Gower. It'll take a pound to move him, what with that touchy keeper they got, dealings with the Guildhall—'

'Wonderful,' I said. 'We'll deduct it from your balance.' Tugg was still down to me many pounds; another handful of shillings would make little difference.

'See here, Gower—'

'Nothing to see, Tugg. I have your debt, I have your note. And I have the most horrendous bit of—'

'Ludgate, then,' he said, with another thick sigh. 'He'll be there till delivery.'

I gave him a hard look. '*Live* delivery.' He nodded.

Outside Newgate I retrieved my pattens, then trudged through the walls and up the muddy way to Holbourne, breathing shallowly on the bridge as I neared the outer reaches of the ward. Before the churchyard at St Andrew a wild-haired man preached to the drizzle, his only parishioners a crescent of nosing goats. I caught a snatch of verse as I ducked into the narrow alley just east of Thavie's Inn.

'Full long shall he lead us, full rich shall he rule,
Through pain of pestilence, through wounds of
     long war.
Yet *morire* is matter all sovereigns must suffer.'

All kings must die. True enough, and the lines were well wrought, though the preacher soon lapsed into the usual fare. Corruption, gluttony, lust, the coming holocaust of the unfaithful. I wondered how long the poor man would last before joining Blythe in his cell.

At street level Monksblood's stood open to the weather, a brick wedged beneath the alley door. I leaned in and gave a nod to the keeper. He tossed me a jar. At the foot of the stairs sat his daughter, a slight thing of about eight. With her foot resting on the next cask, she angled my jar beneath the tap and carefully turned the bronze spigot. I dropped a few pennies in her little palm. A wan smile, tired eyes bright for a moment beneath her shining brow, then she looked past me and up the stairs, waiting for her father's next fish.

With the sour ale on my tongue I surveyed the undercroft

tavern, lit weakly by a row of lanterns dangling from heavy beams. The tables were nearly empty, just two groups of men clustered along the hearth. Masons, fresh from work on the bridge. I got a few sullen looks. Steam rising from damp clothes, the muffled clatter of boots overhead.

In the far corner my friend sat alone, frowning into his jar as his finger traced a slow arc around its mouth. He seemed coiled on the bench, his brow knit, his eyes narrowed in concentration, the whole of him tensed against some unspoken thought.

'Geoffrey,' I said, and moved forward.

Half-turning with a start, he rose, his face blossoming into a smile. '*Mon ami*.' He spread his hands.

As my arms wrapped his frame I felt the familiar surge of anticipation: for court gossip, for poetic banter, for news of mutual acquaintances. Yet beneath the thin coat I also felt ribs, hard against tightened skin. Chaucer had lost a couple of stone that winter; there was less to him since his latest return from abroad, and his unfashionable surcoat, of undyed wool cut simply with straight sleeves, lent an almost rural aspect to his bearing. Normally he would dress like a bit of a fop. I wondered what explained the change.

For a while we just drank, saying nothing, two hounds sniffing around after a long separation. Eventually he leaned over the board. 'How has it been, John? You know . . .'

I looked away. 'Let's not bleed that wound, Geoffrey.'

He let that hang, then touched my elbow. 'I hope it has started to heal, at least.'

'I had her things removed and sold at Candlemas – most of them.' Candlemas: purification, purging, the scouring of the soul and the larder. I thought, as I hadn't in weeks, of Sarah's prayerbook, its margins and flyleaves full of her jottings. It was one of the few of her possessions I had kept.

Chaucer moved his hand away. I asked about Philippa.

He picked a splinter from the table. 'Keeps to court, hovering around her sister and the Infanta. It doesn't help that I'm travelling all the time. Calais, the cinque ports.'

'And this recent trip, to Tuscany and Milan? The custom was able to spare you?' Back in November Chaucer had arranged for a deputy to step in for him at the customhouse. His trip south had been planned hastily, and for reasons he had kept to himself.

'Some negotiations for the chancellor: a bribe here, a false promise there.' He pushed a lump of talgar across the table. The Welsh cheese was an epiphany on my tongue: tart, rich, deliciously illegal. 'Though this trip was a bit less official than the last. *Inglese italianizzato, diavolo incarnato.*' He feigned a sinister smile.

An Englishman italianized is the devil incarnate. 'A judgment you inspired, I suppose?'

'You've been practising!'

I hadn't, though the odd lesson from Chaucer in recent years had taught me a few useless phrases. '*Donde il formaggio?*' I said awkwardly, pretending to look around for the cheese.

He smiled. 'It's *dov'è il formaggio*, John, not *donde*. Where *is* the cheese, not where is the cheese *from*.' He pushed the talgar my way.

'*Dov'è*. Right.' I knifed another wedge.

He went on about his trip. 'And the books! In the Visconti libraries you can't reach out a hand without—Speaking of books, I've brought you a little something.' From his bag he removed a volume and set it between us. '*Il Filostrato*. A work that has reminded me of you since I first read it years ago, though I can't quite say why. It's a tragedy of the Trojan War, and a story of love. Not to your usual tastes, though I have a feeling you'll enjoy it. And it will give me an excuse to teach you more Italian.'

I thanked him and stroked the embossed spine and cover. Calf, dyed a deep purple, cool and smooth. 'The writer?'

'Giovanni Boccaccio,' he said. 'I tried to meet him once, but he wouldn't see me. A recluse, practically a hermit.'

'Boccaccio.' A name, like the talgar, worth savouring. I mouthed the rubrics as I leafed, admiring the ghostly thinness of the abortive vellum. No full-page illuminations, but the larger initials were ornate, with gold flourishes, a full palette of inks, descenders reaching out to curl around the peculiar beasts in the margins. There was a poem on the second leaf, a single stanza in a hand I knew well.

> Go, little book, to our unfathomed friend,
> Above his silvered head to build a shrine,
> Retreat of Wisdom, Ignorance to mend.
> Full oft there shall you comfort and entwine
> His long limbs in bookish fetters benign.
>   Thou shalt preserve those aquamarine gems,
>   Or Gower's friend shall cast you in the Thames.

As always Chaucer's verse captured its subject with the precision of a mirror. My thinning hair, shot through with spreading grey. My long frame, which had two lean inches on Chaucer's, and he was not a short man by any measure. Finally the eyes. 'Gower green,' a limner I once knew named their shade, claiming no success in duplicating it. Sarah had always likened them to her native Malvern Hills at noon, though she had died without fathoming the truth about these eyes, and their diminishing powers. Only Chaucer possessed that knowledge, expressed in a touching bit of protectiveness in the couplet.

I looked up to see him staring vacantly at the far wall. I closed the book.

'Why did you want to meet here of all places?'

'I'm less known in Holbourne,' he whispered, in French, teasing, 'where there's smaller chance of recognition than within the walls.'

'Ah, I see,' I replied, also in French. 'I am the object of a secret mission, then. Like your visits to Hawkwood and the Florentine *commune*.'

His smile dimmed. 'Hawkwood. Yes. You know, I spent some time with Simon while I was in Florence.'

'God's *blood,* Geoffrey!'

He looked uncomfortable. 'You didn't write to him after Sarah died.'

'No.'

'He's your son, John. Your sole heir.'

The child who survived, when three others did not. I drained my jar, signalled the girl for another.

'Have you heard from him?' he asked, reading my thoughts.

A fresh dipper, and I drank deeply. 'Tell me about your sons instead,' I said, in a feeble change of subject. 'How is Thomas faring at the almonry?'

'Well enough, I suppose,' he said.

'And little Lewis?'

'With his mother, the little devil.' He gave a half shrug. 'Some call *him* the devil, our Hawkwood. But I suppose our king knows what he's doing when it comes to alliances.'

'What few of them he has left,' I said.

He looked at me, smiling. 'No King Edward, is he?'

I held up my jar. 'Full long shall he lead us, full rich shall he rule.'

His smile faded. 'Wherever did you pick that up, John?'

'A preacher, versing it up out on Holbourne just now.'

'Our sermonizers are quite poetical these days, aren't they?' he scoffed. There was a certain strain in his voice, though I thought nothing of it at the time.

'Fools, if you ask me, to versify on that sort of matter,' I said.

'Better to stick to Gawain and Lancelot, I suppose.'

'Or fairies.'

'Or friars.'

We laughed quietly. There was a long silence, then Chaucer sighed, tapped his fingers. 'John, I need a small favour.'

Of course you do. 'Go on.'

'I'm looking for a book.'

'A book.'

'I've heard it was in the hands of one of Lancaster's hermits.'

I watched his eyes. 'Why can't you get it for yourself?'

'Because I don't know who has it, or where it is at the moment.'

'And who does know?'

He raised his chin, his jaw tight. I knew that look. 'Katherine Swynford, perhaps. If a flea dies in Lancaster's household she'll have heard about it. Ask her.'

'She's your sister-in-law, Geoffrey.' I felt a twinge of misgiving. However innocent on its face, no request from Chaucer was ever straightforward. 'Why not ask her yourself?'

'She and Philippa are inseparable. Katherine won't see me.'

'So you're asking me to approach her?'

He took a small sip.

'Why me?' I said.

'How to put it?' He pretended to search for words, his hands flitting about on the table. 'This job needs a *subterranean* man, John. A man who knows this city like the lines in his knuckles, its secrets and surprises. All those shadowed corners and blind alleyways where you do your nasty work.'

I gazed fondly at him, thinking of Simon, and so much else. It was one of the peculiarities of our intimacy that Chaucer seemed to appreciate talents no one else would value in a friend. Here comes John Gower, it was murmured at Westminster and the Guildhall; hide your ledgers. Hide your thoughts. For knowledge is currency. It can be traded and it can be banked, and more secretly than money. The French have a word for informers: *chanteurs*, 'singers', and information is a song of sorts. A melody poured in the ears of its eager recipients, every note a hidden vice, a high crime, a deadly sin. Or some kind of illicit antiphon, its verses whispered among opposed choirs of the living and the dead.

We live in a hypocritical age. An age that sees bishops preaching abstinence while running whores. Pardoners peddling indulgences while seducing wives. Earls pledging fealty while plotting treason. Hypocrites, all of them, and my trade is the bane of hypocrisy, its worth far outweighing its perversion. I practise the purest form of truthtelling.

Quite profitably, too. The second son of a moderately wealthy knight has some choices: the law, the royal bureaucracy, Oxford or Cambridge, the life of a monk or a priest. Yet I would rather have trapped grayling in the Severn for a living than taken holy orders, and it was clear that my poetry would never see the lavishments from patrons that Chaucer's increasingly enjoyed. Yet I shall never forget the thrill I felt when that first coin of another man's vice fell into my lap, and I realized what I had – and how to use it. Since then I have become a trader in information, a seller of suspicion, a purveyor of foibles and the hidden things of private life. I work alone and always have, without the trappings of craft or creed.

John Gower. A guild of one.

'You can't be direct with her about it,' Chaucer was saying. 'This is a woman who takes the biggest cock in the realm between her legs. She's given Lancaster three bastards at last count – or is it four?' He waited, gauging my reaction.

'What is this book, Geoffrey? What does it look like? What's in it?'

His gaze was unfocused and vague. 'To be honest with

you, John, I don't know. What I do know is that this book could hurt me.' He blinked and looked at some spot on the wattle behind me. Then, in a last whisper of French, 'It could cost me my life.'

Our eyes locked, and I wondered in that instant, as I would so often in the weeks to come, what price such a book might extract from my oldest friend. He broke the tension with one of his elvish smiles. 'If you can do this for me, John, get me this book, I'll be greatly in your debt.'

As you are so deeply in mine, he did not say; nor did he need to, and in his position neither would I have. I left Monksblood's that morning bound to perform this 'small favour', as Chaucer had called it, for the one man in all the world I could never refuse. The man who knew my own darkest song.

TWO

Gropecunt Lane, Ward of Cheap

Eleanor Rykener grunted, spat, wiped her lips. The friar covered his shrivelled knob. Wouldn't meet her eyes, of course. Franciscans, they never liked to look. He dropped his groats on the straw. 'Why thank you, Brother Michael,' she said, her voice a sullen nip. The friar stared coldly at some spot on her neck, then shrugged on his cowl, edged around the old mare, and left the stall.

When she had dressed, Eleanor stepped out into the light rain, looking down toward the stone cross before St Pancras. The friar wouldn't give that a glance either as he slunk around the corner of the churchyard toward Soper Lane. She raised her face to the sky, cleansing his piety from her tongue.

'Regular as these little oinkers here.' Mary Potts leaned against a post, gesturing to a dozen pigs nosing street muck.

Eleanor tossed her gossip a tired smile. 'And never has the good grace to render me confession after I grant him service.'

They stood in silence for a while, watching the flow of

late-afternoon traffic up along Cheapside, the creak of old wheels, the low calls of sheep, the urgings of hucksters, though the din seemed always distant from the ladies of Gropecunt Lane, a quiet byway of leased horsestalls and abandoned shopfronts that absorbed sound the way a dry rag absorbs ale, and as central as St Paul's to the human business of London. Every now and then this business would be theirs, as some desiring man, face to the ground, mind on slit, would make the turn and find a maudlyn to take his groats and squirt. Despite the lane's reputation, the girls kept things tidy, raking the dirt and pavers themselves, cleaning up after animal and man alike. It was their own small piece of the city, where jakes plucked coin from their purses and maudlyns tucked it into theirs, the ordinances be damned. A simple thing.

'Afternoon, m'pretties!'

Eleanor turned. Joan Rugg lifted her skirts as she hopped from stone to stone in a vain attempt to avoid the mud.

'What now what now what now,' Mary Potts murmured.

With a final grunt, Joan heaved herself on to the pavers fronting the stalls and straightened her dress, a shapeless thing of stained wool. The Dun Bell, Joan's girls called their bawd, with three chins stacked against her neck, lips full and always moist, beady eyes that moved more quickly than any other part of her, and a mass of matted hair entwined through the band of a wide hat she never removed. This, a splendid circle of leather and wool adorned with flowers of faded silk, had been given to her by a lover in her youth, she liked to recall. On that misty day its perch lent her large form an air of botanical mystery, as if the viewer were approaching a mountaintop garden above the clouds, or some strange, Edenic island in the sea. 'You ladies seen our Agnes?' she asked.

20

'Not today,' said Mary Potts.

'Thought you sent her up Westminster on Tuesday,' said Eleanor, suddenly concerned. As far as she knew Agnes Fonteyn had been consorting with one of the king's sub-stewards, a long-time jake who would request Agnes's company for a few days at a time during royal absences.

'Didn't come through.' Joan raised her sleeve to scratch at her forearm. 'But I had a particular request for her this morning, from a fine gentleman of the Mercery. And a procuratrix'd like to make arrangements, right?'

'You talked to her mother down Southwark?' Mary asked.

'Sign of the Pricking Bishop,' Eleanor added quickly, naming a common house in the stews where Agnes's mother had long peddled flesh.

Joan scoffed. 'Would've had to wait in line a half day to get a word in. That whore's swyving makes her daughter look like St Margaret.'

'Did you try her sister?' Eleanor said. 'Lives up Cornhull.'

Joan wagged her head. 'Took a peek in her fancy house, asked about a bit in Broad Street, but no sight of her ladyship.'

A dungcart turned up from St Pancras on the way to the walls, banded wheels groaning under the weight, the waste of man and beast souring the air. When the clatter receded, Joan turned back to them. 'Can't have my maudlyns vanishing on me, not with Lents about to pass, appetites built up as they are. Forty days of nothing, then a week of everything, in my experience.'

Mary groaned, her arms wrapping a post. 'Shoulda been a nun, shouldn't I, maybe took vows with them Benedictines?'

'Ah, but then you'd *really* be getting it in every hole, my dear,' said Joan wisely.

The two of them shared the laughter for a bit, attracting a few looks from other girls up the lane as Eleanor clasped her hands in worry. Joan put a hand to her chin. With a sidelong glance at Eleanor, she said, 'Agnes got a little spot, though, don't she? Out in the Moorfields.'

'A small walk short of Bethlem,' said Eleanor with a natural shudder. 'I've been there with her.' This was Agnes's 'lair', as she called it: an old hunter's blind outside the city walls where some of her wealthier jakes liked to take her, along with any other maudlyns they could cajole. They were, for the most part, young, reckless men with too much time and coin on their hands. Or fellows whose names might start with *Sir*.

'Go have a look then, will you?' said Joan. Her sweetest wheedle.

Eleanor hesitated. 'Rather not go alone.'

Joan heaved a shoulder at Mary. 'Take the child with you. Be back bell of six, or shortly after. Sky looks to be clearing, so we'll likely be busy tonight, the blood of London rising strong.'

Mary, playing the genteel, crooked her elbow. Eleanor took her arm, and they left Joan Rugg standing beside the stalls. 'Bell of six now,' the bawd called after them. Eleanor waved an acknowledgment, only too glad to escape her sticky work for a few hours, though quite worried for Agnes.

A muddy trudge in the drizzle took them along Cheapside past the Standard at le Vout, where two vagrants hunching in the stocks chewed at tack as a one-armed boy softened the biscuits in ale. A straight course up Wood Street and they were at Cripplegate. Eleanor looked up as they passed beneath the gatehouse, the prisoners idling behind the high grates, the keepers giving the two mauds barely a glance. Agnes likewise would have strolled from the inner half of the ward to the outer without a second thought

22

from these men. Strange, that she would have let off her work for longer than a few hours, let alone a full day; she seemed always wanting more shillings, the busiest girl on Gropecunt Lane and happy about it.

Strange, too, that she'd said nothing to Eleanor about her plans, for the two maudlyns had long been intimate, swapping jakes, lending a coin here and there, looking out for one another in their carnal trade, and always mindful of the situations that had led them to it: Eleanor, an orphan, her younger brother apprenticed to a Southwark butcher who beat him mercilessly; Agnes Fonteyn, who had fled her mother's bawdy house in the stews for a higher cut of her skincoin. *Tightest yoke a' mauds you'll ever see*, Joan Rugg liked to say, and it was true.

Once past Cripplegate they skirted the northern wall past the bricked-up postern at the foot of the causeway and soon came to the edge of an overgrown orchard. Here the lane opened out into the broad expanse of the Moorfields, a linked series of marshy heaths that formed London's nearest hunting grounds, mostly deer and fowl. A few drier, higher bits could handle cows at pasture, though for the most part the whole area was a fen. That late afternoon Eleanor and Mary saw no one moving among the high tufts of moorgrass.

The first path off the causeway led to a spot beneath a large, lone oak. From there a smaller path branched off to the east. Ahead loomed the mass of Bethlem Priory, its walls heightened and buttressed since the order started taking in lunatics the year before. Eleanor recalled her last visit to Agnes's lair, the mix of routine coupling and utter terror. The desperate gropings of an ageing squire, the loose spread of his gut on her back like a jelly blanket – then a sound that shrivelled the squire's cock, and her own as well: a lunatic's

23

scream, echoing from the Bethlem walls. Since that night Eleanor had heard similar accounts of the priory's madmen, fighting their chains as the canons extended their charity to the wrong of mind.

Eleanor saw the white rock that marked the final turn. They pushed through the heavy foliage until they reached a high wall of hawthorn. A strong scent of primrose masked a sweeter, sicker smell beneath. Mary touched her arm. Eleanor held her breath and stepped into the dense brush. A flash of bare skin on the ground, glistening, moist. Eleanor pushed aside the last branches. They saw the body.

She was face down in the wetness, naked, her skin marbled with mud and rain. Her hair, caked in soil, had spread into three slicked highways from the crown of her crushed head, opened to the vermin. Beside her left hand lay a shoeing hammer, its handle resting carelessly over a root. Eleanor, in a daze, picked it up, felt its killing weight. As she stood feeble guard, Mary, with a heavy sigh, squatted in the mud beside the body. 'Oh, you poor thing,' she said. 'Oh, Agnes you were so lovely, oh my beautiful.'

'Turn her over then, get her face out of the peat,' said Eleanor, hammer still at the ready. Something didn't make sense. Agnes's hair—

Mary pulled at the girl's shoulders. With a suck of mud she came free. Once she was flipped Mary used her hem to wipe the dark patches from the girl's ruined face.

They stared down at her, at first disbelieving what they saw. Eleanor glanced into the hunter's blind. A pile of women's finery thrown over a stump: an ivory busk, a taffeta cape trimmed with fur, more silk than she and her fellow maudlyns could ever hope to afford, all in a style that Eleanor – who had a poor girl's eye for new jet, could tell you who in town sold the latest dresses from Ghent and Bruges – had rarely seen in London. She looked back at the face.

This dead girl was indeed lovely. She was not Agnes Fonteyn.

THREE

La Neyte, Westminster

Wat Tyler. Jack Straw. The city as powerless as a widow, Troy without its Hector, the commons running like barnyard animals through her streets, taking her bridges, torching her greatest houses, storming the Tower and murdering the lord chancellor and the lord treasurer. Though it had been four years since the Rising swept through London, the memories still haunted our great but tired city, pooling beneath the eaves, drifting along narrow alleys with the continuing threat of revolt.

No one had been more affected by the events of those grim weeks than John of Gaunt, Duke of Lancaster. After stealing everything worth taking, Tyler and his gang burned Gaunt's Thames-side palace to the ground, and the ruins of the Savoy would sit along the Strand for years: a charred reminder of the brute power of the commons, and the constant threat embodied by the city's aggrieved poor.

Now the duke avoided London as much as possible, centring his life and his business around the castle of Kenilworth far to the north. When his presence was required in the city Gaunt would appear for a few days or a week at a time, the grudged guest of those magnates willing to tolerate his household, and betting on his survival. Often he would lodge at Tottenham, though that Lent he was residing at La Neyte, the Abbot of Westminster's moated grange a mile up-river from the abbey, and it was there I would be granted an audience with his sometime mistress, arranged the day before.

The duke himself was just leaving the abbot's house as I arrived in the upper gateyard, his retainers gosling along behind him. He half-turned to me, his brow knit in fury as he acknowledged my bent knee with a curt nod. Those around him knew better than to speak, as did I.

In the summer hall I moved slowly along the wall, mingling with the line of bored servants as thick hangings brushed my cheek. The chamber teemed with lords of various ranks who had been seeking a word with the duke before his abrupt departure, and I tried to go unremarked by those remaining. My eyes, uncooperative, failed to spy a drip bucket, full of rainwater from the porous ceiling. It surrendered its contents to my left foot, then clattered across the floor. There was a hush. It was Michael de la Pole who broke it in his graceful way. 'Not to worry. The abbot has ordered some silken buckets,' said the lord chancellor into the silence, giving me a slight nod. Laughter, though not at my expense, filled that portion of the hall, and the baron resumed his conversation.

Standing behind the baron, shifting a little as the hubbub returned, Robert de Vere, the Earl of Oxford, gave me an ugly look. I glanced away, though not before noting his discomfort. De Vere had likely been the target of Gaunt's ire, and now here's John Gower, come to brew more trouble, as if the particular group of magnates clustered in the hall at La Neyte that day did not promise enough. A duke, an earl, and a baron, a tensile triangle of mutual suspicion and dependence. Gaunt was still furious at de Vere for turning the king against him at the February tournament at Westminster, where a plot against the duke's life was only narrowly averted – and this after all the business the year before at the Salisbury Parliament, where Gaunt's supposed plot against his royal nephew nearly led to the duke's hanging on the spot. The plot was spun of gossamer, of course, the invention of a Carmelite friar who was afterwards seized on the way to his cell and tortured to death. One year, two imaginary plots, and great trouble for the realm. De Vere, the young king's current favourite and a notorious flatterer, was taking every advantage he could of the widening rift between the king and the duke, gathering nobles to his side in an open attempt to wrest power from the much older Lancaster. Caught in the middle of it all was the Baron de la Pole, chief financier to old King Edward and now lord chancellor, determined to keep the peace at all costs – and, it appeared to me, losing ground by the day.

Oxford had now turned his back on de la Pole, suggesting that he had taken the chancellor's kind gesture toward me as an insult to him. Sir Stephen Weldon, chief knight of the earl's household, noticed his lord's vexation and excused himself. I set my face for the encounter. This took some effort, for Weldon's most distinguishing characteristic was a crescent scar on his chin, a jagged curve of whitened skin. Whenever I saw it I imagined a line of Oxford's wretched tenants hooked by their necks, swinging in the wind.

'Gower.'

'Sir Stephen.'

'Our fine town should consider itself gilded indeed whenever John Gower deigns to abandon Southwark to tread Westminster's humbler lanes.'

'Even as these avenues acclaim your own passings through with their every voice.' How I hate this man.

28

Weldon assessed me, a peculiar glint in his eyes. 'You look awful, Gower. I'd thought it was your wife who was sick.'

I stared at his scar. 'Sarah died last year. The week of Michaelmas.'

He raised a hand to his mouth. 'I'd not heard.'

I said nothing.

'You must forgive me, John,' he insisted. 'It is inexcusable.'

'Though unsurprising, Sir Stephen.'

His eyes narrowed. He was about to say something more, then thought better of it. They usually do, even the higher knights. He inclined his head, spun on a toe, and rejoined the cluster around Oxford, leaving me wondering why the man had approached me in the first place.

Someone coughed, stifled it. Katherine Swynford was descending from the abbot's chambers, given over to Gaunt for the duration of his stay. Her skin glowed with the duke's recent departure, the cut of her gown too low by a coin's span, her hood trimmed in a silk brocade that matched her emerald eyes. Stretching her compact frame, she looked about until her gaze settled on me. With a subtle toss of her head she directed me to the wide oratorium off the summer hall, where a group of five other ladies sat at their embroidery.

'Why did you want to see me, John?' she said when I joined her. She glanced over her shoulder, already impatient.

I recalled Chaucer's anxious state at Monksblood's. *You can't be direct with her about it*. I opted against obedience. 'Apparently Geoffrey thinks you might know about a book he's seeking.'

She let me stand in silence, leaning over to correct a companion. 'Unravel that. Less of an arc, more of a triangle. Lovely. Then pin out the *roet*.' Dame Katherine never failed to amaze me in those days, commanding the duchess's ladies-in-waiting as if they were already her own.

At length she gave me her attention. 'Always on the lookout for the next little book, isn't he?'

'Too true.'

'What's special about this one?' She took up a narrow strip of cloth of gold, which she proceeded to pick apart from the edges.

'It's – delicate,' I said, hiding my ignorance behind a veil of discretion.

'Well of course it is, John, or it wouldn't be you standing before me but my own brother-in-law!' She continued to pick. 'What a worm.'

I silently conceded the larger point. Gaunt's subtle favouritism toward Chaucer was well known and had been ever since Geoffrey composed an elegy upon the death of Duchess Blanche some years ago. Katherine viewed him as an unworthy rival for the duke's attention. The current duchess certainly wasn't getting much of it, despite Gaunt's vow after the Rising to forsake his mistress in favour of his marriage. The duke had seen the rebellion as a warning from God to put away his long-standing consort, and indeed for several years the two had succeeded in avoiding one another's presence, even as the duke plied her from afar with luxurious gifts, properties, and pounds. Now, by all indications, things were boiling up again, their liaisons increasingly out in the open, as they had formerly been for so many years.

Yet I remained one of Dame Katherine's greatest admirers, both for her restraint and for her admirable fortitude in the face of so much calumny from her detractors. Despite what must have been nearly irresistible pressure from Lancaster, she had never broken her vows while her husband lived, even when Sir Hugh Swynford was abroad. That Lancaster was now breaking his own was the duke's problem, not hers. She seemed determined in those years to see him through another duchess, whatever the cost to her reputation and prospects.

'So . . . what makes him think the book is here?' she said, giving me a look.

'He heard it indirectly from one of the duke's hermits, so he says.'

'Oh? And did he bother to say which one?' She swept an arm toward the terrace doors. 'Lancaster has hermits to spare. Richard of Chatterburn, John of Singleton, Gregory of Bishop's Lynn – David of the Ditch, Tom of the Tavern, Peter of the Privy, as common as friars. Dozens of them, popping their heads out of their holes like rabbits, sniffing for nobles whenever Gaunt opens his purse.'

'He didn't say.'

Her gaze lingered for a moment. 'Will you play cards, John?' From a side table she removed a stack of parchment ovals.

'Cards?'

'You haven't played such games?' She spread the cards across the table at her knees, and I marvelled at the colourful shapes: blue swords, golden hawks, red plums, and purple thistleflowers, all arranged in differing numbers and patterns. 'They are quite popular in Paris, though this pack comes from Florence. A gift from Chaucer, and now it's my second.' She pointed to another deck, stacked neatly on the table, and to all appearances identical to the one she held.

I asked how the game was played.

'There are many games of cards; it seems I learn a new one every week.' There were four suits, she explained, each numbering thirteen. Pips from one to nine, then the four faces in each suit: the Prince of Hawks, the Duke of Plums, the Queen of Swords, the King of Thistles, and so on.

'Fifty-two cards in all, then,' I calculated.

'Plus the trumps, a dozen of them.' She laid out another row. 'The Wheel of Fortune, the Magician, the Bleeding Tower, and this is the Sun.' An exquisite rendering of Apollo in full splendour.

31

'What part do the trumps play?'

'They wrestle with the pips and one another in various ways, depending on the rules of the particular game.'

Like the queen in chess, I observed.

'Though the queen has worthy rivals.' She laid out more trump cards. 'Fate, the Devil, the Fool – and, most powerful of all, Death.' A skull, leering at the viewer, the skeleton mounted on an emaciated horse. She explained the rules to a simple game involving points doled out for each pip and face card, with the trumps acting as foils. For some time we played in silence, and I noticed her agility with the parchment shapes, a sleight of hand that involved a deft use of her palms and knuckles to deal and reposition the cards in play. Eventually, as I learned the rhythm, I relaxed back into the conversation.

'Perhaps the Earl of Cambridge might know something about this book?'

Swynford raised a shoulder. She caught me looking at her bare skin, didn't seem to mind. 'Our dear Edmund Langley?' She played the Four of Hawks, a shrewd move, evidently.

'The Infanta and her sister are at court this month, I've heard.' The wives of Gaunt and Langley, the eldest of Edward's surviving sons. I went to take her four but flubbed my draw. She smiled as she swept the table clean in one movement and laid out a new play.

'Ah yes, the *hermanas español*. Those dark bitches are my little hell.' Swynford looked up with a worried smile. 'What a tangled web you spin for me, John Gower. Are you here to torture me or amuse me?'

'Your choice.'

She narrowed her eyes. 'Let's have a different game, a simpler one.' She picked up the cards again and laid ten of them face-up on the table. 'Choose one. Any card at all.'

'What determines my choice?'

'Merely the condition of your soul.'

Feeling mischievous, I leaned forward and tapped the Devil. She puckered her lips. 'But that is Chaucer's card.'

We shared a laugh as she gathered the cards into a loose pile, though just as quickly her face clouded. 'I know something about this book.' She looked across the hall to the humming circles of gentry. 'There have been whispers of a theft. A strange manuscript, stolen from La Neyte last week.'

'Silver I could understand, or plate. But who would steal a book?'

'It was a young woman, passing as a lady-in-waiting to the Countess of Bethune. Now she's dead.'

I stared at her.

'Someone skulled her, out on the Moorfields.'

'The Moorfields? I can't imagine—'

'And, John,' she breathed, leaning forward, her eyes attractively wide, 'I think I may have seen her. Coming out of the abbot's private chapel, right before she lifted it.'

'What sort of a book?' I asked, trying to keep up.

'I know nothing of its content, I swear to you. Only rumours.' To my surprise I believed her. 'And now Braybrooke is involved, asking my duke all sorts of ugly questions. You know how suspicious everyone is since the council, and that crazed friar's rantings last year. As if my duke and the king are mad dogs in a ring, circling one another, waiting for the next chance to lunge for a neck.'

This gave me pause. 'Why would the Bishop of London be after the same book as Chaucer?'

'Suppose it's less innocent than you suspect. Not one of those romances everyone is reading. Not a saint's life. But a book of prophecies.' She narrowed her eyes. 'Heretical prophecies.'

'Prophecies.' I recalled the preacher spewing his verse out on Holbourne, and Chaucer's agitation when I recited the man's words. 'Wycliffe's work?' John Wycliffe: a heretic, thoroughly condemned and recently dead, but all the more dangerous for that.

'Lancaster doubts it, though—'

Swynford's chin lifted. She stood. I twisted my neck as I rose to see the figure of Joan, Countess of Kent and the king's mother, standing at the arched doorway. Greying hair pulled back from slivered eyes, widow's weeds on a figure to make any man pause despite her considerable age. High cheekbones, set beneath a wide brow, and cobalt eyes that flashed as they settled on Swynford.

'Where is my brother?' she demanded as she approached, four of her attendants stepping aside. 'He summons me up from Wickhambreaux, yet I am kept waiting at Westminster half a day.' I winced inwardly at Gaunt's treatment of his sister-in-law. In the nine years since the death of Prince Edward, Gaunt's elder brother and former heir to the throne, the countess had seen her status slowly decline. Had her husband survived the ancient King Edward, she would have ascended to queen consort, and helped the younger Edward rule with the same flawless grace and deliberation she had shown so many times on public occasions. Though still the most beloved woman in the realm, Joan was becoming more and more of an afterthought.

Katherine put a hand to her breast. 'He just left us, Countess. An appointment at Fulham.' She straightened her skirts and retook her seat, the other ladies doing the same; a subtle insult.

Joan's lips tightened. 'Tell the duke my patience wears thin. I shall return to Wickhambreaux tomorrow.'

'I will tell him, Countess,' said Swynford.

Turning to leave, the countess looked at me. She sucked in her cheeks. 'John Gower.'

I bowed deeply. 'Your servant, Countess.'

She regarded me closely. 'I've gazed into your mirror, Gower.'

'My lady?'

'I have read your great work, the *Mirour de l'Omme*.'

My cheeks flushed. 'You surprise me, Countess.'

'Why is that?'

'I would not expect such a humble work to make its way to so noble a reader as yourself.' Nor its writer's name to be remembered.

She waved a hand. 'Rot, Gower. The breeding of Death and Sin, the bastard births of Hypocrisy and her sisters – why, you could be describing the household of Lancaster!'

Swynford gasped, staring in hatred at her lover's sister-in-law.

The countess gestured with her chin and turned away. Chaucer's book forgotten, my head swimming with the rare flattery, I followed her through the gauze curtains and out on to the small terrace.

'I am too hard on Lancaster, you know,' she said as we circled. 'It was a unique humiliation for a man like Gaunt, to bounce his king on his knee.' She walked along the parapet, pausing to pick dead leaves out of a pot. 'Though it has to be said that there are not many so powerful yet so willing to sacrifice their ambition. You would agree?'

'The Duke of Lancaster's modesty is universally admired, my lady.'

She spun on me, eyes darkened. 'Watch yourself, Gower. The ears of Westminster are as plentiful as scales on a herring.'

'Yes, Countess,' I said, chastened.

She stared at the lines of barges plying the Thames in the distance. 'My son has many enemies. Enemies who openly question his legitimacy.'

She paused with the ruffle of curtains. In the open doorway to the upper gallery stood Swynford, the gauze draped across a bare shoulder. One of her sons had wandered to the terraces, it seemed, his gaze now following a bird. Gaunt's youngest child, a girl they had perversely named Joan, she held by the hand. Seven and counting, some Gaunt's, others her late husband's – the entangled promises of a future none could yet foresee.

Swynford, after an amused glance between the countess and me, whisked her children away. The countess watched the curtains flutter in their wake.

'Be inventive with your next work, John Gower,' she murmured as the curtains stilled. 'To see my son stand before Parliament, with his slutting uncle at his side? A spectacle worthy of the mysteries.' With that she left me.

In the distance the river was a plane of drifting pieces. Barges, wherries, a raft of sawed logs soon to be swallowed by the city below. To my weakening eyes they appeared as so many living forces, moving against each other in ways I could then only dimly understand: an enigma in motion, like Swynford's foreign deck of cards. I stared at the water with a growing unease, thinking of a dead girl and a missing book, wondering what strange burden Chaucer had laid on my shoulders.

FOUR

Cornhull, Ward of Broad Street

'Please put it on my tally, Master Talbot.' Millicent Fonteyn nodded at the spicerer, willing him to wrap her purchases before his wife came to the shopfront. Between them sat four equal measures of prunes, almonds, currants, and dates. 'Oh, and a measure of the apricots,' she said, unable to stop herself.

George Lawler reached for the jar, shook his head as he tonged them out. He twined the lot together. 'Last time, Mistress Fonteyn.'

'You're kind, Master Lawler. We'll settle after Easter, if that suits. Now—'

'Oh, that suits us fine, m'lady, just fine.' Jane Lawler pushed through the alley door. She was a spindly woman, with dark brows set close and a small nose she fingered at will. 'Fine to settle after Michaelmas, fine to settle after All Saints, and, by Loy's bones, it'll be fine to settle after Easter. Why, it's only coin, isn't that right, Georgie? And if we lose it all, why, we'll get the Worshipful Company of Grocers to provide out of the common money, aye?'

Lawler sheepishly handed Millicent the bundle.

'Why, that's it, George!' his wife went on. 'Let's pack up some raisins for her ladyship. Saffron, too, cypress root, nutmeg – why, let's crate it all for the virtuous madam and have done with our livelihood.'

Millicent, shamefaced, turned to leave, Mistress Lawler tagging her heels. 'After Easter, she says. After Easter!'

Millicent was on the street.

'As if the Resurrection of our Lord'll be enough to put a single farthing in her graspy little palm.' Millicent took a sharp right out of the shop, her shoulders stooped with humiliation. 'You walk 'neath this eave to pay your debt, Millicent Fonteyn, nor never walk 'neath it again, nor any grocer's eave of Cornhull!'

Londoners turned their heads, cruel questions in their glances. Millicent kicked through a cluster of hens by the well before St Benet Fink, fluff and feathers scattering with her haste. She stopped on Broad Street, calming herself with her back on the rough wood of a horsepost. The damp air settled around her, drawing the moisture from her skin. By the time she pushed herself off the post her dress was soaked through, with dark stains at her middle and beneath her arms.

Millicent's house fronted the longest row of tailors' shops in London. For two years now the Cornhull house had been hers, the annual lease financed by Sir Humphrey's lust and largesse, and the dwelling had matched her aspirations in every detail: a keyed door, two floors, a glazed window at the front. She loved the walk along West Cheap and through the Poultry, her back to St Paul's as she strolled along the widest street in London, with its double gutters and raked pavers. A singlewoman without profession, kept by a wealthy man for his weekly dalliances. There were far worse fates for the elder daughter of a Southwark maudlyn.

Or so she had once thought. Two pounds five was the happy

sum she had possessed on the day of Sir Humphrey ap-Roger's death. Now it was nearly gone, with no provision made in the knight's will for her keep. His homely widow had got every penny of his fortune and every hand's width of his lands, leaving nothing to keep the woman he had truly loved free of penury. Millicent picked a spiced apricot out of the grocer's package, chewing but not tasting it as she approached her home. She removed the chained key from her neck.

'Why *there* you are.'

Millicent tilted her forehead against the door, sighed, then put on her best smile as she turned. Denise Haveryng, proprietress of her own late husband's thriving shop and a boastful freewoman of the city, wandered over with a tray of flans. 'Dame Haveryng.'

'You've been to Lawler's, I see.' She inspected the opened package in Millicent's hands, clearly disapproving of the indulgence. The weeds on this widow were dark only in colour: gauze sleeves flounced at her wrists, a belted sash with a leather buckle that almost glistened at her waist, and the damask lappet on her brow beneath a short-coned hat would not have looked out of place on an earl's wife.

Millicent, though not hungry, reached for a flancake.

'You've had visitors,' Dame Haveryng began. 'Three of them.'

'Ah?' Millicent opened her door. Denise herded her inside.

'Been like the Whitsunday procession. First there was Master Pratt, third time this month.'

The house's owner, clerk to the merchant taylors' guild, after her for weeks over the lease.

'Very well.' Millicent removed her hood, once a subtle latticed affair trimmed in silk, now fading and patched.

'And Jacob. To see about back wages, the poor dear.'

Millicent winced at the reminder. Even her former servants were her creditors now. 'And the third?'

'Your sister.'

Millicent froze.

'Takes after you, though dresses a bit downward from your station.' Denise paused in her glee. 'Wasn't aware you *had* a sister, dear.'

'We – we are not close.' Their last meeting, nearly two years before, had been a chance encounter on the wharfage, Agnes waiting to board a common wherry, Millicent and Sir Humphrey passing by to hire a private barge. They had exchanged quick smiles; Millicent remembered Agnes's hand jumping from her side, though she had settled for a furtive nod before turning away.

Ignoring the flan tray, Millicent pushed Denise from her house and shut the door. Out back she took the stairs two at a time. The door to the rear bedchamber was ajar. She entered to see her sister huddled against the wall, clutching a bolster, wrapped in a coverlet.

'What are you doing in my house, Agnes?'

Her sister looked dreadful, her skin ashen, her hair a tangled mess. Her eyes would not meet Millicent's until she had walked over to the bed and sat, the old straw pallet giving beneath her weight. Agnes looked up at her sister, her eyes darkened with sleeplessness and, Millicent thought, fear. 'I'd nowhere else to go, Mil.'

'Not to our mother's?'

'Said I'd made my choice, now I'm on my own, like I wanted it.'

'Why do you need anyone's help?'

'"Though faun escape the falcon's claws and crochet cut its snare, when father, son, and ghost we sing, of city's blade beware."'

'Are you sick, Ag? You're talking no sense.'

'She gave it me before she died. That's what she yelled.'

'Our mother has died?'

40

'"*Doovay leebro*", he said to her. "*Doovay leebro*", like he was singing.'

'Who was singing? Is our mother dead, Agnes?'

She shook her head. 'Not Bess Waller. That poor girl by the fire. Man with the hammer killed her.'

'Man? What man?'

Over the next while, as Millicent sat with her sister and calmed her down, Agnes haltingly told her all that had happened: her assignation in the Moorfields with the abbot of Bethlem, the holy man's departure after a short swyve, the silence as she dressed, then the crash of shrubbery before the beautiful girl burst into the small circle of firelight. 'She tried to talk, to tell me something, I could see it, but the poor thing was out a' breath, and the man was just behind her. So she shoved me her bundle and pushed me into the hawthorn and put a finger over her lips. Then he was there.' Finally the girl's death: the exchange of words in two tongues, the fall of the hammer, the killer's silent departure from the clearing.

Millicent listened with a growing disbelief, torn between sympathy for Agnes's plight and fury at her sister for bringing this darkness into her home. When Agnes had finished she stood and staggered over to a large chest, one of the last household items Millicent had to sell. She reached down behind it and withdrew a rectangular object wrapped in a heavily embroidered cloth. She looked down at the bundle for a long moment, then handed it to Millicent.

'I suspect he'll be wanting it back.'

FIVE

St Laurence Lane, Ward of Cheap

Joan Rugg slapped the constable's wrist. 'Not so pinchy there!' she cackled. The constable gave the bawd a hard shake as he led her toward the beadle's shop, where two men bearing heavy sticks stood to the sides of the door. Joan goosed them in the ribs. 'Valued jakes of the ward, these ones,' she teased. 'My best regulars.' The men traded denials.

Eleanor Rykener entered the shop behind them, a heady mix of ash and smelt in the air. An image of St Dunstan hung over the door out to the smithy in back, while wooden shelves at various heights displayed the goldsmith's newest wares. Gleaming plate, necklaces with inlaid gemstones, silver spoons laid out on silk. On the facing side were objects brought in for repair: a bishop's crozier, a set of clasps, embossed cabinet panels, a rich man's wine jug. That jug alone would buy my cock and arse for a year, Eleanor mused. Joan, she could see, was having similar thoughts about the rings.

Two apprentices tooled a brace of gold plates. For a while, as the constables shuffled their feet, the maudlyns sat and listened to the *tap tap tap*, the rough joining of common tools and precious metal, until the guildsman came in from the back. Eleanor looked up and into the nose of Richard Bickle, beadle of Cheap Ward and richest goldsmith north of Cheapside. The eyes and ears of the ward, a man who knew everything about anyone worth knowing anything about. Past master of the city's guild, Bickle was wrapped in a gown of red wool trimmed in sable, his lean face atop a neck chafed by a recent shave. 'Ladies.'

'Master Bickle,' said Joan.

'Let's cut through the elegances.' Bickle's voice was clipped, severe. He rubbed his palms. 'Two of your unspotted virgins been seen, Joan, heading into the Moorfields, coming out all spooked. Now we got a dead lady found not a hundred yards from where they come out the moor.'

Eleanor toed at a gap in the rushes.

'Hope you'll see it as we do, Joan. Girl's killed in one ward, possible witnesses whoring it up in another. City politics be a tricky business.' He spread a paternal smile. 'But no need to take this to the Guildhall, yeah? Avoid complications. Wouldn't want to shut down Gropecunt Lane again, send you and the Blessed Sisters of St Pox down Southwark way for trimming your hoods in budge.'

'Course not,' said Joan, wagging her head. 'Who's the dead girl?'

Bickle shrugged. 'Not for the likes of us to know. Some intimate connection to mustard, is all I'm told.'

'French girl then?'

'Looks like to the coroner,' said Bickle. 'Some fancy lady taken to the Moorfields, brained in the prime of life, left for the crows. Sad story, but not ours.'

'Right right.' Joan fingered her chin. 'And why they pulling your poor knob into this mess, Master Bickle?'

'Pressure from above and beside: the alderman, getting it

43

from the mayor, getting it from the bishop, getting it from the – ah, St Tom only knows. I do as I'm told.'

Joan turned to Eleanor. 'What about it, El? Tell the little man what he needs to know.'

Bickle bristled at *little man*, but held his peace. He turned to Eleanor. 'Good then. Firstwise, what were you doing out on the Moorfields that time of day? Bell of five, was it?'

'Thereabouts,' said Eleanor, in no hurry to help.

'What brought you to the moor? Strange place for a pair of mauds to go a-wandering.'

She shrugged. 'Sometimes the men like it, that little shed out there near Bethlem. They can be – free with themselves.'

'Lets them scream for the teat, like the hungry babes they be,' Joan put in helpfully.

Bickle's scowl softened. 'Haven't changed a bit, Joan Rugg.' She gave him a girlish grin. He turned back to Eleanor. 'So you were heading out that way with some jakes, you and—'

'Mary Potts,' said Joan.

'You and this Mary Potts, right, taking some fellows out there, was it?'

Eleanor shook her head. 'We were looking for somebody.'

'Looking for somebody. And who were you looking for?'

Eleanor said nothing.

'And who were you looking for then?'

'Tell him, Eleanor,' said Joan, her voice hardening. 'You tell him or I will myself, girl.'

Eleanor hesitated, feeling protective of Agnes.

He edged closer. 'This isn't only about a murder, now. This young lady went and stole something from the very Duke of Lancaster before she got herself killed. A book, is what it was. A *valuable* book. And from what I seem to be hearing from your pretty little mouth, could be your *somebody* went and stole it from *her*, yeah? Went and stole it from that girl, then killed her, yeah?' Bickle grasped her chin and turned her face to his. There was a plug of mint in his lip, his breath strangely pleasant, though his hands smelled of metal.

Eleanor tried to shake her head. 'I know less than nothing about the Duke of Lancaster, nor about some old book.'

'Could be, could be,' said Bickle. 'But I suspect your *somebody* might.'

'I – I couldn't say naught about that, Master Bickle.'

'You couldn't say naught.' He leaned in. 'A dead lady's one thing, *Edgar*.' He spat her man name in a tone that terrified her, then gripped her forearm. 'French lady of means dead on the Moorfields, you got the whole city asking questions: constables, subconstables, beadles and aldermen, the coroner and his deputy, all the way up to the king's household wants to know.' His grip tightened. 'But a dead maudlyn? Who'll give half a mind to that, hmm?' His gaze swept her face. She saw the flicker of revulsion. 'Dead swerver like you, floating in the Walbrook with the cats?'

Swerver. And that's what I am, like it or not. A man in body, a woman in soul. One day a *he*, the next a *she*, a stiff cock for some, a tight arse for others. Provided they could pay, Eleanor would do all and be all for her loyal jakes, and she had plenty who liked taking it and giving it every which way. Sometimes as a man, sometimes as a woman, sometimes as both at once, though that could get complicated. Why, just last week there was this gongfarmer, big-muscled and hairy as you could like, but get him in the stall and he starts to whinny like a gelding. Or a mare, more like, wants to take—

'Speak to the man, El,' said Joan Rugg. 'You speak, or I will.'

As Eleanor sat on the goldsmith's bench, her own life threatened over the death of a stranger, she felt her fear turn slowly to resentment, then to anger. She knew it wasn't Agnes who

45

killed that girl on the Moorfields. Yet who's Agnes Fonteyn to leave such a mess for Joan's mauds to clean up behind her? A book, the beadle says. A *valuable* book, stolen from Lancaster. And now Agnes has it. What's that whore doing with a book? Worse, she's keeping it to herself, after all I've done for her these years, the coin and bed we've shared, now here *I* am on a beadle's bench, getting *this*?

Eleanor's lips were inches from Bickle's ear. 'Agnes,' she said. 'Her name is Agnes Fonteyn.' And Eleanor Rykener, she did not add, will find her first.

SIX

Florence, near Orsanmichele

'You leave tomorrow. You will join the delegation at Bologna.' Adam Scarlett found a more comfortable position on the stool, one of four in the low single room that served as the friar's occasional dwelling. His left foot rested on the floor, his right on the hearth, scattered with ash and meal. As he spoke to Paolo Taricani he rocked himself slowly back until his head touched the stone wall, the cool on his neck a pleasant contrast to the chamber's stuffy heat.

'I will not do it.'

'Of course you will.'

'No.'

'Brother Paolo—'

'Send Teti. Or Efisio. Efisio makes sense. He is quick, young. Gets it up and in and twisted before the florin hits the floor.'

Scarlett ignored the hurried pleading. 'But you are the best, Paolo. And Ser Giovanni knows it. That is why he has chosen you for this extraordinary task.'

'I am *Il Prescelto*, then.' Taricani's sarcasm was thick, and Scarlett worried this could get difficult.

He sighed, recalling what Hawkwood had told him. *Take him as far as you can, Adam. If he's still balking bring him to me.*

He tacked right, appealing to Taricani's ego; left, to his civic pride. Nothing worked. Finally Scarlett stood. 'Let's go, Brother Paolo.'

The man frowned suspiciously. 'Go where?'

'San Donato a Torre.' Hawkwood's villa that season, a short ride to the north.

Taricani shook his head, still showing no fear. That could change, and quickly, but for the moment Scarlett let him prattle on. 'I will not go. I will not do this – this "extraordinary task", and I will not go with you.' He spat on the floor. His own floor. He looked tense, about to spring. His hand moved to his belt.

Scarlett spread his arms, slowly, and raised his hands to his sides. He gave the man a conciliatory nod. '*Bene*,' he said, and left the tenement, hating what he had to do next.

Taricani's house sat at the ass end of a narrow alley leading south from Orsanmichele. At the other end waited three of Hawkwood's roughest men, unmounted at the moment, their horses posted out in the piazza. Scarlett gave them the signal, then went to wait in front of the church, selecting the sharp corner at Via dei Pittori as his spot. The crumbling house of the Bigallo loomed overhead, knots of thirsty pilgrims draped around the plinths, waiting, like Paolo Taricani, for a miracle that would never come. On a high scaffold an old painter and his apprentice were at work retouching a David, hurling his stone at the giant. Scarlett wondered whether the outmatched Paolo, too, would fight, and if so, for how long. The man had too much to lose, though, and it was not long until he stumbled into the piazza, his hands bound at his waist, one eye blackened, the other cut and swollen.

Hawkwood's men had fared no better. One of them had

earned a long gash across his cheek, which he wiped with a quiet fury as the others threw the friar over a horse and set off across the piazza. Scarlett took his time, arriving back at San Donato a full hour after the others. Hawkwood had waited for him, though, and as Scarlett walked through the yard toward the house the *condottiero* was just coming out the villa's entrance. The men had bound Taricani to a chair, an ornate, high-backed seat brought out from the hall, and the man's thin face now showed a few more bruises, a second black eye.

Hawkwood stood before the chair, fixing Taricani with a friendly smile. 'You were Bernabò Visconti's swiftest knife for years, Brother Paolo. Why he let you retire I'll never know.'

Taricani shrugged. 'The *signore* has his methods, Ser Giovanni.'

'Indeed,' said Hawkwood. 'Might be interesting to plumb them with you someday.'

Taricani bunched his lips, exuding confidence. 'At your pleasure, Ser Giovanni.'

Stay humble, Scarlett silently warned the man.

Hawkwood knelt in the dirt. He placed a palm on each of Taricani's knees, looked up at his face. 'You have a beautiful woman, Brother Paolo.' He let that sit, then, 'And a daughter who ripens by the day. My men have seen her at the markets, Paolo. She can't be more than, what, ten, eleven?'

Taricani nodded, his eyes darkening.

'And her name, Paolo. It is memorable, isn't it, but I seem to have forgotten it. Help an old man, Paolo. What is your daughter's name?'

'Pic-Picco-Piccola-Piccolamela, sire.'

Hawkwood chuckled at Taricani's difficulty. 'Piccolamela. Now I remember! "Little apple" in my native tongue. An exquisite name for an exquisite girl, this virgin bastardess of an uncelibate friar. Did you choose this name yourself, Paolo?'

'My – her mother chose it, sire.'

'Well good for her. Piccolamela. How about that?' Hawkwood clapped his palms on Taricani's thighs, reading the new terror on his face. 'Though it's a strange coincidence. For do you know what my favourite fruit is, Paolo?'

Taricani shook his head.

'Can you guess?'

He shook his head again. Less confidence this time.

'Apples, Brother Paolo. I like apples best.'

Taricani's tongue flickered across his lips.

'And you know how I like my apples, Paolo?'

The assassin was still.

'Green, Paolo. I like my apples green.'

Taricani pressed against the ropes, then the pleas started. *No, Ser Giovanni, you wouldn't, Ser Giovanni, she is only a girl, Ser Giovanni, oh mercy, Ser Giovanni, mercy mercy mercy!* Scarlett listened for a while, then looked off into the hills until the begging faded into the familiar moans of a newly broken man.

Hawkwood stood, all business. 'The fate of your daughter's virtue is entirely up to you. If you refuse us we'll have her in hand this evening, and your whore as well. I'll make you watch, Paolo Taricani. I'll taste your little apple first, then hand her to my man Scarlett here, then we'll bring the garrison up from the river. I'll cut off your eyelids if I have to, but you'll watch every man take her, one by one, and in every way imaginable. You know I'll do it, too. You've seen me do worse. By God, you've *helped* me do worse, Paolo. And if you fail in your mission, if I get word you've bungled the thing, or fled, why – why then I will take your Piccolamela to Venice and sell her to the Turks. Little apples fetch a handsome price in the doge's slave markets.'

He bent over the puddled friar. 'On the other hand, Paolo, if you do this, know that I will take care of your daughter,

50

and your woman too. They won't be short of florins, and no one will lay a hand on them. And if you don't come back I will still protect them. Your daughter, though the illegitimate spawn of a half-lapsed friar, will marry well.'

Scarlett could see the resignation on Taricani's face, the defeated angle to his shoulders. But only for a moment. Taricani was a professional, after all, and this was a job like any other. Just a job. Scarlett watched him take a deep breath, nod at the ground, and look up at Hawkwood, his eyes lit with the cold flame of a born killer. 'At your service, Ser Giovanni.'

Hawkwood clapped the man on the shoulder. 'Very well, then.' He started to untie the knots, freeing Taricani from his chair. 'The rendezvous is set for Bologna. You'll have four spears of ours, in addition to any accompanying the delegation. From Bologna up to the Aosta pass and over to Geneva, then on the Rhine from Basel to Cologne. Next a hard ride to Hamburg, where you'll sail to Dover. The French are likely massing in Flanders, so there's no getting through by land to Calais.' Even as Hawkwood rattled off the sites along the itinerary Scarlett could hear the mix of wistfulness and anticipation in his lord's voice, thick with longing to make this journey his own.

'You will arrive in London the third week of May or thereabouts, and the thing is set for – well, Scarlett here will fill you in on the details. Should be a beautiful spring day.'

Hawkwood walked inside. Scarlett spoke to Taricani for a while longer, then hailed several of the men who had brought the man up from Florence. 'See him back to Orsanmichele. And, Paolo, this is for your woman, and for Piccolamela.' He tossed a purse on the dirt. Taricani rubbed his wrists, reached for it, and peered inside. He looked up at Scarlett. A grim nod. The job would be done, and done well, despite the cost. With that Paolo Taricani was taken back to Florence, for a final farewell to his family.

Inside the villa Hawkwood was staring up at the arms of his father, Gilbert Hawkwood, now his brother's: a lion rampant above a bend, the tendrils curling up the sides and the centre. The Inheritor, Hawkwood liked to call his brother. The *condottiero*'s own arms, much more prominently displayed on the east wall, consisted of a lone falcon poised above a tangled forest of vines.

'My father was a strange man, Adam,' Hawkwood said into the gloom. 'Imagine having three sons, and naming them all John. The eldest son, heir to the name, and all that comes with it. The youngest, also John Hawkwood, has the luck to die young. And the middle son? That's right: John Hawkwood.'

He sniffed. 'Middle John, my mother called me. "Does Middle John want his cider now?" "Time for Master Middle John to get him to his lessons!" And it all stacks on, doesn't it? Thornbury and the others, fled back to suck on Lancaster's teat with scarcely a word of thanks. My son-in-law takes my daughter away and now sits in Parliament, one of the highest men in Essex. Then all this business with Chaucer . . .'

'You've bought up half of Essex, John,' Scarlett said. 'Sible Hedingham, the lands around Gosfield.' He put a hand on Hawkwood's shoulder, a gesture to frame the familiar use of the *condottiero*'s first name. Hawkwood permitted it when they were alone, though Scarlett rarely took advantage. 'You own more of England than your brother ever could, let alone Coggeshale.' The son-in-law. 'Are you absolutely sure this is the wisest course? This is what you want for yourself, to reclaim your legacy under such circumstances?' He had been trying for weeks to turn the *condottiero* from his dark purpose; one last try, however weak, could not hurt.

Hawkwood reached up and patted Scarlett's hand, clasping it tightly as he nodded at his family's arms. 'It is not about me any more, Adam. It is about my son.'

'Your – your son, sire?'

'He's in Donnina's belly. I can *smell* him in there, baking away.'

This was news to Scarlett – and, he suspected, a bit of wishful thinking.

'The next Sir John Hawkwood will be a baron, Adam. Perhaps even an earl, belted by the king himself. And I won't curse the poor fellow with a brother, either. Perhaps I'll name him George.' He smiled, looked at his friend. 'Or Adam.'

Scarlett felt it, more deeply this time. The warm glow of inevitability and fate. Sir John Hawkwood was a hard man, the hardest he had ever known, but this plan of his, despite its ruthlessness, was melting the great mercenary into a soup of sentiment. 'His given name hardly matters, John. It's his surname that will bear his nobility.'

'Well spoken, Scarlett.' Hawkwood turned back to his family's arms, his eyes verdant with the ambition of a much younger man. 'England, Adam,' the *condottiero* said. 'It is time to go home.'

SEVEN

Temple Hall

Dozens of struggling lamps cast a hellish glow on the huddled apprentices, all stomping their feet against the raw air, their eager faces greyed by the smoke lowering down from those few chimneys rebuilt in this precinct since the Rising. I slowed in the middle of the courtyard and just watched them: their pent-up energy, their fear of rejection, their tentative pride at this rite of passage, all readable in the nervous poses struck as they waited. Forty young men, no more than half to be utter barristers by the evening's end.

Fifteen years had passed since my own, less formal initiation at the Temple, yet the occasion could still raise the hairs. As I stepped beneath the row of arches along the cloister a familiar voice stopped me. 'Is that you, John Gower?' I turned to see Thomas Pinchbeak hobbling along from Temple Church, with Chaucer holding an arm. 'Wait there.' He wiped his high forehead, exposed by the tight-fitting coif worn by his order. A capped stick bore part of his fragile weight.

'Good evening, Thomas. Geoffrey.' I took his stick and his other arm, my hand brushing the silk rope belted around his banded robes. Pinchbeak was a man who had grown into his name, with a long, sharp nose that jutted forward above lips pursed against some unnamed offence. Behind the serjeant-at-law's back Chaucer gave me a meaningful look, which I returned with a subtle shake of my head. We hadn't spoken since Monksblood's; I had no real news yet about the book, and I didn't want him to think I was avoiding him.

'Lurking at the fringes, I see,' Pinchbeak said to me, and I smiled at the ribbing. My ambivalent ties to the legal world were a matter of occasional amusement to Pinchbeak, newly a member of the Order of the Coif, one of the most powerful lawmen in the realm and now a royal nod away from appointment to justice of the King's Bench.

'You are one to talk.' I gestured across the lane at the last of the crowd straggling into the hall. 'Late, as always.'

'Ah, but I have the excuse of a wound,' he said, though something in his eyes belied his easy manner. A compact and wiry man, Pinchbeak had taken an arrow in his left thigh at Poitiers yet stood and fought for hours after, an incident that had rendered him both lame and legendary. When he gave the gold and ascended to serjeant not a soul in the realm begrudged him the honour. Yet his face that evening was troubled, and he seemed about to say something more when a small group of other serjeants-at-law surrounded him, hustling him gaily into the throng.

Chaucer watched him go in, then turned to me, his face lined with concern. 'Nothing?'

'Not really.'

'What did Swynford say?'

'Very little,' I said, deciding to mention nothing about the book's theft, nor about Swynford's peculiar suggestion regarding its prophetic nature. I needed to learn more first, and I was not in the business of giving away information, even to an intimate friend. 'She doesn't have it, if that's what you want to know. She'll do some discreet asking around.'

'I see,' said Chaucer, looking at me dubiously.

'I've only started searching, Geoffrey,' I said, wanting to give him something. 'London is a big place. A book could be anywhere.'

He gave me a tense nod.

'Just one question.' I pulled him out of the human flow. His eyes darted to the hall door, then back to the lane as I leaned into him, my mouth inches from his ear. 'What do you think this book is, my friend? What do you know about it that you haven't told me?'

I felt his breath on my cheek. 'Less every day, it seems.'

'And you're aware you're not the only one looking for it?'

'I suspect not,' he said. 'But I need you to find it first, John.'

I backed away, found his eyes. 'You know me, know my skills. If it's there to be found I'll find it.'

His shoulders rose slightly, and he grasped my arm before turning for the feast. We parted at the arched doorway into the great hall, where hundreds of lawmen were already at table, ladling soup, picking flesh from lavish trays of sauced cod and porpoise. At the front of the space stood the pageant wagon, covered in a cloth that obscured everything but the wheels. As I found a seat the men around a far table lifted their glasses in song. The crowd joined in, the din rising to the rafters and the darkened spaces high above.

> *Twice two full quarts we lawyers need,*
> *To fill a legal jug.*
> *With one, we're gay, with two, we teach,*
> *With three, we prophesy.*
> *And four good quarts it takes to bind*
> *Legal senses, legal tongues,*
> *A lawyer's hands and mind.*

Cups and flagons clashed on the last word, drink sloshed, the sobriety of Lent set aside for an evening. The clamour stirred a familiar longing. Though I had spent two formative years at the Temple, my father had not allowed me to remain in the profession. For an esquire's son the practical application of law was regarded in those days as a rather low trade. Had I been born ten years later I might well have been sitting that night with Pinchbeak and the serjeants instead of on that crowded bench, shrouded in ignorance.

The line of nervous apprentices formed for the tap. As the first hopeful presented himself, the presiding master leaned forward and plucked at his gown, the mark of unsuitability. The young man turned away, his eyes already moist at the prospect of another year before his next chance at admittance. Other unlucky souls followed him out over the next little while until the successful class stood at the front of the hall to great applause. A few pompous speeches, then, with cake and ale served out, the main event began.

Up stood Stephen FitzWilliams, master of the utter barristers. Delighting in his role, he pushed himself on to the pageant wagon, his legs swinging freely between the wheels, his gown hanging loosely on a gaunt frame. He spread his hands above his head, gathering silence.

'Gentlemen of the law,' he intoned. 'I bid you fair evening, and good fare made of our moot!'

'*Huzzah! Huzzah! Huzzah!*' the crowd replied.

'As your new-appointed liege, your sovereign, your emperor and king—'

Someone threw a fish spine.

'Leave that off!' He loudly cleared his throat. 'It has fallen to me to determine our evening's weighty matter, to be mooted before you.'

'*Huzzah!*'

'Last year on a similar occasion we mooted some obscure clauses of the Statute of Merton, did we not?'

'*We did!*'

'Our disputations involved the writ of redisseisin. In the Latin of our beloved Parliament, *Et inde convicti fuerint* et cetera et cetera. Which is glossed, in our Frenchy cant, *Ceo serra entendu en le breve de redisseisin vous vous cadew hah*oo *haloo* and thus and so. Shall we revisit this well-trodden ground, as dry as pestled bone?'

'*Nay!*'

'Perhaps we should dabble in the assize of novel disseisin.'

'*Nay!*'

'In default of a tenant *en le taile*?'

'*Nay!*'

'In the wrongful appropriation by a tortious patron?'

'*Nay!*'

'In theft?'

'*Nay!*'

'In misprision?'

'*Nay!*'

'In the law of bankruptcy?'

'*Nay!*'

'Well then, you leave me no choice!' A master of delivery, FitzWilliams had brought me and everyone else in the great hall to the edges of our seats.

'Our subject for this year's moots shall be a matter of universal and urgent concern.' He leaned forward, an air of suspense in his thrown whisper. 'Methinks the matter of our March moot, my matriculating men, must be . . .' The pause lengthened until finally FitzWilliams, his head bent back, his nose pointing to the ceiling far above, screamed, '*MUST BE MURDERRRRR!*'

A collective whoop went up from young and old alike, followed by a round of sustained applause. As the claps and stomps faded and the men retook their seats, I glanced over at the upper benches, where the serjeants-at-law sat in high station. Thomas Pinchbeak, I saw, was leaning forward and speaking with some urgency to two of his colleagues. I could understand their consternation, as even the more festive moots generally treated the finer points of property and torts. A murder trial would not be unprecedented, but it would require the substitution of mere spectacle for legal rigor. I was somewhat surprised that the young men had opted for such a subject.

FitzWilliams hopped down and grasped a corner of the drapery. 'Servants of the law,' he shouted, his eyes wild, 'I give you the evening's bench!' In one flourish he pulled off the canvas. The applause was thunderous as the crowd took in the mock court on the wagon: the stern judges in a ponderous line, the pompous bailiff, a hunch-backed recorder, and finally the accused, bound standing to a rail by his legs and wrists, his teeth gnashing, his face twisted in mock agony at the imagined hanging in his near future.

The most remarkable part of the spectacle was the scene laid out on a narrow platform jutting forward from the left front of the wagon. A scraggly hawthorn bush, potted in an oaken tub, suggested the outdoors, as did several inches of loose dirt spread around it. On the soil, face down, lay a young man, his torso bare, his waist and legs clad in a flesh-coloured costume, the buttocks exaggerated with padding.

'Our victim, if you please!' FitzWilliams called out over the roars of approval. The actor rose to his knees, cutting a ghoulish figure. His chest had been shaved clean and painted with wide crescents traced to suggest breasts. Between the legs of the suit had been sewn a triangle of animal pelt. And from his head, adorned with a wig of long, dark hair, a dried shower of red paint descended in a glistening path, its source a crusted wound mocked up in gruesome detail.

I looked again at the cluster of serjeants. At least five of the powerful men were now visibly agitated, their gestures conveying strong displeasure at the subject of the performance. There was clearly some disagreement, though: I guessed that several of them wished to halt the murder moot, while others felt reluctant to take action, with all the objections this would raise. Yet why, I wondered, was this spectacle provoking their concern at all, given the usual tenor of plays at the Temple? Such pageants were notorious for their bawdy and even violent content, some of them ending in blows; this one appeared no different.

FitzWilliams had pressed a cluster of utter barristers into service as the jury. He held up his hands.

'Let us review the facts of the case,' he said. 'First: before us lies a young woman. A virgin, I'm told – though I have not, personally, performed the requisite inspection.' He put a finger in the air, drawing earthy calls.

The victim sat up, pursed his rouged lips in a kiss, then, with a wan wave, collapsed. 'Her head crushed,' FitzWilliams continued, 'her fair body stripped of its dress, her raiment laid carelessly over a rock. So far a straightforward matter, no? A fair maiden wandering in a place where a woman should never venture alone. Attacked. Perhaps ravished. Surely killed.'

An exaggerated frown. 'But consider the complexities of the case before us. First, where did this act most foul occur? Not in London, but outside the walls – indeed in the Moorfields, hard by Bethlem Priory, where the wood are wont to wander.'

A crowd along a side wall sent up a wolfish howl, and my skin went suddenly cold. Katherine Swynford, at La Neyte. *It was a young woman . . . Someone skulled her, out on the Moorfields.*

My vision blurred as FitzWilliams continued. 'The location

of the crime introducing, then, the matter of jurisdiction, which some will place under the abbot of Bethlem. Others will contend that the Moorfields as a whole lie within an outer ward of the city. In what court, then, and by whose authority shall this matter be adjudicated?'

A movement to my left. Pinchbeak had summoned two pursuivants.

'More central to our purposes this evening, though,' FitzWilliams continued, 'shall be the nature of the crime: how are we to determine whether we are facing a killing *ex malicia praecogitata*, or an accidental death? Was she killed with a club to the skull? Or' – he held up a knife, then placed the blade against his chest – 'with a steely thrust to her heart?' At this last word FitzWilliams plunged the knife into his chest and doubled over.

A few shouts of alarm from the more gullible and drunk, but mostly laughter as he withdrew the wooden blade. For me the moot had lost all its humour.

'Ah, but wait!' The murmurs died down. 'We must now reveal the identity of the accused.' He dug a hand into a pocket. 'Why, what's this?' He pulled out a parchment, waved it before the room. 'The indictment, honourable gentlemen! Inscribed by His Honour himself, Justice Beelzebub Barnes of Brixton!' He stood at the top of the aisle between the rows of tables. 'In this document,' he shouted, 'is written the very name of the accused!'

'*Huzzah! Huzzah!*'

'As well as his profession, our next matter for rumination. And what is the profession of our accused, you may ask? A moment . . .' He held the document up to the lamplight. 'Our alleged killer is – a highwayman?'

'*No!*'

'A street vagrant, then?'

'*Nay!*'

61

'How about – how about a friar?'

'*The friar*! *The friar*!'

FitzWilliams shook his head, shining an exaggerated sadness around the great hall. 'Incorrect, gentlemen of the bar, the killer is not a friar!'

General laughter, and as it crested, then ebbed, I noticed a small stir from afar, rendered peculiar only by its timing. In the hall's north corner Chaucer rose from his seat, nodded an apology to his benchmates, and ducked through the low doorway leading to the buttery. As the door closed to on his back FitzWilliams adopted a more serious look. 'Our alleged murderer is not a priest, nor a bishop, nor a cardinal. He is neither a cooper nor a cordwainer, neither a mercer nor a shipwright, neither a pinner nor a—'

'Let's just have it, then, Fitzy!' someone shouted from the back.

FitzWilliams looked up, affecting offence. More titters. I sat forward, confused by Chaucer's departure at the height of the apprentice's spectacle. With a flourish, FitzWilliams gazed across the crowd. 'Have it we shall. Our murderer is, rather, a p—'

'*Huzzah! Huzzah! Huzzah!*'

Loud shouts, drowning out FitzWilliams's revelation with the force of a gale. The serjeants-at-law, twenty strong and with Thomas Pinchbeak hobbling in the lead, rushed the pageant wagon as a single dark-robed mass, their gowns spread above their heads like bat wings as they mobbed the players. Three of the younger serjeants climbed on the wheels and proceeded to demolish the set, kicking apart the flimsy rails, ripping the robes from the judges, releasing the accused from his bonds. Two others grappled the 'victim' off the side platform and stripped the costume from his flesh, leaving him only in his braies, then sent him into the crowd with a jar of wine over his head.

Utter pandemonium: screams of delight and alarm; cups, jars, and flagons flying overhead, to shatter against the walls; serjeants and apprentices alike screaming to the rafters, some enjoying the skirmish, others frightened nearly for their lives; the wagon overturned on the floor, its spoked wheels and siderails broken on impact; the melee thrown in long shadows by hooped candelabra casting pantomimes of disorder against every surface.

Even the wildest revels must end, however, and eventually, as the tumult subsided and the barristers and apprentices surveyed the results, there was a general quieting through the hall, an almost embarrassed assessment of the state of things. I watched and listened to the reactions. Many held that the disruption had been coordinated between the utter barristers and the serjeants, perhaps as a staged commentary on the poor quality of the recent moots. Others avowed that the serjeants saw murder as inappropriate for mooting, and broke the spectacle up accordingly. There were still others who had observed what I had during the lead-up to the interruption: the anger of the serjeants-at-law, the whispered conferrals among England's most powerful lawmen, the decision taken to rush the players before their moot had even begun.

Yet there was something more that had disturbed me about the spectacle, something I would scarcely admit to myself as I lingered in the great hall. I sat at my bench for a long while, watching the overturned wagon as the space emptied of barristers, of serjeants, of apprentices and guests, until only the servers were left. Around me they swept up broken bits of glass and clay, gathered the leavings of the students' extravagance into buckets that would now feed pigs, dogs, their children in the tenements. As the hall emptied my certainty deepened, and a tingling of unease began at the bottom of my spine, moved up my back, and settled into my heart as a coiled suspicion.

My memory replayed the course of the abbreviated moot: the introduction of the case, the gaudy spectacle of the victim, Chaucer's unexplained departure through the kitchen door – and finally, the naming of the accused. In that moment before the serjeants shouted him down, I could swear with a near certainty that one final word had escaped FitzWilliams's mouth. *Our murderer is, rather, a p—*

It seemed unlikely in the extreme that the man had suggested such a thing. Yet I had heard it from his lips, was sure of it: the one word that could most have affected me as I took in the lewd spectacle of a young woman's violent death. *Our murderer is, rather, a p—*

One word: *poet.*

✠ ✠ ✠

Worshipful Sir, and Our Most Intimate Friend,

Your muse finds herself in peril. Upon your return from Rome you will fondle not her supple skin but this rough parchment. Here on the banks of the Arno it will await you, just as my flesh awaits reunion with your own.

Those pleasures must be delayed, for in the morning I leave our Tuscan Eden for the coast. From there I shall arrange passage to that faraway island our histories call Albion, and you call home.

You are a lover of stories. Stories of love, lust, and loss. Of wars, rivalry, and revenge. Of the commonplace and the unlikely. The story I must now tell you is woven of all these threads, and more besides.

You know its characters, some better than others, though you cannot know, as I do, the depths of their perfidy and the heights of their nobility. Even to commit this tale to writing is to subject you, its reader, to the same peril that stalks me now. For Hawkwood's talons are sharp, his vision is keen, and his enemies tend to die young.

I can delay no longer. Time is short, and there is much to relate.

Here, my only heart, is the story.

✠

Once, along the Castilian marches, beyond the Crown of Aragon, there lived a knight. Not a great knight; no one would have mistaken him for a Lancelot, a Gawain, a Roland, though where he fell short of these famed knights in ferocity, he matched every one of them in honour. To his lord he was a model of duty. To his own men he was the very mirror of chivalry: swift of sword, moderate in judgment. Toward his people he acted fairly and wisely in all things.

Our knight kept a castle. Not a great castle; no one would have mistaken it for the alcázar of Pedro the Cruel, nor for Avignon's

65

papal palace, nor England's palace of Westminster. Yet its walls of broad stone and heavy mortar kept our marcher lord well defended from the occasional marauder.

Our knight had a wife. A beautiful wife indeed, so beautiful one might well have mistaken her for Helen, or Guinevere, or for the Laura of Petrarco. She was the daughter of a minor count of questionable lineage. A family of Moorish blood, not a few whispered, keeping the faith of Mahound while miming love of the Cross. Yet as the knight was trusted by his people, such whisperings were soon quieted, his small, dark wonder of a wife accepted into the circles of Castilian ladies gathered on occasion at court.

Soon a daughter arrived. She was, like her mother, dark and small. She captivated her parents. The knight, of course, wanted a son. The wife was still young, and though the years went by with no further issue, there was little doubt that God would someday reward them.

It came to pass, when the daughter was approaching her seventh year, that the knight was summoned by his lord to battle. Not a minor border skirmish, but a major campaign in a larger war that threatened to conscript every able-bodied man from the Pyrenees to the port of Cádiz. You will know of this war: of Pedro the Cruel and Enrique de Trastámara, of brothers divided against themselves. When Pedro called, our knight gathered the might of his men, leaving only a small garrison behind.

Word soon came of a bloody battle in Nájera, a battle in which King Pedro won back the crown of Castile from his bastard brother. Though this victory was to be short-lived, the tidings brought considerable joy to the castle and town, despite the additional news that the lord's return would be delayed many months as King Pedro led his army to further battles against the lingering enemies of the crown. In her knight's long absence the lady saw to the needs of his property and people, with an added touch of feminine grace that delighted those around her.

On the Day of St Dominic, as the lady and her daughter strolled in the castle's herb garden, the scents of rosemary and lavender mingling in the hot calm of an August afternoon, a blotch on the northern hills caught the little girl's eye. She squinted against the sun.

Dust, yet not from a storm. The road from Burgos was dry, and any single horse would kick up a mass of saffron powder that might linger for hours.

The cloud she saw now filled the horizon. Forty horses, perhaps fifty. She tugged at her mother's dress. They gazed together at the approaching force, their hearts lifting against a darkening sky.

The Day of St Dominic. The day the strangers came.

EIGHT

Rose Alley, Southwark

The Pricking Bishop. Edgar Rykener shook his head at the painted sign, amazed that the Bishop of Winchester allowed such pictures in his liberties. Lord Protector of Whores, they called him up on Gropecunt Lane, defending his right to run as many houses as he pleased across the river in Southwark while the hard-working maudlyns of London got constantly harassed by the law. Joan Rugg would go on about it for half a day. Unlike Gropecunt Lane, the stews of Southwark embraced their natural filth, the half-pipe gutters stopped up with brackish water of a murky green, the conduits to the river long forgotten by the bishop's underworked ditchers. Wobbly shacks had been built out into the streets to claim space for shops, while the oblong fishponds at the western end walled off the great houses on the riverbanks beyond. No sweepers or rakers to maintain the streets, nor regular dung carts to haul away the most offensive waste.

On the Bishop's front steps sat a withered old maudlyn, barely there beneath her shift and smock. St Cath was her name, Edgar recalled, still alive after half a century on her back. A dozen cats wandered in and out of the half-opened door, pressing against St Cath's side or darting past while she ignored them.

'Is Bess about?' Edgar asked her. The old woman said nothing. 'Bess Waller, be she about?'

St Cath shifted against the step. 'Bess Waller,' she said, as if speaking the name of a stranger. Her face, crossed by a thousand lines, registered no emotion.

Edgar tapped his foot.

St Cath spat. 'The matter of it?'

'Not your concern.'

'Nor be Bess Waller none of yours.'

Edgar stood on his toes and peered into the doorway.

'Not a peek more,' said the woman, pushing away one of the cats and struggling to stand, 'but you proffer your pennies like the fine gentlemen of the parish.'

He snorted. 'For the love of St Thomas, woman, all I'm about here is looking out for Bess's daughter.'

'Millicent?' she said quickly. 'Hunting Millicent Fonteyn in the stews?' St Cath shook her bent frame and wheezed, wagged her small head. 'Won't find that knight's trull in Southwark. Best look up Cornhull for Millicent. *Duchess* Millicent by now, for all we knows over here.'

Edgar thought over the woman's response. Something about it didn't sit right. 'It's not Millicent I'm about. It's Agnes.'

'Agnes?'

Not this again. 'Yes, Agnes, you withered hag, sometime maud of the Bishop. Is Agnes Fonteyn about, or'd your witchcraft turn her into one of these cats?'

St Cath glared at her. 'Agnes hasn't been about since Epiphany time.'

'That's right.' Bess Waller, bawd of the Pricking Bishop, leaned against the doorsill looking Edgar over. Despite two daughters and years of swyving, Bess had angles to her face that could only be boasted by the mother of Agnes Fonteyn; also the same lithe form, the same golden hair still radiant as she neared fifty. 'You're El—Edgar Rykener, are you not?'

'I am,' said Edgar. They'd met last year, soon after Agnes had left the Southwark stews and joined Joan Rugg's crew in Cheap Ward. Bess Waller had come after her younger daughter with a club while the bawd was away, trying to beat Agnes back to the Bishop, pleading the strength of family and roots. But Agnes had stuck to Gropecunt Lane, and now she was pure London.

'As I was telling your lovely serjeant-of-the-gate here, I need to have a word with Agnes. She about?'

'She's not,' said Bess. 'We miss her round the stews though, that right, St Cath?'

The old woman nodded. 'Miss her all right.'

'Agnes had the cock lining up at the door,' said Bess. 'Something in the sweet air off her, that way she got with her head. That toss, you know?' She mimicked it perfectly. 'And always had since she's a girl. Sweet piece of sweetmeats, that one. Still sucking it off up Cheapside?'

Edgar rested a foot on the step, stretched his tired thighs. 'Our bawd's Joan Rugg.'

'Joan Rugg!' Bess cackled. 'Taught that fat hen everything she knows about the cock. How to fondle it like one of St Cath's kittens here, how to clamp it atween her thighs for the while of a paternoster. The gentle cock's your false idol, Joan, I tell her, and treating it right will bring you all the riches you can want. A fast learner, by St Bride. Just like Agnes.'

And what a homily to motherhood Agnes had in you, Edgar thought. 'So,' he said. 'Not a sight of her, then?'

Bess wiped her nose. 'Why you seeking out my Agnes?'

'Had some little business to pestle with her.'

70

'Business.'

'Thought she might've stepped over the river. If not, then . . .'

'Then . . .?' Bess raised her eyebrows.

Edgar took a step back, his gaze moving up the façade to the second-storey windows, one of them wedged open. A giggle, a slap, a moan.

Bess clucked. 'Best you be off, pretty boy. Got some gentlemen coming by next bell. Don't want my jakes inconvenienced.'

'I'm thinking the same,' said Edgar, also thinking there was more going on here than Bess Waller would reveal. He gave the bawd a meaningful look. 'You tell Agnes her Edgar come by, though.'

'Sure sure,' said Bess. 'Though could be Easter, could be All Souls all I know. But I'll tell her you were by. You give Joanie a Jesu palm on the arse from her Bess, hear?'

Edgar turned and walked down Rose Alley to the bankside. There he paused and looked back at the Pricking Bishop. Bess Waller's arms were in the air, her face beet-red as she let St Cath have it, for what he didn't know.

On the bridge he purchased a farthingloaf and pinched off pieces of coarse bread, washing them down with some warmed beer. As he crossed the Thames he thought of the peculiar twinge of suspicion he'd felt on first telling St Cath why he was there. What was it about the old woman's words that had unsettled him?

Millicent.

Bess Waller's older daughter, Millicent Fonteyn, lived in a decent house along Cornhull, had some money and wanted more. She'd had nothing to do with her mother nor her sister for a long time. While Agnes had only recently left her mother's stewhouse for the streets of London, Millicent Fonteyn was no more than a distant memory on Rose Alley.

Yet the moment Edgar had asked St Cath whether Bess Waller's daughter was about, the old woman had responded swift as you please.

Millicent? Hunting Millicent Fonteyn in the stews?

Which meant what? Which meant St Cath, flustered at Edgar's prodding, was covering for Agnes. He nodded, sure of it now. Agnes has been at the Pricking Bishop, he thought; may be there still, the little tart. And who, he wondered for the hundredth time, was that poor dead girl on the moor?

NINE

Two appointments set for that morning, the first with the wife of a disgruntled notary to the king's secretary with a copy of a royal writ to sell. We met in an alley above the stone wharf. She had brought a maidservant along for appearance's sake, and perhaps to impress me. As the servant dawdled at the end of the alley she sidled up close, wanting to flirt. She was an attractive woman, with soft curls peeking from beneath a loosened bonnet, full lips, cheeks pinched a bright pink, and I felt an unfamiliar stir that I promptly pushed aside.

'The writ?' I finally said, taking a small step back.

'Here, sir,' she said, offering it to me. The original, or so her husband claimed, had been sent under the king's own signet, a sign of Richard's increasing tendency to bypass set procedures in the administration of the realm. I read the hurried copy carefully, scanning for that useful detail. *The king to Sir Richard de Brompton, greeting. I command you to do full right without delay . . .* A knight of Shropshire, a mercer of Shrewsbury, and a debt of nearly two hundred

73

pounds. Yet I knew Brompton, a notorious debtor I'd had occasion to pluck a few years before. This was nothing new.

I shook my head. 'Sorry.'

She looked at me, a promise in her moist eyes. 'Not even a shilling, Master Gower?'

I suppressed a shudder. 'Nor a farthing, I'm afraid. But do tell your husband to be on the lookout for this sort of thing. You never can tell what might rise to the top. He knows how to reach me.'

She mumbled something, tightened her bonnet, then slunk off toward the palace with her maidservant. I followed them at a discreet distance and watched as they merged into the crowd around the south doors.

In the great hall I looked about for Ralph Strode, my second appointment in Westminster that morning, but when I reached our meeting place before Common Pleas at the north end a sudden silence swept the chamber. King Richard, in from Eltham Palace for the day, showing himself off. I went to my knee like every other man in the massive space, watching as the king came to the centre of the hall, paused with a practised deliberation, then gestured for all to rise and go about their business, though as always in his presence the talk was subdued. He wore long robes cut in the French fashion, a wide collar squeezing his thin neck. His fair hair, shoulder length and uncovered, swept from side to side as he spoke to his minions and those seeking a word. The king's impromptu entries into Westminster Hall were of a piece with his increasing love of ceremony, these portentous shows of authority that brought him in ritual touch with his subjects as often as he liked. If he caught your eye on one of these occasions you took a knee, no questions asked.

Yet there was a strange gentleness in the young king's bearing, a warmth of gesture and look I had never felt from his father, whose princely arrogance had surpassed even Gaunt's among old King Edward's sons. Though barely into his nineteenth year, this man had real reverence for the crown and its regal history, in ample evidence around the space. King Richard had recently commissioned statues of England's past kings to be installed around the hall, with his own likeness culminating the series. The Confessor already stood in splendour against the south wall, his robes and crown gilded luxuriously, and a limner at work on his feet.

I leaned unobtrusively against one of the hall's great pillars, watching the king, when his head turned in my direction. His eyes found mine, and sparkled with what looked like affection. It took me aback: since his coronation I'd had perhaps three brief interactions with the king, none of them remarkable in any way. Surprised by this sliver of royal attention, I went to my knee and held the pose until King Richard released me with a slight, boyish smile and a swivel of his chin. It was a moment of genuine connection I would hold in my mind in the weeks ahead, as I learned of our intertwined fates.

'Quite a mess up there.' Ralph Strode had come up behind me. He grasped my arm. We gazed together into the vaults, the moist flakes of sawdust descending in thin streams, stirred up by work on a platform high above. For years there had been talk of an entire new roof, though for now all was timber and shingle, the ceiling playing a constant game of catch-up against rain and birds, bats and wind.

King Richard left the hall, the accustomed din rising again in his wake. As I turned to walk with Strode I was struck by his appearance. The common serjeant's skin was deeply veined, his eyes rheumy, his skin puffy and pink. He barked a wheezing cough into his sleeve.

'You're the busiest man in London, Ralph. I appreciate the time.'

He shook his head. 'For you I'd renegotiate the date of Easter with the Greeks!'

We strolled along the booths as I told him why I was there. For months I had been tangled up over my lands east of Southwark. A wealthy merchant, building a house on a neighbouring lot, had sued for ownership, claiming that certain acreage fell within the boundaries of his property. Though the case hardly threatened my livelihood, it was requiring more of my time than it deserved, and I could find nothing to use against the man. Strode had just the sort of urban pull to finesse a transfer of jurisdiction from the bishop's court across the river. He was one of the few men in London's upper bureaucracy I could honestly call a friend, and he owed me a stack of favours as high as the north tower. 'The short of it, Ralph, is that I want to get this moved to Westminster, into Common Pleas.'

'You'll need a writ of *pone*, then,' Strode said.

'There may be some complications.'

He asked about the deeds, security, documentation, clarifying several matters. At the end he shook his head dismissively. 'None of this should present a problem for writ of *pone*. I'll put James Tewburn on it when I get back to the Guildhall.'

I inclined my head. 'You're a big gem, Ralph.'

'Believe me, it will be my most pleasant task of the week, and if I can use it to avoid other entanglements . . .' His stride stiffened a bit, a hint of trouble in his eyes. 'Especially this Bethlem mess.'

'Oh?' He was turned away and didn't see my reaction.

'The killing up there,' he went on. 'Quite a foul business.'

'So I understand.'

'Didn't help to have the whole thing played by those student hoodlums the other night. For days I've heard clusters of barristers bragging on the affair: the first moot ever busted up by the serjeants! The mayor's courts at the Guildhall are

76

buzzing with it, then I come out here and the murder and its mooting are the talk of Westminster.'

There did seem to be a certain thickness in the air, several animated conversations nearby clearly occupied with more than the usual legal matter. Michael de la Pole, whom I had last seen at La Neyte, stood in the middle of one of them. The chancellor gave me a slight nod when I caught his eye. 'Has the killer been apprehended?' I asked Strode.

'No, nor the victim's identity discovered. No name, no associates, no claimant to her body.' His voice lowered to a near-whisper. 'She was last seen alive at La Neyte. Now it's rumoured she was an agent of Valois.'

'A spy? Here in England?' I thought back to that moment with Tugg at Newgate, which was supposedly filled with French spies.

'So it seems.'

'Why do they think she's French?'

He shrugged. 'Her clothing, for one. And those who heard her speak claimed her accent smacked of Provence. Avignon, perhaps.' A word with grim associations: the schism of the church, a holy empire divided against itself, and France's ally against the true pope in Rome.

Our circles had brought us through each arcade twice, and we now approached the opened doors to the north porch, looking out on the yard. Strode gazed across the line of tents pitched along the hedges. 'War's coming, John. You can see it in the king's face. All this business with the Scots, the truce nearly at an end.' The royal delegation had recently left for negotiations to extend the peace, though no one expected anything to come of them. 'Imagine a French fleet, an invasion force, pulling its way up the Thames.' He looked over the shapeless mound of his nose and across the space. 'Ten thousand Frenchmen set on revenging their countrymen starved at Calais, or slaughtered at Crécy. What would such a host do to Westminster, to our children?' He leaned over a balustrade, elbows on the stone. 'To have their spies infiltrate London itself? Unthinkable.'

I needed more. 'And the girl?'

Strode shrugged his heavy shoulders. 'At La Neyte she was flitting from room to room, admired but unremarked. She was there a whole day, pretending to be a lady-in-waiting to the Countess of Bethune, one of Gaunt's guests. Bethune and the countess had already left for Kenilworth, you see, so no one was there to discredit her. And her story was unassailable. She stayed behind, she told everyone who asked, in order to procure a particular variety of Flemish cloth desired by the countess. At last, by asking the right questions of the right people, the girl found what she was looking for. She stole it and fled, presumably to hand it over to another spy. No one knows whether she succeeded.' He licked his lips. 'Then she was killed.'

'In the Moorfields.'

'Yes.'

'Who found her body?'

'I don't know.'

'Who examined it, attempted an identification?'

His nostrils flared. 'Tyle.' The coroner of London, Thomas Tyle, a man Strode had long despised. Lazy, incompetent, sloppy in his record-keeping, Tyle was an intimate of the king's chamberlain, and let everyone within hearing know it at every opportunity.

'Strange,' I said into the clamour of starlings angling toward the riverbank. 'A murder in the Moorfields? That's outside the walls. Not Tyle's jurisdiction.' Ralph knew this as well as I did, and as I studied his face I could tell the irregularity had been gnawing at him.

He looked at me. 'Nor Tyle's usual practice, to show up and do his actual job.'

'True.' In cases of unnatural deaths, it was the subcoroner

78

who nearly always performed the inquest. Why, then, had Tyle himself taken over the scene? I posed a final question, trying to keep my tone light. 'And what did our French beauty steal out from under Lancaster's nose?' Katherine Swynford had already told me, but I wanted to test Strode's knowledge.

He gazed through the cloud of starlings, black slashes against the sky. 'A book.'

TEN

Broad Street, Ward of Broad Street

'A nun and a maud, and here we are together again.'

Millicent looked at her sister, huddled in the darkness. Agnes had stayed in the Cornhull house that morning while Millicent went out to sell the bracelet her sister had found on the body in the Moorfields. The tiny piece had fetched a few shillings on Silver Street, enough to keep them fed for a week or two, though what they would do after that was a mystery. She sighed. 'I was hardly a nun, Agnes.'

'Well, you lived among them out at St Leonard's Bromley. Got their speech, learned to read like a master.'

'Not quite,' said Millicent. 'But I darned their robes, smoothed their wimples.' She stared at the book, wondering at the peculiar motivations of its maker. 'Then Sir Humphrey ap-Roger came along, and they put me out as a concubine.'

'Girl who lives as a nun *is* a nun, leastwise in my book. Not that this is my book now, by the cross.'

Millicent had just struggled through a second reading of this dark work: a difficult book, filled with words and turns of phrase the Bromley sisters had never taught her. *An educated laity is our order's highest aspiration, Millicent,* Prioress Isabel had reminded her many times. *To know that God's teachings are well water to the thirstful – this is one of the central works of our contemplative life.* Millicent had cut her teeth on the devotional texts made available to her by the Bromley sisters, though she had never read anything like this. The verse was bumpy, like her heartbeat, with repeated letters throughout and four hammering thumps to each line. Like a minstrel's romance, sung in the halls of lords.

> *The bone that he breaketh be baleful of harm,*
> *Nor treachery's toll with treason within . . .*

> *A woman with womb that woes him to wander*
> *For love of his lemman, his life worth a leaf . . .*

Such lines, as she murmured them to her sister, carried dire threats, each one of them tuned to the fate of an English king. Yet much of the work remained obscure, its lines heavy with symbols she couldn't decipher. Hawks, swords, thistles, and much else.

'So what's it all mean, Mil?'

Millicent thought for a while. 'Twelve prophecies, and I think I've undressed most of them. From the songs the minstrels sing, the plays they put on at Bromley Manor, St Paul's, everywhere.' The sisters knew these stories well, as did all Londoners: lays of olden kings, ballads of Harold and William the Conqueror, the story of the Lionheart, dying in his mother's arms. 'Twelve kings of England, Ag, all dead in the very way the minstrels say they went. Age, battle, disease, a poker in the arse.'

'Kings can die a lot of ways, eh?' Agnes shook her head.

'The great question, though, is, what will be the *next* way?' Millicent found the passage on the final pages that most concerned her: twelve lines of verse, speaking with a terrifying force of her own moment.

Agnes looked confused, so Millicent read through several of the prophecies and glossed along the way. 'I hardly know all our kings, Ag, but as for the ones I do know, the book seems to have it about right. And now we have here, in these last lines, the thirteenth prophecy.'

'The thirteenth prophecy?'

'The death of King Richard himself.' Millicent recited the most baleful passage in the work.

> 'At Prince of Plums shall prelate oppose
> A faun of three feathers with flaunting of fur,
> Long castle will collar and cast out the core,
> His reign to fall ruin, mors regis to roar.
> By bank of a bishop shall butchers abide,
> To nest, by God's name, with knives in hand,
> Then springen in service at spiritus sung.
> In palace of prelate with pearls all appointed,
> By kingmaker's cunning a king to unking,
> A magnate whose majesty mingles with mort.
> By Half-ten of Hawks might shender be shown.
> On day of Saint Dunstan shall Death have his doom.'

'There it is then,' said Agnes, her face brightening.

'There what is?'

'It lays out the place of the killing, doesn't it? "In palace of prelate" and "by bank of a bishop". A palace by a river. A bishop's palace.'

'Braybrooke?' Millicent remembered a float with Sir Humphrey to the Bishop of London's riverside residence.

'Or our own Wykeham,' said Agnes. William Wykeham, the Bishop of Winchester, whose palace in Southwark stretched along a fair span of the Thames. 'Then it gives the killer's method, aye? Nesting with knives in hand, then springing forth—'

'"At spiritus sung",' Millicent finished for her. 'What's that mean, then?'

Agnes shrugged. 'Prayer, could be, ending in *spiritus*. Like a signal.'

'A signal.'

'"Cause they'll have help, won't they?'

'From a "kingmaker",' said Millicent. 'A magnate whose majesty is mingled with *mort*.'

'Who's this Mort?'

'Not who but what, dearheart,' Millicent said gently, stifling a laugh. '*Mort* is France's word for death.'

'Ah.' Agnes frowned. 'But the book tells who wants the king dead, or at least how to know them for what they be. The shenders'll show themselves by "Half-ten of Hawks", whatever that might betoken.'

'Five hawks, then,' Millicent said.

Agnes frowned. 'Why not say five?'

'*H*alf-ten. *H*awks.' Millicent emphasized the common first letter of each word. 'It's the verse.'

'So the killer of our king will be carrying five hawks on his arm?'

'That's a lot of hawks for one arm,' Millicent mused.

Agnes crawled forward on the rushes, took the cloth that had covered the book in hand, and spread it over the floor. 'Five hawks, the book says, and there they are, clustered around the shield. Now I see it, Mil!' She turned round to her sister. 'It's like wool and a spinning wheel.'

Millicent squatted by the cloth.

'Without the wheel, the wool is just wool.' Agnes cradled an imagined basket. 'What good be a basket of wool if you haven't made it into thread yet? But once you've wound it on the spindle, started turning your wheel' – her hands spun the air – 'why, the wool starts to twist itself together, and soon you got so long a length of thread as you like.'

'I don't see it.'

'It's all on the cloth, isn't it?'

Millicent had thought little of the piece of embroidery apart from the shilling or so it would fetch on Cornhull. Yes, it was an extraordinary sample. But what did it have to do with the book?

She surveyed it now, looking more closely at the marks of livery embroidered across its span. She had noted them earlier, when Agnes first unwrapped the book for her, yet now their significance hit her with real force. Around one of the shields had been embroidered a careful pattern – a circle of five hawks – while the other sat in the midst of a triangle formed by three delicate white feathers. The cloth, she realized, told a story, a story whose main characters were embodied by the livery set between its edges. And what a story it was!

If she had learned her reading from Isabel of Barking, Millicent had learned her heraldry on the lap of Sir Humphrey ap-Roger, who had loved to point out the subtle variations signifying relations of rank, status, and depth of lineage: fields and divisions, charges and crests, beasts rampant and supine. In the difference between a blue lion on an argent field and an argent lion on a blue field lay whole histories of conquest and submission, Sir Humphrey taught her; *learn these histories and the livery that tells them, Millie darling, and you'll go far.* Yet the heraldry on this cloth required no great knowledge, for she recognized most of it instantly. The colours of the king and his uncle were depicted in a battle of some kind, with swords, knives, and arrows surrounding their emblems and supporters.

Millicent clasped her sister's hands. 'Without the wheel, then, the wool is just wool.'

Agnes nodded. 'And without the cloth,' she said, continuing the thought, 'the book is just . . .'

They said it together: 'A book.'

There was one final piece. Millicent read the last line of the prophecy to her sister. '"*On day of Saint Dunstan shall Death have his doom.*"'

'Dunstan's Day,' said Agnes. 'Nineteen May, or I'm a fool.'

Millicent calculated on her fingers. 'Six weeks, Ag,' she said into the darkness, the meaning of the prophecy chilling her limbs. 'Our king has but six weeks to live.'

They had sat in silence for a while, absorbing the prophecy's dire meaning, when Millicent saw a flicker of something cross her sister's face. 'What is it, Ag?'

'The faun,' she said, a faraway look in her eyes.

'What about it?'

'Right before that man killed her. She looked up at the sky, and she cried it out. A rhyme. 'Though faun escape the falcon's claws and crochet cut its snare, when father, son, and ghost we sing, of city's blade beware!' I remember it like my Ave Maria, her voice was so clear. It felt like she was screaming it to me, *to me*, while she's kneeling there, waiting to die. It's been stuck in my head since, just like that man's *doovay leebro, doovay leebro*. So what's it mean?'

'Say it again.'

As Agnes repeated the rhyme, Millicent scratched it on to the last page of the manuscript with a nub of coal in her unpractised, spidery script. The words did nothing to clarify the rest of the prophecy, but writing them down seemed to calm Agnes somewhat.

'Whatever it means it's only words, Ag. And we can't eat words.' Millicent stood, the manuscript falling from her lap. 'Nor a cloth, nor a damned book.' She slammed the chamber door behind her, clomping down the outer stairs, her hopelessness rising with each descending step. Her sister in her bed, the two of them together for the first time in years, yet Millicent felt more alone than ever. City's blade indeed.

ELEVEN

Basinghaw Street, Ward of Basinghaw

In London, if you die of unnatural causes, your corpse will be inspected not by the coroner himself but by his deputy, who gathers witnesses, orders the beadle to summon the jury from around the ward, and performs the inquest at the site of demise. The procedures are well established, and in theory should function smoothly.

Things are somewhat messier in practice. Though he works on behalf of the city, the coroner reports to the king's chamberlain, not to the mayor – a bureaucratic peculiarity I have found immensely useful over the years. Officials of city and crown can always be stirred against one another, and divided loyalties are to my vocation what a hammer is to a smith's. Since the last year of Edward's reign, the commons had been complaining regularly in Parliament about the coroner's office and the mischief this arcane arrangement could cause. To have a city official unbeholden to the mayor of London? A scandal, and an opportunity.

As usual Thomas Tyle, king's coroner, was absent when I

arrived at his chambers on Wednesday of Easter week. The location spoke of the office's tenuous relation to the city government: just outside Guildhall Yard but within shouting distance of the mayor's chambers, and the common serjeant's, though I had sent a boy ahead to confirm the common serjeant's absence from the precincts. Seeing me here would raise uncomfortable questions in Ralph Strode's mind, and I needed him on my side.

Two clerks, facing one another over a double-sided desk. Neither looked up.

'Is Symkok about?'

The one to the left raised his jaw slightly, eyes still on his work. 'He's in there.' The back room, which I'd visited more than once. It was a dark space despite the bright day, the shutters closed nearly to. I found Nicholas Symkok, chief clerk to the subcoroner, hunched over the end of a table, a ledger opened before him. A crooked finger followed a column downward. The curve of his back seemed part of the furniture, a bony arc some carpenter hadn't thought to trim.

Nick Symkok was my first. It still startles me to think of how natural it all seemed when it began. Just a few years after the great dying, half of London beneath the soil, the city abuzz with news of the Oxford riots. That summer I found myself performing occasional clerical work in the Exchequer under the chancellor's remembrancer. Though I hardly needed the money, my father had promised my temporary services to the treasurer, to whom he owed a favour.

It was during the Michaelmas audit when one of our counters came to me with a messy sheaf of returns from Warwick's manors near Coventry. It seemed a sheriff had been drastically undercounting the number of tenants in his hundred, with the resulting decline in revenues from that part of the earl's demesne. I received permission from the remembrancer to take a discreet trip out to the Midlands to investigate. A careful comparison with the original returns soon showed that nothing was amiss in the earl's record-keeping. The guilty party, I realized, had to be one of our own.

A few days of digging back in Westminster turned up Nicholas Symkok, an auditor responsible for the embezzlement of nearly twenty pounds from the king's treasury over the last several years. Not only that, but Symkok had been using these enormous sums to purchase the flesh of the boy choristers singing for a prominent chantry attached to St Paul's.

When I confronted Symkok he melted in front of me, begging me to say nothing to the chancellor or the remembrancers – asking me to save his life. I agreed, on one condition. Symkok, I told him, would hereafter provide me any and all unusual information that came across his desk: the shady business of earls, the questionable holdings of barons, the conniving of knights. He was to digest all of it, slipping me anything of possible interest. I paid him, though just enough to keep him dangling on my hook. For several years after I left the Exchequer, Symkok was my main conduit, giving me my first clear look at the private lives of the lords of the realm.

Those years taught me much about the peculiar arts of *chantage*, and it was from the steady flow of copied documents in Symkok's hand that my small reserve of knowledge gradually expanded to encompass the vast store of information it would become. The arrangement seemed to crush Symkok, though, and he was never the same man. His ambitions stifled, he had spent the last twenty years floating through a series of clerical positions in the London and Westminster bureaucracies, all of them happily useful to my own purposes, if not to his career. At present he worked for the coroner of London, counting corpses.

I watched him until he felt my presence. He turned slowly on his bench. His eyes widened. 'Gower.'

'Hello, Nick.'

'What brings you here?'

'Death, of course.'

'Whose?'

'A girl's.'

'Lots of dead girls in London.'

'Not like this one.'

'What's her name?'

'Medusa? Persephone?' I said wryly.

'Name unknown, then?'

'To me it is.'

'And when did she die?'

'A week ago, perhaps more.'

'How?'

'Clubbed, or stabbed,' I said. 'I'm not sure.'

'Murder, then.'

'Yes.'

'Where did she die?'

'The Moorfields.'

It was as if a flame blew out in his eyes. His face went flat, expressionless.

'She was killed in the Moorfields, two weeks ago or more,' I repeated. 'I take it you know the circumstances?'

Symkok looked down at the ledger, his jaw rigid. 'Can't help you, Gower. Not on this one.'

A dog barked from Guildhall gate, a muffled sound that carried through the outer room. I let the silence linger. 'But I think you can, Nick.'

He shifted on his bench. A vacant stare toward the shutters, and finally that reliable nod. From a cupboard at his feet he removed a wooden box and placed it on the table, then reached inside and withdrew a heavy roll. He spread it across the surface, the worn wooden handles gleaming with the polish of many hands, until he found the entry in question.

'Be quick about it.' He left the room, with the coroner's roll opened on the table. In this document would be transcribed the original report, which was written out at the scene of the inquest. The roll, then, was the official copy of all the coroner's investigations of unnatural deaths in London during the term of his appointment. A rich and morbid archive, I had found over the years. I read the inquest report.

Friday the eve of Lady Day, ao 8 Richard II, it happened that a certain woman, name unknown, lay dead of a death other than her rightful death beside a certain low wood building in the Moorfields, in the rent of the holy priory of St Bethlem. On hearing this, the coroner and the sheriffs proceeded thither, and having summoned good men of various wards – viz. James Barkelay, Will Wenters, Ralph Turk, Thomas de Redeford, mercer, Simon de Saint Johan of Cornhull, draper, Laurence Sely, Simon Pulham, skinner, John Lemman &c. – they diligently inquired how it happened. The jurors say that on some unknown day before said Friday, said woman was beaten in the face and struck on the head and bloodied, feloniously murdered by an unknown assailant. When asked who found the dead body, they say a certain Adam de Hoyne, carter, did raise the hue and cry upon discovering the lady in her natural state. Upon inquiring further they did learn that no witnesses were found to be present at the said woman's death, nor did they find that anyone about knew her name, nor her station, nor her land of origin.

The corpse viewed &c.

Clothing appraised at 2s.

The surrounding inquests contained nothing out of the ordinary. I read the report again, memorizing certain details. The body had been discovered some days after the murder, it appeared. The woman had been beaten, her death apparently caused by a blow to the skull. She had been found 'in her natural state', or unclothed. No witnesses, no identifying belongings. The appraisal of her clothing was high, though not unusually so.

In the outer chamber Symkok was conferring with his fellow clerks. When I emerged he gestured me outside. We reached the middle of Cat Street before he opened his mouth. 'So?'

'Seems simple enough,' I said.

'Murder usually is, in my experience.'

'Tyle himself held the inquest?'

He nodded.

'Bit unusual.'

Symkok shrugged. 'Though not unprecedented. When an earl dies on us, or a knight—'

'A nameless girl, stripped to the smooth? Hardly an earl, Nick.'

He wouldn't meet my gaze.

'Tell me, Nick.'

He straightened his back, his chin high. 'Nothing more to tell, Gower.'

We stood for a time, Symkok squirming in his discomfort.

'Do some digging, then,' I quietly said. A cart passed behind him, a low groan from its wheels. 'I need to know why Tyle took this one. Who told him to do the inquest himself rather than fob it off, like he usually does? And what did he find?'

He swallowed, his lined neck rippling with the effort.

'Be discreet about it, Nick.'

He swallowed again. 'Always am, Gower, at least where you're concerned.'

I left him there, gnawing at his past.

✛

Back at St Mary Overey a letter awaited me in the hall. I took it up from the tray where Will Cooper would leave all my correspondence, expecting a bill from a local merchant, or a report from the bailiff of one of my estates. I was surprised at the letter's weight until I turned it over and saw the heavy seal. The wax bore the impress of Robert Braybrooke, Bishop of London.

Rather unusual, to send a sealed missive across the river when the bishop's messenger could have said a simple word to my servant. After a moment's hesitation I broke the wax. The note was short and to the point, and in his chief secretary's hand. The Lord Bishop of London requested my presence at Fulham Palace this Monday, at the hour of Tierce, upon his return from a visitation up north. The letter left the subject of the appointment unmentioned. London and I had had our moments, though all of that was far in the past, and I wondered what the bishop could possibly want with me. I thought about it for a while, ticking off a mental list of current complexities but coming up with nothing aside from Katherine Swynford's brief mention of Braybrooke at La Neyte, and his distress over the book sought by Chaucer.

Whatever its subject, the bishop's was an invitation I

was in no position to decline. In my study I scribbled a reply at the foot of the letter, melted some wax, and left the missive in the tray for Will, who would arrange its delivery for that afternoon. Five days, then I would know more.

TWELVE

Cutter Lane, Southwark

The knife landed in muscle with a wet spit. A second blade quickly followed, nearly touching the first. The carcass swayed, and Gerald Rykener clapped his hands roughly on his tunic. 'Have that, Tom.'

The other apprentice stepped up to the line, a blade pressed between his fingers. His wrist bent, his arm rose, and with a flash of metal the knife was buried in the flank just inches from Gerald's. The second landed a half foot higher on the beef, missing its target. '*Damn* it to queynting hell,' he said, then with a scowl handed Gerald a coin.

Eleanor watched her brother pocket it, and for a moment the simple joy of victory on his face turned him back into the sweet boy she remembered. Then Gerald saw her.

'Ah, by St George. Swerving again,' he muttered to his companion, his contempt for her undisguised.

The other apprentice looked over to where she stood by the fence. 'What do you think, Gerald? Your brother a mare or a gelding?'

'A mare with a cock?' Gerald taunted. 'A gelding with a queynt?'

'Either way she-he's got enough riders to keep him-her filled with oats 'n' mash till the trumpet sounds, from what I hear.'

'Aye that,' said Gerald, ignoring her as his fellow turned for the barn. Gerald wiped a long crimson smear across his cheek, then from beneath the carcass removed a bucket of blood. He took it to a heated cauldron at the far end of the yard. Gerald was fourteen, yet already moved with a tradesman's confidence that would have been endearing if he hadn't turned so foul. His apron was cut small in the style of the craft. *We butchers pride ourselves on leaving our aprons white*, he'd explained in those days when he cared. Now it was stained a brownish red, his loose breeches slimed with gore.

When he returned to the fence she saw the latest bruises had faded. His lip, too, had mostly healed. He was close so she went for his neck, the line of faded scar tissue running from his jaw to his nape. He knocked her hand back but she reached for his head and felt a new knot. Size of a peach pit. 'What's that about?'

He ducked away. 'He swings the mallet around, you know, got those teeth on it. It's wood, though, so. But Grimes'd never hit me with the metal one. Not ever.'

'Not yet,' she said. 'And when he does you'll be dead as that beef side hanging behind you.' Why Gerald took his master's part so often she couldn't reckon, though Nathan Grimes had been his effective father for going on three years, and children could develop peculiar loyalties.

He looked at her purse. She handed him the coins she'd come to deliver. 'It's hardly much. A shilling and five. Keep it somewhere, use it only in your most needful moments. Not for candied gingers on the bridge, now.' She half-turned to go, but something in his eyes held her back. 'What is it?'

Trying to sound impatient: she needed to be tough with him, tough as he was with her, or he'd never make it to his majority. 'What is it, Gerald?'

He snarled and spat in the filthy straw. 'No matter. Go away, Edgar.'

As her brother returned to his work Eleanor watched him sadly, marvelling at how much the boy had changed. They had been separated since their mother's death, when Gerald was seven, Eleanor thirteen and starting to discover her second life. A man in body, but in soul a man and a woman both, a predicament that made her wardship a domestic hell: a wife who tormented her with the hardest household labour, a husband who wouldn't leave her alone once he found out what she was. She had taken to the streets at sixteen. Gerald, though, had seemed to be getting by, floating from guardian to guardian, some good, some bad, yet all carefully regulated by the city, with appearances before the mayor himself once a year. Eleanor managed to see him nearly every month as they grew up. Finally, at his eleventh birthday, the office of the common serjeant arranged for his apprenticeship to a freeman of London and master butcher, and all appeared set.

Then, not six months after his apprenticeship began, the city passed the butchery laws, and Gerald's master moved his shop across the river to Southwark to avoid the fines and fees. There not only butchers but guardians operated on their own authority, with little legal oversight from the town, and no common serjeant to take the orphans' part. 'Never heard no law against a butcher moving shop to Southwark,' Grimes had said when Eleanor confronted him. He turned instantly cruel upon the move across the Thames: Gerald was on his own there, surrounded by meat yet starved for bread, beaten regularly and with no recourse. Eleanor had tried to intervene, but the laws of London, it was said, have no house in Southwark.

Soon enough Gerald was turning into one of them, these Southwark meaters, a nasty bunch of Cutter Lane thugs without guild or code, sneaking rotten flesh into the markets and shops across the river. The Worshipful Company of Butchers, London's legitimate craft, had been trying for years to quash the flow of bad flesh into the city to no avail, and now that Gerald had been caught up in their illegal trade he, too, was slipping down the path to a hanging. It often seemed to Eleanor that Gerald's entire self had changed, as if the Holy Ghost had sucked out his soul and the devil had blown in another.

'Best be off,' she said. He shrugged indifferently. From behind her, a whisper of straw. A pig, she thought. Gerald's back was to her as he scraped at a pile of hardened dung. 'May be a stretch before I can get out here again.' She recalled the beadle's questions, the threats, and thought of Agnes. Two sparrows perched on the side of the stall flitted off. Gerald started to turn. 'There's been some trouble on the lane, and I might have to be—' He faced her now. His eyes widened.

Eleanor's neck snapped back, her hood wrenched violently downward by an unseen hand. She was spun around into the face of Nathan Grimes, taking in his ale-breath. 'Trouble on Gropecunt Lane? For a lovely boy-princess like yourself?'

'You let my brother go, now!' Gerald screamed, backing away. 'You just let him go, Master Grimes!'

Grimes was a stout, boar-like man, with well-muscled arms that flexed as he held her. 'I'll let it go all right.' With a hard push against her head, he shoved Eleanor to the stall floor. She backed up against the boards, then came to her feet, her breath shallow.

Grimes gestured toward Gerald. 'Get inside, boy.' Gerald stayed where he was. Grimes raised a hand. '*Inside*, boy.' Gerald looked at Eleanor. She gave him a reassuring nod.

He backed away, pushed open the pen gate, and walked reluctantly toward the house. The butcher leaned over Eleanor, toying with Gerald's knives.

'I know what you be, Edgar Rykener,' said Grimes, with a small lift of his chin. 'No place for swervers in a respectable butcher's shop, now. Let your brother learn his craft in peace.'

'Peace?' said Eleanor under her breath; then, more loudly, 'He getting any peace by *your* hand?'

'Getting fed, isn't he?' Grimes retorted. 'Getting schooled in hogs and calves, learning the way of the blade, got some thatch over his head. More'n you can say for lots of boys his age, in London or not.'

'And getting a mallet to the skull in the bargain.'

Grimes spat in the dirt. 'Boy needs to learn respect he wants to be a freeman like me.'

'You took an oath, Master Grimes,' she seethed. 'In the mayor's presence himself you swore to God you'd protect my brother, keep him from harm. Now you'd as lief kill him.'

Grimes lifted a cleaver, fingered its edge. 'Never cut up a maudlyn in all my day.' He looked over at the beef carcass. 'Can't imagine there's much trouble to it, though.' He smiled. 'Now get back to London, sweetmeats.'

She edged out of the stall with a final glance at Gerald. He stood in the doorway to the apprentices' shack, his face so much older than it should have looked. Once she was gone Grimes would paint it good. The burden of it all settled on her: a murder, a missing friend, a brother liable to be brained at any moment and clearly troubled by something he wouldn't reveal.

Yet there was one man who might be capable of putting things right for Gerald, Eleanor speculated as she walked up toward the bridge, get him out of all of this. A kind man, from all she'd heard. A man with the authority to remove her brother from his Southwark dungeon and put him with a kinder master in London. As she passed back over the bridge she thought about this man, knowing, at least, where to find him; trusting, for she had to, in his kindness.

THIRTEEN

St Mary Overey, Southwark

On the morning after Low Sunday I rose early, awakened by the buzz of the priory bell, cracked and unreplaced since the belfry fire two years before. My appointment with Braybrooke would not be for hours, but I left the house anyway, absorbing the quiet din of these Southwark streets at dawn, already alive with the work that sustained the greater city over the river. Here the trades commingled with none of London's attempt at logic, the shops of haberdashers and carpenters, tanners and tawyers, fishmongers and smiths, coopers and brewers all side by side, spewing smells and sounds and petty rivalries even as small creeks of rubbish spilled out of alleys between them. I stepped into a baker's shop and purchased two sweetbuns for the trip. At the river landing I paid my pennies and hopped on a common wherry, joining a few others westward bound.

I found a seat for the float to Fulham, and as the wherry passed St Bride's on the north bank I squinted across the wide span at a group of young men in skiffs. They were tilting, I realized, their target a square of beaten tin suspended from the lampstick of an anchored barge. Four oarsmen per skiff made wide circles around the craft, the lanceman at the bow, loose on his knees; then, a speedy approach, the lance held at the shoulder, the skiff keeping steady over the rises; and finally impact, as the dulled point of the lance struck the tin, the noise carrying over the water. An awkward game, yet several of the young men were quite skilful with their lances, taking the applause of their mates with exaggerated pride.

These, I thought with a shudder, would be the first Englishmen killed were a French invasion force to sail up the Thames from Gravesend and destroy the bridge. How would these boys spend their final moments? Would they turn tail, ditching their skiffs on the bank, fleeing through the streets? Or would they stand and fight, tilting at warships in a futile attempt to save London?

At the quay of Patrisey I changed wherries and thought ahead to my appointment with the bishop. Knowing Braybrooke as I did, I could expect a meeting full of venom and insinuation, of parries and feints. Tread softly, I warned myself.

With a slow turn toward the north bank, we passed lines of oak and elm towering over the terraced lawns leading up to the bishop's great house, which commanded an enviable position over the river. Above the dock was a pavilion trimmed in banners of silk, cloth of gold, and sable, displaying Braybrooke's mascles over his personal barge.

As the bank came into view I saw not only Braybrooke's colours, but the Earl of Oxford's as well. The wherry bumped in just up-river from Braybrooke's barge, and as I stepped up the bank I saw Robert de Vere striding across the lower terrace. Normally Oxford moved about with a larger retinue, yet his only companion that day was Sir Stephen Weldon. I bowed as the earl approached. He looked me over, his discomfort apparent as he waved me to my full height.

'Gower,' he finally said.

'Your lordship.' I nodded to Weldon. 'Sir Stephen.'

Weldon returned the nod.

'How is his lordship the bishop?' I asked them.

'Supervising plantings on the upper terrace,' said the earl, forcing a smile. 'Seems there are some questions about the rigor of the vines he's got in from Bordeaux. But he's still determined to pull a decent *clairet* from our English clay.'

I winced. *'Prêtres anglais ont toujours aimé le vin.'*

'As long as I'm not forced to sample the result,' said Oxford.

Weldon feigned choking, a comic gesture that broke the awkwardness. 'I do miss the wines of Italy,' the knight said, his eyes crinkling with the memories. For years Weldon had served with Sir John Hawkwood before his permanent return to England in the fifth year of Richard's reign. Weldon was taller than Oxford, and thinner, with a studied casualness to his stance. He wore little in the way of livery, a small badge on his right breast the only mark of his station. 'Perhaps England's next war might be fought over France's vine rather than its cities.'

'A welcome suggestion,' I said, choosing to take Weldon's courteous demeanour as sincere. 'For that I'd happily lift a sword.'

With these elevated nothings we parted, and I was left wondering what business the earl could possibly have at Fulham. To my knowledge, all Oxford and London shared was a mutual hatred of John of Gaunt.

I was directed to an upper side terrace, reached after a circuitous route through a network of gravel walks. I found the Bishop of London on his knees, thinning roses. At a discreet distance stood two servants bearing bowls, flagons, and gardening tools for the bishop's use, and, closer, four additional men holding his robes, mitre, and cap: two friars, a canon of some kind, and Fulham's head gardener, the last with his hands crossed tightly in front of him as Braybrooke assaulted his art with the unpractised hand of a knight shearing sheep. The canon, noticing me, cleared his throat. Braybrooke turned.

'Gower.' The bishop was a man of awkward, treeish height; to see him on his knees, his meaty hands scooping dirt from the ground, was something new.

'Your lordship.'

Braybrooke loosened a stone. 'How's Gaunt?'

'I would not know, your lordship,' I said. 'I caught a passing glimpse of him the other week at La Neyte, but that is all.'

Another stone, a spray of soil. 'Can't be comfortable for the duke, can it, being a constant object of suspicion?' I listened as the bishop muttered over the royal troubles of the last year, still the talk of the realm. He had been at the council tournament in February, and I learned a new detail about the aftermath of Oxford's plot against Lancaster. If not for the peacemaking interventions of Countess Joan, the bishop claimed, either Gaunt or King Richard would surely have been dead by now. And with the king still young, always gullible, and increasingly unpredictable in his alliances, things could only worsen.

'What about you, Gower?' the bishop said. 'You're content with your own alliances?'

'I'm for the king, your lordship,' I said cautiously. 'From whatever faction he comes, I'm for the king.'

'An easy vow.' He packed dirt into the new hole. 'For a man who takes such stark moral stands in his verse, you're remarkably reluctant to choose sides.'

My jaw tightened.

'The lines are being drawn, Gower. Two popes, two churches

– some would say two kings.' The bishop looked up, his eyes cold. 'Your friend Geoffrey Chaucer, too, would do well to clarify his allegiances. Not a lover of friars, that one.'

I glanced at the two Dominicans. 'Chaucer is a lover of the good,' I said. 'He loves good friars, as he loves good bishops such as your lordship. Good wine, too, and good lawyers.'

Braybrooke barked a laugh. He clipped and dug for a while, then looked up at me again. 'This book you're looking for has a name.'

I blinked.

'You think I'm a fool, Gower? You make a wide-eyed request of Katherine Swynford, the yawningest mouth in the realm, and you expect her not to gossip?'

'A fair point,' I conceded.

'*Liber de Mortibus Regum Anglorum.*'

'My lord?'

'*Liber de Mortibus Regum Anglorum.* That's what this work is called.'

'"The Book of the Deaths of English Kings",' I translated.

'A book of prophecy, written by a certain Lollius during the reign of the Conqueror.'

'That long ago? What relevance could a book three centuries old have in our day?'

'The *De Mortibus* prophesies the death of every English king since William. The houses of Normandy, Plantagenet, with the circumstances of each royal death rendered in detail. The time, the place, the means.'

'I've never heard of this Lollius. Are people taking this seriously?'

'The book is being read by Wycliffe's minions, Gower. They gather in conventicles and recite the prophecies one by one. Thirteen kings, thirteen prophecies, thirteen deaths, all foretold and retold as a goad to revolt.'

105

'I loathe Wycliffe's teachings as much as the next fellow, your lordship. But he never questioned Richard's legitimacy.'

'I suggest you learn a bit about this book before you dismiss it, Gower. One of my friars here has mingled with the Wycliffites during their readings. He's got a bit of the work in his head.' He looked over his other shoulder. 'Brother Thomas, a taste. The death of King William, if you please.'

One of the friars stepped forward with a bow. At a nod from Braybrooke, he spoke the requested lines.

> *A bastard by birth, of Brittany bane,*
> *A duke rendered king by Deus decree,*
> *With fury so fierce all England will fight,*
> *Shall matins and masses restore to all men,*
> *Then in Mantes to muster his might shall appear.*
> *Unhorsed by his hand this sovereign full hale*
> *On pommel full pounded from saddle shall pitch,*
> *And goeth to ground to giveth the ghost.*
> *At sovereign of swords in death swoon he will,*
> *No more to flee mors, his reign an end make.'*

The friar stepped back, assuming his position, still by the tree. Something about the lines sounded familiar.

Braybrooke sat on his heels, prompting the gardener to step forward hopefully. The bishop waved him off. 'Thus shall die the first of thirteen English kings.' Braybrooke wiped his brow. 'Let me correct myself: thus *did* die the first of thirteen English kings, this one at the great battle at Mantes, of which we read in our chronicles.'

'Of which this Lollius read in our chronicles, unless I'm an utter fool,' I muttered, unswayed by the bishop's lofty tone.

He glared at me. 'If you're sceptical, Gower, keep listening.' He nodded to the friar, who began a second series of lines.

> 'With seven of swords to swing at their will,
> To chasten with chattel, and chase their king down.
> In Gloucester will he goeth, to be gutted by
>   goodmen
> With rod straight of iron, in arsebone to run.
> With pallet of pullet, his breath out to press,
> And sovereign unsound for Sodom be sundered.'

My hand went to my gut. 'The second King Edward.'

'And his disgusting execution,' Braybrooke said. 'Lying on a feather pallet, a poker shoved up his arse. A fitting death for a Ganymede king. And finally the more peaceful death of good King Edward.'

The friar spoke a third time. I could not hide my surprise at his opening words.

> 'Full long shall he lead us, full rich shall he rule,
> Through pain of pestilence, through wounds of
>   long war.
> Yet morire is matter all sovereigns must suffer.
> This long-lived leader, beloved of all,
> At three of thistles shall suffer his fall;
> Gold bile shall him bite, with bitter wound wide,
> At Sheen will be shent, last shrift there to render.'

Braybrooke scrutinized my face as I remembered where I had heard these lines before. At Holbourne cross, shouted into the drizzle by that deranged-looked preacher. The man had spoken this very verse.

'Some say the gomoria took him,' the bishop said, turning away with a smile, 'though I believe the old fellow had a simple stroke.' With the rocks removed and the ground cleared, he knelt to address the large rose bush before him. The gardener was trying not to weep.

'The prophecies, if that's what they are, are full of enigmas, Lord Bishop,' I said, wondering how Braybrooke could be swayed so easily. 'What are the "three of thistles", the "seven of swords" in the account of Edward, or the "sovereign of swords" in William's case? These sorts of symbols don't appear in the chronicles, not in the ones I've read.'

The bishop pricked a finger, brought it to his mouth. 'The thistle is important to the Scots, I'm told,' he said with a smack of his lips. 'Perhaps some new Robert de Bruce is on the rise.' His voice sounded almost jocular now, as if he were putting me on.

I looked at his rounded back. 'With respect, your lordship, the work your friar just recited is written in a modern fashion – its style, its rhythm. It sounds like the story of King Horne, or that vision of Piers the Ploughman that was so much in favour around the Rising. I have to say, I'm surprised so much is being made of an obvious forgery.'

He turned to look at me. 'The thing could have been written by anyone schooled in our nation's chronicles. Is that what you are thinking, Gower?'

Finally some sense. 'The church is familiar with false prophets, my lord.'

With an audible crack of his long spine, Braybrooke stood, flicking dirt off his hands. 'Your scepticism is admirable, Gower, and matches my own.' An attendant stepped forward with a bowl. Braybrooke dipped his hands and wiped them on a cloth. He turned to the friars and canon, who robed and capped him. He waved off his mitre like a cat refusing tack.

'We are men of the law, Gower,' he continued as we walked to the river. 'I serve the church now, but I still have faith in our earthly institutions. The crown, Parliament, even the courts. You know all too well how my trust was once challenged in this regard, John, and I'm still grateful for the compassion you showed.'

It was a rare moment of candour from Braybrooke, whose ambition often outstripped his memory. I murmured my thanks.

He puffed his cheeks, blew air. 'My contempt for Lancaster is no secret.'

'I've witnessed it.'

'Heresy and war arrange us in peculiar alliances.' He said nothing of Oxford, though I assumed he was thinking of the earl. 'If the reports I have received are accurate, the thirteenth prophecy is known only to a few.'

'The thirteenth prophecy?'

'England has had thirteen kings since the conquest.' He waited a moment, then said, 'Thirteen, *including* William.'

'Yet if William—' I stopped walking, finally understanding, and feeling like a fool.

He stepped down on to the Fulham quay. 'Now you know why a man in my position would be anxious to root out this book before the thirteenth prophecy becomes known, let alone realized. My friar, Brother Thomas back there, has heard only whisperings of its content, but apparently it implicates someone quite close to the king. Who that might be we don't yet know, though one can guess. So you see it hardly matters whether the *De Mortibus* is a genuine work of prophecy or a clever forgery. If word of the last prophecy were to get out . . .' He looked at me.

'Yes, my lord.' A missing book, a girl murdered in the Moorfields, and now this. 'The thirteenth prophecy, then, concerns—'

'The death of King Richard. Still a boy, really, but with all the world on his shoulders.' He gazed across to the far bank. 'Whatever Chaucer is paying you to find this book, I will give you double if you bring it to me instead, Gower. Triple.' With that the Bishop of London turned from me, walked up the embankment, and was gone.

FOURTEEN

Cutter Lane, Southwark

Hook out the belly, knot up the guts, snip out the anus – all that was fine, but Gerald still had trouble with the hiding. How to keep it one piece when it wants to split apart at the shoulders, that was the thing. As Grimes liked to remind him, a split hide wasn't worth half a whole, *and you'll get the hole, boy, get it right through your pate 'f you split another vellum on me.*

This time it worked. Gerald grunted happily as he felt the spine, pared to the haunch, begin to loosen against the gored skin. Spines had their own smell, too, that chalky air of fresh bone. He pulled it free. Hard part of this calf was done. He felt his arms loosen, the knife working its magic as he sliced and split with the ease of a stronger, bigger man.

Gerald loved butchery, felt he was born to cut up these beasts. Only bad part was Grimes. His master was inside now, prattling with that priest. He'd first shown up two weeks ago. This was his third visit. Gerald could hear them all the way from the cutting floor, their voices raised in an argument of some kind. Same as last time.

The priest's comings and goings were putting Grimes in a bad state, even worse than usual. More blows to the cheek, more boxes to the ear, more threats of worse to come. Part of him knew his brother was right – well, his sister – his broster, his sither, whichever way in God's name Edgar–Eleanor was swerving these days, it was true that Grimes's shop wasn't a safe place for a boy Gerald's age. Better to be back in London, with its laws. But what could *he* do about it? What could Edgar do, for that matter – let alone Eleanor? He shook his head, trying to put it all out of his mind and concentrate on the carcass swinging in his face.

Tom Nayler came in, wiping his hands. 'I'm off, then,' he said, tossing his chin in the direction of the high street. 'Got a coney to slit up the market. This'll wait, yeah?'

'Suit yourself,' Gerald said, wondering who the lucky girl was this time. Tom had a way with the daughters of oyster-mongers and maudlyns. 'I'll finish this one up. Not a lot left.'

Tom ambled off. Gerald sliced and cut contentedly for a while longer. Flanks, legs, heart, with the offal for the dogs. The master's shop had grown quiet, though he hadn't seen the priest leave. He stepped off the floor and glanced up the alley. Tom Nayler was long gone. After a look in the other direction he wiped his blade, set it down on a board, and stared at the shop, his thoughts churning.

What was it with Grimes and this priest? Wasn't a parson of the parish, that was sure. Gerald knew the local parson, just like he'd known the parson at St Nicholas Shambles in his younger days. No, this one wasn't a Southwark man. Not even a Londoner. A northerner, maybe. Or a Welshman. Talked with a gummy twang, like his words were tangled up in brambles and couldn't get out.

The only window on this side of the shop was shuttered, as usual when important visitors came to talk to Grimes. The butcher liked to keep his inquisitive apprentices at bay.

Taking his time, Gerald walked over to the shop, found the right spot, and pressed his ear to the gap between the boards. More than once he'd saved his hide this way, catching snatches of the master's complaints about his apprentices and correcting himself accordingly.

He heard the priest, speaking low. At first none of it made sense. A lot of talk about how Grimes had to listen, had to do this and that, think about his future. Then, a stream of verse. 'Listen to it, Nathan Grimes. It's you this prophecy is talking about, you and your cutters over here.

> By bank of a bishop shall butchers abide,
> To nest, by God's name, with knives in hand,
> Then springen in service at spiritus sung.

Butchers, Nathan. Butchers bearing knives. They're to be the blood of it, and you the heart.'

Grand words. But what did they mean? Gerald heard Grimes clear his throat. 'Lots of butchers in London, Father, over in the Shambles and such. There's nothing in the verse to say it's to be a Southwark meater, is there?'

'Not exactly, no,' said the priest slowly. 'But "bank of a bishop"? And later it reads "In palace of prelate with pearls all appointed." That's Winchester's palace, my son, you know it as well as I. And who's the closest master butcher to Winchester's palace? Nathan Grimes, that's who.'

'Nathan Grimes,' said the butcher, tasting his name.

'That's right. "By kingmaker's cunning a king to unking." Do you see?'

'Well—'

'It's plain as the shining sun, Nathan Grimes. Look in the glass. You're to be the kingmaker, sure as I'm standing here.'

'The kingmaker,' Grimes repeated.

'Wouldn't be the first time you've been at the centre of

such great events,' said the priest, lowering his voice. 'You were on the bridge with Wat Tyler, Nathan. You walked right behind him. And I saw you myself on Blackheath, standing at Ball's feet. You could have taken out King Richard at Mile End, with a cleaver or a long knife.'

Gerald felt a chill, finally understanding the priest's cryptic talk. It had been four years since the Rising, when the commons of Essex and Kent, infuriated by the poll taxes and the harshness of their levy, had flooded London by the thousands, burning buildings, beheading bishops and treasurers and chancellors, imprisoning the young King Richard himself in the Tower and nearly executing him at Smithfield.

The butchers of London and Southwark had marched along with the rest, and Gerald could still remember the exuberance on the streets as word spread of John Ball's sermon on Blackheath. *When Adam delved and Eve span, who was then the gentleman?* Words of hope, and a promise of a better life for England's poor. Though things were now much the way they had been before the Rising, its wounds were still fresh, the city and the realm braced with suspicion of the commons. You could still see it on the faces of the beadles and aldermen, in the tense stance of lords and ladies as they rode through the streets, trading hostile glances with clusters of workers breaking stone, or lame beggars idling by the gates.

Now, it seemed, the talk of treason was back. That priest in with Grimes, he was trying to convince the master butcher to raise arms again, and this time have a real go at the king. He thought of the priest's verses. *By bank of a bishop shall butchers abide.* Not *one* butcher, not Nathan Grimes alone, but *butchers*. So what did that mean for him, Gerald Rykener?

The scrape of a bench. Gerald turned his head so his eye was against the gap. The priest rose and clapped Grimes on the back. 'This is fate, my son. It's prophecy, as sure as the

Apocalypse itself. God sees our futures and our glories in ways we mortals cannot, Nathan. This is yours. Embrace it, my son!'

Grimes sat there, staring at the far wall of his shop, kneading his swarthy chin. Gerald watched him, almost seeing the muddled thoughts in his master's brain, like a rocker churning cream. Then the butcher looked up at the priest, a gleam in his eye. He stood, inhaled deeply, and nodded.

'I'm in, Father.' His nod strengthened as his certainty swelled. The priest stepped in and embraced him.

Gerald felt his stomach heave. He turned away, his eyes cast at the ground as he trudged back to the kill shed. He leaned against the rough board wall, pondering what he'd heard.

The butchers of Southwark. A new Rising. Knives and cleavers and axes and a crowd of meaters, massing over the bridge, intent on killing the very King of England. To what end? He shook his head, the answer as clear as his memory. A rain of arrows, the swish of a garrison's swords, and it would all be over. A slaughter in the streets, the blood of the poor running between the pavers. Just like last time.

And who would the hangman come for first, once the king's men discovered who sparked this certain treason? Gerald looked up, the fear clenching at his middle so he could hardly stand straight. Nathan Grimes, that's who – and his two apprentices, all of them about as safe as the butchered veal calf hanging there before him.

FIFTEEN

Broad Street, Ward of Broad Street

A rock, hitting the streetside shutters. Millicent did her best to ignore it but then another struck the wood, throwing a hollow *crack* into the back room where she lay with Agnes. She glanced at her sister, who was still asleep, then threw off the covers and walked to the front room, pushed open a shutter, and leaned out. On the lane stood a young woman in a faded wool dress, hands planted on her narrow hips.

'What is it?' Millicent called down.

She looked up, her hand angled against the sun, tendrils of dark hair circling a moonish face beneath her hood. 'Millicent Fonteyn?'

'Who wants to know?'

'Eleanor Rykener. Searching out your sister. She about?'

Millicent willed herself not to look over her shoulder. 'Agnes hasn't been up Cornhull in five seasons.'

'That right?'

'What do you want with her?'

Eleanor lowered her voice. 'Beadle of Cripplegate's been asking questions, and she's been gone for a while now.'

Millicent said nothing. 'Tell her I been by. I'm worried for the poor thing.'

Millicent was about to reply when Denise Haveryng came out of her shop, making clear she'd been listening to the exchange.

'Saw her last at the wharfs, if I remember,' said Millicent quickly, trying to end the conversation before Denise opened her mouth.

'That right?' said Eleanor.

Denise loudly cleared her throat. 'Though you might check up Gropecunt Lane, or Rose Alley over the bridge,' she called out. 'Those be more her haunts. Millicent's as well, I imagine, before too long.' She looked up at the window with a sweet smile, as if expecting Millicent to thank her for saying nothing about Agnes's presence in her house.

Millicent slammed the shutter, jammed her palms against her eyes, and leaned back against the sill, cursing her sister and her own penury for the tenth time in as many days. Ever since Agnes showed up in her bed with that damned book Millicent had felt frozen, unable to make a decision about anything, even what food to purchase with her few remaining pennies. Nor was Agnes any use, huddled up as she was, afraid to set foot on Cornhull, let alone return to Gropecunt Lane and earn her skincoin.

They'll be after me, she had sworn up and down. *Constables, sheriffs, the man who killed that girl. Don't make me leave, Mil. Let's stay here. I feel safe here, Mil.*

She wasn't, of course. For someone wanted this book enough to kill for it – and if one man wanted it so badly, surely others did, too. Yet here they were, sitting like harts in a field as the hunters closed around them. Even that Eleanor Rykener had known where to look, and if what she'd just said was true, the authorities in Cheap Ward were now asking after Agnes.

They were in danger. Something had to change. She took

117

a deep breath, and the decision stole demon-like into her mind. She woke Agnes.

'We sell it, Ag.'

'Whah?' Agnes yawned, rubbing her eyes.

'The book. We sell it to the highest payer.'

Agnes shook her head, coming awake. 'Having it here in your house's already a dangerous thing, Mil. Like holding a flaming log. And now you want to sell it, spread the fire when the source be us? Better to toss it in the Thames.'

'Wrong.' She pressed her sister's hand. 'We have to sell it, and sell it soon. It's the only way out of this hell, Ag. My debt, your life – why, sell it to the right man and we'll have riches to spare.'

'But who would purchase such a thing, Mil?'

Who indeed? Through the morning hours Millicent thought through every interaction she could recall with members of noble retinues from her years as Sir Humphrey's consort. Since his death these connections had been entirely broken, for a singlewoman without blood, wealth, or station could hardly seek the company of counts, knights, and ladies and expect to meet anything but disdain. It was not the nobles themselves they would approach, she decided. Rather it was the working members of their households: the armourer to the Baron of Yorkshire, the steward to the Duke of Lancaster, the clerk of wardrobe to the Earl of Oxford. The men with the most intimate access to their lords, and the means to persuade them that this book of prophecies would be a most worthy purchase.

Agnes still looked doubtful. 'Suppose they turn us over to the constables, or the beadle?'

'They won't,' Millicent said confidently. 'Who'd believe them, claiming some maudlyns are going around London peddling a book of prophecies?'

'I suppose you're right,' said Agnes. 'Though we don't have

to do this, Mil. Our mother, she still might take us in. Even you, even after all these years.'

'A generous soul, that Bess Waller,' Millicent scoffed.

'You're her daughter too, Mil. Could be she'd give us our old rooms to ply the swyve, let us keep more of what we earn. The Bishop wasn't so bad, and we'd be together. Our mother's got, what, another ten years, then the place can be our own.'

Millicent shook her head furiously. 'I'm never going back. Never. And you can't live the life of a maud into your old age. You want to turn out like St Cath, that withered sheath? This book, this is all we've got.'

'Not true, Mil,' Agnes pleaded. 'We got these' – she grabbed her breasts – 'and this' – palmed her crotch – 'and as long as they work we'll get skincoin. You know that well as I!'

Millicent looked at her sister, her small body still unruined. Agnes had always carried her beauty well. When their mother started selling Millicent's flesh at fifteen, all those quick, rough lessons in womanhood, Agnes had slipped about the Bishop with a beguiling sense of her own virginal charms that provoked Bess Waller's eager jakes. 'I'll wait for *her*' was a common refrain, their eyes following Agnes even as their legs followed Millicent.

Only one man had ever openly preferred her to Agnes: Oswald, the prior of St Mary Overey. Millicent had come as close to loving him as she had any man, even Sir Humphrey. An old Austin canon of forty-eight when she met him, what he wanted most was to run his nose and fingers up her bare sides and along that warm space between her breasts, never get inside her and grunt away his groats like all the others. She remembered the gentle ambitions of his lips and fingers, the firm pleasures of his clerical tongue. He talked to her of his life, his sin, his

119

ambitions for a bishopric that would never come – provoking jests from her about bishops' pricks and why he'd ever want one in the first place, given how soft they all were.

One morning Prior Oswald asked her what *she* wanted most. She told him: a way out. So he purchased it for her, and gave her the news the last day she saw him. *You shall be a laysister of St Leonard's Bromley, my dear Millie. You'll learn to garden, to embroider, perhaps to read – and you'll never have to spread your legs for another man (though if the prioress herself demands a ride, you probably shouldn't refuse).* He had made the arrangements that very week. She never saw him again.

In the years since Oswald's death, Millicent had come to understand the fragility of it all, and her dependence on the wealth of flawed men for the needful things that had given her life whatever coherence it held. Prior Oswald had lifted her from the life of a maudlyn, buying her a position in a revered religious house. Then Sir Humphrey ap-Roger came along, giving her access to the greatest halls, to say nothing of this house and its furnishings. Yet his wealth, too, had been a passing force in her life.

First her prior, then her knight, and now – who next? Who would step into this frightening void and fill it with apricots, and almonds, and good meats, and a strong tongue, and wine and houses and—? Yet even as she asked herself such hard questions she was filled with guilt at the stir of gluttony and lust and covetousness in her soul. She heard the voice of Prioress Isabel ringing through her mind. *God frowns on extravagance, Millicent. You must temper your desires for worldly things, stamp them underfoot along with the demons who provoke them.*

Millicent closed her eyes, vowing to heed Isabel's warning,

the moral charge of the nun's sobering words. She would live a measured and moderate life, yes she would, just as soon as she could afford it.

She turned on Agnes. 'We sell it, or I'll burn it myself.'

SIXTEEN

Gropecunt Lane, Ward of Cheap

Eleanor had slumped herself over the low fence, trying to ignore the soreness in her feet. It was early afternoon, not a jake in sight, though the tedium only sharpened her worry. For hours she had been hanging next to Mary Potts, going over the same ground as her foot traced lines in the dust. Agnes still missing, her brother's life threatened by a cruel master, that girl's body never leaving her inner sight.

At the moment her thoughts were all on Gerald, though she couldn't help commingling her concerns. '"Only a wooden mallet," he says. "Never hits me with the metal one!" You hear that? He's got to get out of that cutter's shop, Mary. Grimes'll brain him sure, or he'll lose an arm for bad meat. But now I'm afraid to leave Gropecunt Lane in case Agnes comes back, not that there's much chance of that, plus then the beadle'll start asking more questions. But if I don't seek out the common serjeant soon, get Gerald moved back to London – why, he's dead sure as we stand here, like that girl on the moor!'

'Just *go*, El,' said Mary. 'You been twisting your teats about

122

the thing for days now. What's the worst can happen? Mayor'll throw you out on Cat Street and you'll be right back here, doing what you love. I'll be here the whole time, waiting on Ag.'

Eleanor felt a nudge of hope. 'You'll cover for me with the Dun Bell?'

'If Joan asks I'll say you went off with King Richard and Bolingbroke to teach those boys how to keep their young wives happy.'

Eleanor kissed her, grateful for Mary's practicality. She slipped off through an alley; replaced her dress and bonnet with the breeches, hose, coat and cap she kept hidden behind a horse stall; manned her hair and face in a trough; and was soon in the crowded precincts surrounding the Guildhall. It was market day, though despite the morning fires the westernmost hulk of the college threw the loud press of Basinghall in a cold shadow that pimpled his arms. Passing the eastern gatehouse Edgar came out between the chapel and the library into the more open expanse of Guildhall yard, where he paused to survey the inner precinct.

The common serjeant might have been anywhere, so Edgar chose a position outside the west doors to the side of the porch, edging near a clutch of women selling hand food. He was used to leaning against posts watching men's faces for long stretches of time. No different than swyving. He settled in for a wait, studying the trawl of tradesmen and bureaucrats and hucksters moving in and out of the doors and gates.

Edgar had encountered the common serjeant of London once before, at the procedure terminating his wardship upon his majority. An ample man. Reddened cheeks. A massive nose. The man had treated him with a genuine if cursory kindness on that earlier occasion, and Edgar's hope was that he would be similarly disposed toward Gerald.

Now here he was, coming right toward him. There were

three men, deep in conversation, and as they stepped up to the porch Edgar took a few idle steps in their direction, picking up a fragment of their exchange.

'. . . could not have been clearer,' one of them said, 'though the mayor's lost his patience.'

'All of us have.'

'Don't have much of a choice, though, do we?'

The shortest one walked through the Guildhall door with a grim nod to the others. Ralph Strode and the first man huddled together, their voices too quiet to make out, then the other man followed his colleague into the great structure. Strode turned about and made his way along the south side of the building, waving off the hucksters thrusting buns and pies at his face. Edgar followed him as he angled for a cluster of lower timber buildings at the far side of the Guildhall.

He quickened his pace. 'Master Strode.'

Strode looked down at him but did not slow. 'Busy just now.' They passed along the western edge, the scent of roasting chicken in the air from the spits in the side yard.

'Pardon, Master Strode, but there be a matter of some urgency that requires your attention,' said Edgar, trying to sound proper.

'Some urgency,' Strode said, his voice strained. 'How many times have I heard those words this week?'

'It concerns my brother, Gerald. He's but fourteen, sir, and I worry for him.' He stayed at Strode's heels through a narrow passage between two of the outbuildings. 'He was one of your charges, Master Strode, an orphan of the city. Now he's a butcher's apprentice and his master beats him, beats him somewhat awful. With a *mallet*, sir. I fear for his life.'

Strode stopped in mid-step, his frame swaying like an overfilled cart. Slowly he turned. 'Tell me your name,' he said, his robed bulk looming over Edgar in the shadows.

'Rykener. Edgar Rykener, and my brother's Gerald Rykener, butcher's apprentice of Southwark.'

'Rykener.' A voice resonant and deep. 'Edgar Rykener. And your brother is Gerard, you say?'

'Gerald, sir. Gerald Rykener.'

He waved him along with a heavy sigh. 'You've found the right functionary to your purpose. Step in here. We'll have the matter out.'

Edgar followed him into a two-room stone-and-timber building with parchment windows on the outer walls. In the front chamber were three desks, a small hearth currently cold, and a generous amount of crammed shelving. Two of the three desks, the largest one against the far wall, were occupied by four young clerks, one huddled over each side and all busy scribbling on to the parchments, papers and ledgers spread before them. Iron-looped oil lamps dangled from chains of varying lengths, like a strange tree bearing fruits of smoky light.

The clerks sat up at the common serjeant's entrance. Strode summoned one of them with a raised hand and a snap. 'Tewburn.'

Edgar started and blushed, recognizing the clerk immediately. James Tewburn was one of her more frequent mares. Liked to take it as a woman, mouth and arse alike. But he was always tender, always paid well. He didn't recognize Edgar in mannish garb. Not yet.

'Mark what this young fellow says, James,' Strode ordered the clerk, without noticing Edgar's discomfort. 'Take his name, the location of his brother's shop in Southwark, the name of his master – all the pertinent details. Write them up as an appeal to Wykeham and keep at it until the matter is resolved.'

'Yes, Master Strode,' said Tewburn, looking right at Edgar, though still without a trace of recognition.

Strode flashed an easy smile. 'Pardon the lawyerly cant,

125

Edgar. I've explained to Tewburn that we must make an appeal to the Bishop of Winchester, William Wykeham, in order to transfer wardship of your brother into the City of London. Southwark is out of my jurisdiction. But I know Wykeham well. I can't imagine he'll have a problem with our request.'

Edgar nodded, overwhelmed by the man's generosity. 'I – I don't properly know what to say, Master Strode, nor how to thank you.' He could think of some improper ways, though the common serjeant didn't seem the sort.

He waved a hand. 'Keeping our city's wards free from harm is my greatest duty. I do it happily. Just confer with Tewburn here, and he'll have it settled.' He disappeared into the inner chamber.

Tewburn led him over to his desk, where Edgar stood as the clerk shuffled through a mess. The man was younger than he looked, with shoulders already sloped and a discernible hump midway up his back. His eyes, small and round like little black beads over his thin whiskers, took Edgar in with a bureaucrat's scrutiny.

'Your brother is apprenticed to whom?' he asked, his swollen knuckles poised above a ledger.

'Nathan Grimes, master butcher.'

'Of?'

'Cutter Lane in Southwark.'

'Your brother is to be a butcher, then?'

'Yes, sir.'

'And he's in what year of his apprenticeship?'

'His third, sir.'

'Age?'

'Fourteen, sir.'

'I'll take up your brother's wardship as quickly as I can,' said Tewburn, a ready warmth in his voice as he discerned the depth of Edgar's concern. 'Come round in a week or so.'

Still no flash of recognition, and Edgar left Guildhall yard with a tentative hope that Tewburn would truly help his brother.

Later Eleanor crossed the bridge to risk another visit to Grimes's yard, where she found Gerald alone, shovelling dung. His arms, bare and glistening with sweat, showed a patchwork of fresh bruises, and a gash on his brow had recently scabbed over. His eyes when he looked at her were empty, his shoulders slumped.

After she greeted him he wiped a forearm across his brow. 'Might be time after all.'

'Time for what?'

His shifted on his feet. 'To find me another station. Butcher's shop back in London.'

She slapped him, hard. 'So *now* it's time, is it, when I been saying the like for two years?'

Gerald shrugged, not defensively but with a sort of sullen fear, the coldness gone from his eyes. 'Grimes got himself in some deep stick, Edgar. *Real* deep.' He looked over his shoulder at the butcher's streetfront office, separated from the slaughterhouse by a series of narrow pens, each containing a few animals just shy of the knife. 'You got to get me out of this, and right soon.'

'What kind of stick, Gerald?' she said, not wanting to hear the answer.

'This priest, he shows up time to time. Been four, five times now, to meet with Grimes. They pray and get to talking about another Rising. Grimes was on the bridge, you know, with Wat Tyler. He's still got plate he took from the Savoy before they torched the place.'

'But that's wood talk, Gerald,' she said, wanting to believe it.

'They say Wat Tyler should've quartered King Richard when he had the chance. Now it's like to be *their* job. They're

127

butchers, after all, quick with a knife. Grimes keeps mumbling about his fate, how he's been chosen for it by God. That's what the priest told him, so he says when he's in his ales. Butchers, biding by a bishop's bank, then springing out to kill the king.'

Eleanor took this in with a mix of contempt and fear. On the one hand, the notion of these Southwark butchers plotting rebellion was ludicrous on its face. Yet when it came to treason the king's men wouldn't deal in niceties. If a butcher was conspiring on the death of the king they'd take his apprentices along with him, and happily hang them all. 'Grimes is a lunatic, Gerald,' she said, trying to sound convincing. 'Man doesn't have the brains to start a revolt of the mutton against the cows.'

'Still,' he said, 'I want out of Cutter Lane, Eleanor. Get me back to London, yeah?'

She looked at his face, set with genuine fear. Gerald only called her by her she-name when he really wanted something. 'It may be a stretch of time before I can get it done, Gerald.'

'But soon, Eleanor,' Gerald said. He hefted his shovel. 'Soon, yeah?'

Eleanor swallowed, the fear for Gerald eating at her as it never had. 'Soon as I can, Gerald. Then you'll be free.'

SEVENTEEN

Colbrokes Quay on the Thames, Tower Ward

The Ides of April, and the river's surface churned beneath a pale sun as I walked the last length of the wharf toward the custom-house, a hard knot in my chest. The book was out of Swynford's hands, God knew where it was, and Chaucer had no business with it. Seditious, Braybrooke had called it. A traitor's book. The sensible part of me wanted to warn Chaucer off before the whole thing got us both strung up at Tyburn.

Yet my motives were hardly pure. From everything I had learned the *De Mortibus Regum Anglorum* could become the single greatest piece of information I would ever acquire. To possess this book of prophecies and learn the identity of the king's supposed assassin? The manuscript would open doors I had been working to unlatch for years: to the Privy Council, to the lord chancellor, to the court's uppermost magnates. It was clear that Chaucer had been less than honest with me about this book – and I had little enthusiasm left to put it in his fumbling hands.

The door to the customhouse stood open, though no one was inside. Around the near quay a crowd had gathered beneath the highest crane on London's waterfront. The Goose, the machine was called, its charge to raise with pulley, crank, and the sweat of ten men the most massive arrivals at the city's port: great slabs of Kentish stone, casks of iron shot, the occasional mast. Chaucer stood there waving his arms up at the crane. From its hook, over the wide deck of a merchant barge, was suspended a large bale of cloth, the subject of a dispute. I went inside to wait.

Surveying the office, I marvelled that the crown collected any customs money at all. I'd long been amazed at the administrative burden Chaucer had taken on with this post. Virtually no surface was free of the slips that marked every collection of fee in the port going back years. There were thousands of them, spilling out of drawers and crates, papering the seats of stools, leaving a single narrow path across the floor. *The countless cockets crowding my craw*, Chaucer once put it. The line hadn't made it into his verse.

As I looked across the littered office of the wool custom, it occurred to me how closely this documentary rat's nest resembled the disordered sprawl of Chaucer's poetry. Stories of mundane dealings between men, accounts of every imaginable human exchange, recorded on these slips of skin just as they filled his poems with the endless flow of his imagination.

On the far end of the desk sat the quire I had sent over a few days before. It was our private game, the difficult glue of our friendship. Months could go by between our poetical swaps, yet then we'd sit right down, berating one another for a tenuous metaphor, an ill-chosen trope, a lazy rhyme. That morning Chaucer was to critique some of my elegiacs, fragments of a long Latin work I had been composing since before the Rising and still had not completed. I expected to leave the customhouse with some new writing of his.

Nothing, I felt confident, would divert us from this ritual

we had both come to cherish. Not even murder. Not even treason.

'John, you're here!' Chaucer stepped into the customhouse, his eyes going to the bag at my side. He gave a few instructions to a waiting clerk, signed a bill of some kind, and sent the man back to the wharf. 'Let me dig out my little book.'

The air thickened immediately. He wanted to know. But our practice was always to begin with the poetry. He dug through the mess on his desk and emerged with his 'little book', as he called it: the familiar pigskin bifold in which he would keep only those quires of parchment currently in use. It was Chaucer's custom, once he had filled an existing quire with his writing, to remove it and slip a fresh one within the covers. So familiar was his old, faded bifold that it took my poor eyes a moment to see he had replaced it with a new one.

'Lovely, isn't it?' he said, showing off the elaborate tooling and the shiny leathern cover, dyed a striking red. 'It's goat. From Africa, swears a leatherworker I know in Florence. He does great work for the Bardis.' He opened it and took out two loose quires wedged between the fixed pages. 'These verses are a small taste of a larger compilation I've been tossing around. The idea is a pilgrimage, a – well, the frame is unimportant. Two tales here, each to be preceded by a prologue. One is earnest, the other's all game, and next time I'll expect a devastating *sed contra* to both.'

I tucked the parchment quires into my bag while Chaucer started humming distractedly and knuckling his desk. I waited.

'Have you read them, Geoffrey?'

He frowned.

'My elegiacs, on the virtues and vices?' I felt almost childlike, waiting for his attention.

A reassuring smile. 'Of course, John. Pardon my distraction.' He sorted through the loose sheets on his desk, found my own booklet of verse. 'Here we are. Let's just see . . .'

He scanned his notes in the margins, his lower lip tightening in displeasure. 'Rather stark, wouldn't you say?'

'The lines weren't written to be light, Geoffrey. Not like these fabliaux.'

'As you'll soon learn.' He gestured at my bag, and the work he had given me. 'Honestly, though, they could use some leavening.' He took on a preacher's voice, gazing at me over the folios as he spoke my Latin lines. '"The schism of our church has cursed us with two popes, one a schismatic and the other legitimate." And the next couplet: "France worships the schismatic and holds him in awe, but England is a defender of the true faith."' He set the booklet down, a wry challenge in his gaze.

'Should I be amused or offended by your tone?' I asked him. 'The church *is* divided: we're allied with Rome, France with Avignon.'

He shook his head. 'Take these next lines, on bishops. Listen to yourself, John.' He went on in my Latin.

'*As I seek for followers of Christ among the
    prelates
I find that none of the rule survives that was once
    in force.
Christ was poor, but they are overloaded with gold.
He was a peacemaker, but they are war-mongers.*'

His voice had taken on a sing-song cadence, rising before the caesura, then falling toward the end of each line, as if my elegiacs were some child's rhyme.

'*Christ was generous, but they are tight as a closed
    purse.
He was occupied by labour, they have an excess
    of leisure.
Christ was virginal; they are like maudlyns.*'

132

He stopped. 'I won't go on – nor, I think, should you.'

I felt my fists clench, and my vision starred. 'You're parroting my lines, as if their faults chirp for themselves. I thought you approved of taking the clergy to task.'

Chaucer squinted down at the quire, wetting a quill. 'Perhaps if you lightened up a bit, added a dash of humour to your biting satire?' He dipped, blotted, scratched. 'We've talked about this before. In your poetry, everyone is either good or bad. There's no room for moral ambivalence, no accounting for the complexity of character that renders us the fallen humans we are. It's as if you are firing arrows blindly at the entire world.'

'Are you saying the lines aren't true to their subject?'

He sighed, then turned to me. 'Much worse, John. They are not true to *you*.' I blinked. He leaned forward, his hand clutching his crowded desk. 'You're a dazzling Latinist, John, and your elegiacs could be taught as paradigms of the form. But why can't you take some *risks* in your work? Your verses always preach the upright line while you spend your own life scurrying through the shadows, ratting up useful bits of information you turn to your own advantage. Do you write this way because you see yourself as some white-clad incorruptible, standing on a high place upheld by excellent moral foundations? I hardly think so. Do you pen lines like these to obfuscate, to keep us all looking away from what you do? Because no one who writes like this could be as devious as John Gower, *mon ami*. Whatever your reason, your making doesn't come from your heart, from that place that makes you *you*. It doesn't ring true. It never has.'

I could say nothing. He looked at me for a long moment, a mix of puzzlement and affection in his eyes – and, as I think back on it now, a shadow of pity. 'You are a stubborn man, John, and the stubbornest poet I know.' He nudged me back my booklet and turned to his desk, straightening a small corner of the untidy surface. 'Keep writing like this and you're bound for oblivion.'

Though his responses to my poetic making could often be harsh, Chaucer had never spoken to me like this. I sat there, goaded into silence by this cold assessment of my work, feeling something between long regret and immediate fury. Then one of Chaucer's clerks put his head in the door, asking several questions about the transaction down at the quay.

When he was gone I plunged straight in, my voice tight with anger. 'The book you're looking for is a work of prophecy. You didn't think to tell me this?'

'Prophecy,' said Chaucer, his bright eyes unreadable. 'What sort of prophecy?'

'Braybrooke claims the book is treasonous.'

He bent his neck and looked at the rafters. '"Treason" is a word tossed around like pigshit these days. Though considering the source I suppose I shouldn't be surprised. For the Bishop of London, thought itself is treason. Pose a few curious questions about the sacrament, get a hanging for your trouble.'

'Don't cling to Wycliffe, Geoffrey,' I warned him. 'Gaunt adored the man for some reason, but he was a heretic, and a dissident. His teachings have been roundly condemned.'

'God help us. And now Braybrooke is convinced this book is heretical? From everything I have heard it's just a light satire. A well-crafted look into England's royal past, with a peculiar twist here and there.'

I shook my head. 'Believe me, Geoffrey, this is not a book you want to be associated with. There's already been loads of trouble about it: at court, at the inns, with the bishops – foul circumstances that surround it on every side. Even a young woman's death.'

'*What?*'

134

'Murder, Geoffrey.' I told him what Swynford and Strode had told me, and reminded him of the disrupted pageant at the Temple Hall. I said nothing about the business with Symkok, keeping that bit of information to myself.

His hand went to his mouth. It trembled there, then went back to his side. 'Who was the young woman?'

'An agent of the French crown, by all appearances.' He was still. 'So you see, it's not Katherine Swynford who is responsible for the disappearance of the book. This is much bigger than her.'

He stared at me. Were those tears welling in the corners of his eyes? 'But *why*, John? Why would anyone kill a young woman over a book?'

'The work concerns the deaths of kings,' I said, pushing on. 'Of *English* kings.'

He blinked. Yes, tears. One of them escaped, tracking down his left cheek.

'By statute of Parliament it's treasonous to compass or even *imagine* the death of the king,' I went on. 'Yet this work – and I've heard parts of it, with my own ears, from Braybrooke's friars – this work prophesies the deaths of England's last twelve sovereigns, as well as—'

'Ha!' He gave a short, frantic bark of a laugh. 'How is it that a work can prophesy deaths that have already occurred?'

'I asked Braybrooke the same question. According to the bishop, it was written many years ago.'

'Yet again, how—'

'Its prophecies reflect the chronicles accurately. Consider the prophecy on the death of the second Edward.' I repeated the memorable lines I had heard from Braybrooke's friar.

'In Gloucester will he goeth, to be gutted by goodmen
With rod straight of iron, in arsebone to run.

135

With pallet of pullet, his breath out to press,
And sovereign unsound for Sodom be sundered.'

As I spoke the lines Chaucer stood and walked to the opened door, where he leaned on the sill, his shoulders rising and falling to the shouts on the embankment, the clap of boards from an unloading barge.

I gazed at his back. 'I haven't told you the worst. The thirteenth prophecy foretells the death of King Richard.'

A dismissive cluck. 'No no no, that's wrong, Richard does not—' He froze, his eyes widening as he turned to me. His face paled, going the colour of sunbleached bone. I approached him and took his hand, the earlier cruelty forgotten for the moment. 'Geoffrey, what is it?'

'It cannot be,' he said, his voice just above a whisper, the tears giving way to something I took then as fear. 'This explains – but it simply cannot be.'

'You are making no sense, Geoffrey.'

'But of course. Of *course*!' Tears streamed down his face, his entire frame shaking with the strangest abandon.

Baffling. 'Why are you laughing? These are grave matters.' And what are you not telling me?

Chaucer calmed himself, placing a hand on my shoulder as he wiped the other across his eyes. 'The book, John,' he said. 'Get me the book, and all shall be well.'

'This is blind idiocy, Geoffrey. The Bishop of London himself says it: this is a burnable book, a work of high treason certain to destroy any man who holds it.'

'Get me the book. At any cost.'

'You're acting like a little boy now. Do you want to see your reputation ruined over all this?'

'*Reputation*,' he said, as if the word were a rotten river oyster. 'My *reputation*, you say?' Suddenly back from wherever he had been, Chaucer leaned into me, his face a red mask of cruel intention, his neck a foreign bulge of tendons and veins. 'You *will* find this book for me, O Moral Gower. I know it, and you know it. In a city where everyone owes John Gower, Esquire, a favour, Geoffrey Chaucer may be the only soul to whom he owes one himself. Quite a large one, too. And in a city in which John Gower, Esquire, has information on nearly every man of importance, it may be useful to call to mind the small matter of your son's count—'

'*Enough.*' I stepped away. 'How *dare* you threaten me like this?'

He grabbed a pile of cockets from his desk and threw them in the air. The parchments snowed around our heads. His lips curled into a puerile sneer. 'Call it a threat if you like. Whatever the case, your position is exceedingly weak. Do not test me, Gower.'

I stared at him, waiting for him to retract the malicious threat behind his words, but his lips seemed frozen in place. 'You've finally stripped the veil, my friend,' I said, a trembling whisper. 'Now you are no better than I am. At last you know what it's like, to have a man's soul in your hands.'

The look Chaucer gave me then was the coldest I had ever seen. 'Poets don't traffic in souls. That is the work of priests. The sooner you learn the difference the better a poet you shall be.' On that cruellest of notes he turned away. 'Find the book. Find it, bring it to me, and just maybe you will see your son in England again.'

As I left the customhouse and paced back along the wharfage, I carried Chaucer's words as a profound weight on my spirit. Yet from our abrasive encounter one deeper question lingered, a question that concerned neither the viability of this deep friendship nor its tenuous basis in our poetry. The question concerned, rather, the young woman on the Moorfields, this alleged French agent murdered over the very book my difficult friend sought with such singular focus – and to whose death he had reacted with such exaggerated surprise that it seemed feigned. It was a question about Geoffrey Chaucer himself, and it had been haunting me for a week and more. A question no longer avoidable.

Could Chaucer kill?

✛ ✛ ✛

The dust cloud grew as the company approached, massing into a great orb that filled the northern sky, as if God had obliterated a portion of the earth from His sight. Even from that distance the lady could recognize the arms borne by the herald: the livery of the king. The gate, she ordered, was to remain open, the defences unprepared. Castile is arrived, she told her husband's men and her servants. Make the castle ready! Open our larders and cellars to his needs! Her orders carried out, the company arrived, to be greeted with the lady's open arms.

Yet once they had reached the castle gates and their leader stood before her, she realized she had been deceived. This was not King Pedro, nor was her husband among the company. These men wore livery she had never seen, spoke in a language she could not comprehend. The banners of Castile they flung carelessly to the ground.

Their lord, a prince from a northern land, was a hard man, with a pale face that might have been cut from stone. A forked beard fell from his chin like two waterfalls of molten lead, and in him the lady sensed a certain cruelty, a flow of dark intention beneath the rituals of courtesy the situation demanded. He groused loudly of King Pedro's unpaid war debts, and the poor condition of his troops.

The prince had arrived in the company of his younger brother, a duke. Taller by half a head, this lord was a man of few words. He was of nobler bearing than the prince, and seemed almost ashamed by his older brother's disposition.

For weeks the lords remained in the castle, their troops garrisoned along the walls. The lady learned that a much greater force, thousands strong, was encamped near Burgos, growing hungry and ill as the foreign prince awaited payment of Pedro's debts. As the unwelcome visit lengthened, the prince let the lady know her place at every opportunity.

Your husband is in my debt, he said. And your husband's lord, and his lord, and his lord in turn – all are in my debt. All that your

139

husband claims to own shall properly be mine. Mine the harvest gleaned from the earth beneath your feet. Mine the flocks rutting and grazing in these fields. Mine the small treasure guarded in this castle's hold. And mine—

The prince did not say it, but from the moment of his arrival she had felt it. His eyes upon her constantly, his conversation crudely suggestive, his hand lingering too long upon her own at their moments of formal greeting.

She made sure she was never alone, trailing her daughter with her wherever she went, ordering a maidservant to remain in her bed through the night. She bent her back to please the visitors. There were slaughters to order, hunts to organize, horses to water and feed. Her husband's *senescalo* went nearly mad as the soldiers' demands increased.

The lady called on her villagers to help, appropriating their animals, their grain, their bodily labour to ensure adequate food and drink for the visiting lord and his men. *All shall be returned to you in droves,* she promised them. They gave willingly, that their lady's honour might remain intact.

Yet those hardened folk of the Castilian marches, their wisdom deep as the soil, understood what she did not. The darkest law of chivalry.

When a great lord arrives at the home of a lesser, whether his vassal or not, the lesser shall consider all he owns to be the just property of the greater. All should be surrendered to him freely and without objection.

And what the lord does not receive willingly, he is entitled to take by force.

PART TWO

Faun of Three Feathers

Day xiv before Kalends of May to Nones of May, 8
Richard II
(18 April–7 May 1385)

EIGHTEEN

St Mary Overey, Southwark

Two stories: one of lust, one of murder. One of revelry, of adulterous love, of untroubled joy in the flesh. The other of a young boy's faith, of treachery, death and resurrection.

In the first story, a randy student seduces a carpenter's wife, deceives him with a false prophecy of a second flood, and causes a household disaster. There is also a parish clerk, a fop who seeks the wife's favours for himself yet wins only a fart as his reward. The tale is told by a miller, who delights in the flaws of every character he portrays.

In the second story, a young chorister hears a sacred song being performed by older boys and vows to learn this gorgeous antiphon on his own. As he moves back and forth through a Jewry, the song fills his throat. The offended Jews conspire against him, causing his murder and throwing his corpse in a privy. As his mother searches for him, the boy is miraculously resurrected. The narrator of this tale is a prioress, a holy woman leading a community of Christian nuns.

Two stories, both scrawled in Chaucer's loose hand in the

quire he had given me at the customhouse. On a first reading no two stories could have been more unlike. The thought of compiling them within a larger work made no sense, yet such was Chaucer's plan, inspired by the same Giovanni Boccaccio who wrote the tragic romance Chaucer had brought back from Florence.

The more I thought about these stories, though, the more I came to see what, in Chaucer's bent imagination, they might have in common. Both dealt with the consequences of sin and fallen flesh. Though the prioress's story more directly concerned death, martyrdom, and persecution, this miller's tale cast its own shadows: another Noah's Flood, the degradation of the marital sacrament, hints of sodomy. As art, then, the stories seemed congruent, eerily so. Once again Chaucer had proven himself a superior teller of tales.

Or a compelling liar. I sat back, my spine finding its worn place on the study wall. We had spoken often over the years about the proximity of poetry and deception. To write a great poem, Chaucer insisted, you have to be a greater liar. You must convince your readers that your characters are flesh and blood rather than words on dead skin, that their loves and hatreds and passions are as deep and present as the readers' own. Your task is to delight, to pleasure, to lift your reader to another sphere of being and then strand him there, floating above the earth and panting for more lines.

This long struggle with my own poetry? Perhaps it's just that, I thought: I don't deal in colourful lies, but in plain truths, however coarse and hidden. What need is there for deception when the truth is so much more compelling, so much darker in its attachments?

The truths before me now, though, were hidden beneath an impenetrable veil, despite all the damning facts and obscure information I had accumulated over the years. A prophetic book I hadn't read and couldn't find. A murdered woman I didn't know and couldn't name. A friend I couldn't fathom and shouldn't trust. And all the while a city I thought I'd mastered suddenly strange and alien to me, coiled like a serpent across the river, its tongue whispering a threat I could not comprehend.

Caught up as I was in these clouds of enigma, it took me a few moments to notice the hard knock from the front of the house, followed by faint voices and the stomp of boots. A visitor, admitted by Will Cooper at the hour I defended most fiercely for my writing. I sighed, looked down at my quill, and stood. Thick clouds had been toying with the sun that morning, casting the interior of the house into peculiar shades that created illusions of presence in empty corners. It was for this reason that I thought at first I had imagined the man in the lower hall, as if a phantom of his form had flared up from Hell to burn through my very door.

He turned, looked everywhere but into my eyes, his smile tinged with everything that had passed between us.

'Father,' he said.

✣

Nearly three years had passed since that dreadful Trinity Sunday, a feast Sarah particularly loved. She would order up everything in threes for the supper. Three soups, three wines, three meats, three sweets, enlisting every taste in the celebration of Father, Son, and Holy Ghost. The messenger arrived mid-morning, as we were returning from early Mass. Our house stood back from the priory walls on Overey Street by a good twenty feet, with two broad yew trees towering over a gated yard paved with riverstone. A young man waited within the courtyard. I recognized him as one of Chaucer's clerks from the wool custom.

He bowed slightly. 'I must speak with you, Master Gower,' he said, his eyes wandering toward Sarah. 'I come direct from Master Chaucer, and at his orders.'

There was an awkward moment which Sarah smoothed over by going inside. No one else was about, save a few churchgoers gathered farther down. The shops were closed, the street appropriately silent for the morning of a feast day.

'Is Chaucer in some kind of trouble?' It would not have been the first time.

'Not – not Master Chaucer, sir. I'm here about your son, Master Simon.'

'Simon? What has Simon got to do with your business at the wool custom?'

'It might be best to leave such questions for Master Chaucer.'

I pressed the man as we walked to the Southwark wharf and boarded the waiting skiff.

'There's been a killing, sir.'

My heart thrummed in my ears. 'Simon?'

He shook his head. 'Your son is safe.' He would say nothing more, and my worry turned to dread as we floated toward the Tower. I sat back on the board seat, willing the small boat across the river.

Chaucer was waiting at the quay. Above the water, as the skiff angled toward him, he stood still as a carved apostle, his face pale, his eyes swollen with exhaustion. When I stepped up he broke his stance and grasped my arm. We walked in silence to one of the warehouses down the wharf. At the door Chaucer stopped me. 'Go easy on him, John.'

The air inside stank of sheep. Bales of wool were piled high to the rafters. A thin shaft of sunlight outlined a peculiar shape on the floor, reflecting upwards to create a luminous sphere around Simon's bowed head. He sat at the end of a long counting bench, nearly doubled at the waist. Low moans came from his chest, his body shaking with pain and fear. Against the near wall, just inside the door, rested the corpse: a form wrapped in sailcloth, a thatch of dark hair visible at one end, a trace of blood on the board floor.

Chaucer signalled to the watchman to leave us, then shut the door from within. I approached my son.

'What have you done?'

Simon was filthy, his clothes torn, his flesh reeking of ale. He looked up. His face was an utter mess. 'I killed him, Father. And . . . there's more.'

The moment stretched, my rising anger mingled with a helpless confusion. I turned to Chaucer. Back to Simon. Finally I approached the corpse and uncovered the face. I recognized it as belonging to a constable of Tower Street Ward, a man I had encountered once or twice, though I didn't know his name.

Simon, in his stuttering way, and with Chaucer filling in the last several hours, revealed everything.

For some months, Simon told me, he had been involved in a counterfeiting ring, forging half-nobles with the help of a goldsmith and an under-master at the King's Mint. The smith would concoct a weak alloy, the under-master having sneaked one of King Edward's obsolete stamps out of the Tower, and Simon would rough up the fake coins with bricks, trading them up for genuine nobles or down for groats and pennies. Too many of the three-shilling-fourpence coins appearing in London all at once would arouse suspicion, so Simon had arranged for quantities of them to be put into circulation at the markets in York, Hull, and Calais, as well as on deposit with two of the Italian banking houses on Lombard Street.

As he explained his logic and actions, I stared at his mouth, spewing these numbers and calculations as if he had been born a criminal. I had always hoped Simon's prodigious talent with numbers and words would open doors to a respectable career, perhaps on the logic faculty at Oxford, or in the law. Never would I have imagined my son conspiring with such men to forge a royal likeness on gold coins. Yet the scheme had been turning a handsome profit for some months, due in large part to Simon's astute sense of the money supply.

Their luck turned when a constable of Tower Street Ward stumbled on to their operation while chasing down a petty thief, who had taken refuge in the back of the goldsmith's shop. Rather than turning the three counterfeiters over to his superiors, the constable had attempted to extort part of their profits, threatening them with exposure should they refuse him. So, with the approval of his partners, Simon had arranged a large payoff, setting the exchange for just after curfew at a rough alehouse on the wharf. The negotiation had grown heated and was taken out to the bankside, where the men came to blows. Simon described the fight, his fists flying at the man's face, taking his own hits, then delivering the final blow that sent the constable reeling backwards on the wharf, his head meeting an iron shipping-hook as he fell. Hearing the commotion, two watchmen at the wool wharf had come running, one of them tackling Simon to the ground, the other attempting to revive the fallen man.

Too late. Rather than summoning the authorities, they had sent for Chaucer, controller of the wool custom and something of a tyrant in his management of the wharf. At his direction the watchmen had hauled Simon inside, along with the constable's body, and there they had waited for Simon to recover from his drunkenness before questioning him about the incident.

'I made him tell me all of it before I sent for you,' Chaucer explained. 'I thought it best to limit the surprises, make sure Simon had all of this straight so we could get to the truth without a lot of hemming and hawing.'

I nodded vacantly, the enormity of it all dawning on me. My only surviving child, a counterfeiter, and a murderer.

Simon broke again, burying his face in his hands. 'I'm sorry, Father, you – you have to appreciate my—'

'You'll get no appreciation from me, Simon. Nor forgiveness. *Counterfeiting*? Did you think for one moment of your honour, and my reputation?'

He looked up at me, his eyes lit with a righteous clarity that seemed drastically out of place. 'You're right, Father. Perhaps I should have pursued a more honourable trade. Are you taking apprentices?'

I hit him. Not a smack but a hard punch that sent him flying backwards to land on the filthy surface.

'*John!*' Chaucer rushed forward and reached for Simon, who was sprawled across the floor. Chaucer helped him to his feet, then stepped back, grasped my arm, and led me out to the wharf. He pushed me roughly against the side of the warehouse. 'If Simon is taken – if there's even an inquest – he'll be hanged. Perhaps not for murder, my men will attest it was an accident, but for the coining. It's treason to counterfeit the King's Mint.'

'Treason,' I said, the word bitter on my tongue.

'We can fix this,' Chaucer said in an angry whisper. He looked up the wharf. 'The constable never told anyone else what he found out – otherwise he couldn't have used the information against Simon. Do you see?'

I nodded tightly.

'As for my men, they'll stay silent. They're well paid, and God knows they keep enough secrets as it is. So really this all comes down to destroying evidence, and staying mum.'

Chaucer's focus on the practical had a calming effect. I looked at him. 'So what do you suggest we do?'

There was no real choice in the end. The corpse was disposed of by the watchmen. A sack, four large stones, a skiff up to Stepney Marsh, the weighted body over the side and into the reeds. Simon, too, needed removal from London lest tongues start to wag. Chaucer would make all the necessary arrangements: passage to Tuscany; a letter of introduction to his old friend Sir John Hawkwood; a promise to check on Simon within a twelvemonth, as his business for the king would surely take him back to Italy before long.

With dire threats, I forbade Simon from speaking any word about the matter to Sarah. I would tell her of an unexpected opportunity for him in the south, an offer of employment in the king's service, working on behalf of Hawkwood, the great mercenary and Richard's newly appointed ambassador to Rome.

He left for Italy without bidding farewell to his mother. I thought it best that she remain ignorant. Within five days of the killing on the wool wharf, and with barely a whisper of notice in London, Simon's presence in Southwark, and in our lives, was only a memory.

✥

Now, with all this coming back to me in an unwanted rush, I watched Simon unbuckle his belt, remove his surcoat, line up his boots on the doorside block in the same way I had seen him do hundreds of times. The elegant movements of his hands, the distinctive lines of his face, the almond curves of his eyes, curls as neat as if an iron had pressed his hair: all still spoke of that insolent boy who could never please his father. Yet Simon's gaze was not, as it had been the last time I saw him, floating toward Gravesend for a new life in Italy, defiant or proud. Instead it was tired, or defeated. He wouldn't meet my eyes.

'Why have you come back, Simon?'

Simon bowed his head. He was wearing a short gown, the sleeves long and wide in the Italian style. 'I should have written ahead, Father, but with the roads, the French – I decided to come ahead on my own. I have taken a leave from Hawkwood's service, with his consent, though I am not at all sure whether I shall go back to Italy. When Chaucer told me my mother had died I couldn't help thinking of you, and of our home.' He looked around at the hall, though still would not show me his gaze. 'I don't imagine I shall be much comfort to you, but it seemed the right time to come back to England, after so long abroad. I should like to find a position in London, or if you don't want me that close I have contacts in Calais. I think my skills could be useful there.'

He continued on in this vein, and more than anything else it was his pathetic curiosity about Sarah's death that began to stem my anger. When did she first show signs of sickness? Did she speak lucidly to you, Father, in her final hours? Did she have any last words for me? Because Chaucer never said. Was her suffering great? It was as if Simon, within his first hours back in Southwark, became the voice of my own, unspoken sorrow, now so mingled with his.

It was at some point in those hours that I found myself thinking of the Duke of Lancaster, and wondering where in his tangled relations he found the most comfort in the face of so much loss. John, Edward, the second John, Isabel, four of his children with Duchess Blanche, all of them buried in Leicester years ago; another John with Duchess Constance, felled by fever before his second year. Such childhood deaths harden a man, whip his heart with chill and heat even as he bites his lips to keep the pain from speaking for itself. Now this one boy who had somehow clung to life was here, with me, and despite all that he had done the feeling that almost overwhelmed me in that moment I can only describe as a grateful, joyous calm. The calm of kin, I suppose.

We sat in the garden, eating a midday meal I barely tasted. As Simon devoured his food I turned the conversation to his life in and around Florence, at the service of the English *condottiero*. His position, as he described it, seemed to consist in a variety of clerical tasks for Hawkwood's company: contracts for service, purchases of supply, provisions for garrisoned troops around the peninsula. At one point in our conversation his face darkened.

'What is it, Simon?'

151

He hesitated. 'I should tell you as well, Father, that I was betrothed.'

'Was?'

His lips tightened. 'She died. Fever. We never made it to our vows.'

'How long has it been?'

He slightly shrugged. 'Months. But every day I wake up imagining she's still alive.'

'What was her name?' I asked, thinking she might have died right around the time Sarah passed.

He closed his eyes. 'Her name . . . her name was Seguina.' He could barely utter it, and when he had he started weeping, not the cry of a man with an eye to his status, nor a boyish mewl, but a ripping keen, the phlegm pouring from his nose to glisten his lips and chin, his chest and shoulders heaving in a haphazard rhythm, animal-like chokes barking from his throat. In a strange way I found myself feeling almost jealous of his pain, its comfortless depth. I had never wept with such abandon for Sarah.

'Seguina,' I finally said.

'Seguina d'-d'-d'Orange,' he hiccupped, still a boy in that moment.

'A beautiful name,' I said, and just like that it was settled. I still marvel at the ease with which Simon slipped back into my daily life, like a hand-warmed coin into a silk purse. Often I wonder how everything would have turned out had I gone with my first impulse, sending him away from Southwark with an oath and a boot. Or if I had demanded to search his meagre luggage.

But Simon was my sole heir, as Chaucer would not stop pointing out, and with all the stir around the book and the Moorfields killing, the lingering emptiness left by Sarah's death the year before, I suppose I was looking for some source of comfort in those turbulent weeks. No one can be blameless in such circumstances, and I now understand why I remained ignorant – was kept ignorant – even as the clouds thickened above. Yet as I look back on our reunion that day I can still be sickened by my self-deception, my blithe acceptance of its terms.

That, I am afraid, was my own doing. For never once did I think to question the timing of my son's return from Italy. Nor its meaning.

NINETEEN

San Donato a Torre, near Florence

Adam Scarlett, hungry, muddy from the road, in no hurry to deliver his news, leaned against the stable wall and watched the battle unfold. Three lancemen, shields held high, began their charge at the small artillery company, who waited until the last moment to launch the payload. Clods and stones peppered the attackers, then the trebuchet broke, sending a cracked feed bucket rolling between the ranks. The five boys traded screams and blows, coming together in a loud melee before collapsing in a heap of giggles and sweat. The farrier, mumbling about the yearlings, came out and chased them off.

Scarlett turned away and started his ascent to the villa, the scene replaying in his mind as the scent of freshly turned dirt rose from beneath his riding boots. War never ended in the communes, it seemed, every season grinding its hundreds of young men into the clay. Soon enough these boys, most of them sons of bought soldiers, would be riding out themselves, bound for a seasonal cattle raid, or another pillage in the Romagna.

In the gallery Hawkwood was dressing down one of his chief men, a *tenente* from the garrison near Perugia. Scarlett had arranged the man's summons and transfer to Florence several weeks before, after Taricani's departure, and now he was here to face due punishment. Private deals with a Jewish banker, sums moved off the books. Scarlett found his usual place along the south wall, within easy sight of the *condottiero*. With the mess he had in hand he was happy to wait.

'Please, sire, if you would only—'

'Silence, pig.' Hawkwood was enjoying himself, and the kneeling man seemed to know it. Scarlett watched as the soldier's cheek paled, his fright like a layer of wash swept over a fresco.

'You think I haven't had enough of this from my countrymen already? First Cocco, pulling his little *truffa*. And now you, Antonio?'

'But, sire, the Raspanti—'

'Ah, the Raspanti. Blame it on the poor, shall we? That's the best you can do?'

'Yes, sire – I mean no, sire—'

'Enough,' said Hawkwood, quietly this time, and in English. 'Enough.' He turned and his gaze found Scarlett, who gave his master the slightest of shrugs. A *what-did-you-expect?* sort of shrug. The *condottiero* widened his eyes in agreement, his irises white flecks on brown, hues of frosted mud, of winter campaigns and Yule sieges.

Hawkwood reached down to his side for the stick. *La Asta*, the Rod, a notorious forearm's length of hard elm, its core drilled out and filled with a pour of lead. He palmed it gently, looking from his hands to the *tenente*, now a whimpering dog waiting for a boot. With one movement Hawkwood brought the stick up, across, and the man's head whipped to the side with a hard crack of bone.

Wretched moans, lots of blood, and when he brought his head back to centre Scarlett could see the ruined jaw hanging by a slab of torn skin and ripped muscle. Hawkwood leaned forward and cupped the broken bones, shoving them back into place with an excruciating thrust. Scarlett winced for the *tenente*.

'Keep this shut for a while, Antonio,' he said, back in Italian. 'Take the silence I've imposed on you as an opportunity, hmm? To think about virtue, about service, about loyalty and the consequence of what you've done. We'll talk again next year, when your mouth works again.' He jerked the loose bone to the side, and the *tenente* fell to the floor, writhing in pain.

Later, after Hawkwood had sorted through the day's correspondence with Pietrasanta, his chancellor, they walked through the gardens, looking at the week ahead. Scarlett was procrastinating, and badly. He listened to his master going on about the Perugia situation.

'I've grown sick of these southern men, Adam. The heat makes them lazy, and now all this conjuring with the Jews. Really, I've taken all I can take. Give me an Englishman over these rude peninsulars any day. Or even a Scot.' He paused to look across the ravine to the north. 'It will be good to see London, won't it? And after so many years.'

Scarlett took a breath, another, then said it. 'The book has disappeared.'

Hawkwood froze. 'When?'

'Five weeks ago Monday, my lord. Our messengers have just brought the news from Westminster.'

Scarlett told him the rest of it: the incident at La Neyte, the pursuit in the Moorfields, the fear spreading like fire among the English gentry. The messenger had been sent on his way within a few days of the theft, with instructions to

156

spare no expense in bringing the news to the great *condottiero* in Florence with all due speed.

'I shudder for the poor horses,' Hawkwood said absently. He turned and looked at Scarlett. 'You're telling me, Adam, that a French spy has stolen the book from under our beak, and Lancaster's?'

'All we know is that it was pilfered by an unidentified woman,' said Scarlett, letting the implication sink in. 'Now she's dead.'

'A woman.' Hawkwood's eyes widened. 'Could it be—'

'That is my assumption, sire.'

Hawkwood considered this for a while. 'Resourceful little thing, isn't she?'

'Wasn't she.'

Hawkwood smiled thinly. 'And the others?'

'That's not known,' said Scarlett. 'Yet.'

Hawkwood continued walking. 'The last dispatch spoke of the work's popularity among these Lollers.'

Scarlett paced behind, watching his master's face. 'The late Wycliffe's disciples, and friends of Lancaster. Some of them have it by rote, and by the time of its disappearance it had become the most notorious writing in England. A book of ghostly prophecies, with dark portent for the fate of the realm! But now no one can find the original manuscript, nor the cloth. And I worry – well . . .'

'Tell me, Adam.'

'I worry that this may be Il Critto's doing.'

'Oh?'

'I do not like coincidences. First Il Critto takes a leave, suddenly, and without warning. Then this young woman, who was nearly betrothed to him, disappears without a trace from her father's house. Next your slinky poetical friend comes back from Rome. You know the gossip, sire. He was seducing her. Then *he* leaves us – quite distraught, from the

157

servants' reports. And all of this just a few weeks after the book leaves our hands. A book now missing.' They took a few more steps. Scarlett was the one who stopped this time. 'I don't like it, John. I don't like it at all.'

Hawkwood's face was hard to read at that moment, though it soon broke into a serene smile. 'Well, there's little we can do about it now, eh? And in some ways the theft may be the best thing that could have happened.'

'Oh?'

'This will only draw more attention to the book. Soon enough every man and woman in London will be singing these prophecies from the towers. Then what will our long castle have to say for himself? This changes nothing, Adam.'

Scarlett could see Hawkwood's point about the theft, though he did not share the *condottiero*'s confidence that all would be well. With the book on the loose and the prophecies bandied abroad, there was no telling where all of this might end up.

He thought again of Il Critto, as they had dubbed him soon after his arrival in Hawkwood's circles. Young, ambitious, sizzlingly brilliant. A charmer, but Scarlett had distrusted him from the first instant. Il Critto had distrusted Scarlett as well, especially after that unfortunate misunderstanding over the faked dispatch from London. It was merely a loyalty test, and the young man had passed it admirably, though he had taken the whole thing as a personal affront, an assault on his honour. Scarlett had tried to make peace, but Il Critto would hear none of it, and the young man had spent the next two years in Florence despising the sight of him.

It had been weeks since Scarlett had given Il Critto more than a passing thought. Now he was concerned. *Non tenet anguillam, per caudam qui tenet illam.* A bit of wisdom ground in by long experience among these venomous communes. 'He who holds a snake by the tail doesn't have it under control.' And at the moment, Scarlett worried, we don't hold even the tail.

Hawkwood, feeling none of this, gave his most faithful man a fond smile. 'And now, Adam, you will join your king-maker in a game of cards.'

TWENTY

St Paul's churchyard, Ward of Farringdon

'Will he recognize you?' Agnes Fonteyn asked her sister.

Millicent ignored the question as she gazed across the expanse of the great churchyard, where swift clouds bowled shadows among the hucksters, pilgrims, guildsmen, and idlers. With her gut tightened in fear, every sight and sound reached her with an acuity that cast the peril of their situation in sharp relief. The line of swearers spilling out the south door, clutching contracts as they awaited their turn at the altar to sign or make their mark. Construction at the south end on a line of dwellings for canons: the pounding of hammers, the loud claps of boards, carpenters' swears. The banter from the steps, bakers' daughters and fishwives hawking from their leased stations around the broken cross, and every word bounced off the stone.

River mallard, roast bittern, five roast larks for two, here here, sir.

Cristina Walwayn's pigeons're putrid, sir, hardly fit for pasties.

Don't y'purchase from that station, good sir. That's Evota there, Our Lady of the Stale Buns.

Fish, sir, roast fish? Henry Holdernesse be my master, trustiest monger in town, sure. Not like Tilda Cooke over there, she'll sell you a flat a' pigshit and call it a herring-cake. Mine goes down easy, sir, and sells easy as well.

Though selling a book, Millicent had discovered, was more difficult. Over the last week she and Agnes had become industrious fishers of men, posing as middling singlewomen of Cornhull, their hook baited with the only worm they possessed. This book, Millicent firmly believed, would bring a high price from the right man – a man ambitious enough to use it for the unique sort of personal gain its contents promised. A few whispered conversations at service gates, furtive proffers at tavern doors, a handsome profit.

Yet none of these men had taken the bait. Not a one of them had even understood the significance of what she was offering them, nor the grave threat the book represented to the realm. That morning Millicent had made a decision. Their next prospect would be a greater man. Not a lord, but something like a lord: a man belonging to the Order of the Coif, a serjeant-at-law with deep connections in the king's affinity.

Thomas Pinchbeak had once been close with Sir Humphrey ap-Roger, who had relied on him for a number of legal matters. She had met the lawman at a mummers play along the embankment, Sir Humphrey showing her off on a Midsummer Eve, the shore fires painting the river with a devilish sheen. That was nearly three years ago. Pinchbeak might recall her face, though surely not her name, as she hadn't encountered him again since well before Sir Humphrey's death. What would he think of her, she wondered, approaching him with such a peculiar offer – or, depending how he received it, such an unsettling threat?

With the book concealed in her coat lining, Agnes turned to wait at the top of the south stairs while Millicent approached the gate. Pinchbeak stood with two of his fellow

161

serjeants-at-law within the parvis, a low-walled area before the portico enclosed as a small courtyard. The lawmen were engaged in a light-hearted dispute of some kind, with Pinchbeak the wry observer and mediator, two of the younger serjeants more animated. On the stone benches that lined the sides of the parvis sat several other lawmen conferring with visitors – two wealthy burgesses and a knight. To the side of the gate stood a young man of perhaps seventeen, gangly, tall, puffed with his minor station.

'A word with Master Pinchbeak, please,' Millicent said, giving him her most winning smile.

He spat in a gutter. 'The serjeants have little time for hucksters or women, nor women hucksters. Be off with you.'

Millicent looked down at her dress, now shabbier than any garment she had worn since St Leonard's. 'But it's known that the serjeants-at-law gather in the parvis to serve *all* the citizens of London. You'd deny a freewoman of the city such privilege?' Her raised voice attracted the attention of the lawmen. Pinchbeak approached the low gate, then leaned out to address the young man.

'Let her in, Dawson.'

The young man bowed his head. 'As you wish, Master Pinchbeak.'

Pinchbeak gestured to Millicent to follow him, and she matched his slow progress toward the far wall of the parvis. He walked with a stick, topped by a carved skull of ivory that looked small beneath a massive hand, which belied his compact frame. He didn't look at her until they had taken a seat, and he said nothing once they were settled, merely raising an untamed eyebrow.

Millicent reached into her bodice and removed her medal, the silver replica of St Leonard that still identified her with Bromley. She displayed it for Pinchbeak. His expression softened. 'As you see, Master Pinchbeak,' she began, 'I was

162

once a poor laysister of St Leonard, no more than a peeler of roots to that great house. Yet I come to beg the indulgence of a lawman famed across England for the wisdom of his counsel.'

Pinchbeak, ignoring her flattery, studied her face, his gaze wandering freely over her features and down to her breast. 'We've met before.'

'I don't believe so, Master Pinchbeak,' she quickly said. She stole a glance at his collar, a band of chained silver about his neck with a pendant badge below, bejewelled with the livery of his affinity: a single white star, opposed fields of gold and red, the whole surrounded by ornate tangles of vines, leaves, and flowers, the subtlest metalwork to be had in London. The gifting of this collar had been a sign of singular distinction, marking Pinchbeak as a prestigious member of that extended network of knights, squires, freemen, and servants orbiting Robert de Vere, Earl of Oxford.

Pinchbeak tilted his head. 'I'm rarely wrong about such things. But no matter. State your business. Always happy to help out a sister of Bromley, whether lay or avowed.'

She spoke of the book. His face remained impassive as she described the volume and its poetry, the dark histories inscribed in its strange verses; the cloth and its heraldry, the incriminating livery woven in its strands. She recited the four bits of prophecy she had learned by rote, including the one that mattered most, on the death of King Richard. She said nothing about the manner in which the book had come to her, nor about the murdered girl. This piece of the story, she suspected, might prove more useful at a later point.

All the while Pinchbeak observed her with a practised calm, his fingers steepled before his sharp nose. She could not read the lawman's eyes even as well as she had read the book, though in their depths she sensed genuine concern. The hollow of his neck created a dark well of stubbled skin

163

that pulsed as he listened. She was watching a vein throb beneath his chin when he finally spoke.

'To whom else have you uttered these lines?' He leaned forward slightly.

'You are the first,' Millicent lied. 'The very first, Master Pinchbeak.'

She waited. With a shuddering groan, the bell struck in the St Paul's belfry far above, wrapping Millicent in its deep throb and shaking her guts like jelly in a bowl.

Pinchbeak remained still through the last of the clamour, his gaze on Millicent far from kind. 'You deal rather freely with these prophecies,' he said into the final, dying tone.

'Though freely is not how I hope to part with them, Master Pinchbeak,' she countered.

His frown was severe. 'You haven't the devil's idea what unholy hell you've dug yourself into, Mistress—'

'Rykener,' she said on an impulse, thinking of the Gropecunt maudlyn showing up at her door. Through the parvis gate she saw Agnes, lingering by the stairs. 'Eleanor Rykener is my name.' Her sister would flay her if she knew she had betrayed her friend in this way, yet giving her own name would lead the authorities right to her door.

'Mistress Rykener,' Pinchbeak said, attempting patience, though she could now see the cords in his neck standing out against his skin, which had coloured to a deep purple, 'I've heard noises from others about this book. A hideous thing, and if what you say is true, if you really have it, why, you've dug yourself a pretty little hole. The very words you've uttered in my presence – the words alone are treason.'

Millicent subtly smiled. She had Pinchbeak just where she wanted him. 'Though they are not my words, good sir. Nor my treason described in the prophecy.'

'Not your words,' Pinchbeak said, sitting back. There was a challenge in his gaze, perhaps even a small degree of admiration. 'Yet whose words are they? That's the question, hmm?'

She shrugged. 'Though to my purposes a useful one only insofar as it aids me in their sale.'

'Your purposes will best be served by bringing this book to me. You'll receive a handsome fee, I assure you.'

At last. 'And the size of this fee, Master Pinchbeak?'

He thought about it. 'Four marks.'

Millicent sniffed. 'Four marks? Four marks, when a prince's ransom would hardly suit? Think of your own reward, Master Pinchbeak, should you deliver this book of prophecies to your lord. And the penalty should he learn that you were presented with the opportunity to recover it – but failed.'

He sputtered for a moment, but he knew she was right. 'Let us be clear on this, Mistress Rykener. The line you quoted concerning the day of the regicide, the feast of St Dunstan. The thirteenth prophecy is clear on this matter?'

Millicent nodded and repeated the two lines:

'By Half-ten of Hawks might shender be shown,
On day of Saint Dunstan shall Death have his doom.'

Pinchbeak rose with some difficulty, his right arm shaking on his stick. 'What's to prevent me from having you seized this very moment?' he asked. 'Here you are, *femme sole* in the presence of a serjeant-at-law, with no husband to shield you. Newgate is full of traitors this season, man and woman alike.'

Millicent had anticipated this. 'I have made certain arrangements for the disposition of the book in case I'm taken, Master Pinchbeak. It's safely hidden.'

'I see,' he said, looking sceptical. 'And you intend to approach every prominent man in London with this book until you find one ready to snap it up?'

'Only those known for the keenness of their discernment. Their wisdom in making difficult choices.'

He gave her a thin smile, then leaned forward awkwardly, his breath warming her cheek as he wedged his stick between his chest and the parvis pavers. 'Come see me next Friday, Mistress Rykener, in my rooms at Scroope's, the serjeants' inn at Ely Place. By then I will have inquired about these prophecies. If I learn there is anything to them we'll discuss a suitable price.'

Millicent, delighted, rose from her bench while Pinchbeak turned away for the company of his fellow serjeants. She rejoined Agnes at the south porch and they headed back to Cornhull, talking excitedly about the fortune that awaited them. Though she felt a nagging worry that Pinchbeak's inquiries might lead him to spurn her offer, Millicent had been stirred by the encounter, and had no intention of waiting until the next week to inquire with Pinchbeak about his price. Why, the serjeant-at-law could make an offer for the book along with other gentlemen interested in its purchase. They had settled on the next wealthy man to approach when Agnes tugged her sleeve.

'What do you suppose he wants, Mil?'

'Who?' The turn for her house was just ahead.

'Man over there. Spicerer, looks like.'

Millicent looked to see George Lawler, standing before his shop and urging them over. He was agitated, his gaze shifting left and right. Arm in arm, the sisters crossed over and cleared the gutter. 'Yes, Master Lawler?' Millicent said when they reached him.

'Men've come.' He peered back into his shop. 'To your house, and also here.'

'Pratt, sure, and his son,' Millicent said. 'He'll have what I owe him, as soon as I've settled with you.'

'Not Pratt.'

166

'Who, then?'

'Loy if I know. Constables? But not of our ward, that's certain. Had the long knives at their sides, no badges. Asked after the sisters Fonteyn, do I know them, know their whereabouts.'

Millicent gasped. 'The *sisters* Fonteyn?'

'Knew that one of them, the rich one, frequented Lawler's. With a fondness for sugared things. And that the younger one's a mau—' He stopped himself. 'Didn't know you had a sister.'

Millicent turned to Agnes, her fury rising. 'And how could *they* have known, Agnes? Spreading rumour of your famed chastity about the city, hoping it would burnish my name?'

Agnes stepped back as if struck. 'I been gone from Gropecunt Lane weeks now, Mil. So they're looking for me, looking for the b—'

'Stop!' Millicent cried.

They all turned at a harsh laugh from Lawler's shop door. Mistress Lawler, arms folded, taking it all in. 'Look at the shiny side of the coin, your ladyship,' she said as Millicent felt herself redden. 'Least now you'll have an honest way of working off your debts.'

Millicent turned and strode off, Agnes hurrying behind her.

'Never had a doubt about that one, Lawler,' she called to their backs. 'A maud's a maud, wherever she gets her pennies. Let that be a lesson to you, George. The wisdom of wives, deep as the sea is green.'

'Aye,' she heard Lawler mutter. 'And just as cold.'

They reached the corner. Millicent had to force herself to place one foot in front of the other.

'Mil,' said Agnes, working to keep up. 'Mil, what if the men are still about? Shouldn't we get away from here?'

The visitors had been thorough in their inquiries. It seemed London's entire cloth industry was staring at them as they slunk past the colourful displays and hangings lining the lane: dresses, smocks, hoods, coverlets, and a host of other goods that now made Millicent feel trapped by the opulence rather than a part of it. Finally they reached her house.

The door stood ajar. Heedless of Agnes's warnings, Millicent entered, surveying the destruction. In the front room, chair cushions had been torn apart, feathers and straw scattered across the floor, wooden shelves torn from the walls, leaving gaping holes in the plaster; in the kitchen larder, already-empty barrels were broken on the floor, her recent purchases from Lawler's studding the rushes. She raced up the back stairs and into the rear bedchamber. Her trunk lay in pieces, hacked apart with an axe or sword. It seemed that nearly every garment she still owned had been sliced in two and tossed about the room.

She turned to Agnes, who had followed her up the stairs. 'Dearheart,' Agnes said, holding out her arms.

Millicent pushed her away. 'This is on *you*.' Her fall from wealthy consort of a peer to penniless sister of a Gropecunt Lane whore had been short but steep; now it was complete.

'But, Mil—'

'*Shut* it, Ag.' Millicent's hands shook as she gathered up those few items that were whole and stuffed them in a handled basket she kept for laundering.

Agnes was peering down at the street through a gap in the front shutters. 'They'll be after us, sure. Folks are already staring up here, lot of talk in the street.'

Millicent nodded tightly. 'We'll go then,' she said. They left her house for the last time, stealing along the alley to Spinners Lane. There they paused as Millicent adjusted the load and hefted the light basket that contained all her earthly possessions: an extra bonnet, two faded dresses, the few shillings left from selling the dead woman's bracelet, and the book, still wrapped in its cloth.

There was only one place to go, a destination neither of them had to name. They walked silently to the river and over the bridge, then made the turn past St Mary Overey. Millicent felt her shoulders sag with defeat, and as they entered Rose Alley it seemed that every raw moment of her former life as a maudlyn assaulted her with a thickening of memory and shame.

The neighbourhood hadn't changed a bit. Same drab storefronts and sagging overhangs, looming over the lane like sullen birds of prey. Same sluggish gutters, carrying filth from house to pond and pond to river, filling the air with the stink of dead fish and tired whores. Same forlorn women and girls affecting cheer as they peddled their flesh to tradesmen, friars, and worse. No better than slaves, Millicent thought, and though I swore I would never return, now I'm all but one of them again.

She glanced over at Agnes. Her sister walked tall, no shame on her face, appearing almost excited to be coming back to their childhood home. The strength of the girl, Millicent thought. Where does she get it?

Finally they were in front of the Pricking Bishop. Millicent nearly gagged at her first sight of St Cath, the spirals and slashes of withered skin. The old woman looked at Agnes, then at Millicent, letting her wizened gaze wander slowly over her breasts and down to her thighs and feet.

St Cath snickered, bobbing her chin. 'It'll be an honour, Lady Queynt, an honour to put your fair cheeks and teats to work again for the Bishop. Bess'll be thrilled.'

'Thrilled and gashed and swyved,' said Bess Waller, appearing at the door. Millicent looked at her mother's face for the first time in five years. More lines in her skin, more grey dusting her hair, but the Southwark bawd was as fetching as ever.

Agnes seemed about to say something but Bess held up a

169

hand. 'Middle back room up top. Yours for a fortnight, but after that it's suck or scram. Hear?'

'Yes, *mère*,' said Agnes, nodding dutifully.

Millicent could not make a sound. Her mother stared at her with something between pity and contempt, then let out a thin whistle. 'My, my, my. How the wheel of Lady Fortune turns.'

Millicent gritted her teeth and pushed past her mother, entering the Pricking Bishop and hating herself for having to.

TWENTY-ONE

St Mary Overey, Southwark

We quickly settled into a pattern. Always an early riser, I nibbled at bread in the kitchen, where I would sit by the hearth until Simon came in from the hall. We would exchange a few words, he would eat a little something, then he tended to go to the solar to read or scratch on a tablet for the rest of the morning. The first few days he never left the house. I would catch him staring vacantly out of a window, or sitting in a dark study by the hall fire. Invariably his smile would return when he noticed me, and soon enough he would start peppering me with questions about my affairs. He wanted me to take him to St Paul's and Westminster, where I could introduce him around. Despite my reluctance I gave in the third time he asked.

Simon had a new and easy way about him, open yet respectful as we spoke with these familiar clutches of lawmen and bureaucrats. He never seemed too free, his bearing modest and unpresumptuous, and I began to think these changes in him were genuine. Within days of his return to Southwark Simon was simply *there*, my natural son and only heir, more a part of my daily life than he had ever been before that night on the

171

wharf. If his crimes were not forgotten they had diminished with time, miniaturized, I suppose, by the simple fact of his presence, and the brittle persistence of his mother's last words.

✥

There is a particular image of Sarah that can slip from my memory for days or weeks at a time, only to reappear at the most unguarded moments, taking away my breath, nibbling at my conscience.

It was Epiphany time, over fifteen years ago now. We had lost Elizabeth to fever the week before, this after the death of John, our eldest, that autumn. Now our two younger children, Alison, eight, and Simon, just shy of six, had fallen ill. Simon's birth had been difficult. There would be no others. Unable to sleep over the rattles of his troubled breaths, I had crept from the lesser bedchamber down to the parlour, using the outer staircase so as not to disturb Sarah.

My feet were carelessly bare. I remember the rough edges of cold stairs, the indifference of a January moon. In the parlour I slouched on a long bench against the western wall, thinking blankly of our dead, our barely living. At some point I drifted off.

When I awoke Sarah was at the east window, framed against the night. We would often leave that window unshuttered, as it gave on to the far corner of the churchyard, and was thus in that part of the Overey house that lay within the priory's walls. There was a high stool there, nestled in an angled nook that allowed its occupant to lean against a broad wooden post. It had been Bet's favourite place to sit. Birds watering at the polygonal fountain, new buds on the gillyflower stems, Austin canons sneaking past to slip her a plug of mint: over this private world our elder daughter had sweetly reigned for most of her eleven years.

Standing there in her nightclothes, washed by a half moon,

her mother looked like a glassed saint in a church window, pious and steady, every strand of her thick hair tucked properly beneath her night bonnet. Since our elder son died I had grown increasingly resentful of Sarah's composure, which seemed only to have strengthened with Bet's passing. She would reveal nothing of her grief, greeting friends and family with a sympathetic smile and a warm embrace, as if *they* were the ones needing comfort. My own state over those months could hardly have been worse. I would find myself weeping at a moment's notice, bawling in a corner like a whipped schoolboy.

Not Sarah. *Great in a crisis, our Sarah*, it was said among the women of the parish. A new Job. She had always been so, a tower of womanly strength as she bathed the foreheads of the dying, comforted the living with rote phrases from the prior. That night, as I watched her stand before the window, I felt a flash of fury and wanted to shake her, to scream some feeling into that placid skull. Instead I simply sat, mute and still, as if nailed to the bench, diminished by my wife's stout quietude.

Then the contortions came. Her entire frame gave a single heave. A choking sound rose from her throat, stifled as soon as it began. This convulsed her further, her arms spasming like the bound limbs of a criminal on a noose.

Thinking she was ill, I was about to rise when she went to her knees and reached for the window. Her fingers stretched along the sill. She put her face to the bottom of the opening. Her cheek moved slowly along the rough board. I watched her, the strange sweeping movements of her hands as they whisked from the wood to her face, as she sniffed like some chained lunatic at her fingers and palms.

It came to me then, the meaning of Sarah's actions. She was gleaning the dust of our daughter. Discovering those places where Bet's hands had played, gathering the last particles of her skin, the final remnants of her scent as they lingered on the windowsill. As if to take them in, and store them somewhere until the two of them could meet again.

My breath stopped, yet I was too stunned by the change in my wife to go to her, despite the rush of sympathy swelling my lungs when I could breathe again. Sarah next turned away from the window and clutched the wooden stool. Flattening her cheek against the surface, she embraced the legs so tightly I thought she must be hurting herself. All the while she continued to draw indistinct moans from somewhere in her chest, which hummed with the pain of a dying animal.

Now she was prone, writhing on her stomach, clutching at the rushes. Now on her back, groaning at the ceiling beams. This went on for an indeterminate time until I thought she was done. She had curled herself against the wall, still heaving, puddled in grief. I took a deep breath, preparing to rise.

Then her voice, stealing from some shattered place, broke the room's silence. 'Not Simon . . . please not Simon . . . not Simon too . . . oh God not my Simon not Simon not Simon not Simon . . .'

I frowned. What about Alison? Why wasn't Sarah praying for our daughter, just as close to death as her brother? My thoughts darkened. Simon had always been Sarah's favourite; it was obvious from the moment of his birth. She had been a model mother to all the children, in her way. Yet our youngest she treated differently. Lifted him more often, shouldered his governess aside at night, gentled him in ways she never had the others.

It showed in him, too. Simon was a defiant, stubborn boy. Spoiled, coddled, contrary. Though astonishingly quick at his lessons, he could be an incorrigible brat, the object of numerous complaints from his schoolmasters and tutors, never willing to sit still and learn, whether sums from his teachers or bits of wisdom from his father. The very opposite of Alison, my child of light, seemingly born to please with her delicate embrace, her shy nods, her willing smile. She had been my only source of comfort over those awful months, as her older siblings died and her mother grew increasingly remote from everyone but her son. It was as if our family had been separated by some fathomless chasm, Sarah and Simon teetering on one side, Alison and I on the other, the voices of our departed sounding from the void, willing us to jump.

Yet here we are, still among the living, and we must manage somehow. The thought guided me back to the present. Despite the favour Sarah had always showered on Simon, I could not believe she would ask God for his life over Alison's. I waited for a prayer for our daughter. None came. Sarah continued her moaning for Simon, a thousand desperate pleas thrown into the night. Still nothing for Alison, not a motherly word.

I ground my teeth, close to screaming at her, cursing her for preferring Simon even at a time like this. Instead I remained silent, and channelled my fury into my own, darker prayer. No, Lord God, I prayed inwardly, take him. Spare *her*, God. Spare my daughter, I beg of Thee, and take my son. In the name of Your own Son, my God, grant me my daughter's life. Take Simon if You need another, so long as Alison lives.

At the time these words seemed only natural, a bid for Alison's life against her mother's wishes. I imagined our warring prayers mounting to heaven, curling into God's ears, and I felt a rush of righteousness as I asked Him for the life of my beloved daughter, at whatever cost.

Sarah never saw me sitting there that night, feebly watching the spectacle of her sorrow.

Alison died the next morning. My reaction was a tearless silence, as I shuffled about the Overey house, heavy with failure. Two days later Simon's fever broke and he was out of bed, jumping about as if he had never been ill. Instead of joy in his recovery all I felt was the bitter unfairness of it, that Alison should die so Simon could live. For it seemed to me then that Sarah had traded something for Simon's life that night, that some vital portion of her spirit had passed into him with all those spasms and wracks and grotesque snifflings, none of which she had spared for Alison.

So I turned against her, against the good and against life, embracing the nothing that belongs to this world. She had God on her side, after all. She certainly didn't need me. That chain of early deaths pulled me from my moorings, dragged me downward into that amoral place where I have dwelled for so many years. Once a loving husband who doted on his wife, I became a reserve of cold severity, indifferent to the comforts of intimacy and the pleasures of the marriage bed. Once a fair and judicious father even to Simon, I became distant, demanding obedience from a son whose very life I secretly resented. Once a poet of youthful love, I became a scribbler of cranky moralism, my writing nothing more than a means of access to high men and hidden information, much as I had once wished to craft such things of beauty as Chaucer gave the world.

As for Sarah, Alison's death and Simon's survival seemed to have no effect on her, and as the years passed and our sole child grew from a boy to a man, she remained unflinchingly loyal to him, even as he proved himself again and again unworthy of her indulgence, drinking in the street, consorting with maudlyns, boxing with labourers, trying his thumb on the blade of the law. It would come as no real surprise when his juvenile indulgences culminated in the killing of another man. A fitting turn in a life of such frivolous waste.

Then, within eighteen months of his departure for Italy and Hawkwood's service, another death. A shallow cough one day, a fever the next, and Sarah was gone. There was a moment near the end, as I sat beside her, when she reached for my hand, her own a patch of warm parchment, loose against my palm. I blinked at her fading eyes, leaned down to catch a ragged whisper. 'Try to love him, John. Just try.' My head bent in a feeble nod. She never spoke again.

Regret paints the memory in infinite hues, all blurring to a leaden grey with the passing of time. What future would have become possible had I gone to my Sarah that night in our parlour, had I pulled this wracked woman into my arms, cleared her nose with my thumb and finger, helped her gather up our daughter's invisible dust? What could our remaining life have been, had I shown a half-ounce of compassion for this shattered mother, praying for one small life out of four?

For only now do I see how much greater Sarah's burden was than my own, and what Simon's survival must have cost her. Only now do I see that her turn to God that night was done out of desperation, not spite or unthinking preference for one child over another. That her prayer for Simon's life was in part a prayer for me, for our family, for the survival of the male heir by which every man judges his worth and ensures his legacy. That in that darkest of places she remained the most loyal of wives, even to the extent of praying to God, in the only way she knew how, for the survival of her husband's name. That Sarah Gower, unlike her husband, never asked for a child's death.

Now, with her son back in our home and so many past roads converging, I found myself burning to speak to that shimmering woman in the window one last time, and ask for her forgiveness. Not for the way I treated her all those years. Sarah, in her stolid goodness, would not need to be asked for that measure of grace. I had seen it in her eyes as she passed, and knew it was mine to take with me to the grave.

The forgiveness I sought was on behalf not of Sarah, but of Simon. For half a lifetime I had blamed my son for the extinguishing of his sister's life, and for the slow moral decay of my own. All his life Simon Gower had carried that heavy load I had laid on his narrow shoulders so many years ago: the impossible burden of the unchosen child.

Try to love him, John. Just try. I felt the womanly pressure of Sarah's last words, the charge they gave me to live up to some modest ideal. *Just try.* That, at least, I could do.

✢

Word from James Tewburn arrived from the Guildhall. There was now definitive news on my property matter, and he hoped to deliver it in person. I called for Simon, thinking to bring him along, but he had already left the house. By noon I was on Basinghall Street, then in Guildhall Yard, which was busier than usual that day.

There was a long board bench along the pavers outside Strode's chambers. On it sat a typical collection of Londoners seeking attention: three starved-looking children, their clearly drunk guardian giving them the occasional head slap; a short row of bored apprentices over on legal business from Westminster or the inns, their robes hiked up to their knees to gather air; a young man tapping his foot, likely a ward nearing his majority; and a hollow-eyed man in faded hose clutching a sheaf of documents. All had business with the common serjeant's office, and all had arrived before me.

Ignoring the glares, I leaned in. Four of the common clerk's scribes filled the cramped space, busily filling ledgers and rolls with the city's affairs. Though employed by the Guildhall, these were also scribblers for hire, young fellows with good eyes, men you could rely on to copy out a quire or a book when you needed a quick and steady hand. I had commissioned their services more than once in recent years, so my face was well known around these inky precincts. 'Is Tewburn about?'

The nearest clerk shook his head. 'Been summoned to

Westminster.' He turned. 'Chancery, Pinkhurst?' he called to one of his counterparts.

'Chancery, right,' the man called back. 'Expect him back at two or thereabouts. But you'll catch him before then at the Pin-and-Wheel.' Sometimes it seemed that London's clerks and lawmen spent half their lives in taverns.

At Cat Street the way narrowed and bent to such an extent that even an experienced Londoner might find himself lost, though I never minded this part of the city. Nowhere else were so many trades practised, so many goods sold and resold with such spirited rivalry. Silks of Lyon, hanging from poles of polished elm jutting out over the close lane; olives of al-Andalus, displayed in shortened barrels and scooped out with great pomp by a shopkeeper's girl; cinnamon and cloves from who knew where, filling the air with exotic scents – and all available at a stone's throw from the knit hose and rough leather work-gloves crafted across the river in Southwark.

Outside a leatherworker's shop, as I stooped to examine a row of tooled belts, I saw Ralph Strode coming up Cat Street from the church of St Lawrence. With him was Sir Michael de la Pole. James Tewburn walked behind them, and as I watched the trio approaching I wondered what would bring the chancellor to these precincts. The baron's finger was aimed at Strode's wide chest as they walked, thrusting sidewards to reinforce his points. All three appeared agitated, Tewburn's face in particular clouded, the corners of his mouth pulled back in what looked almost like physical pain. Not wanting to get caught eavesdropping, and with nowhere to conceal myself, I stepped from behind the display.

'Gower!' Strode called, suddenly all cheer. The chancellor's manner had also transformed, and after my bow arms were grasped all around. Tewburn, said Strode, had good news.

The clerk turned to me with a forced smile. 'Only this

morning, Master Gower, I secured the writ of *pone* necessary to move your property matter into Common Pleas.'

'I'm pleased to hear it,' I said. 'Thank you, James, for taking care of it so quickly.'

'I'd wager your adversary will drop the matter soon.'

'Let's hope so,' I said.

The clerk bowed. Strode dismissed him. Tewburn's face fell again as he turned for the Guildhall, giving the impression of an unresolved conflict. Strode watched Tewburn's back until the man disappeared. 'A peculiar one, our Tewburn,' he said distantly. '*Deficit ambobus qui vult servire duobus.*'

'Surely he regards you as his primary master, Ralph,' said the baron.

'Perhaps,' said Strode, his face clouded. 'In any case . . .'

'Yes,' said the chancellor with a brisk tone. 'Thanks as always for your counsel, Ralph.'

'At your pleasure, your lordship.'

The baron turned to me, his brow arched. 'I understand your son is back from Italy, Gower. He sounds like a promising young man.'

'Thank you, my lord,' I said, wondering how such information could have reached the chancellor so quickly. The Baron de la Pole was by reputation and action a fiercely independent man, one who had earned the friendship of old King Edward and now spoke for the House of Lords with persuasion and quiet force. It was he who had arranged King Richard's marriage to Anne of Bohemia several years before, and though he came from a lesser family than most of those in his circle, there was no one in the realm who commanded more respect. I decided to be direct. 'You know, my lord, he is eager to find a position in the government – perhaps too eager, given that he's just returned.'

'Do send him my way, will you?' said the baron. 'With all the ruckus over levies it would be good to have some steadier hands among the ledgers. The court of Chancery has never been busier.'

I bowed. 'Simon would be delighted to serve in any capacity, my lord. He'll call at your chambers tomorrow.'

The chancellor said his farewells. We watched as two of the baron's guards, who had been shadowing their master as he walked along Cat Street, converged on the chancellor in the middle of the lane and proceeded with him toward the river.

'Simon is back in England?' Strode asked when the baron had left us. 'When did he return?'

'Not a week ago,' I said, still wanting to know the purpose of his colloquy with de la Pole.

Strode glanced down the street. 'The Bent Plough, if you aren't pressed for time, John?'

'If *I'm* not pressed?'

'Be good to have a sip,' he said. 'Hear your news, your latest connivings.'

Ralph Strode was hardly one to spend the middle of a workday in idle chat. Yet he seemed eager to speak, though I would have to tread lightly. I gestured back toward St Lawrence. 'The chapel would be fine, if you wouldn't mind.' Strode used the chapel of St Eustachius within the church as a secondary chambers of sorts, conducting all kinds of business from the dim space. If we went to the tavern, as he had suggested, I would get nothing else done that afternoon.

'So be it.' His heavy arm wrapped my shoulders and we made our way into the church. The nave was mostly empty, though the clink of silver from up ahead suggested some lingering business. In the Eustachius chapel I half-sat on one of the misericords, a row of narrow seats that had been moved to the side after their replacement some months ago. Eight of the displaced wooden chairs, grouped in two rows of four, rested vertically along the chapel's north wall, their underseats carved with scenes of rural life: a wife wielding the distaff against her cowering husband, a rotund fellow at the hurdy-gurdy, a ploughman sodomizing a goat.

'You look troubled, John,' he said with no preface.

'Simon's return has me a bit thrown off, I suppose.'

'Not a pure source of joy?'

Strode knew nothing about the accidental death on the wharf. 'For the last two years he's been working in the White Company. The clerk of a mercenary, blood for hire. Not the career I would have chosen for him.'

'I had understood that his position with Hawkwood was more in the clerical line.'

I leaned against the cool wooden back of the misericord. 'Sir John hires out his troops to anyone. His last client before Florence was Clement of Avignon, when he bought himself a papacy. The man led the slaughter of an entire village in the Romagna. To imagine Simon notarizing and sealing bills for such an alliance of convenience – not a settling thought.'

'I speak from experience when I say that the servants of great bureaucracies rarely have an effect on their policies. Don't be too hard on him, John.'

'I've already been too soft. When I saw him standing in my hall I wanted to strangle him.' I shook my head. 'To return from Tuscany with no message ahead, no warning?'

'"For youth," as our good friend writes, "shall have neither guide nor straight line".'

'"Nor old age dewed grapes to pluck from the vine",' I replied, completing Chaucer's couplet.

Strode chuckled and sat back. It was time to broach the other subject. 'You know, Ralph, may I draw on your knowledge for a moment? I need the ear of an Oxford master.' Before moving to London and taking up his current office, Strode had enjoyed a long career as a theology fellow at Merton, where his connections were still quite deep.

182

'You flatter me, John,' he said, looking amused.

'There's a certain author I need to know more about, an ancient writer,' I said. 'You know I'm not boasting when I tell you I'm pretty well read in the authorities. But this man is an utter mystery. I've never heard of him.'

Strode shifted on the misericord. 'What author?'

I watched Strode's eyes. 'His name is Lollius.'

He blinked.

'The name means something to you?'

Strode toyed with a loose button, his jowls working a tooth. 'You're testing me, I can see it in your eyes. Yet I know you well enough to take no offence. So I'll take your test, then you'll tell me whether I've passed it.'

Pleased at the frank reaction, I grasped his near arm. 'You just did, Ralph.'

'Good, then.' He cleared his throat. 'When we met at Westminster, I mentioned a murder. A girl, slain in the Moorfields.'

'I remember.'

'What she took from La Neyte, it's said, was a book. This book contains a number of prophecies written by this Lollius. Twelve of them foretell the deaths of our past kings.'

'And the thirteenth,' I added, 'the death of King Richard.'

Strode studied me. 'You are well informed.'

'Braybrooke.' This prompted a brisk nod. 'The bishop is confounded, has no more idea about Lollius than I do. Without having seen the work I can't speak to its accuracy, of course – but I have my suspicions.' I lowered my voice. 'From all I have heard, this *Liber de Mortibus Regum Anglorum* must be a forgery.'

He frowned. 'A forgery?'

'To write a prophecy about times already past is hardly a challenge,' I said. 'What would prevent a living man from tracing back through our chronicles the means of these royal deaths, and "prophesying" accordingly?'

Strode nodded slowly. 'Then simply writing a new prophecy about King Richard.'

'What better way to trouble the realm than to predict the manner and means and even time of its sovereign's death?'

Strode's eyes caught flecks of candlelight from the chapel's altar. 'I have thought about the name "Lollius" a good deal myself. Is there a taste for Lollius's work in Wycliffe's circles, among these Lollers?'

'Braybrooke thinks so.'

'I'm not surprised, though I've heard nothing of it from my former colleagues in Oxford.'

'I can't help but think I might have better luck than Braybrooke's men in identifying this Lollius. But I need an excellent library, Ralph. A library with the – ah, the muscle to bear up under the inquiries of a dogged man.' I thought of Chaucer's account of the Visconti library, the immense holdings that had furnished him with the Italian writings that inspired so much of his current making. 'The problem is, there's little time, and I can't go abroad.'

Strode, always up for an intellectual challenge, adjusted his bulk and sat forward. 'There are libraries aplenty in Oxford, Gower, of more variety than even the great monkish collections at Bury or St Albans. In fact, now that I think on it, there may be a collection of books in Oxford uniquely suited to your purpose.'

'At Merton?'

'No indeed,' Strode said. 'The library I'm thinking about is in an outbuilding behind the Durham grange. A roomful of trunks and crates. I know little about the collection beyond the fact of its existence. Yet I do know its keeper. A cantankerous old man, but we are on friendly terms, and I'd be happy to write you a letter of introduction. The man in Oxford you'll want to see is Peter de Quincey.'

'And he'll admit me, even though I'm not a monk?' Durham was a small Benedictine college, and the order was jealous of its privileges.

Strode shook his jowls. 'Quincey is a lay brother to the order. His late master was Richard Angervyle de Bury.'

'Bishop of Durham?'

'And a great lover of books. You'll have read his *Philobiblon,* of course.'

I gave a chagrined frown, feeling ignorant as I often did in Strode's presence. 'I haven't, though the title intrigues me. Do you own it?'

'I do,' said Strode. 'I'll have my copy sent round to St Mary's in short order. As for the collection, well.' He looked up at the vaults, as if searching the ceiling for the appropriately lofty words. 'The most mysterious collection of books in England, some say, though I've never plumbed it. Few in Oxford have, though it's the subject of endless speculation.'

'And Angervyle himself?' I asked.

'He was quite the figure: Clerk of the Privy Seal, a noted emissary at Avignon before this disastrous break with Rome. Peter de Quincey was his most trusted clerk. He's an old man now, though with a letter from me he should give you a friendly hearing, despite the whiff of suspicion in the Oxford air these days.'

This took us to the subject of rising heresy, and the disturbing news out of Oxford. Strode had mixed feelings on the matter of Wycliffe's emergent sect. 'The condemnation of Wycliffe before his death has divided my colleagues on the faculties of logic and theology,' he said, getting to his feet. 'Every syllogism is now parsed for heretical content. The old freedoms are being threatened.'

He led me out of St Lawrence and on to the street. 'The

185

effect is chilling, Gower. You have to wonder how long it will be before the same scrutiny comes to the inns, and infects how we teach the very laws of England.'

'It surely won't come to that,' I said, considering this dire possibility. I struggled to match his pace. 'Would you recommend against this visit to Oxford, then? This Lollius could be anyone.'

'One has to start somewhere,' said Strode. 'Take our students, who must entertain absurdities of the most outrageous sort when they're first learning to theologize. "Suppose God revealed Christ not to be His Son. What then would be the authority of the sacrament?" "Suppose it were discovered that the faculty of intellection resides in the stomach. Could a hungry man think well?" Such inquiries aren't threatening. They merely *pretend* to question our beliefs precisely in order to strengthen them. Consider the nature of the irrelevant proposition. Such a proposition must be greeted with scepticism, and yet we cannot discard it entirely, can we?'

I hesitated, not sure where Strode was taking me. 'I suppose not.'

'Suppositions are exactly the point in the case of an irrelevant proposition. If the proposition proves useless, we simply ignore it. If, on the other hand, it proves itself worthy to think with, why, we should do everything we can to exploit its use. There's hardly heresy in that.' We had reached the porch at the Guildhall, where Strode indicated that he would leave me for an appointment with the mayor. 'It's a lesson,' he said, 'we would all do well to remember. In dialectic, even what seem the most irrelevant propositions can lead us to the truth.'

'Or truths,' I muttered, feeling glum.

Strode paused on the first step, towering over me. 'Tell that to Braybrooke, Gower. The Bishop of London should cultivate a taste for tolerance to match his enthusiasm for gardening.' He took the shallow steps in one move, his long robes fluttering in his wake.

Back through Guildhall Yard. A flash of colour before the eastern gate, and a few scattered laughs. On approaching I saw the cause: a bit of street theatre of the sort often seen in the city's larger gathering places. With Strode's concerns still preoccupying me, I paused, distractedly, to watch.

The mimes were performing a play about the first King Edward. Longshanks, the Hammer of the Scots. The company had reached the deathbed scene, performed with the king prostrate on a mat, his lords gathered round. The speaker stepped to the front to interpret the scene for the crowd.

> 'As he lingers his last, with lords all about,
> By six-less-two swords he shall say as he dies,
> "My heart you must heft toward heaven on earth,
> To Jerusalem journey, joy to enjoin,
> And my bones against Bruce to be borne into war,
> My gravestone to graveth: Leave Gaveston gone."'

The mime playing Longshanks put a hand to his forehead, chortled out a last breath, and expired, to the warm applause of the circle of Londoners gathered around the actors. He leapt to his feet, the mimes collected small coins in their caps, and the scene broke up as quickly as it had gathered, the company heading for St Paul's or the bridge with the heat of the day.

My own skin had gone cold. *By six-less-two swords he shall say as he dies*. Seven of swords, sovereign of swords, prince of plums, three of thistles – and now six-less-two swords, another numbered symbol echoing with the voice of the *De Mortibus* prophecies. Even this rough street spectacle of Longshanks's death had drawn its language from the book, which now seemed to be everywhere I turned. A street preacher, the bishop and his friars, the common serjeant, and now the mimes of London, all speaking the morbid idiom of Lollius, the whisper of kingly deaths on their lips.

It was at that moment that I started imagining the prophecies as a kind of pestilence, raising boils on the vulnerable body of the realm. Despite the laughter of these Londoners, the image stayed with me the rest of that day, as the book spread its ill portents through the city and the realm.

Men of our time have a peculiar fascination with a form of story. It is the story of raptus, of ravir, of ravissement. It has various names, in the Moorish tongue the muwashshah, in Spanish the serranilla, most commonly in French the pastourelle.

A simple story, always the same. A young shepherdess strolls in a field or on a road. A knight on horseback swoops in and seeks to seduce her, beguiling her with poems, or clever words, or promises of fame. She resists his advances, resists yet more, until eventually his desire goads him to force himself upon her, destroying her virtue. There are variations here and there: the shepherdess is carried off by an evil knight or a murderous giant, so her gallant rescuer saves her life even as he sullies her flesh. Often there is a rival involved, and one knight must defeat another to win the lady.

Yet however the matter falls out, the young lady remains silent about her rape, her tongue as useless as Philomel's after it was severed by Tereus. So acceptable a part of lovemaking is this vile act that even Father Andreas, in his Art of Courtly Love, enjoins noble men to delight in it without thought: 'Remember to praise them lavishly,' he writes, 'and should you find a suitable spot you should not delay in taking what you seek, gaining it by rough embraces.'

Yet where is the woman's sovereignty, her choice in the matter? The woman never writes her own story. She is rather like the lion in Aesop's little fable, who sees a painting of another lion being strangled by a man. But who paints the lion? Tell me, who?

He who paints the lion claims to know the lion, and with his brush he may colour whatever lies he wishes. The power of the teller, you see, is inestimable.

And so it is with women in these pastourelles, these tales of rural virgins who know not their own desire well enough to keep from resisting the rapes they must suffer with all the inevitability of death. I have heard them in the langue d'oïl, I have heard them in the langue d'oc, in the tongue of Juan Ruiz, in the tongue of Dante, and translated from the tongue of the Jews. In every human language, it seems, men have depicted the joys of ravishment, and never with consequence for the ravisher. Just one time I would like to hear a version with a righteous end, one in which the perpetrator—

—I flee my matter.

One morning, as the girl sat with her mother in their bedchamber, learning to pin out a broad stitch on her frame, there came a pounding at the outer door. They heard voices, then one of the servingwomen entered.

'The prince requests an audience, my lady.'

'Very well.' The lady gathered her embroidery and placed it in a basket. 'I shall receive him in the salon.'

As she left the bedchamber she turned, stooped down, and held her daughter by the chin. 'Stay here, my sweet. Just here. Do not come out until I call you. Do you understand?'

The girl nodded. Her mother kissed her nose and walked out of her private rooms, closing the door behind her.

Through a knot the daughter watched as the foreign prince entered the salon. Her mother called for her maidservant, moving in frantic circles as she sought to elude his grasp. It happened so quickly: a brief struggle, a hand clamped over her mother's mouth, her dress torn from her shoulders, the horrific sight of the lord in his nakedness.

Through it all the girl obeyed her mother's last command. 'Do not come out until I call you.' And she did not. What could she have done?

The prince, dressing himself, left his victim on a cushioned chair, weeping with pain and humiliation. At the sight of her mother's bruised thighs, her reddened breasts, the little girl let out a whimper of sympathy.

The prince's head whipped round. Before she could move he had flung open the door to the bedchamber, grabbed her small arm, and pulled her violently to the middle of the salon. He drew a knife, madness in his eyes, and made ready to cut the girl's throat.

A crash of splintered wood, and the door to the upper hall burst open. In the opening stood the foreign duke, a short sword in his hand. He took two long strides and held the blade at his brother's throat. No words were exchanged, though the thunderous tension between the brothers filled the salon. Finally the prince shrugged, smirked at his younger brother, and left the room.

That evening, as she walked with her mother through the lower hall, the girl sensed a movement behind them. She turned.

There, in a doorway, with his grey, fish-like eyes, stood the prince. His arms were crossed over his doublet, pointed with the same lions and flowers depicted on his shield. His eyes took in her mother's form, surveyed the bruised and battered flesh he had ravaged. Then he looked at the girl. She gave him her cruellest glare, surprising herself with her childish defiance, and on his face she saw it: a flinch, a smear of utter shame at what he had done.

She felt a dark and secret thrill. For all his brutality, she recognized in that moment, for all his shows of strength, what defines this man above all is his weakness.

A weakness I shall never show.

TWENTY-TWO

The Guildhall, Ward of Cheap

The gentleman the clerks called Gower had departed the Guildhall a while before. Edgar Rykener wondered whether he, too, should put his head in the doorway and ask them for assistance. But he'd overheard that James Tewburn wasn't about, so he gave his name to one of the other clerks and returned to the bench. The wall's dark stone cooled his blood, easing him into an upright slumber untroubled for once by thoughts of all that pressed him: that mess with Bickle the beadle, the dead girl on the Moorfields, his worry about Gerald, the missing Agnes.

He was deep in a dream when a hand on his shoulder shook him gently. 'Edgar? Edgar Rykener? You are here to see me?'

'Ye—yes,' he stammered, waking to the sight of James Tewburn. The clerk's threadbare coat was cinched too tightly, giving his thin fingers no quarter as he kneaded the chapped skin at his neck. His eyes shifted about, darting from Edgar's face to the chamber door. 'As I was in the precincts of the Guildhall, I thought—'

'Right, yes yes, of course,' said Tewburn.

Edgar glanced up and down the passage between the buildings. The bench had emptied during his slumber, though voices floated from the structures on either side.

'Master Strode's chambers are in heavy use today,' the clerk continued. 'Let's find a more suitable spot.' He led them in a circuitous path around several more buildings to a remote corner of Guildhall Yard, obscured from view by a high privet hedge. Had Tewburn recognized him this time? Edgar wondered.

'Here,' Tewburn said. There was a short stone bench slightly apart from the wall. The clerk sat forward with his elbows on his knees. 'There have been some, ah, difficulties in the matter of your brother's wardship,' he rasped.

'Difficulties?' Edgar said with alarm. 'Is Gerald well? Is he safe?'

'I believe so,' he said, though Edgar could hear the doubt in his voice. 'His master knows nothing about the transfer, and he won't know until the day it's to take effect. Our common serjeant is scrupulous.'

'I see,' Edgar said weakly. 'And what's caused these difficulties?'

Tewburn shrugged. 'London and Southwark are discrete cities, with distinct laws, distinct manors, distinct courts. Master Strode has no jurisdiction on the far bank, and though his arm is long, there are limits to the speed and force with which even he can negotiate with his counterparts there. In Southwark he's nothing.'

'But what—'

'We must find an accommodating judge in the Southwark manor court wielding jurisdiction over Grimes's shop. And even to determine in whose authority Cutter Lane lies presents a considerable difficulty. The lane runs along the boundary between two Southwark boroughs, dividing them as prettily as Pythagoras himself could bisect a circle.'

The flood of details overwhelmed Edgar, for what did he know of borough courts and jurisdictions, of bisected circles and Pythagoras? What he did know was that Gerald needed to be moved out of Nathan Grimes's shop, and moved soon.

He also suspected there was something Tewburn wasn't telling him. The clerk's voice was stiff, too proper even for a Guildhall man. For Edgar knew Tewburn, in that way he knew his most frequent jakes: knew his voice and his manner, the way he responded to certain gestures and inflections. 'When will you know more, Master Tewburn?'

'We should receive official word by Monday, I'm told, Tuesday at the latest, and we fully expect a resolution—'

'James,' Edgar said, his voice soft but severe.

Tewburn stopped, then turned slowly, his eyes widening with recognition and desire. Tewburn knew that tone, asked for it every time.

'I – how—'

'James,' he said again. 'If you have something to tell me, tell it now, or there won't be much of this in your future.' He took Tewburn's hand and put it on his breeches.

The clerk's face reddened, his tongue flicked his upper lip, then he sprang to his feet.

'What is it, James?'

He put a hand to his eyes. 'Ah, hell with it all.' He gazed through the privet, making sure they were not being observed, then blew out a long breath. 'The truth is your brother's mixed up with some foul men. The butchers seem to control that whole manor over there. They've paid off the judges, the bailiff, the prior for all I can tell. They're a hard bunch, waylaying cattle and sheep before they're driven to market, scaring off the inspectors. No one knows who's in charge, and whenever I push for an answer on who has the authority to approve the transfer I get a spin on somebody's finger.'

Edgar considered telling the clerk what he knew but

decided against it. Too risky. No reason to muddy the waters with all Gerald's talk of treason, which could interfere with the transfer of wardship. 'Anything else?' he asked.

Tewburn shrugged. 'I'll know more in a few days, after I've met with one of the Guildable justices. It looks to me like Gerald's kept himself clean, but Grimes is thick in it. I'll have it sorted by Monday. We can talk then.'

'Here?'

'Better that I come find you. Our usual place?' Tewburn took the sacrament most often in the north churchyard at St Pancras, a disused and overgrown spot of land lying between Gropecunt Lane and Popkirtle Lane and running nearly up to Cheapside. The newer yard to the west of the church was now the parish's burial plot, so the maudlyns tended to use the older one with certain jakes who were uncomfortable coupling in the horsestalls.

Edgar nodded and stood. 'Monday, then, just after the Angelus bell.'

Tewburn peered through the privet, then back at Edgar, going to his knees with a questioning glance. Edgar allowed him to reach up and unlace his breeches. The clerk was eager, and within the short whiles of three paternosters, said in his mind while he was sucked by Strode's clerk, his seed was in Tewburn's mouth, Tewburn on his feet, and they were winding back through the mayor's outbuildings. Edgar refused his offer of a groat. This one, he told the clerk with a grateful smile, is on my tally.

As he left Guildhall Yard Edgar pondered the troubling encounter. Whatever Tewburn had learned across the river about Grimes and his gang of butchers couldn't be good for Gerald. He shuffled along Cheapside back to Gropecunt Lane, his gloom returning. Perhaps Master Strode, for all his might and goodness, wouldn't be able to help after all.

No surprise there. Tewburn, after all, worked for the City

of London, and Strode worked for the City of London, and Bickle the beadle worked for the City of London – yet the City of London, Edgar Rykener thought with a grim sense of his own place in this hateful town, most surely did not work for him.

TWENTY-THREE

St Mary Overey, Southwark

Distraction, deception, subterfuge, mendacity, all those unspoken tools of the subtler crafts: government and trade, diplomacy and finance. For someone in my line of work these are tools ready to hand, and I wield them with an implicit confidence in my own mastery of any given transaction. Only rarely are they used against me, and when they are I generally recognize them before any harm is done.

But not always.

'You could write an algorism for it,' said my son.

'What is an algorism?'

Simon looked at me almost pityingly. 'A procedure for calculating something. Put an equation together with a few rules and you have an algorism. Named for al-Khwarizmi, one of the great mathematicians of Araby.'

'Oh.'

'The metre of a poem is a measurable quantity,' he went on.

'Right,' I said.

'Whenever you choose a word or a combination of words

in putting together a line, you're also choosing numbers. Any given elegiac couplet contains six feet, then five feet, with a finite variation in syllable count across the couplet.'

'Finite. Like my patience.'

Simon laughed, though I could tell he would not give it up. It was the day before the St George's morrow feast out at Windsor, and we were eating a sparse midday meal together in the hall. Onion soup, drawn beans, a loaf of wastel, and a tart with an orange conserve that Simon had purchased at a spicerer's on Bridge Street. An extravagance, I thought, but he intended it as a small gesture of gratitude; I decided to take it in that spirit. We had discussed his new employment with the chancellor, and he had just been asking me about my latest writing. I had complained about the drudgery of elegiacs. He was responding with this arcane defence of poetic metre.

'An algorism would allow you to calculate rate of change in the metre, whatever sort you're employing.'

'But what would this information give you?'

'A glimpse of the poet's mind as he writes. How often does Cato craft an irregular line? With what frequency does a poet writing in elegiac couplets choose a spondee as opposed to a dactyl as the first foot of the hexameter?'

'Again, though—'

'You could do it with chronicles, too, starting with very simple calculations. What's the most frequently used dactylic word in Vergil? *Numine*? *Volvere*? *Omnibus*?'

'So one could tell a lot about a poet's taste in images, say.'

'Exactly. Or whether there's less metrical or syntactical variety toward the end of a work.'

'Suggesting what?'

'That the poet grew lazy the closer he got to the end?'

I looked at him, sensing a subtle shift in tone. 'I take it you had lots of time for this sort of thing in Italy.'

He shrugged. 'It's how my mind operates, I suppose. At the moment I'm working through a similar sort of puzzle for the chancellor's secretary.'

'Oh?' Simon's appointment with de la Pole's office had gone well, and the chancellor had given him some materials with which to assay his skills.

'He asked me to prove my accounting skills on an old audit book.' He rubbed a palm over the worn leathern cover of a small booklet. 'Reconcile this sum, justify that expense, and all of it's written in the most crabbed hand you can imagine, with these unique abbreviations I have never seen before. It's like a code. Quite a mess, though I've almost got it cracked.'

He went on for a while in this vein, and as I watched him eat his tart I wondered at this strange combination of genius and whimsy that defined so much of his person. Simon had killed a man, and his history of counterfeiting spoke to a capacity for deception that could still give me chills. Yet as Chaucer had once pressed me to recognize, the death was unintentional, an accident, and Simon had clearly been changed for the better by his two years in Hawkwood's service. Gone was the arrogant self-confidence, the defiant puerility. In this new role as the dutiful son, he was capable of helping me to forget, even for a few hours, the subject of Chaucer's murderous book.

The respite ended abruptly when Will Cooper came in with a small bundle under his arm. 'A delivery from the Guildhall, Master Gower. Compliments of the common serjeant, the Honourable Ralph Strode.'

'Ah, the Angervyle.' Remembering Strode's promise, I eagerly untied the rope thongs binding the cloth around the volume and started to browse.

'What is it?' Simon asked, craning his neck.

I hesitated, unsure how much to say. 'It's a book about

loving books, I suppose. The *Philobiblon*, by Richard Angervyle of Bury, who was once the king's envoy to the papal curia in Avignon.'

We spent the next several hours in the solar, Simon sprawled in the south oriel overlooking the priory garden, I seated on a broad-backed chair along the northwest corner absorbing Angervyle's bracing account. Written in Latin prose of an easy gait, the *Philobiblon* began with several straightforward chapters on the affection due to books, the wisdom they contain, their considerable cost. 'No dearness of price ought to hinder a man from the buying of books,' Angervyle wrote, 'if he has the money that is demanded for them.'

Angervyle possessed a strong sense of history, citing examples of renowned book-buyers from the past, including Plato and Aristotle, as well as some negative *exempla* of those who spurned their volumes. There was also a long discussion of the treatment and storage of the bishop's own books. Dripping noses, filthy fingernails, pressed flowers, cups of wine brought too near the precious folios: all of these represented destructive forces to the volumes in his collection, which he sought to preserve and protect against the ravages of their many potential abusers. To this end, he wrote, his plan was to endow a hall of books at Oxford, a chamber that would lend out his collection, rendering it a great public good to the entire Oxford community. 'The treasures of our books,' he wrote, 'should be available to all.'

Eventually I came to a chapter containing stories about certain notorious haters of books. I read it, then read it again, associating Angervyle's story with the events of the last several weeks: prophecies, threats, the burning of books.

An old woman came to Tarquin the Proud, the seventh king of Rome, offering to sell nine books of prophecy. But she asked an immense sum for them, so much that the

200

king said she was mad. In anger she flung three books into the fire, and still asked the same sum for the rest. When the king refused, again she flung three others into the fire and still asked the same price for the three that were left. At last, astonished beyond measure, Tarquin paid for three books the same price for which he might have bought nine. The old woman disappeared, and was never seen again.

My thoughts raced. The story of Tarquin spoke directly to Angervyle's interest in books of prophecy, and his acute awareness of the value of such volumes even to kings. Could one of his own books have contained the prophetic work of Lollius, this manuscript it seemed everyone in England was seeking – this work that had already led to a young woman's violent death? Despite my conviction that the *De Mortibus* must be a forgery, the cryptic mode of Angervyle's treatise was giving me a taste for the hunt.

'Prophecies, Father?'

I looked up, realizing I had been murmuring. I tend to translate aloud as I read, an old schoolroom habit, and Simon had caught a word that tickled his curiosity.

'Just an old Roman tale,' I said.

'Though I'd be happy to hear it, if you wouldn't mind.'

'Well – fine then.' I translated Angervyle's account.

'Fascinating,' said Simon.

'How so?'

'I was just doing a little calculation here, for the chancellor's secretary, on the price of barley during a drought year.' He tapped the book on his table and set aside the tablet he had been using for his sums. 'The smaller the supply, the greater the cost – or so you would think. In fact, though, like the old sibyl's books in your story there, the price will often stay constant even when the supply diminishes suddenly. What

201

do barley and books have in common? Well, if we look at your typical bill of sale . . .'

And we were on to another exchange about the predictive virtues of numbers and algorisms, the weak proofs of mere words. Soon enough I was caught up in it myself, amused by his serious tone though aware of how much he knew about a subject utterly foreign to his father.

What struck me most about that afternoon, though, was the distracting ease of our conversation, despite following so closely on Simon's unexpected return. I realize now how pathetically grateful I was for his renewed presence in Southwark. I even felt reluctant to depart for Oxford in a few days' time, so warmed was I by his company after those bleak months. My guard was down, the air thick with questions I never thought to ask: what Simon was scratching on his tablet, the nature of the book he held throughout our long hours together, the purpose of all this talk about algorisms and the price of barley.

Surely, I see now, this was Simon's intent. For by the time I returned to reading, the one moment of curiosity he had shown about Angervyle's book was entirely forgotten.

TWENTY-FOUR

Watelyng Street, Cordwainer Ward

Eleanor spent the afternoon preceding her rendezvous with Tewburn away from Gropecunt Lane, taking it from a wealthy merchant down from Coventry. Joan Rugg had sent her to the man's inn at half-Sext, and by Vespertime her tongue, her lips, her arse, even her cock ached from a day of hard use. She needed cider, and she needed it cursed soon or she might's well nail herself to the side of the stable and let every freeman of London have his turn with her corpse. She shed her dress and pulled on her breeches. It was that sort of a day.

The Painted Lion off Watelyng Street was fairly packed at that hour; seemed half the workingmen of London lined its benches, calling for ale. Edgar was able to nudge himself a space on the broad hearth, where he sipped contentedly and watched the crowd.

The talk was all of labour statutes and poll taxes. He heard names and titles he recognized, all spoken in contempt. The Duke of Lancaster, the Earl of Oxford, the Duke of Dung and let him rot in his privy.

My brother Joseph, farms out Suffolk way for Sir Rillardain.

What he tells me, the pollers are counting his very children.
Twelve groats per to the royal coffers, if you please, and not
a penny left for bread.

Where's the injustice in that, hey? Suppose if you be the
mighty Duke of Lancaster you need gold to pave the steps
of your new palace, the Savoy being torched and all.

Can't have our dukes goin' penniless now, can we?

Nor our good king.

Where'd our England be without the king has enough
gilded hawks to hunt Waltham Forest?

And enough of our blood to spill for the sodden fields of
France?

But thank St Lazarus we got the Parliament to sort it
for us.

Got me there. A blessed shining lot of common profit for
the nonce.

A handsome statute it was, too, the poll tax. Makes a fleet
of good common sense.

Your married pardoner paying twelve shill, your Mayor of
Chester paying forty and six, your widowed second cousin
of the third son of the alderman's clerk-in-chief of Bridge Ward
paying three shill four – why, what could be simpler than them
sums to figure up in the Ex-cheker?

Edgar laughed along with them, raising his jar to the Prickling
Pickled Pricks of the Poll Tax, though the men's words went
right around and over his muddled head. The workings of
Westminster and the Exchequer were a fathomless mystery to
Edgar; no reason to start plumbing them now. For a while
longer he sat with the labourers, listening to the discontented
talk of tax and toll, of collections and conscriptions, until he
reckoned it was time.

The Angelus bell had already sounded from St Martin le
Grand by the time he turned up Soper Lane toward St Pancras.
The ward watch generally left the maudlyns and their jakes

alone after curfew, though he didn't want to risk further delay. He angled on to Popkirtle Lane, avoiding Joan's crew and the prying eyes of the bawd, then went through a narrow gap between storefronts and over the low wall.

Beneath a waxing moon the St Pancras churchyard could assume an unearthly cast, as if the bodies below its soil were reaching up for the ankles of those who passed above them. Long grasses whisked at his hose. Under his shoes he could feel forgotten graves, and there was a faint musky smell carried on the churchyard air. When he reached the meeting place he stopped and leaned on a tilted slab, a stone rectangle that served well for coupling. No sign of Tewburn yet. It was a peaceful night in the parish. The gentle breeze was cool on his face and a blanket of quiet settled among these stones.

Too quiet. Normally at night, until hours after the curfew bell, the churchyard would hum with the giggles and groans of maudlyns at their labour, with catcalls from the two whoring lanes to east and west as jakes wandered their length. Even on slow nights the ladies would fill the air with a low chatter that could easily be heard in this grassy space behind St Pancras. That night Edgar heard nothing.

A rustle in the grass, low and to the right. He turned and backed away, heart pounding. Only a bird, picking at something – a carrion bird, at its foul work. It gave him an ugly look as he stepped toward it. He stamped the ground. The scavenger flew sluggishly away.

Edgar moved forward several feet, then retched in the high grass. He turned back and looked. Before him lay the ruined body of James Tewburn. His head had been half-severed from his neck, now a gaping valley of torn skin and blackened flesh. The skin above, pale under the quarter moon, was a ghoulish lantern, glowing brightly among the looming stones. One of clerk's eyes was already gone, the bird's easiest meal.

Squatting in the grass Edgar closed his eyes again and said

a prayer. After a careful look around he stood and crept between the stones to a gap in the western wall, thinking only of reaching the safe company of his fellow maudlyns. A few more steps brought him out to Gropecunt Lane.

He shrank back with a gasp, now understanding the silence. The narrow street was abandoned, as if Joan Rugg's sturdy gaggle of maudlyns had simply fled. Doors sat askew, their hinges broken apart. A pendant-lamp lay on the pavers, its glass shattered, the frame bent. No candlelight from the stalls or beneath the eaves.

Edgar huddled against the corner of a horse barn. Sure, the mauds got their share of grief from the authorities. Once a season or so the alderman might send his men down to make a few arrests, usually at the behest of an abbot or prior. Curfew violations were a way of life, though every once in a great while there would be some trouble about it.

Yet this was more than the typical hassle from the constables. The maudlyns were simply gone. Vanished, like Agnes Fonteyn, and now James Tewburn was dead in the churchyard.

From the darkest shadows to Edgar's left a figure stole out on to the narrow lane. From his belt he pulled a short sword, the blade glistening in the moonlight. Edgar quickly calculated the distance between them. He looked over his shoulder at the churchyard. Back at the man. The stranger paced slowly forward, peering beneath the eaves.

Then, from the top of the lane, a flash from a torch. Night watchers, patrolling the ward. 'You there!' one of them shouted, seeing the man in the lane.

For a moment it looked as if the intruder would turn and run, but he decided against it, clearly not wanting the entire parish after him. If he was Tewburn's killer, Edgar thought, flight would cast immediate suspicion on him once the body was found. He discreetly sheathed his blade and approached the watchers, his hands raised. 'Just out for a bit of queynt, good fellows. Where are all the mauds?' A gentleman's voice.

The first walker clucked his tongue. 'Not here, that's sure. Popkirtle Lane and Gropecunt Lane both. Busted up earlier today, sluts hauled away, and who knows when they'll be back.'

'How unfortunate,' said the man.

'Aye,' agreed the first walker with a rough laugh.

There was a pause. 'Sir Stephen, if I'm not mistaken?' said the second.

'The very same,' said the man, his voice taut with the recognition. Edgar heard the jangle of coins as the man prepared to pay off the walkers for their poor memories.

As the chatter continued Edgar edged backwards, away from the arc of lamplight, until he was at the end of the alley leading back to the churchyard. He took a final glance at the trio on Gropecunt Lane. At one point the stranger shook his head with a laugh, and it was then Edgar saw it.

A hook on his chin, a whitened scar. And a face he would remember. *Sir Stephen*. Edgar turned and made for the wall.

TWENTY-FIVE

The palace of Windsor

On the evening following the Feast of St George the palace was lit like a box of polished jewels, the guests just as gaudy. Simon and I had arrived from Southwark late that afternoon and were staying at the mill inn by Windsor Bridge, and had joined the crowd streaming through the west gate. The secretive St George's festivities on the eve and the feast day itself had been restricted to the twenty-four knights and twenty-odd ladies of the Order of the Garter, as custom dictated. Over the last four years, though, and at King Richard's initiative, an additional, much larger feast had been thrown on the morrow, largely to show off the extensive renovations at Windsor. Each of the Order's lords and ladies was permitted ten guests for the closing feast, though the size of the crowd indicated that the figure had been interpreted rather loosely.

That year and the last I had been the guest of Sir Lewis Clifford, a Knight of the Garter who had happily approved the addition of Simon to his list. Next to Gaunt himself, Clifford was perhaps Chaucer's greatest supporter in these high circles, a friend to poets of diverse quality and fortune, and it was Geoffrey who had introduced us years before during my time at the Temple. Clifford and I had an interesting history: a missing shipment of Lyonnaise silk, a discovered bribe, a quiet conversation about one of his crooked associates. In gratitude he became my entrée to these circles, a trusted source when I needed him, and a fount of unending courtesy when I did not. When we entered the great cloister I saw him near the grange, speaking to Nicholas Brembre, Mayor of London and one of numerous royal and civic officials present at the annual gathering.

'A stew of bureaucrats and secretaries,' I mused to Simon. 'Generously spiced with aristocrats,' he said quietly.

The Windsor steward had opened up the tower at the top of the Spicery Gatehouse to the guests, who moved up and down the stairs as sconced torches lit the darkening sky. The tower commanded a vast panorama of the surrounding countryside, which was settling into dusk. Outside the walls and far below, the commons were already ankle-deep in mud, enjoying the order's bounty: casks of ale, spiced cider, roasted mutton by the score. The lower tables stretched into the night, the nearby hamlets and villages emptied of their residents as the king purchased their goodwill toward himself and the Garter. We descended to the hall for Richard's entrance. Despite the deepening factionalism in the realm, for these few days the cream of English chivalry was to set aside its squabbles and resentments and unite for a festival of prayer, unity, and reconciliation. A charade, of course, though always a useful one.

'Why are you smiling, John Gower?' Katherine Swynford, sidling up as Simon wandered off. She wore an uncharacteristically modest dress, a taffeta of deep purple cut just below her neck, an arched and almost coif-like hood covering all but the frontmost span of her hair. With her stood Philippa Chaucer, also dressed down, though where Swynford wore

209

modesty as a peasant wears ermine, on Philippa this understated attire looked natural. Chaucer's wife had a prominent chin below a pleasant, honest face, and eyes that sparkled with a wit whose quickness she shared with her sister. 'Plotting some nasty satire, I suppose?'

I bowed to the sisters. 'Simply admiring the royal view, my lady, and appreciating the feel of the royal stone beneath my humble feet.'

Swynford tightened her lips and dismissed me, looking around for someone more important. Not difficult at Windsor. Everyone knew that Gaunt's mistress aspired to the Order, and these occasions gave her the opportunity to win favour with the knights in hopes of getting her name put before the king once Lancaster was in a position again to ask for royal favours. Swynford's attention was on the terrace doors and the duke's coming entrance. She stood several feet in front of us, showing no interest in our talk.

'You are looking well, John,' said Philippa, her soft voice patterning a warm familiarity.

I inclined my head. 'Nice to see you down from Lincolnshire, Philippa.'

'Have you heard from Simon? How is he faring?'

I was used to hearing this question from Chaucer's wife, who had no knowledge of my son's dark past. 'Why don't you ask him yourself?'

She looked surprised. 'Simon is back in England?'

'Right there, talking with Ralph Strode.' I nodded at him, standing nearby with the common serjeant. 'Geoffrey hasn't mentioned it to you? Perhaps he hasn't heard either.'

'The things Geoffrey Chaucer fails to mention to his wife would fill an ocean.' She did not say it bitterly, though her eyes hinted at her sadness. Over the last two years Philippa had been spending more and more of her time at Kettlethorpe Hall with her sister rather than in London with her husband.

'But I'm glad to hear you are reunited with your son, especially now.'

'Thank you, Philippa.'

'Has he brought a wife back from the south?'

I hesitated. 'Actually he had been betrothed. The young woman died. Fever.'

Philippa put a hand to her neck. 'And Simon so young!'

'Though I must say, she seems to have changed him for the better.'

'What was her name, the poor dear?'

'Seguina. Seguina d'Orange.'

As if a keg of powder had exploded behind her, Katherine Swynford's nose traced a swift arc through the air until she faced me, her torso twisted in the effort. She glanced at Philippa, then our eyes locked, and for an instant hers scorched me, a loss of composure so uncharacteristic of the Swynford I knew it left me breathless. Her gaze lingered another instant, then, recovered, she spun from me and walked toward the gate.

I turned to Philippa, who also looked unaccountably troubled. 'Seguina d'Orange. What does that name signify to you and your sis—'

The trumpets sounded, and my question faded into the loud stir from the gates. Heralds stepped forth first, announcing the royal entry into the king's cloister, eight trumpets blaring as the king and his queen, the duke and his duchess moved out among the kneeling crowd. The company fell into two double-deep ranks. I joined the second, all eyes on the young man whose life seemed so delicate as his subjects pressed around him. The king's fair skin set off the feeble beard. His robes were pounced with heraldry, white harts in chase around his shoulders and waist. The queen, a tiny scrap of a woman who rarely spoke, wore a gown trimmed in a sable-silk brocade that she fingered absently as she paced.

King Richard walked slowly across the room, pausing before every third or fourth visitor to speak a few words. Lancaster and the duchess followed, the duke's mouth fixed in a tight frown.

Behind them walked a large company of magnates, the most important among them the earls, including Thomas of Woodstock, Earl of Buckingham and Gaunt's younger brother, and the Earl of Oxford with his burgeoning entourage, including Sir Stephen Weldon. Other knights of the king's affinity followed – Philip la Vache, Nicholas Dagworth, John Clanvowe, Richard Abberbury, and Simon de Burley, all jostling for position in the press of bodies, cloth, livery, and banners as the throng slowly moved through the fawning crowd of lower gentry.

The last man out, appearing as the lines were already disintegrating, was Chaucer. He walked alone, his gaze on the spectacle before him bemused and authorial. Spying me with his wife, he raised his chin and approached.

'Philippa,' he said.

'Geoffrey,' she said, and walked away. Chaucer looked after her, resigned rather than offended.

'The height of courtesy, as always,' I said, his cruelty at the customhouse still on my mind. 'What gives you licence to treat her like that?'

The skin around Chaucer's eyes creased. 'There's a fine line between licence and licentiousness, John. I've crossed it more than most: to the stews of Rose Alley, to Gropecunt Lane and back again, mistresses taken with her full knowledge.' He looked away, a hint of regret in his stooped shoulders. 'Philippa thinks our marriage is a pageant, nothing more. Since that Cecily Chaumpaigne mess she won't let me touch her.'

Chaucer's notorious troubles with women had sparked more than one unfortunate episode over the years, including a disturbing accusation of abduction and rape some time ago. The young woman, a baker's daughter, had officially released him from the initial charge before things got too serious. I was away from London that season and had never learned the truth of the matter, though I had seen what he was capable of in other contexts and had long wondered whether the accusation were true.

'Candour suits you, Geoffrey,' I said. 'Though you could have shown more of it earlier in your marriage.'

'Perhaps,' he conceded. 'But then, candour goes only so far, don't you think? There must also be love.' A shadow passed over his face, a hint of longing or regret in that sad smile. 'Ah,' he said, tripping past the admission, 'and here is Weldon. What about *your* many loves, Sir Stephen?'

'Too numerous to count, and always more in line.' Weldon's scar was at full jut. Ignoring me, he gave Chaucer a pointed look. 'I need a word.'

'You may have a dozen or so,' said Chaucer. He turned to me. 'If you will excuse us, John, a customs officer's duty is to his dutifulness. Oh –' he stopped, his voice measured as Weldon strolled ahead – 'and that surely wasn't Simon I saw just now, having a chat with Ralph Strode?'

'It was,' I said, with a hint of defensiveness.

'I thought so.' He looked at me strangely, then turned away and strolled with Weldon toward the palace. I watched them recede into the crowd, then went to look for Simon. It took a while to find him, and by the time I did the bell had sounded for the feast.

As the ladies separated for the lesser hall, we retired into the St George's range, a space of opulent magnificence that seemed to be trying too hard to awe those who entered. There were a few courteous words from the king, a prayer from the archbishop, then the chatter resumed. Simon sat to my left, and to his left was Thomas Pinchbeak, who peppered both of us with news from Westminster and the Inns as we made our way through a roast piglet, the crackled skin slipping easily from the tender flesh. Chaucer was seated at the next table. I felt for the queen and the duchess, the only women remaining in the great chamber. They ate in gloomy silence next to their husbands on the dais. They never spoke to one another as far as I could see.

The extravagance of food and plate was distracting, and it was not until much later, with the serving of cakes, sweet wafers, and a spring pudding as minstrels and players filled the front of the hall, that I thought again of the book. It was Pinchbeak who did it, leaning before Simon to ask me the most peculiar question.

'And the blood, Gower?'

'Pardon?' I said, assuming I had misheard him. Simon was sitting back, trying not to interfere with our exchange.

'The blood, on the robes.'

I stared into Pinchbeak's eyes as the words of the coroner's inquest came back to me: *said woman was beaten in the face and struck on the head and bloodied, feloniously murdered by an unknown assailant.* 'What about it?'

'Your son and I were debating the point. Are they using wine for the blood, do you suppose?' He nodded toward the front of the hall. I turned my head and realized Pinchbeak was referring to the pageant playing out before the dais. A play of St George and the Dragon, with one boy taking the part of the sacrificial virgin and four others bearing the painted beast on their shoulders. Two robed youths, bloodied, dead, trying not to wriggle, lay sprawled on the floor before the dragon.

My pulse slowed. 'Beet juice, I'd guess.' Pinchbeak gave me a vague smile, then turned to the man on his other side with a comment about the cakes.

'Too dark to be sheep's blood,' Simon mused.

It all came back then – the book, the murder, the play at Temple Hall, broken up by Pinchbeak and his fellow serjeants. As I looked around at the babbling guests I wondered how many of them knew of the *De Mortibus*, of the alleged French spy murdered in the Moorfields, of the king's prophesied death. The exchange reminded me to visit the coroner's chambers to have another word with Nicholas Symkok, who had acted so dodgy with me. I wouldn't have time before my Oxford trip, though it would be at the top of my list upon my return.

After Richard's departure the crowd started to thin. Lancaster remained on the dais, enjoying the attention, though the duchess excused herself, as did several of her attendants. Swynford entered with a small clutch of other ladies. The doors to the lower stairs were propped open; guests began to drink more seriously, many filtering out to the yards; and a pleasant evening cool descended on the hundreds still remaining.

I wandered among them, speaking to acquaintances, until I came upon Sir John Clanvowe, a knight of Richard's chamber and a poet of modest accomplishment. He stood with Sir Lewis Clifford, our host for the evening, before the entrance to the Spicery stairs.

'I understand you'll be travelling to Oxford?' Clanvowe asked me. The knight's loose cotte, dyed a simple grey, bunched around the belt girding his waist. Of my height and age but a wiry stick of a knight, Clanvowe was like an eager bird, his head moving in small, distracting jerks at each phrase. His voice was high and sing-songish, falling at the end of every sentence like a crow's fading caw.

'I am, John,' I said without the honorific, as Clanvowe preferred. 'I leave at dawn, and Simon will be going back to Southwark.'

'You know, I will be in Oxford by Wednesday or Thursday,'

Clanvowe said. 'Travelling with Clifford here, who's taking up the constableship at Cardigan. I'm on my way back to Hereford for the summer. Perhaps you'll let me feed you one evening while you're in town?'

'I'd be delighted,' I said, meaning it, for I had always felt a companionable warmth toward Clanvowe, a man of real wisdom who was never his best at court. We parted with a promise of supper the following week in Clanvowe's rooms at the Queen's College, and I thanked Sir Lewis again for his hospitality in inviting us to the great occasion.

Growing tired, I started to search out Simon, wandering past a canopy festooned with gay flags and branches of flowered crepe. Beneath it, in the glassy light of four hanging lamps, Katherine Swynford sat at a low marble table, laying out her cards. Her opponent in the game was Sir Stephen Weldon. A crowd had gathered around their table to watch, and there was much murmuring about the beauty of the cards. I recalled the rules of the game Swynford had taught me, though this one was different.

Swynford laid down four cards. I leaned in to see which they were: the Two of Thistles, the Eight of Swords, and the Four and Duke of Hawks. Weldon countered her move with a trump card, the Wheel of Fortune, which Swynford took with the King of Thistles. Weldon's next play was the Prince of Plums.

I stared at the card, my vision starring.

The Prince of Plums.

I went cold, nearly breathless with the realization. As the game continued lines of verse burned through my mind, the letters searing my memory like a hot coal on skin.

> *With seven of swords to swing at their will . . .*
> *At sovereign of swords in death swoon he must . . .*

Seven of Swords. Sovereign of Swords. Three of Thistles. The strange phrases from the prophecies referred not to arcane symbols or figures of allegory, but to the suits of the playing cards of the sort dealt by Katherine Swynford.

The faces of the guests gathered around the card table took on a sinister cast. In the front rank stood Robert de Vere, the earl's mouth set in a bemused grin at the sight of his knight losing badly to Lancaster's concubine. Behind him loomed the imposing bulk of Ralph Strode, taking in the game with a slight frown as Thomas Pinchbeak watched over his shoulder, bent forward like a raven at a fresh corpse. Beside him Sir Michael de la Pole, the chancellor, cold in the April evening, arms wrapping his frame. A dozen others surrounded the pair, all transfixed by this unfamiliar game: the cards from Tuscany, the strategies from Lombardy, yet the players wholly English in their allegiances.

I imagined myself watching them from above, these lords, magnates, diverse bearers of the nation's fortune. Had anyone else with knowledge of the *De Mortibus* made the association with the cards? Or was this my knowledge alone, shared only with those plotting against the king? And, I now wondered, was Katherine Swynford one of them?

'Not if I can help it, *damn* it all to hell, and now with all the rest . . .' A familiar voice, raised and angry, had barked from the cluster of shrubs at the range-end before fading into a loud whisper. Heads turned.

Chaucer, his features twisted in anger, strode past me without a look. At the sight of the lofty crowd beneath the canopy he recovered himself and affected a tired smile. He bowed to the assembled company, then without a word shot through the gateyard postern. I turned back to see Simon slinking away from the foot of the range. The light was such that no one else in the vicinity seemed to note my son as the target of Chaucer's wrath.

217

Later, as we left the palace grounds and rode to the mill inn with a small company of other guests, I struggled for words. I suspected I knew the source of the dispute but wanted to make sure.

'Simon,' I eventually said, my voice low. At my initiative we were riding last in the group and wouldn't be overheard.

'Yes, Father?'

'You had words with Chaucer.'

'I did.'

An owl hooted somewhere behind us.

'We talked about Hawkwood, and my homecoming,' said Simon. 'Chaucer had – Chaucer *has* warm feelings regarding my decision to return to England.'

'What feelings?'

'Hawkwood—' He let out a breath, his head angled skyward. 'Chaucer feels I haven't acted in good faith toward the White Company. That I've made him look terrible in Hawkwood's eyes.'

'Ah,' I said, my suspicions confirmed.

'Chaucer said it wasn't easy to set me up in Hawkwood's service after – after what happened,' he said, stumbling. 'Said he had to call in quite a large favour with Sir John in order to obtain a position for me. And that my unexpected return to England suggests that I haven't shown the trustworthiness he would expect. That it smacks of youthful indecision, as he put it.'

'He has a point,' I said wryly. 'Rather a strong one.'

'I suppose he does,' said Simon. 'But I was truthful with Hawkwood about the reason for my departure. He told me he would be happy to accept me into his service again if I return.' He turned to me. 'Have I acted in bad faith?'

I thought for a moment, pleased by this unexpected request for fatherly wisdom. 'Not toward Hawkwood, at least. You have given him two years of good service, and he's invited you to return. But you *have* acted in bad faith toward Chaucer. The courteous thing would have been to write him in advance, informing him of your decision to return. Seeing you at Windsor while thinking you were still in Italy? That must have been quite a shock.'

He nodded. 'I see that. But what can I do to make it up to him?'

We had reached the courtyard door and now stood in the road. The other palace guests were handing off their horses to the stabler and his boy. 'If I know Chaucer, it should be a simple matter. A letter. Doesn't need to be long. Short and sincere. Once he reads it he'll forget the whole thing.'

'Let's hope so,' said Simon, holding the heavy door.

Simon slept deeply the first part of that night, snoring on his bolster as I thought back through the Garter feast, wondering what I had missed. It had been an evening of tense encounters and interrupted revelations: Swynford's peculiar reaction to the name of Simon's lover, my epiphany about the cards and the prophecies, that ugly spat between Chaucer and Simon. Though I knew more about the prophecies than I had that morning, I felt my ignorance like a bad meal in the stomach. For the first time in my life, it seemed that knowledge, which had always been my privileged coinage, was failing me. There were things I was not being told, knots my mind seemed incapable of unravelling. And always before me the murder on the Moorfields, and the deaths of kings.

It was at some point during the smallest hours when I awoke to the bark of the keeper's talbot in the courtyard. The dog was quickly silenced, and I realized that Simon was no longer in our bed. I sat up, listening intently, and heard a series of low murmurs from below. One of the voices belonged to Simon. The other was too soft to recognize. I could make out nothing of the conversation. I went to the door and opened it a crack.

The hinges threw an angry squeal across the courtyard. The talk ceased abruptly. I crept back to bed and waited until Simon climbed the stairs, then listened as he pissed, loudly, from the upper landing down into the courtyard. He cleared his throat, spat. He entered our chamber quietly and slipped beneath the covers.

'Everything all right?' I whispered.

'Just a trip to the privy. That onion soup . . .'

'Right,' I said, feeling uneasy.

Hours later I awoke with a start, the sound of Simon's piss, and his obvious lie, ringing in my ears.

TWENTY-SIX

Rose Alley, Southwark

Eleanor wedged herself between the barrels, her attention back on the Pricking Bishop's alley door. No sign of Agnes yet, but she'd seen Millicent, airing a blanket out the second-storey window. It was only a matter of time before the sisters would make their move. And when they do, she vowed, I'll make my own.

Out of a larger house along the bankside stepped a rail-thin woman, a basket of laundry in her arms. She set it down on the street side of the gutter. A boy followed her out. They walked together toward the high street, leaving the basket of clothing for a servant to wash. Eleanor glanced up and down the lane. She stepped across and pulled a few garments from the basket. In the far alley, bouncing on her toes to avoid the filth, she shoved first her left foot, then her right down the stolen breeches. The grey doublet fit snugly.

It was not an hour later when Edgar finally got what he'd been waiting for. The Fonteyn sisters, their hoods cinched tight, left the Pricking Bishop and strode with purpose toward the bridge. Despite the welter of affection and relief he felt at seeing Agnes alive and well, Edgar was also newly furious at her, and he was tempted to jump out and confront her right there, though he remained in place. When they had turned he took a deep breath and walked across Rose Alley.

St Cath sat at her usual place. A loud snore shot from the old woman's mouth. He waited for another, then stepped around her and slipped inside.

He stood in a small antechamber, dim with no windows. As his eyes adjusted he heard the choir: soft moans from the room to the left, rhythmic thumps from above. He crept through the lower level to the makeshift bakery. A squat oven, where Bess Waller's crew baked wastel and other breads for illegal sale across the river in London. A cutting block with an upside-down mashing bowl. Two high tables with four stools. The heavy door to the rear yard was bolted shut, though the trapdoor to the undercroft stairs was open. From the space below rose a pale cone of candlelight and two voices.

'Pickled twenty pots and here it be George's week with only two on the shelf?'

'Girls like the leeks and garlic, Bess. Gets the blood up, stiffens the cock.'

'Tell them to ease off a bit.'

'Sure.'

'And you'll see about the cod? Half a barrel gone to rot, and the Bishop out good coin. As to the cider . . .'

Edgar stopped listening as he surveyed the room. He made his way carefully along the walls, peering into the shelves past the crockery, the warmth of the oven on his skin. On a shelf above the hearth rested a small array of pious items: a copper candlestick, a small pewter cross, both of which he pocketed; a wood painting of the Magdalene, which he left. He had nearly circled the room when his foot struck a pan, sending it to clatter across the floor.

'St Cath! That you?' Bess Waller hollered up the cellar stairs.

Edgar held his breath.

'Agnes? Mil, that you, girl?' Bess's bonnet came into view. 'Can't let a damned bawd sort her cellar without a rotting racket, by St Bride.' She looked up. '*You*!' she screeched, legs already pumping.

Edgar bent down to lift the edge of the cellar door. Bess ran up the stairs to beat him to it. He took more than a few splinters in his fingers as the trapdoor rose from the floor. When it passed the midway mark he let go of the heavy board.

Whump. The board slammed down on Bess's hand. A rough scream from the bawd, who slipped her fingers from beneath the weight. Edgar stomped on the board to the pounding of Bess's shoulders and fists from below. He reached for the cutting block and dragged it until it rested halfway over the trapdoor.

The women's cries were muffled now. Given the kitchen's separation from the main house there was little chance those within had heard the commotion. Nor was there a direct street entrance to the cellar, as far as Edgar knew. He had some time. He resumed his look through the shelves, peering into pots and pans, knocking plate and crockery to the floor with an abandon that gave him more angry satisfaction than he'd felt in weeks, since finding that corpse on the Moorfields.

Four grain barrels occupied the final bit of floor space beneath the shelves. He knocked the first barrel to the floor and reached for the next as the brown dust of wheat flour filled the air. Two more barrels, and now millet and barley dust rose in great clouds. The final barrel, quarter full with rough-cut and mouldy oats. He knocked it down, then stood, panting in the bready air. No dust from the oats, but a lot of mess on the floor, take a full day to—

He saw it. A lump beneath the rancid grain. Pushing his dusted hair aside, he bent to the pile and pushed through a few inches of oats. He felt cloth. He grasped a leather thong and pulled, recovering a thin rectangular bundle, wrapped in embroidery. He felt its width and length, pressed his palms on the flat surfaces.

A book.

He stared down at it, scarcely believing his fortune. The girl in the moor, stripped of her clothing, creatures at her flesh; the beadle of Cripplegate, Richard Bickle, his gold-smelling fingers grasping Eleanor's cheek; poor James Tewburn, slain in the churchyard with no one about. And this book, a book Edgar couldn't read to save his soul, yet a treasure worth a lot of killing and coin.

Edgar wiped flour from his eyes. After a last glance around the kitchen, he crept back to the Bishop's front, squeezed on to Rose Alley, and headed for the bridge, the oldest maudlyn in Southwark still snoring in his wake.

TWENTY-SEVEN

Holbourne

Coming up from the Fleet River the sisters slowed, looking across at the imposing façade of Scroope's Inn and the armorial bearings on the windows, the tracery spidering from the central medallions. The inn of the serjeants-at-law was a solid block of stone, framed by two gardens and two small houses but with no front courtyard welcoming visitors. It would have to be entered directly from the street, in open view. Two wagons came from the left, a cart and a few riders from the right, though the wide street was relatively deserted on this sunny day. Millicent took Agnes's arm, crossed to the high door and, no one stopping them or asking a question, pushed against the heavy oaken barrier.

With a deep yawn of old iron, the door yielded, giving way to the cold gloom of a long rectangular chamber. Little light penetrated through from the high windows. Before them on the east wall was painted the figure of a massive robed woman, a cloth binding her eyes, a set of balanced scales hanging from her left hand. IUSTITIA, the Latin inscription above her read. In Scroope's Inn, Millicent mused, justice isn't a pretty painting, for here the law sees everything, and the scales are always tipped. It could be no mistake that Pinchbeak had directed them to his own domain, the chambers of the serjeants-at-law, the most powerful legal officials in the land. There were fewer than thirty of them, king's appointees all, with their own set of privileges, their own style of robe and coif, their own grand inn up on Holbourne. Sir Humphrey ap-Roger had known several of them, dined with them in this very inn as a guest on occasion, though even he, a knight of ancient lineage, had felt intimidated in the serjeants' company.

Doors off the front hall led out to a central courtyard, where a series of covered staircases on the outer walls rose to two levels of apartments. They reached another chamber, smaller though equally high. In an alcove off the far corner stood three writing desks arranged around an aged clerk, his bent form crammed between them. A mounted arc of candles hung chained from a lower rafter, rendering the man's head, uncapped and bald, as a glowing orb.

He did not look up at their approach. At his desk Millicent said, 'We seek Master Thomas Pinchbeak, sir, serjeant-at-law. Where may we find him, if you please?'

Still without moving his head, the old man replied, 'First back stairs, top level, eastern corner rooms on the south side.' Then he looked up, taking them in with something like terror. He sputtered a bit, shook his head, and gave them a stern frown. Millicent could almost hear his bones creak as he rose. 'Women are not permitted in Scroope's, nor in any of the inns of our art. You must leave at once.'

'But Master Pinchbeak himself summoned us,' said Millicent. 'And here we are.'

'Summoned you, did he?' the man thundered. 'Summoned the pair of you, and not tell old Wilkes? Couldn't be bothered to – not that I – well . . . ahhhh.' His voice weakened and his eyes shot upward, catching the flames. 'Though do I recall something about . . .' He grimaced down at his desk, his hands sorting through the loose sheaves around him. 'Your name?'

'Rykener,' said Millicent. 'My name is Eleanor Rykener.'

Agnes gasped. Millicent silenced her with a look.

'Eleanor Rykener, Eleanor Rykener,' the old man intoned, patting around his desk. Millicent heard the clink of coins. He help up a felt purse. 'This is for your troubles, an advance left for you by Master Pinchbeak. The serjeant had an urgent matter at the bench.'

Millicent, torn between frustration and greed, took the purse, opened it, then showed it to Agnes, who reached inside and pulled out a small handful of coins.

'Two marks of silver, that be,' the old man said, 'and not a farthing less. With the balance to be paid upon delivery, says Master Pinchbeak.'

Millicent started to protest. They hadn't brought the book with them, fearing some form of deception on the serjeant-at-law's part. Their plan had been to gauge Pinchbeak's seriousness and see the money before returning to the Pricking Bishop to retrieve the manuscript.

'And this balance, good sir?' Agnes asked in her pleasantest tone. 'Its size?'

He pursed his lips. 'Master Pinchbeak said nothing to me about its size, my pretty. He requests your return tomorrow with the item in question.'

Outside they considered the exchange as they walked back through the walls and toward the bridge. 'Merely an advance, that man said,' said Agnes. 'And tomorrow we'll collect the balance, eh, Mil?'

'So it appears,' said Millicent, though without her sister's optimism. If Pinchbeak truly wanted the book, why would he have left a mere two marks, and why would he have put them off like this? Something about these dealings with the serjeant-at-law didn't sit right, though Millicent couldn't sort it before Agnes started pressing her about the Eleanor Rykener business. Millicent explained, telling her sister about Eleanor's visit to her Cornhull house, then her use of Eleanor's name in her meeting with Pinchbeak at the parvis.

'It just happened, Ag,' she said. 'I couldn't very well use my own, could I? Hers was in my head, and it spilled out when Pinchbeak asked me my name.'

Agnes, visibly furious, said nothing all the way to the bridge, then across to Southwark, with Millicent tagging her heels. On Rose Alley their steps slowed at the sight before them.

A small crowd of maudlyns, spilling on to the lane. The girls, some of them wearing only unlaced shifts, had gathered unexpectedly in the street, while others had dressed themselves in their shabby finery; few heads were covered.

St Cath, arrayed in a faded purple gown and a hood four sizes too great for her shrunken head, sat with a cat on her lap, glowering up the alley. As her daughters approached Bess Waller turned to face them, her arms crossed tightly, her jaw set in anger.

'What is it?' Millicent asked, fearing the worst.

'Thing's gone.'

'What's gone?' Agnes asked. 'What thing?' Millicent asked at the same moment.

'The book,' Bess said. 'Nor will you credit who's robbed us of it.' She told them the details: Eleanor Rykener, all manned up, sneaking by St Cath and appearing in the Bishop's kitchen. The slammed cellar trap. The spilled oats. Finally Bess's release by one of the girls.

Millicent spun on Agnes. 'And it had to be that Eleanor Rykener, didn't it?' she spat, no longer regretting her use of the maudlyn's name with Pinchbeak. 'I hope that swerver hangs for treason.'

Agnes gasped. 'What – how could you—'

'She stole it from us, Ag. Out from under our chins. And with it our only chance at a future.'

The sisters turned away from one another, silent in their mutual fury.

'So there it is, then,' said Bess eventually. 'What's a biddy maud like Eleanor Rykener hope to do with a cursed stack of parchments?'

It was at that moment that St Cath looked up from her trance. Her face shone with the confidence of a prophetess. 'Only one place in London an unlettered maud could hope to sell a book,' she croaked. 'Leastwise in my experience.'

They all looked at her, wondering what strange memory had provoked the old whore's intervention.

'And where's that, St Cath?' Bess Waller asked her with the patience the woman's years deserved.

'Ave Maria Lane,' St Cath went on with a sage nod. 'Hard by St Paul's. Had it off there with a limner and his apprentice upon a time.' Her eyes sparkled with the recollection. 'Or Paternoster Row. That's where I'd look for the tarred slut.'

TWENTY-EIGHT

Broad Street, Oxford

'How much for the copying?'

'Three and two.'

'And the subwarden let you have it for the week?'

'"One of only two copies of Master Albertus in Balliol,"
he tells me. "Mind it well, young Pelham, mind it well."'

'And you will?'

'I'll keep it chained to my wrist.'

'And basted with your annotations.'

'Basted, roasted, ruminated—'

'And shat on Shitbarn Lane.'

'Into the privy of theology—'

'We call Balliol College.'

The three students erupted in laughter as they walked by,
sparing no glance for a robeless Londoner seated on a stone
wall. One of them looked a bit like Simon, the same sparkle
of wit and ardour in his eyes, brains and charm to burn.
They passed beneath the arched gate into Balliol yard.

With a heavy sigh I rose, feeling, as always in Oxford,
like the slow third wheel of a swifter cart. Though I had

travelled here several times in recent years, I was neither a former student nor, like Ralph Strode, a master, my education having led me to the Temple rather than to Oxford or Cambridge. I knew men who had studied in both towns, Strode among them, and Chaucer always swore I could have been a fine philosopher or logician. But I had admitted to myself years before that certain dimensions of these disciplines were beyond me.

Though what, I wondered as I looked up Broad Street at yet another ruined façade, can come of theology when its greatest home lies in rubble? The town of Oxford seemed to have declined since my last visit into a haven of thieves and whores, stealing and swyving in the empty plots and fallow fields along the London road, keeping company with the hanged. Yet as the keeper of the inn at St Frideswide's had remarked, for every structure being pulled down outside the walls another two were going up on Cornmarket Street. Even the Durham monks had ambitions to expand their manse into a full-fledged college, with its own degreed faculty. As Will Cooper had observed to me on our way along the high street, Oxford was a confused town, it was plain to see: uncertain about its future yet eager to scrape away its pestilential past, caught in that strange land between decay and renewal.

I walked through the outer doors of the Durham *hospitium* as the monks were concluding Tierce. The voice of the abbot dismissed the monks to their work, and outside they broke up into smaller clusters.

One of the last to leave the oratorium was an old man in lay garb. His hose were cut tight around his ankles, tucked into rough boots that wouldn't have looked out of place on a ploughman. He wore a loose jacket of thin brown wool, unbuttoned over a simple shirt dyed a dark red, and from its collar jutted a neck of remarkable length made all the more striking in contrast with its owner's head, which seemed to block the sun as he approached me from across the quadrangle. Though deep crags lined his brow, his skin lay drum-tight against his cheeks, as if pulled by an unseen force somewhere behind his ears.

'Master John Gower?'

'The same.' I half-bowed to the man. 'You are Peter de Quincey?'

'All my life,' was his reply. 'Come to sniff through the bishop's books, have you?' He asked a few other pointed questions, referring to the letter from Strode I had sent around the day before. Apparently satisfied, he led me to a far corner of the outer manse, where a narrow doorway opened to the dormitory passage.

'Bishop Angervyle, Strode tells me, was a great man,' I said to his back.

'The greatest,' said Quincey as he stepped along the narrow passage. 'His lordship served as the king's cofferer, as dean of rolls, as bishop of Durham, even as envoy to Avignon, to say nothing of his station as lord chancellor. A lustrous life.'

'Though I've heard, too,' I said, sensing his eagerness to expand, 'that Angervyle was instrumental in the deposition of the second King Edward. That he was forced to hide out in Paris for a time.'

A secretive smile over his shoulder. 'I will not deny it. He was a man of powerful associations. An adviser and emissary to kings, emperors, and popes. But above all Richard Angervyle was a devoted collector of books. An *amasser* of books, one of unparalleled devotion. You undoubtedly know about the more immense holdings in our realm. Bury St Edmunds, St Albans, the libraries at Winchester and Worcester . . .' We left the grange through a rear door facing on the walls. Fields and orchards beyond, workers toiling in the distance. 'And the great libraries of Christendom: the holdings of King Charles of France, the curial libraries at Rome and Avignon.'

'Yes, of course,' I said, thinking of Chaucer's account of the Visconti collection. Our apparent destination was a small, detached building positioned against the north wall and surrounded by a thick cluster of trees and shrubs. The building's walls formed a hexagon of timber and stone.

'Yet these libraries, while great in number, have no *soul*.' Quincey pulled a long key from its dangle by his waist; it reminded me of Tom Tugg's grotesque key to the Newgate cells, though more finely wrought. There was a click, then, with a reluctant breath, the door swung open on well-oiled hinges.

'Such collections,' Quincey continued as he stepped inside, 'are rich men's baubles, serving the purposes of vanity. Even the most sober monks regard their books as a reflection of their order. These men, Master Gower, collect books as the Duke of Lancaster collects palaces. And bastards.' He gestured for me to enter.

The first thing I noticed about the dark space was the smell: rich, deep, gorgeous. Cardamon, I thought, and cloves and cinnamon – and old parchment, and leather, and boards, and dust. It was overwhelming; I had to step back out for a moment to sneeze. Quincey, meanwhile, had taken a pair of wicksnips from a shelf and busied himself lighting several new candles. Despite the opened door the room was not well lit, the shutters having been nailed fast. Old, rickety-looking shelves lined five of the chamber's six walls. All were empty. Angervyle's books, I assumed, were stored in the many trunks arranged around the room, of varying sizes and laid out like a labyrinth of low walls.

'You'll pardon the spice,' said Quincey. 'An excellent preservative of books.'

Though perhaps not in such quantity, I thought.

'Bishop Angervyle's library was different. Distinctive in every respect. Richard de Bury, you see, collected only those books that matter most to our modern minds.' He rubbed his hands and approached one of the closer chests.

'I've been told that the bishop was quite particular about his selections,' I said. 'No law texts, for example.'

Quincey nodded. 'The bishop had no patience for law, nor even for much theology, and those subjects he did favour did not exactly endear him to his superiors. The abbot here in Oxford – and this was before Angervyle's elevation to the bishopric – was unwilling to give over a room to his manuscripts. He regarded the books, and also Angervyle himself, as vulgar.'

'Vulgar?'

'Supposedly it demeaned the order to be seeking out wisdom in the works of pagans. In lewd poems, in the spectacles of Seneca, even in the obscenities of Juvenal, one of his particular favourites. So here they are, left to rot in chests, with no dedicated library to house them, despite the talk of all the new building to come. I worry that these, these *monks*' – he shuddered, as if swallowing a spider – 'will ruin his legacy. That on my death the collection will be destroyed.'

I surveyed the chamber, wondering if Quincey would let me buy the whole lot.

'Or divided, with some books going to one college, others to another. The bishop's fondest wish was to have all his books housed in a single room, made available for lending.'

'So he writes in the *Philobiblon*.' I looked around at the many chests, feeling greedy. 'Did he make a catalogue?'

'After a fashion. But the bishop's own lists were organized into rather eccentric categories: books lending themselves to happiness, books sorting virtue from vice, books concerning animals. So I took it upon myself in the years after his death

234

to systematize the collection. Even so, the handlist I've assembled leaves much to be desired, I'm afraid.'

He led me to a standing desk. On it was a volume of moderate thickness, its clasps locked, its binding chained to the wall. Quincey inserted a small key into the clasp lock, and the tight straps sprang apart at the buckle. 'Here, then.'

I peered down at the neat lists, alphabetized by the author's name if known, by the work's opening words if not. 'This will be enormously helpful,' I said as I scanned incipits.

'I hope so, Master Gower.' He modestly bent his stick-like neck. 'Though perhaps you might save yourself some time if you tell me what you are after. A particular work?'

'Well, I suppose you might know of the author I'm looking for.' I watched the man carefully. 'What significance does the name "Lollius" have to you, or did it have to Angervyle?'

'Lollius, you say.' He rubbed his nose, looking everywhere but into my eyes. '*Lolliuslolliuslolliuslolliuslollius*,' he intoned, his voice running an unmelodious gamut from high to low and back again. 'Do I recall a moment in Petronius, perhaps, or was it Sallust?' He squinted. 'Horace,' he said at last, with a snap of his long fingers.

'Horace?'

'Wrote a famous *epistola ad Lollium*.'

'A letter to Lollius?' I said. My hand twitched.

'And an ode. Do you know Horace?'

'A bit.'

Quincey walked to a trunk against the far wall and came back with a moderate volume opened to a middle folio. With a growing excitement, I moved to a position near the door and sat on a trunk to read the Horace as Quincey puttered around the chamber, dusting the empty shelves, straightening the trunks, fooling with the latches. Lollius, I discerned from the ode's first lines, was evidently a judge, consul, and well-regarded public figure in Rome. Horace had written the ode as a kind of promise to save the man's memory from oblivion. The lines were also a paean to good and virtuous service for the state: Horace praised Lollius for his keen sense of ethics in his work, bending decisions to the right, turning away from bribes, facing down death while spurning the rewards of wealth.

I turned the page and frowned. Where I had expected more lines to Lollius, a new poem began, this one the epistle to the same man, which the scribe had inserted between the two Horatian odes. I read it quickly. It largely duplicated the content of the first ode; the second was addressed to another man altogether.

Neither the epistle nor the ode said anything about Britain, nor kings, nor cards; not a word about prophecies, nor assassinations, nor conspirators. Horace's Lollius, as I should have realized when Quincey first mentioned him, could not possibly be the same man who allegedly authored the *Liber de Mortibus Regum Anglorum*. The Roman poet was writing during the lifetime of Christ Himself, fully a thousand years prior to the demise of the Conqueror, the first kingly death prophesied in the *De Mortibus*.

No cause for despair, though. I had been in Angervyle's library all of a quarter hour and had already acquired a significant bit of information. I looked over at Quincey, who was inspecting a binding. 'Do you know of this Lollius's poems?'

He shook his head. 'Only his memory, and only in that Horatian ode and letter.'

'No other Lollius, then? An English one, perhaps?'

'Doesn't clap a bell, I'm afraid.'

'Though perhaps his works are mentioned elsewhere in Angervyle's library.'

'Anything is possible, Master Gower.' With this enigmatic reply Quincey set the volume back in its trunk and rose, brisk and businesslike. 'In any case, you're free to inspect the collection at your will.' He pointed to two trunks near my knee. 'These crates contain all the bishop's holdings in *historia*. Chronicles of England, of times past, and the writings of the ancient historians of Rome, Lucan and such. And here we have books of science.' Four trunks, arrayed against the western wall. 'Aristotle's *Physics*, treatises of Galen and Hippocrates, even the works of al-Kindi on astronomy and cryptography, translated from the Arabic.'

'Cryptography?'

Quincey gave me a queer look, his left brow edging up his broad forehead. 'The art of secret writing, Master Gower. Transpositions, ciphers. Such techniques are employed mainly by alchemists, dabblers in magic, that sort. And spies, of course.'

I felt a quiet thrill. Tom Tugg at Newgate, Ralph Strode at the Guildhall, and now Peter de Quincey here in Oxford, all quick to invoke the shadow of spies, unnumbered and anonymous, spectres of treachery and deceit in a time of war. I thought of the dead girl in the Moorfields – a French spy, according to Strode – and again I had the sense of a connection unmade, of knowledge hidden beneath veils I could not part.

Quincey soon left me alone in the chamber – as alone as I could be with hundreds of books around me. I decided to begin with the histories, selecting four volumes from the first trunk and taking them to the reading desk. Settling on the stool and adjusting the candles, I arrayed the four manuscripts before me, admiring the unique embossments tooled on covers of various shades.

No time for pleasure, I reminded myself. My king prophesied to die, and here I sit, plucking at chronicles. Secret writing indeed. First the Bede – no, Geoffrey of Monmouth. With a sigh and a squint at the crabbed script, I read, my vision, for once, unclouded.

The strangers had arrived on the day of St Dominic. They departed on the Saturday following the Feast of the Assumption of the Blessed Virgin.

At first the lady would not admit the truth to herself, and in the early weeks it was easy enough to ignore her condition. The first time she missed her menses she put it off to the trauma of her rape, the evil humours the foreign prince had left within her. After the second time she examined her frame in a glass. Her belly was undeniably growing.

The daughter watched as her mother cursed her fortune, tore her hair, beat at her breasts. She swallowed anise, birthwort, chamomile by the mouthful, hoping with these herbs to abort the child. At one moment she reached for a knife, planning to tear out this foul life. At another she vowed to throw herself off a chalk cliff. Yet each time she would relent, unable to abandon her daughter.

Soon enough it became impossible to hide her condition. The lady sensed her people turning on her. Oh, they would still serve her, carry out her commands in their dutiful way. Yet she had lost their goodwill.

A lady in these times, bearing the child of a lord not her own? Unthinkable, and yet there she was.

With her sixth month came new tidings of the war. A miserable defeat for her lord's king, and as this bleakness descended the lady gave in fully to her despair. On the morning chosen for her death, she sat for a while in the outer courtyard, dandling her daughter one last time. The girl knew something was awry. Yet even as they kissed their farewells, they saw in the distance a cloud of dust, smaller than the last, moving slowly across the marches. The lady squinted against the scorching sun. Bevelled or and sable, six hawks argent ascending the middle rank.

The livery of her lord and husband.

The lady locked herself in her apartments and for two days would not see him, despite his pleas. Nor would his men nor his servants tell him what they knew, though in their averted eyes he read a calamity.

Had she been ill, with pestilence or some other malady? Was she sick even now, afraid to pass on a mortal blight to her lord? Was she disfigured?

Yes, the lady thought. Disfigured. She stripped to her thin shift and threw open the door, awaiting the sword.

Call to mind, my heart, the story of Joseph's trouble about Mary. It is not a story to be found in the Gospels, where Joseph thinks for a mere verse about divorce but then accepts the truth of the incarnation. I speak of the Father Joseph we see in the minstrels' pageants. This is the Joseph our knight knew best: the foolish Joseph, the husband convinced his pregnant wife has sinned with another man.

An angel came to you? Is that your claim? Ha! A man in the likeness of an angel, say I, come to cuckold me in sight of my relations — and you, my fresh wife, claim to be carrying the Messiah, though still a virgin?

Yet even in this Joseph finally relents, his anger calmed by the angel into a cool acceptance of his fate as the earthly husband of the mother of our Lord.

The mores of the time dictated that the knight should have cast her out of his home, exiled her as a harlot and a whore. Instead he listened to his lady's account of her attack by this foreign prince. Though her swollen body was there for all to see, the knight would not put his wife away, as even Joseph was tempted at first to do. Wondrously, he wept with her instead, promising her his enduring love and protection.

It was not to be. On the Tuesday after Pentecost, in the last year of Pedro the Cruel's reign, God poured spirit into the body of an infant boy, and extracted it from the flesh of his mother. The little girl would hear her mother's death-screams for years to come.

240

The new child looked so much like his mother – and, the girl could plainly see, his malevolent father. Yet from the moment of the boy's birth the knight took him as his own. One of the most self-sacrificing, self-denying loves in all history was this lord's for a son not his own. They made a strange family, these three, yet there was a certain nobility to their devotion that inspired awe from more charitable souls.

Love can be sustaining even in the worst of circumstances. Bare life, though, can be passing hard to endure. As the infant grew into a boy, the people started to look upon their lord with ill will. Betrayed by a strumpet of Mahound! And this bastard will be our lord's heir, and thus our own future lord?

No longer did they treat the knight with such solicitous fealty. There were whispers of insubordination, and gossip in the town.

The situation could not stand. So the knight gathered his most loyal men, no more than thirty in number, and with his children left their home. This best of lords gave up his castle to become a wanderer, a knight errant served only by the few dozen men who would join him on the road.

Though weakened in spirit, our knight was still strong in body, more than capable of leading a company of men in battle. He could sell these skills. He became a knight for hire, peddling the might of his men in the wars of that era, from the Straits of Gibraltar to the ports of Marseille and Toulon, adding other wayfaring men to his company as they went.

The knight taught his daughter well in the course of their wanderings: how to butcher a hart, how to fight with her fists and teeth, how to ward off brigands with a knife. By the age of twelve she was a fierce, rodent-like thing, unrecognizable as the daughter of a wealthy lord.

La Comadrejita: the Little Weasel, as she was known among the camp women. Small, lithe, quick on her feet, always sneaking up on the warriors and their women, dodging grasps and slaps, lifting coins and shiny objects from pouches and shelves. These she would give to her brother as tokens of their love, extracting solemn promises from the little boy that he would do her bidding in all things.

From her father's men his growing daughter learned the many tongues spoken around the great inland sea – not only French and Italian but the languages of the Jews and the Moors, and the mixed tongue of sailors. She took a new name, too, after an old Roman town in the Dauphiné where her father's company wintered one year, and after the orange scarf she wore in her hair.

For eight long years she roamed with her father's company among the hills and rivers of many lands. If not the happiest of girls, she was content, though the memory of her mother's ravishment stayed with her always, like an aching tooth too frequently tongued.

Sorrow comes in waves, it is said. In her sixteenth year the girl fell ill along with her father, her brother, and many of their company. The fever slew the weakest among them: a half-dozen ageing soldiers, two camp women heavy with child – and her brother. He was buried on a high cliff above the sea, with no priest to say Mass. So she said it herself for this sweetest of boys, murmuring through narrowed lips those rote snatches of unknown Latin heard so often in her life.

In his bleakness at the loss of his son, and seeing his daughter's devastation, her father made a decision. His child needed a home, a chance at a life worth living.

He had heard tidings of a large company of mercenaries serving the signore of Milan, a much larger assemblage than his own, well managed and organized. So the knight travelled with his diminished company to Lombardy. There he sold himself and his men to this company, a wealthy band of mercenaries hiring their might to the most powerful magnates in the land: kings, dukes, popes.

The leader of this company was a fearsome lord, tall, haughty, quick of wit and quicker of cruelty. Yet he was revered by his *subordinates, and feared by those who hired his engines and his men.*

His name was Ser Giovanni Acuto. In your tongue, my sweet, Sir John Hawkwood.

TWENTY-NINE

San Donato a Torre, near Florence

'It's remarkable, Sir John,' said Adam Scarlett. 'And alarming.'

Hawkwood, fresh from his weekly bath, had thrown on a loose robe. He peered into the mottled glass, shaving his neck. 'Perhaps it's nothing,' he said.

That morning a servingwoman and her husband had been cleaning one of the smaller *villette* to make room for an envoy from Rome. Four of the chancellor's clerks had vacated the week before, having made a mess of the outbuilding, and it needed a top-to-bottom scrubbing. Her husband had been shovelling old coals from the main hearth when he came across a half-burned quire behind the grate. The edges were badly charred, several pages rendered unreadable. Yet there were at least a dozen nearly full sheets with legible letters and mysterious signs scribbled across both sides. The man had promptly brought the quire to the *condottiero*.

'The hand matches Il Critto's, I'll be bound,' said Scarlett, paging through the quire and eager to examine it further. 'This could only have been his work.'

Hawkwood towelled off. 'So what did our friend leave behind?'

Scarlett shook his head. 'Hard to tell, sire. Only one of these pages makes any sense to me. It's in Italian, if it even deserves the name.' Scarlett read it aloud. A short set of awkward sentences conjugating the verb *nascondere*. *I nascondere, si nascondono, si nasconde . . .*

> *I hide my knowledge beneath my words.*
> *You hide your ignorance beneath your power.*
> *He hides his treason beneath his loyalty.*

The fumblings of a man still practising a tongue not his own.

When Scarlett had finished reading through the grammatical exercise Hawkwood shrugged, reached for his hose. 'So he was honing his Italian. What does this prove, Adam? We've never had reason to doubt his loyalty.'

'Nothing, Sir John. Merely that he used this quire for casual writing in addition to his ciphers. As for the rest . . .'

'Well?'

'It's like reading pebbles on sand. None of it means anything to me, and I don't have the quality of mind capable of sorting it out. Il Critto kept his ciphers to himself.'

'As I warned him he should, on peril of his life, and damn me for a fool!' He laughed gruffly, then considered the matter. 'I suppose we need some help, then.'

Scarlett agreed. That afternoon he left for Siena, where he asked around at the *studium*. He was back two mornings later with the sharpest mind on the faculty. A purse, a polite request, a few vague threats: there had been little resistance. With Hawkwood there rarely was.

In the gallery the *condottiero* invited the dazed man to sit with him on the padded bench he used at his desk. The wide surface was taken up in large part with a marked-up map of Tuscany, Lombardy, Romagna, and the Veneto: troop movements and garrisons, debts owed to the company, the intricate web of Hawkwood's empire. He liked to hold his strategic conversations here, where his power could be spread out before him for the benefit of his visitors.

'In what discipline is your training, Maestro Desilio?'

'Law, Ser Giovanni, at Bologna. Though logic is my greater strength.'

Hawkwood glanced at Scarlett. 'Well good, then. We need a logician's mind to crack these rocky nuts. Did my man Scarletto explain all this to you?'

'He did not, Ser Giovanni.'

So Hawkwood did. 'What you see before you, sir, this mess of scorched parchments and half-burned papers? This is all that was left behind by one of my associates.'

'Associates, Ser Giovanni?'

'He left our service earlier this year. His mother dies, he's the sole heir, he thinks of home – the details don't particularly matter. Though his profession mattered a great deal to me, as it soon shall to you. You see, this man was my cryptographer, Master Desilio.'

'Your – your cryptographer?'

'Il Critto, we called him,' said Hawkwood. 'The man responsible for taking my dispatches and letters and casting them into cipher for delivery abroad. To my garrisons, to my contacts in Rome, Paris, London. You are familiar with cryptography?'

Despite the peculiar situation the logician looked intrigued, provoked by the intellectual challenge. 'I am, Ser Giovanni. At the *studium* we have several books on this craft. By Master Roger Bacon, by al-Kindi the Moor, the latter translated into Latin. I've not studied them carefully, but I know the rudiments, and I can certainly loan you these books.'

'Excellent,' Hawkwood said, nodding eagerly. 'Though I have a different sort of loan in mind.'

Scarlett watched them for a while, the way Hawkwood had of warming up his visitors, making them feel comfortable in his presence, even when he was delivering unwelcome news. Yes, you will be my guest here at San Donato, at least for a time. No, you won't be going back to Siena today, nor tomorrow. Better to write a letter, requesting that the books in question be sent back with my man. You will certainly be paid well, and the *studium* compensated for your absence, however extended it should prove.

'Do you have any further questions or concerns about this arrangement?' Hawkwood asked him.

The man paged through the quire, his mouth at a rueful slant. 'Only that this task, Ser Giovanni . . .'

'Yes?'

'These sorts of ciphers do not lend themselves to expediency. Breaking them could take – it could take months.'

Hawkwood's smile stiffened. 'Months I don't have. Weeks? Perhaps. Days? Even better.'

The logician, knowing better than to shake his head, took a heavy breath. 'I will do my best, Ser Giovanni.'

Scarlett watched Hawkwood incline his head. 'I know you will, Maestro Desilio.'

THIRTY

Paternoster Row

From the northwest corner of St Paul's churchyard Edgar peered across the busy lane, his head filled with the muddle and din, his stomach rumbling with hunger. He'd hardly eaten in days, relying on the sparse alms of the parishes as he skulked around the city, trying to elude the constables, and that hook-scarred man on Gropecunt Lane. Swyving was a hard business, yet it was nothing compared to the week he'd experienced as one of the city's thousand beggars: sleeping in abandoned horsestalls, mouldy bread plucked from gutters, the cold anonymity of London's poorest souls, trying to stay invisible or feign lameness so they wouldn't be put out at the gates. Yet now it was time.

He pushed himself off the booth and walked toward Paternoster Row, past several parchmenters' shops. Halfway down the street a shop matron, hair tied back in a simple scarf, bargained with a neat-looking man over a bundle at her feet. A reeve or steward, Edgar guessed, commissioned to purchase parchment for his employer.

'That's too high, Mistress Pinkley,' the man wheedled. 'The

brothers of the Charterhouse toil for the Lord, not for themselves.'

'The sum wasn't too high for my late husband, nor too high for me. You should get a smell of what I charge the friary.' A harsh cackle. 'But for this stack of lambskin? Four shillings a dozen is passing fair for the holy disciples of the Grand Chartreuse, and I'll have not a penny less. The finest lambs of Sunbury-on-Thames in these skins, nor will you find a thinner lot on Paternoster Row.'

Edgar waited while the man paid and trudged off with the parchments. The parchmentress turned to him with a ready smile which faded somewhat when she saw this vagrant at her shop door.

'What is it?'

He looked down at his hands. 'A book, mistress. A book to sell.'

'A book to sell, eh?' She took in the shoddy hose, the frayed cap. 'Most come to Paternoster Row looking to purchase books, not sell them. And what's a bairn like you doing with a book?'

'Came into my possession, willed me by my mother, bless her,' he lied. 'I have no reading to speak of and don't know the matter of it but I believe it's a valuable thing.'

The parchmentress grinned. 'A primer is it, a painted book of hours that's been in your family? A Bible perhaps, or the blessed Psalter?'

Edgar held it out. The parchmentress looked down at the book and took it briskly. Untying the thong with an adept tug, she gave the embroidery an admiring glance, handed the cloth back to Edgar, then smoothed her hands over the volume's covers.

'Thin little thing.' She flipped through the pages without, it seemed, reading a word, inspecting the thickness of the parchment, fingering several of the leaves with an expert feel for quality. 'Heavy, the skins are. Could be scraped, I suppose, yield a clean book to write anew.' She closed the manuscript and slapped it against an open palm. 'Six pence.'

Edgar felt his jaw slacken. Six pennies, for a book sought by half of London? He shook his head. 'Not for this book, madam. Five – nay, six nobles, and I'll have not a penny less.'

The parchmentress just stared, listening to her own words used against her, then burst into great peals of laughter, slapping her leg. 'Six nobles, he says! Not a penny less! Why, aren't you a gamey little fella! Tom! Get out here, friend!'

The neighbouring shopkeeper appeared in his doorway. Edgar reached for the book. The parchmentress released it with a little shove, accompanied by a delighted recounting of Edgar's demand for six nobles and he'll have not a penny less, Tom, not a penny less. Edgar turned away and made for the corner.

So parchmenters, he'd learned, would find no interest in the book. Their interest in books was like men's in maudlyns: of value for the outer aspect, the fineness of the skin. Not so much the words – and it was the words, Edgar suspected, that gave this book whatever value it had.

He was now on a smaller byway cutting down from Paternoster Row. Three-storey houses with shops at the street level, a glaze of sulphur on the air. The tradesmen here seemed to specialize in painting pages with all the florid colours in God's creation. Illuminators' shops displayed fine samples of their work pegged on to smoothed boards hooked beside their doors. Several painters had pulled their stools and desks out on the lane that dry day, and the sun had reached a point in its arc that allowed their work to show to its best advantage. He paused behind a painter crafting an enormous page filled with black marks in square and oblong shapes. At the top left side of the page a cluster of singing monks stood inside a letter *P* – yes, a *P*, Edgar knew that much, and the *P* was coloured in a shade of blue-green he imagined as the hue of the southern seas.

His shoulders sagged as he walked to the end of the lane. For these painters, books were things of beauty. This one had no beauty to it, that was for certain: no pictures aside from the hurried sketches at the edges of the pages, no great letters filled with holy men or dragons, no blue-green hues to ravish you with longing for the oceans of the earth.

He stepped on to a slightly wider lane. Here at least a dozen men sat at desks, in shops and out on the street, pointing ink on to surfaces of varying size. Like Master Strode's clerks at the Guildhall, Edgar thought, putting letters to skin. A street of words.

Halfway up it he stopped to look over the shoulder of a younger man practising his script on a large, rough sheet: a smooth line, a delicate curve, then he scratched it all out and started again, then again, until he noticed Edgar's presence. He half-turned with a friendly smile. 'Help you?'

'You're – you're a scriv—a scrivener, yes?' he stammered.

'This be the shop of Roger Ybott, master stationer of Creed Lane,' he said. 'Tom Fish is my own name, sole apprentice to Master Ybott. Pleased to help you, whatever your wish.'

He considered his reply. 'Is your craft in the words of books then?'

He frowned. 'The words of books?'

Edgar squinted at the writing desk. 'These parts of London by St Paul's be filled with the bookish crafts, all different bits of it. Those that scrape the skin, ready it for writing—'

'Parchmenters on Paternoster Row, sure, sure,' said Tom Fish, head bobbing. 'Though they don't do their scraping in the city, just come here to sell out of their shops.'

'Then there be the painters, colouring the pages with every shade you ever—'

'The limners along Creed Lane.'

'And in this street there's writing,' said Edgar. 'Those who lime and scrape, those who paint, and here be those who write.'

'We do our share of the writing, sure,' said Fish, finally getting his meaning. 'A commission from an abbot or an earl, we'll put pen to vellum quicker than you can say your Ave Marie here on Ave Maria Lane.' He laughed at his own joke. 'Stationer's work's important work, important as you'll find in all London.'

Edgar pulled out the book. 'Would you be so kind as to value this, Master Fish?'

Fish looked surprised, though also pleased to lend his expertise. 'Let us see here,' he said, taking the book and handling it with a careful adeptness. 'Mm . . . hmm . . . ahh, yes . . .' he murmured, showing off. Like the parchmentress, Tom Fish seemed to be examining the book at first only for its physical make-up, tugging at the pages, holding the spine against the sky. Then he started reading from the beginning, at first with a neutral curiosity, then with a slight frown, then, as he read on, with a widening of the eyes that made Edgar want to turn and flee. At one point he gasped softly. He flipped ahead to the final pages and scanned. He took a large step backwards, holding the book out in front of him as if it were a serpent about to bite.

He looked at Edgar, eyes wide with fright. An older man walked out of the shop. 'What's this then?' he demanded. The shop's master stood only slightly taller than his apprentice, though his hewn face matched his craft, his eyes narrowed in a permanent squint, deep lines reaching for his ears. On his thinning hair he wore a round hat of blue silk, embroidered letters in black and white filling every inch.

Tom Fish turned to his master. 'This young fellow here, Master Ybott, he – he wished to have this book examined, and so I've been about it for the last little while.'

'To sell, Master Ybott,' Edgar clarified. 'I have no reading, so books be of no use to me excepting what price they might fetch.'

Ybott took the book from Tom, taking no notice of his apprentice's state. He read selectively through the thin volume until he, too, went pale. He looked at Edgar, then at Fish. 'Well now,' he said, his voice husky. 'Not a book to bandy about, is it? And you've been carrying this on your person? Just walking along with it, not a care for your head?'

'Yes, sir – I mean no, sir,' said Edgar. 'I know not the words nor the meaning of it. But it it *must* be worth more than sixpence, yeah?'

'More than sixpence,' said Ybott, staring at him. Recovering himself, he cleared his throat, leaned toward Edgar, and rested a firm hand on his shoulder. 'How came you by this book, young – what is your name, young man?'

'I am called Edgar, sir.'

'How came you by this book, Edgar?'

Edgar crossed his arms. 'That be no man's affair but my own, sir. The book be rightfully mine now, and I mean to sell it for what I'm able.'

Ybott gave him one of his deep squints. 'You don't know what pile you've stepped into, Edgar. You best come inside.' He held out his other hand, gesturing toward his shop.

Edgar stood his ground, recalling the encounter with Bickle, the beadle of Cheap Ward. He had no desire to enter yet another man's shop, nor to be assayed further about this damned book. 'I'd rather not, sir, if it be all the same to you.' He stuck out his jaw. 'Now give me back my book.'

Ybott tilted his head, holding a tense smile. 'As you wish. Be warned, though, this book is a dangerous thing to its owner, whether an illiterate vagrant, a Cambridge master' – he paused – 'or a young woman taking on a man's role.'

Edgar shrank away from him. Ybott had got it wrong, but not by much.

'We're in the business of books,' the stationer said, pressing him. 'We know what's best when it comes to the worst, yes?' Sensing his hesitation, Ybott went on: 'You appear hungry, or lost. There's a desperate look about you. Come inside, please, and let me lend you whatever bookish wisdom I possess.'

Could Edgar trust him? Even as he supposed the man's warmth to be motivated by something other than Edgar's well-being, he felt his suspicions dissolving – foolishly, perhaps. Yet Ybott was not a constable, nor a beadle, nor, he trusted, a murderer. So he allowed himself to be guided into the stationer's shop, the apprentice close behind. Once the three of them were inside, Tom Fish shut the door. At the sound of the latch Edgar shuddered, wondering what lay before him.

THIRTY-ONE

Ave Maria Lane

From the top of Paternoster Row, Millicent Fonteyn watched the stationer guide Edgar Rykener into his shop. The apprentice followed them inside, his worried glance in both directions telling Millicent all she needed to know.

She surveyed the narrow lane. The trio had attracted little attention from the neighbouring craftsmen, all busy at their work. Yet there was one of them, a man standing in front of a shop just across the lane, who had witnessed the interaction. He was staring at the door with a hard intensity that gave Millicent a prickle of concern. She and Agnes weren't the only ones searching London for a book. There were others on the watch, others working on behalf of whatever forces or factions sought to use its perilous contents to their advantage. Others looking to take, and to kill.

She stepped out and signalled for Agnes to join her. Two other girls waved in relief as Millicent dismissed them with a grim nod. For days now, and at Bess Waller's orders, a clutch of Southwark mauds had taken turns lying in wait for Eleanor Rykener in these precincts, some watching

Paternoster Row itself, others surveying Ave Maria Lane, still others keeping an eye on Amen Lane above Pembroke's Inn. All setting a net for the wretched little fish, the swerver who'd stolen the book out from under Bess Waller's nose and now sought to sell it for whatever it would bring.

Now they'd found her. Him.

Yet it appeared they were too late. How could Edgar be so foolish? Did he have no idea what it was he possessed, how much of his own future might turn on the fate of the book he'd stolen, and now sought to sell to half the book-makers of London? For soon the master stationer would realize he had little choice but to inform the authorities that a book prophesying the death of King Richard had come into his possession. Nor could Millicent steal it from the stationer as Eleanor had stolen it from the Pricking Bishop, for all the master's attention would be on the volume for the duration of its stay in his shop.

Could she and Agnes take the thing by force, grab a few logs on the way in and have at it? Hardly. A master and his young apprentice, hale men both, would be more than a match for them, even if the sisters took them by surprise. Besides, she reasoned, the streets in this neighbourhood were so narrow escape would be impossible. The guildsman would raise the hue and cry, summon a constable. It would all be over within minutes, the sisters taken before they got as far as the Boar's Head.

'So,' said Agnes. 'Let's walk in.'

'What's that?'

Agnes looked at her. 'Let's walk right in there, talk to Eleanor. She'll give it back, come with us.'

'Have you gone wood, Ag? She's the one stole the book from us!'

'She'll listen to reason, if I know Eleanor Rykener. She'll listen to me.'

Millicent scoffed. 'Listen to that man's coin, I'll be bound. That's what he – what she's here for.'

'Eleanor's not like you, Mil.' Agnes's tone was suddenly hard. 'Sure, she wants good shills like any maud of London. But that's not what's most important to her.' She looked away. 'Not like you.'

Millicent, stung, stared at her sister's profile. 'Well,' she said, then looked back up Ave Maria Lane. 'Maybe you're right.'

'No maybe about it, Mil. We go in there, get her, get the book, she'll come right along.'

Millicent smoothed her dress, held out a hand. 'Come, then.'

They walked up Ave Maria Lane with locked arms and furtive looks at the work of the scriveners on either side. When they reached the shop door, Millicent turned to face the oaken surface, which was free of tracery and grillwork; nor was there a lock. Blowing out a breath, she pushed it open.

A one-room shop. Clean, well lit, books displayed on single shelves. Two writing desks faced one another in the middle of the shop. The scrivener, seated at one of them with his apprentice and Edgar standing before him, looked up in surprise. On the desk the book lay open.

'What's this?' he demanded.

'We came for that,' said Millicent, pointing. 'Our book, just there.'

'*Your* book?' Ybott looked from the sisters to Edgar. 'The young man here tells me it's his.'

Edgar raised his chin. 'That it is, sir.'

'Then you two best be on your way,' said Ybott.

'The book is ours,' Millicent insisted. 'It was given to my sister by – it was given to her, weeks ago. You hand it over or I'll summon a ward constable.'

'Will you now?'

'Get out, Ag,' Edgar snarled. 'Both of you, now, *get out*!'

'You know better than that, Eleanor,' said Agnes, conciliation in her voice. 'You know I be your good gossip.'

'That right, Agnes Fonteyn?' said Edgar. 'Leaving me high and dry on Gropecunt Lane, finding that killed girl, that bloody hammer with her brains still on it? That how you treat your "good gossip"?'

Millicent winced at Edgar's use of her sister's full name, and the incautious crowing of their profession. The scriveners, she saw, were taking it all in. Gropecunt Lane, a bloody hammer, a dead girl.

'We are taking the book,' she said quickly. 'This one stole it, and now we're taking it back.' Ybott started to protest. Millicent raised her hand and stepped right up to him, threatening. 'Think about it. Think about a constable, or the ward beadle stepping in here once you summon him. What do you suppose he'll do? Comes in a stationer's shop to find this book of prophecies in your possession, what do you suppose he'll think?'

'Now, look here, by what right—'

'That it belongs to a few maudlyns wandering by, trying to scare up cock on Ave Maria Lane?'

Ybott was speechless. Tom Fish shot a fearful glance at Edgar, then at Agnes.

'Would *you* believe such a thing, sir, if this one here' – Millicent pointed at Edgar – 'hadn't slunk up from St Paul's to sell it to you himself?'

A feeble shrug.

'What you *would* believe is what's before you: a London stationer closeted in his shop with a treasonous book, trying to pin the blame on some poor maud he brought within to swyve of a spring afternoon.'

Ybott turned away. Millicent approached the writing desk,

lifted the book, and dropped it in her coat's broad inner pocket. She turned on her heel and walked to the door.

'Wait, Mil.'

Millicent turned back to her sister. Agnes approached Edgar, whose face registered a mix of confusion and fear. Agnes reached forward and put a hand on his cheek. Edgar's response was considerably less gentle: a hard slap to Agnes's face that rang through the small shop.

'Where you been, Agnes?' he demanded, his voice hoarse with rage. 'Not on Gropecunt Lane, nor on Cornhull, nor in Southwark, nor lying dead on the Moorfields.' He stomped a foot on the rushes. 'Like that girl I thought was *you.*'

Agnes shook her head against the tears. 'Oh, Ellie, I don't know what to say to you, dearheart.'

Millicent opened the door a crack. The tradesman who had been watching from across the street was gone. She stepped forward and grasped Edgar's wrist. 'Come along. You be a part of this now as much as I am myself, and Agnes here.'

He tried to pull away. Millicent tightened her grip. 'Don't be a child.'

Millicent felt Edgar's acquiescence in the loosening of his muscles. She tugged, and he finally allowed himself to be led from the shop. By the next bell they were halfway across the bridge.

They passed the following days at the Pricking Bishop, stowed in a third-storey room overlooking Rose Alley. It was sour in there, the linens strewn across the pallet crusted with the spent passions of the men who dried their parts on them every day. The book rested in an alcove beneath a low shelf, just within the door. Thomas Pinchbeak, Millicent felt certain, was determined to purchase it, despite the delay caused by Eleanor Rykener's theft, and she was equally determined to sell it for the greatest sum she could extract.

✛

On the fourth night, in the stillest hours, they awoke to hoarse shouts on the street below. Cracking a shutter, Millicent looked out to see five men on horseback, dark hoods and cloaks obscuring any features. They were clustered up by Smith's Rents, their animals circling in the darkness. One of them dismounted and approached the Pricking Bishop, his short sword glistening at his side.

The shouts had come not from him, though, but from his unexpected antagonist.

'Y'aren't Southwark men, that be sure.'

Millicent leaned out. Down below stood St Cath, yawping in the lantern-light, a withered arm in the air, her shift billowing obscenely in the night breezes. The old woman pointed up the alley in the direction of the palace. 'By what right do you trounce in the bishop's liberties? By whose warrant?'

St Cath's crazed bravery soon brought company. Three maudlyns joined her on the street to confront the armed man. They were joined in turn by a dozen girls from the other houses, all shouting at the company to leave the stews the way they had come. Soon nearly twenty maudlyns of Southwark had encircled the men, cackling a righteous din to fill the stews. More lanterns were brought out, the lane filling with a shimmering glow.

Millicent moved for a better view, and her elbow pushed the shutter slightly to her right. The movement drew the man's attention. He looked up. His face was covered, all but his eyes and forehead wrapped in a black scarf tucked between his doublet and cape. For a long moment, in the glare of the lamps, she stood frozen by his stare. His eyes, deep and cruel, smouldered as he memorized her face. Then he looked away.

Now more distant cries, the echo of metal on metal, the clatter of hooves, and everyone's attention was drawn up Rose Alley. Joined by Agnes and Eleanor at the window,

Millicent heard before she saw the opposing company bearing down hard past the Vine. The man on foot turned and sprinted back to his horse, joining his fellows in a mad dash in the opposite direction.

For these were the Bishop of Winchester's liberties, the unannounced intrusion by the strange company a violation of ecclesiastical jurisdiction. The bishop did not take such incursions lightly, nor did his men, a company of which had been dispatched from the palace's main guardhouse into the stews. It was an unfair fight, for though the strangers had the advantage of surprise, Winchester's men were greater in number. Within minutes the violators had been chased through Bishopspark and into Winchester's Wild, where they would scatter themselves to the winds.

Once the street had calmed there were sounds of shutters slamming along the way. Bess Waller appeared at the door, her cheeks ruddy in the candlelight. 'You need to leave, all you, at first bell. They were here for that book, plain as the sun.' She did a circuit of the room, shoving their few things into a basket and sack.

'But where are we to go, *mère*?' Agnes asked her as she pulled on her shoes. 'We have no place, nor coin.' Eleanor huddled at her side, watching the exchange.

'Not her concern, Ag.' Millicent was pulling on her own shoes, the once-elegant skins by now full of holes, not all of them patched. 'Our good mother doesn't bother herself with inconveniences like the welfare of her daughters.'

Bess came to stand by the bed. Stooping, she pressed something into Millicent's hand. Cold, metallic. Millicent looked down, hoping for coins. She saw a key.

'Ditch Street by the Split Shill, just within Aldgate,' said Bess, her night breath foul on Millicent's cheek. 'Small place there I've leased four years now. It's empty, has been a good while. They won't look for you there, that's sure.'

This, for Bess Waller, counted as generosity: the loan of an unused hole across the river. Millicent looked at her mother, wondering what moral world those unwavering eyes saw when they peered into a glass. Though I suppose I'm not one to judge, she thought. She closed her eyes, then her hand over the key.

THIRTY-TWO

Logic Lane, Oxford

Sir John Clanvowe, standing at a trestle table, poured wine from a silvered flagon. 'We will have an additional guest this evening.'

I masked my displeasure with a small sip. A seventh unproductive day among Angervyle's book chests had put me in a sour mood. 'Delightful. The wine, I mean, though I'm sure your guest will be as well. Who is he?'

'I shall let it be a surprise.' Clanvowe spread the frayed ends of his coat across his uncushioned chair. 'Let me hear about your week in Oxford. Have you enjoyed yourself?'

'Not particularly,' I said, opting for honesty. Over the first several days I had felt like a starved man at a king's feast. So many new books to plumb with the raw excitement of a child, losing myself for hours at a time in these authors formerly known only by name and reputation. Yet the search had soon grown monotonous, as each new book failed to reveal anything about the elusive Lollius. After all that time among Bury's books I had started to experience the dark building behind the Durham grange as a hermit's cell.

In airing all of this for Clanvowe, though, I stayed vague, telling him I was in Oxford to track down some texts related to my next major work. We sat in his parlour, sparsely furnished with several chairs, a writing desk, and a short shelf of dusty books against one of the whitewashed walls beneath exposed timbers. Paid well for his service as a knight of the chamber, Clanvowe had been a stalwart in Gaunt's campaigns in Aquitaine, Castile, and France, and he was known to be quite rich. Despite his wealth, though, he lived like an Oxford student – if a well-armed one.

His finger traced the lip of our glass. 'There must be more to it than that, John, to pry you out of Southwark. There are plenty of books in London. What is it you hope to find among Bury's manuscripts? What brought you here, to Oxford?'

'I would ask you the same question.' I took the wine. 'I'd have thought you would spend every hour out of court at Radnorshire, honing your Welsh.'

His face loosened into a smile. 'And it's well honed indeed by this point, what with all the diplomacy I'm performing up and down the border for the king. The marcher lords are a restive bunch. Master connivers. As to my own purpose in Oxford? *Byddwch yn dysgu cyn bo hir*, my friend. And I asked first.'

'Impressive,' I said. Clanvowe's yellow whiskers were tensed, gathered in a thick bunch. 'You won't translate for me?'

'You'll learn soon enough,' he said.

'Learn what?'

'That's the answer to your question.'

'Which question?'

'Both of them, I suppose. Now,' he said, leaning forward to refresh the glass, 'to the purpose of your visit.'

I looked away, thoroughly muddled, already exhausted

with all the effort. I took a long drink of wine and watched the flickering shadows play on the knight's eyes. Sir John had come to Oxford fresh from the political turmoil of London, where all the talk was of war, spies, and factions. He was also a knight of the king's chamber, and though he was a friend, there was no question where his loyalties would go should he learn of a threat to Richard. This was precisely why I wanted to speak with him: however Clanvowe might react to the existence of the prophecy, he would do so with the king's best interests in mind. Yet by divulging the existence of the *De Mortibus*, I would be bringing its dark prophecies into King Richard's affinity for the first time, an irrevocable and potentially perilous step.

Making a decision, I turned back to my host. 'Do you know Horace?'

Clanvowe's brow dropped. 'Slightly. Peasants, slaves, philosophizing merchants. Not to my taste.'

'The odes are great achievements, though.'

'Is that so?'

'But very hard to find. Angervyle's must be one of a handful of copies in England.'

'Do you have a favourite?'

'The ninth ode of the fourth book.'

'What is its subject?'

I waited a moment. 'A poet named Lollius.'

Clanvowe flinched. I have you, I thought, pleased with myself. 'You know it, then?'

'I don't,' he said, recovering quickly. 'Though perhaps there's more you want to say about it.'

I was saved from accepting the challenge by the arrival of Clanvowe's other guest, signalled by a soft knock at the outer door, then a quiet exchange with Sir John's sole servant. We stood as the third man entered the parlour.

A priest, capped and robed in russet, a simple belt at his

waist. No other adornment, though the uncompromising blue of his eyes forced attention, as if roundels of lapis lazuli had been painted around his pupils. A beard, bushy and long, caped his neck. I recognized the man, had seen him on at least one occasion but couldn't place him. Clanvowe made his hostly bow and spread his hands. 'Master John Gower, Esquire, let me present the curate of Lutterworth, Father John Purvey.'

I maintained enough presence of mind to reach forward and clasp hands. Purvey was a young man, his grip on my arm strong with the righteous confidence of the fanatic. Secretary to John Wycliffe himself until the master's death the prior December, Purvey was known as a preacher and scholar of radical leanings, and if what I'd heard was true, he had had the main hand in Wycliffe's recent translation of the Bible, a notorious work that was even now being circulated among the conventicles.

The conversation remained superficial until a weak sop was served, at which point Purvey turned to me with a mischievous smile.

'We have much in common, Master Gower.'

'In what way, Father?' The broth, light and unsalted, tasted vaguely of almonds.

'We are both writers, for one.'

'Though our respective subjects speak to our differences.'

'And our commonalities. Your *Mirour de l'Omme* has struck a chord among the men of our persuasion.'

Our persuasion? I swallowed. 'How is that?'

'Well, for one, you're not shy about criticizing the church, even its most powerful sects.' Then, to my horror, Purvey quoted my own French: '"The friars preach poverty to all, but they're always stretching forth their hands for coin. They love their worldly comforts, but never do they seek employment. Instead they wander about in the habit of vagrants."'

266

He sipped, smacked his lips. 'Truer words have never been written about the friars. Not even by Master Wycliffe himself, bless his soul.'

Clanvowe laughed gruffly. Purvey tittered, and I met their amusement with an uncomfortable smile. 'You came prepared this evening, Father. I'm impressed.'

The conversation moved on, the remainder of the meal consisting of overdone rabbit in a mealy pie, with old mustard on the side. I picked at my portion, imagining that every bite had to be taken carefully, as if my very teeth might grind with heresy, though Clanvowe and Purvey were now chatting amiably about the priest's new living. 'Now that I'm at Lutterworth, it's difficult to get back to Oxford as often as I would like. But that may be for the good.' He looked down at his rabbit. 'It's time I remain in one place for a while, tend to the souls in my care.'

'A fine suggestion,' I said. 'After all, priests are as numerous as stars in the sky. But unlike stars, only two of a thousand know how to shine.'

Purvey gave me a nasty look. 'You question my sincerity, Master Gower.'

'Only your memory, Father Purvey.'

He wiped his lips. 'Take Wykeham, your Bishop of Winchester. The man has twelve livings to his name, all going to fund his castle and his liberties in Southwark, his fishing ponds and his whores. Yet how often do you think he visits those parishes? Once a year, if it suits his schedule?'

'He's a busy man,' I pointed out.

'If the priest of the parish can't live a virtuous life, how is he supposed to teach his parishioners to avoid sin? If gold rusts, what about iron? It's like a shepherd smeared with shit herding a flock of sheep, trying to keep them clean.' He pounded the table. 'This is the problem with the higher clergy, Gower. They've become barons, building obscene castles for themselves, taking on concubines and mistresses and God knows what else. This is why I support their disendowment so strongly. Why should our spiritual leaders also be our wealthiest possessioners?'

I looked at the nearest candle, amazed the man would say such a thing in my presence. 'That position has been condemned by the pope, Father. As you well know.'

'Which pope would that be?' he responded.

I looked at him, now truly shocked. To speak of disendowing the clergy was one thing; to question the English alliance with Rome against Avignon and France was quite another.

'These are high matters, gentlemen,' said Clanvowe, waving a hand as if to dismiss them all. 'Matters between our king and his uncle, between parliaments and popes. If Father Purvey errs too far on the side of the crown against the church, others – Sudbury, say – err in the other direction. Yet that's not why we're here this evening.'

'Then why are we here?' I asked, suddenly wary.

He hesitated. 'I am going to be honest with you, John, and I hope you'll forgive me for luring you to my house under false pretences.' He took a deep breath, exhaled. 'I've known all along why you were coming to Oxford.'

I reared back.

'You're after the *De Mortibus*. You and half of England.'

'How—'

'Chaucer told me. At Windsor.'

'But how did Chaucer—'

'That's unimportant,' said Clanvowe. 'The point is, I've invited our guest here this evening to refute to your face the vile rumours connecting Master Wycliffe and his teachings to these prophecies. Your word carries weight in London, John. It's crucial that you understand the difference between honest theological disputation and open rebellion. Wycliffe had strong opinions, true. But he was hardly a traitor, and neither are his followers.'

'I know what Braybrooke must have told you,' said Purvey, leaning in. 'That we commissioned the work's copying, encouraged its circulation. Perhaps even wrote it ourselves, maybe to inspire rebellion against King Richard, install our ally the Duke of Lancaster on the throne. But these are lies, Gower, intended to destroy Father Wycliffe's legacy. However strongly Ralph Strode and his ilk dispute us on matters of endowment, possession, and so on, I'd step into my own grave before promoting or even imagining the death of our king. This *Liber de Mortibus* has nothing to do with our teachings. Why, I believe that the king, not the pope, is the vicar of God! It's from the king alone that the bishops derive their authority and jurisdiction.'

Plain blasphemy. I remained silent, wishing I had a clerk's transcription of the whole evening.

'These so-called prophecies are worth less than the sheepskins they're scribbled on,' Purvey said, pressing on. 'They offend me. They offend me as a Christian, as a citizen of this realm, and as a priest. Most of all, though, they offend me as an intellectual. They are utter trash, the work of a *jongleur*, not a prophet.'

Clanvowe's brow shone as he moved in the candlelight. 'As a poetic maker like you, John, I also have a pretty low opinion of this work. Like our friend here, I regard it as tripe.'

'At least there we can all agree,' I said, sitting back. Despite my better judgment I found myself believing Purvey's account. It was true that this outspoken priest and his ilk had the potential to do great harm in the realm, and I had long wondered what merit Lancaster saw in Wycliffe. Yet the late theologian had never shown himself disloyal to the crown. Then, just as my mind was settled on this version of things, I realized its obvious implication.

'You two seem to know the *Liber de Mortibus* quite well,' I said. 'Well enough to judge the quality of its poetry, the value of its prophecies. How have you become so familiar with such an execrable work?'

A church bell struck for Vespers, struck again, then another sounded in the distance, both carried on the evening air and filling Clanvowe's hall with a low thrum. It's always unsettling to be away from home, where you can't name the bells. Purvey was fingering a last bit of flesh, teasing it round a circle only he could see. He looked up at Clanvowe with the faintest of nods.

Clanvowe grunted. His tight smile broadened when he met my gaze. He said, 'I made a copy.'

THIRTY-THREE

Ditch Street, near Aldgate

'The stews of Southwark be watched.' Eleanor turned from the slitted window, looking down on what had to be the narrowest, filthiest alley in all London. In the bare room behind her Millicent and Agnes sat huddled beneath a blanket on an old furze pallet, the rough gorse spines crackling with their every move. It had been a chill afternoon, and for a fourth day the three women had remained inside, waiting for a constable's pounding at the door. One of Bess Waller's girls had been bringing food and drink to the room, which had seen its last consistent use two years before as a comfort station of sorts for travellers from Colchester on the Mile End Road. No proper beds, just a stack of old linens for warmth. Though the new ordinances had forced closure of this small venture in the flesh, Bess Waller still leased the filthy tenement on and off as a way of maintaining a foothold in this part of the city.

'Gropecunt Lane's being watched,' Eleanor continued. 'The parvis is being watched. Same with Paternoster Row and St Paul's. The eyes of all London are looking about for three maudlyns and a poisonous book.'

'So it is,' said Millicent. 'And we've nearly lost our chance with the one man who has interest in its purchase – thanks to you, Eleanor Rykener.'

They glared at each other. Eleanor didn't trust Millicent Fonteyn the width of a hen's beak, yet here she was, imprisoned in this cursed hole with the uppy trull, and seeing no way out. Unlike Eleanor and Agnes, who'd been living on so little for years, Millicent had plummeted from a condition of genuine wealth and comfort to this dire state. There was a wild, threatened desperation in the woman, like some caged bear on the bankside, baited with a dog, and yet she acted sullen and secretive, casting furtive glances at the book and the stair. Nor did she seem to have any concern for Agnes, who had brought her the book in the first place, put it right in her hands. She treated her sister like a serving-woman, as Eleanor saw it, giving her little commands as if she were some lady at court.

'Selling this book isn't like peddling meat-pies on the bridge,' Eleanor said. 'Why, I seen a man whipped in the street for selling bad herring. Constables catch us at *this*? We'll be lucky if they throw us in the Tun for a month.'

'We can't hold it against Pinchbeak that he was away on king's business when we went to Scroope's Inn,' Millicent disagreed, rubbing her hands together. 'Pinchbeak has wealth beyond our reckoning, ladies, and I for one wish to give him opportunity to lavish it on us.' The two marks were still nearly intact, and Millicent's hope, Eleanor knew, was to multiply the sum twentyfold or more.

Eleanor shook her head, determined to resist Millicent's lust for riches. 'If Pinchbeak had as much interest in this book as yourself, wouldn't he have had something more waiting for you when you went to Scroope's? Besides, you think it's chance that Gropecunt Lane got broken up so soon after you met him at the parvis?'

272

'Oh, so you think it's my doing now, is that it? Listen to the little thief, Ag, just listen to her!' Millicent taunted.

'Oh, *I'm* the thief, is that it, then?' Eleanor's hands balled hotly into fists. 'You two been striding about London these weeks, peddling some other man's book, and Eleanor Rykener's the thief is it?'

Eleanor was now inches from Millicent's nose. Millicent pushed her roughly, then stepped in, ready to strike. Agnes sprang up. She wedged herself between them, a hand on each chest.

'Shut it, you trulls,' said Agnes. 'You want the ward-watch on us?' She gestured to the window. London parishes were small, everyone knew everyone's business, and it would not do to have theirs known by their temporary neighbours. 'If we're not together on this all shall be lost.'

Eleanor turned away, her eyes screwed shut. Millicent's loud breaths slowed.

'Now,' said Agnes, 'let's talk it out. Mill, clamp it for a half-bell and let Eleanor speak her thing. It's the least the girl deserves after what we put her through.'

Millicent shrugged.

'Eleanor, say what you want to say,' said Agnes.

Eleanor calmed herself and spoke. 'There are men we can trust in the city, at the Guildhall. The common serjeant, say. He's helping Gerald, and I don't doubt he'd help us with this matter of the book.' She thought of Ralph Strode, wondering if he had learned of Tewburn's death. 'We can take it to him. Lay out the whole matter as it's pulled us in.'

'Turn ourselves in, then?' said Millicent incredulously. 'Hand the book over, and our bodies with it?'

Millicent's rebuttal began another round of argument that stilled with a sudden noise from the alley.

'Jonah's *cock* it be a hellish walk, and me joints faring poorly.'

273

A familiar voice, the suck of shoes in mud. The three of them froze, then scrambled about for weapons.

'Bear up, Joannie, bear up,' another voice replied. Equally familiar; more reassuring.

Eleanor walked to the door and opened it a crack. Bess Waller, and behind her trudged Joan Rugg, panting heavily, her great dress half-soaked with her exertion. She stopped when she saw Millicent.

'Ah Lord, Bess, you didn't' – she paused to catch her breath, pushing her hands against her lower back – 'didn't tell me to expect her ladyship'd be about.' Once inside she looked around in the candlelight, then chose a stool against the inner wall. 'What finds a grand lady like Millicent Fonteyn dallying with two common women, albeit one her sister?'

'No whore be commoner than yourself, Joan Rugg,' said Millicent.

'Won't give you a *sed contra* to that, my dear.' Here she looked at Bess. 'I'd suppose between the two of us we've sold half the queynt of London over the years, hey, Bessie?' She shifted her bulk on the stool, allowing a slow fart to escape her mounded form.

Eleanor wrinkled her nose.

'There's no body fouler than your own, Joan Rugg,' said Bess.

'Nor no mouth shaped so like a privy,' Eleanor murmured.

Joan showed her suburban rival a charming smile and farted again. 'A verse for you, my dear:

> We *swyve with pride in Londontown,*
> *Those Sou'ark men be thine;*
> For *city pricks be long and thick*
> *Yet Sou'ark's thin as twine.*

My invention, I'll have you know,' she said with considerable pride. 'There be other lines too, if you fancy a hearing on

274

'em. Now,' she said, turning to her basket, 'how about some supper?'

As Joan Rugg dug out a quantity of bread, cheese, and dried meats, she told the others of the dark events on Gropecunt Lane over the last week. Eleanor listened carefully, as Joan's story explained a lot. A raid, Joan said, the street broken up, every one of her girls hauled in for questioning – though not by the constables or the beadle's men.

'It weren't king's or mayor's men, I'll be bound,' Joan said, lipping a stale crust. 'Maybe Lancaster's, maybe Oxford's, or Warwick's for all I know. Four men I never seen before. They hauled us up to Cripplegate jail, cleared out a room for themselves to assay us one by one. Wore no badges, nor said a word about their affinity or allegiance. Kept us for three days they did, all packed in a cell like a barrel of Bristol herring.'

Eleanor recalled the broken lanterns on Gropecunt Lane, the unraked piles of dung.

'Then, the very day we're back at swyving,' Joan continued, 'the constables find a body down Pancras. A clerk of the Guildhall, murdered like that poor thing in the Moorfields.' She looked at Eleanor, her voice lowering. 'That's when I knew, girls. When I seen the coroner down in the churchyard, a crowd of the beadle's men around him – and then the alderman himself shows up.'

'Maryns?' Eleanor asked in surprise.

'Grocer and alderman, the very one,' Joan said with a sage nod. 'Now what, I asks myself, has the alderman of Cheap Ward got to do with it all? Where did my Agnes get herself to, and what about that Eleanor Rykener? And who killed that girl, and that Guildhall clerk? A chain of strange happenings, Joan Rugg. Must be more to the matter than it appears.' She raised her chin, proud of her deductive skills. 'That's when I decided it might be well on time to pay a visit to

Dame Bess Waller here. Figure we queen bees need to consort when numbers of us start disappearing and folks start getting themselves killed. Parliament of whores is what we need. So I step across the river, find me in Rose Alley for the first time in, oh, must be ten year. And there she is, the cheeky little virgin: Bess Waller, in the incarnate flesh of her, and St Cath as well, fresh as the dew on the fleece!' It was at the Pricking Bishop that Joan learned the same company of dark-cloaked men had also paid a midnight visit to the Southwark stews.

'But the Guildhall usually keeps its hands off your lot,' Bess observed. 'So the question is, what's that clerk's killing got to do with all this trouble for us? What's the damned connection?'

Eleanor took a deep breath. 'I am.'

They all turned to her. She told them about her first visit to the Guildhall, how Strode had put her with Tewburn, who promised to get Gerald moved back to London. Then, during his subsequent visits, the intransigence of the Southwark authorities, and Tewburn's troubles with the butchers. 'Tewburn was set to meet with the Guildable justices the very day he was killed. And Gerald thinks Grimes and his boys are up to something. They want the Rising to start again, and this time to kill the king. You should hear the way Gerald went on about it. Butchers, biding by a bishop's bank, then springing out with their knives.'

Millicent's head whipped around, her eyes wide. She looked about to speak when Joan intervened.

'That explains the little lurker on Gropecunt Lane, then,' she said.

'What lurker?' asked Maud.

'This one's brother,' said Joan, nodding at Eleanor. 'Didn't recognize him at first. He shows up that first day back, mean as you could like. Asks about for Edgar the swerver. 'The swerver' he calls our Eleanor, and his own brother! I told him she hasn't been about, he'll have to come back he wants some of that weird queynt. Guess that wasn't what he was after, though by the—'

'Hold it!' said Millicent, springing up and coming to Eleanor's side. 'What did Gerald say?'

'Said that Grimes and his boys—'

'Not that. The part about the bishop's bank.'

'Just what I said,' said Eleanor, taken aback by Millicent's intensity. 'Buncha butchers, biding by a bishop's bank, springing forth with knives.'

Millicent looked sharply at Agnes. 'That's it, then.'

'Sounds like,' Agnes agreed.

'What are you on about now?' Bess demanded.

Millicent went to the low shelf by the door where she had placed the manuscript. Tearing off the cloth, she paged quickly to the final folio and read.

> *'By bank of a bishop shall butchers abide,*
> *To nest, by God's name, with knives in hand,*
> *Then springen in service at spiritus sung.'*

She looked at Eleanor, whose eyes widened with the realization.

Agnes said, 'Seems what your brother's on about is bigger than a lot of talk, Ellie. What do you want to do?'

Eleanor looked at Joan Rugg. 'Did Gerald say where to find him?'

She gave a broad shrug. 'In the Shambles, he tells me. Didn't think much of it at the time. Why would one of my mauds go looking for a little jake like that in the Shambles, of all places? But he says you'll know where to find him if you want him. He'll be there on Saturday morning. Says he can get off of Cutter Lane and over the bridge for a while. Says you'll know the spot.'

277

She did, and Saturday was the day after tomorrow – though would it be safe? She moved again to the doorway, the fear biting at her. She peered out at the gathering night. 'There's no safe place now, not for any of us been privy to the matter. And I keep seeing Tewburn's eyes pecked out, and that man on Gropecunt Lane.'

'What man's that?' Joan asked.

'The man she saw near St Pancras, the night she found Tewburn,' said Millicent.

'A hook-shaped scar on his chin,' said Eleanor, repeating the description she'd given the others. 'Name is Sir Stephen.' Millicent had sworn she'd seen such a chin before, though she couldn't place the man, or so she had claimed.

'Best to lay low,' said Bess Waller, 'give it another week or two, and this whole thing's like to pass by. Forget about the book. Look to yourselves.'

It was Agnes who saw the great moral flaw in their talk. 'Wait, now,' she said. Eleanor watched the beautiful girl as she stepped to the middle of the room, her face aglow with her sincerity. 'We're all thinking about profit, about coin, about Lady Meed and what she'll do for us if we sell the book to the right man,' said Agnes. 'Thinking on our own lives, as if our bodies be the only bodies worth keeping from the grave. Yet here we sit with a book and a cloth speaking the murder of our very king two weeks hence, and what are we *not* thinking about?'

Eleanor nodded slowly, ashamed of herself but with a surge of love and admiration for her friend. 'About King Richard.'

'And our having the means in hand to save him!' said Agnes.

Millicent snorted. 'It's not our lot to save his neck. This whole matter is far above our heads, and has been from the beginning. With the book we can buy our lives back, and wealth for ourselves. *That* should be our aim, and no other. Let someone else look to the king's sorry life.'

'That's not right, Mil,' said Agnes, shaking her beautiful head. 'Just not right.'

'You'd throw away our one chance at new fortune?' Millicent demanded. 'To what purpose, Agnes?'

Agnes tossed her head, her loose hair a noble bonnet of gold. 'To save our king.'

Joan Rugg threw back her head, cackling incautiously. 'Who'd have thought it?' The bawd smoothed her dress over her generous thighs, her chins aglow in the lamplight: a bull-frog's throat on a moonlit pond. 'The very King of England, by the cross, and his life in the hands of five whores!'

THIRTY-FOUR

Ditch Street, near Aldgate

Lifting the blanket as gently as she could, Millicent moved to the edge of the bed and set her feet on the floor. Agnes stirred beside her; Eleanor lay motionless against the wall. Millicent reached for her shoes. The book rested in its nook, hidden by a dirty cloth. She'd oiled the garnets the night before, telling the others she was doing it for their protection: if the watch were about and they needed to flee, better to have the advantage of silence. Before cock-crow, she stole out of the small tenement.

She moved through the city in the pre-dawn darkness, her destination the landmark described on the note she'd sent to Thomas Pinchbeak yesterday. With a stub of coal, Millicent had scribbled the note on to one of the book's blank flyleaves, sliced from the manuscript with a dull knife and folded into a small square, a stableboy on Leadenhall and a farthing enough to get the note to Pinchbeak, who, she felt sure, would show himself at the appointed time and place – or, more likely, send one of his minions.

Reaching the cross above the Puddle-wharf, she peered

down upper Thames Street into the rising dawn. A narrow slice of river glistened in a thin, red line. A heavy breeze from the waterfront pushed her skirts hard against her legs. The bells of St Andrew-by-Wardrobe rang Prime. Few Londoners moved along the broad, unpaved expanse wending down to the water.

She heard a shuffled foot on the pavers, then the roll of a kicked pebble, ticking against the base of the cross. At last, she thought. She took a last turn around the cross and lifted her head with a ready smile.

Eleanor Rykener, her arms folded on her narrow chest, wide eyes flashing in the dawn. 'What's this, then?'

'I'll have none of your suspicion, Eleanor Rykener,' Millicent shot back. 'Look at yourself, why don't you? Taken to following me, tracing my every step.'

'Only when your steps lead the rest of us under the wagon,' Eleanor retorted. She looked her up and down. 'Where is it?'

'Where is what?' Millicent said, not meeting her eyes.

'The book, you cold slut.' Eleanor took a step toward her. 'Where is it? Brought it here to sell, did you?'

'And if I did?' said Millicent defiantly.

'Then we'll have it back, sure,' said Eleanor. Another step. 'And now.'

From around the corner of St Andrew's came a loud flock of sheep, bound for the Friday markets at Smithfield. A river of wool flowed around them as a boy slapped at flanks, his dog skirting the flow in a wide semicircle, nipping with the confidence of an earl. '*Cumbiday, cumbiday,*' the boy called to a few lingerers. In the wake of the sheep walked a man Millicent recognized immediately.

'Watch, now,' she warned Eleanor. The man followed the sheep to the top of St Andrew's Hill, making directly for the cross.

He was no less than a barn's width from the cross when

281

Millicent remembered who he was. Not Pinchbeak but the rude young man from the porch of St Paul's: that gutter spitter who'd tried to bar her entry from the parvis. He stopped ten feet in front of them, hands at his sides, and gave a mocking bow as the last of the flock passed by. 'Fair ladies,' he said, his contempt undisguised.

'Your name,' said Millicent. 'Say it.' He had come alone, it appeared.

'Robert Dawson,' the man said with a pompous air. 'Steward to Master Thomas Pinchbeak, serjeant-at-law in the service of King Richard. You have the book?'

'You have the coin?' Millicent shot back.

Dawson reached into a pocket and withdrew a small sack. He jangled it before her, the coins within mixing dully. He tossed it on the pavers between them. 'Direct from Master Pinchbeak himself. Forty marks, all in gold nobles and halfs.'

Forty marks. Not a fortune, but easily enough to lease a house in Cornhull or anywhere else for a long while, keep them all in food and clothing, purchase their way into a craft of some kind – as seamstresses, embroideresses, or what have you – and take on their own apprentices. Enough to buy a new life.

Millicent felt her shoulders relax for the first time in months. Such a sum was unimaginable for a book, no matter its content. There must be great and wide belief in these prophecies, she reasoned, or a man like Thomas Pinchbeak would never offer such an exorbitant price. 'What do you think?' she said, turning to her still-hostile companion. 'Forty marks – a suitable sum for our effort, and our prize?'

Eleanor glared at her. 'Though if forty, why not a hundred?'

'A good question,' said Millicent, turning on Dawson, feeling giddy. 'Why not a hundred marks, Robert Dawson?'

'Forty marks, says the serjeant, nor a penny more, my

282

lovely ladies.' He leered at them in a manner that stretched his face to look like one of those stone monsters on St Paul's.

'Very well.' Millicent reached into a side pocket and pulled out the book. The embroidered covering was smooth in her hand, and as she palmed it she realized neither she nor Dawson had mentioned it as part of the exchange. As casually as she could she untied the thong and stuffed the cloth back into her pocket. She took a step toward the man and held out the manuscript.

Dawson flipped through the book, then slipped it into a pouch at his side. He said nothing about the cloth. Dawson looked at Millicent for a moment, his eyes narrowing in amusement. With a nod, he turned from them and made his way past the cross and up Thames Street, soon disappearing along the ward's dim byway.

'Well, pillory me,' said Eleanor, shaking her head as she looked after him. She turned to Millicent with a look of bewilderment. 'Forty marks.'

'Forty marks,' Millicent repeated, squatting for the parse. With the coin in hand, she allowed herself to feel some affection for her sister's wily companion, and of regret for endangering her life. For Eleanor had come through her own hell: forced out of her livelihood, pursued through the streets of London half-starving, she'd stolen a book from a brothel and found a corpse in a churchyard – and yet here she was, still standing, about to receive a small fortune. Feeling generous, Millicent shook the purse. 'And a third yours, Eleanor Rykener. Thirteen marks and change? That's a lot of cock, if memory serves.'

Eleanor smiled grudgingly, and together they walked back toward the precincts of Aldgate. 'You were right all along, I suppose,' said Eleanor. 'What do we do with all that coin, now we got it?'

'We'll buy us some finery, purchase our way out of this

pottage,' said Millicent. 'I'll teach you and Agnes to speak like ladies instead of mauds, find you a squire to share between you. Agnes will have him on even days, you on odds, and you'll hump him together at the Nativity, Easter, and All Saints. How's that?'

They stepped up Fenchurch toward the walls, neither of them giving mind to the moral charge Agnes had placed on them. *To save our king.* Yet in the presence of all that gold, now clutched in Millicent's hands and filling their minds with heady visions of new lives, it was all too easy to forget the dark prophecies whose writing and sale had put the heavy purse in their possession. Millicent listened with a new contentment as Eleanor spoke of a future that now seemed miraculously possible. 'Maybe I'll become a chandler, and Gerald'll cut me out the fat – sheep fat, cow fat, pig fat, goose fat, goat fat – and our candles'll be purchased up and down Cheap and Cornhull, maybe even Calais, why not, and by priors and canons and merchant taylors and all of them.'

As Eleanor spoke of her dreams Millicent untied the heavy purse. As soon as her fingers grazed the first coins she knew – and should have known earlier, during the handoff, when these coins had echoed not with the bright ting of gold, but with the deadened clank of lead. She pulled one out and bit it, leaving toothmarks across its centre.

As she clutched the worthless plug her hands began to shake, yet she said nothing to Eleanor, who walked before her with the bounce of imagined wealth in her step. But when? When should she tell her, and tell Agnes, that she had traded their only hope for a bag of lead, fit for the lining of a conduit, or the smelting of a cheap cross for a country church?

They had reached Ditch Street. Millicent looked up through her tears and into an unearthly scene. A large crowd had assembled in the small patch of dirt before Bess Waller's tenement. From the conversation around them they gathered what had happened. A woman's scream in the dark – the neighbourhood roused, lanterns put alight in the rising dawn, the hue raised around the ward against a fleeing man, though no word yet on the outcome of the pursuit.

As they watched dumbly from the edge of the crowd, the victim was borne out to the street, a spill of golden hair, a river of crusting blood along a whitened arm and a reddened hand that seemed to beckon them forward.

Agnes.

Millicent pushed through the crowd and grasped her sister's arm. Eleanor cradled her head, and the crowd pressed in around them.

'*Doovay leebro. Doovay leebro,*' Agnes moaned.

'Oh, Ag—'

'The – the crochet, Mil,' said Agnes. '*Doovay leebro.* It was him.' She raised her hand to her chin, then looked into Millicent's eyes, her own now delirious with pain, and darkened with memory. 'The maid on the moor, her yelling at the moon like that. It's the crochet. His face. 'When father, son, and ghost we sing, of city's – city's blade . . .' Her eyes froze. A final breath.

Millicent heard a splintering keen as she sank to the ground, the sack of lead plugs making a dull thud beside her. A red dawn cast the tenements in a hellish blush, and the sobbing was her own.

THIRTY-FIVE

The Oxford Road

Bone-weary and still five miles out from Newgate, I heeled the mare's flanks and caught up to Will Cooper. He handed me his skin, the warmed ale doing little to lift my spirits. I had left Southwark determined to ferret out the truth behind the prophecies of Lollius. Now, with nearly two weeks passed and the work in hand, I was filled with doubt. Clanvowe had stunned me with the revelation that he had made a copy of the *De Mortibus* after it fell into his hands in London. Yet the knight had offered little advice on what to do with the volume.

Surrender the book to the agents of the king? Hardly: even its possession put me in a perilous situation given the current factionalism in the realm. In my saddlebag was a book that imagined the violent demise of England's king, a work enumerating royal deaths just as Swynford's cards enumerated fates. Despite reading the work a dozen times, I still had not puzzled out the link between the poem and the cards, and there was much in the thirteenth prophecy that made no sense – though some of its words danced before my eyes with a taunting clarity. *Long castle will collar and cast out the core.* It was with this line, and all it implied, that I would begin my return to the city.

As the towers of Westminster loomed before us, I ordered Will ahead with our packhorse. 'I'll be at Overey for a late supper. Ask Simon to join me after the Angelus bell.'

'As you wish, Master Gower,' said Will.

By dusk I was in Guildhall yard. Ralph Strode, as I'd expected, was in. I gave him Quincey's greetings from Oxford. He bent to remove a bottle from a chest at his feet, then poured us a jar of dark wine before easing his bulk on to a chair that groaned with the accommodation.

I looked at him. 'I have the book, Ralph.'

Strode tilted his head, frowned. 'The book.' His eyes widening. 'You mean the book of—'

'*Liber de Mortibus Regum Anglorum.* I have it, Ralph, and I don't know what to do with it. Nor with myself.' I set Clanvowe's manuscript on the desk, where it sat for a long while. Strode stared at the leathern cover as if the book were a dead pig in his bed. At last he sighed, arranged his candles, and opened it.

Ralph Strode was generally a sonorous reader, known to grunt and murmur while shuffling through the many depositions, writs, and other documents that constituted the material regime of his office. Yet he read the *De Mortibus* in silence, the only sound in his chambers the rough whisper of parchment on his thumb. Finally he closed the manuscript and handed it across his desk.

'Your persistence is admirable, Gower.' Robed arms folded at his chest, a still width in the candlelight. 'You found it in Angervyle's library?'

I drank slowly, considering how much to tell him. 'The only whiff of a Lollius to be found among Bury's manuscripts came from the works of Horace.'

287

'"Oblivion, dark and long, has locked them in a tearless grave",' Strode quoted Horace in Latin, his eyes dark and inscrutable slits. 'Of course.'

'That's right.' Though impressed as always by the common serjeant's prodigious memory, I felt, too, that Strode's reaction was skewed, as if I had offended propriety by bringing this book back to London.

'How did you get it, John?'

'It's a copy,' I admitted. 'Made by a friend of ours.'

He narrowed his eyes. 'Clanvowe?' At my nod he looked away. 'I thought I recognized the hand, should have suspected his role in all this. Sir John's connections among Wycliffe's minions are as deep as Lancaster's.'

'We have to take this to the mayor, Ralph, or the chancellor,' I said. 'St. Dunstan's Day is less than two weeks away.'

Strode pushed the volume across his desk and angled his frame toward the wall. 'Are you mad, John?' Closing me off.

'What?'

'I can't have anything to do with this. Nor with you, if you insist on taking this up the ladder.'

'But, Ralph, don't you see it? "*Long castle will collar*"? You and I both know what this means. You have to see reason here—'

'*Reason*?' Strode thundered, coming to his feet. 'You speak of *reason*, and yet you bring this poison into the Guildhall? This work has been circulating among agents of the French, John, I told you that *weeks* ago. And meanwhile you've been picking at justices, bishops, clerks, coroners, Lancaster's own whore, threatening them with God knows what so *you* can find it. To say nothing of the maudlyns.'

'The maudlyns?'

'The corpses are stacking up, John.'

'What corpses? What the hell are you tal—'

'You've heard about Symkok?'

288

This stopped me. 'Nick Symkok?'

'Took a header off the bridge. An accident, Tyle's saying.'

The clerk for the subcoroner, the man who'd been feeding me some of my best information for nearly twenty years. 'He knew something,' I said. I'd seen it in his eyes that day at the coroner's chambers. Why hadn't I pressed him sooner? Then it got worse.

'And my man Tewburn. Asks a few questions around Southwark and gets a slit throat for his troubles.'

'James Tewburn is dead?'

'Murdered, Gower, and left for the birds in the St Pancras churchyard.'

'Ralph, I don't know what to say. Are you sure—'

'Now I learn you've been conjuring with Clanvowe, a known affiliate of Wycliffe and his strongest voice in Richard's affinity! Why do you think the man was sent off to Wales last week?'

'*Conjuring*?' I protested, rising and jabbing a finger at his massive face. 'You listen to me, Ralph. *I'm* the one who's been trying to keep this whole mess from exploding in our faces. This isn't even the original stolen from La Neyte. It's a copy.'

'And all the more seditious for that,' he said, giving me a breath of the half-eaten pie on his desk. 'The talk of a plot against the king is growing more feverish by the day. Now you return from Oxford, from an evening with Sir John Clanvowe, of all people, with the work that sparked it all. I don't suppose Purvey broke bread with you? I hear he's in Oxford. But not even you could be that stupid, John.'

I hesitated.

'No,' he said, backing away.

'Wait – Ralph—'

'Oh for Bart's skin!' he howled at the rafters. 'Where the hell is your mind, Gower? Our nation is on the verge of war again, and you're dallying with budding heretics?' His breath slowed, his voice laden with quiet warning. 'Let's hope those buds don't bloom, Gower, at least not until Dunstan's Day is safely passed.'

With that he dismissed me, his stony silence and averted gaze like twin weights on my shoulders as I left Guildhall yard. The hour was late, and I was badly shaken, in no state for another appointment that evening, though it couldn't be avoided. My suspicion had sharpened since leaving Oxford with Clanvowe's manuscript, and there was one line from the prophecies rattling my skull with the racket of rocks in a jar – the line I had just recited to Strode, provoking his fury. *Long castle will collar and cast out the core*. The 'core', I was convinced, was *cor*, Latin for 'heart', and signified King Richard's personal emblem, the white hart. 'Long castle' was equally obvious: longcastle, longcaster, Lancaster – a young boy could make the connection, and 'Longcastel' was a spelling I had seen on more than one document in Lancaster's own hand.

Worst of all, I had seen this bit of wordplay before. In another poem, an elegy, written some years ago after the death of Gaunt's first wife, Duchess Blanche. And in the great liturgy of information and deceit, coincidence is an unknown song.

I pushed on to Leadenhall, which I took to the city's easternmost gate, still open to the few stragglers making their way into the city from Bethnal Green or Whitechapel, their features alight with the torches along the inner gate. Aldgate loomed over me like a midnight eagle from its eyrie, its single eye a lone candle high above, shining through a glazed window that might have been Chaucer's parlour. The stairways and apartments climbing Aldgate created a labyrinthine ascent to the top, where I went down a quarter-stair and passed through an arched walkway giving on to the high landing before Chaucer's apartments.

I took the heavy knocker in hand, intending to tap lightly, but the bronze lozenge escaped my grasp. A booming concussion echoed through the precincts of Aldgate. The heavy door opened to reveal the frown of a servant. The man looked me up and down, his face twisted with displeasure. I inquired after Chaucer and got a curt reply. 'Master Chaucer's away from London till Monday, sir, his affairs takin' him to port a' Dover.' Three days. I left strict instructions for Chaucer to contact me on his return.

Now over the bridge, the narrow way between shops and stalls. As I passed the open parts of the span, the water rushing darkly below, my hand moved more than once to my bag; I felt a mounting temptation to cast Clanvowe's manuscript into the Thames and be done with the entire affair.

I knew something was wrong before I reached the gate to Overey close. Will Cooper stood just outside, a sputtering lantern suspended from his fingers. When he saw me he moved in big strides up the lane. One of his eyes was blackened. A line of blood had crusted on his upper lip.

'Master Gower!'

'What is it, Will?'

'They've taken Simon, sir.'

'Who?'

'King's men, looked like.'

'Whatever for?'

'Treason's what they said.'

'*Treason*?' My hand went to my mouth. The counterfeiting. Someone must have slipped news of Simon's transgression to an agent of the crown, and after all this time. As I stood there I vowed revenge – even on Chaucer, if he proved my betrayer. 'Did they have a warrant?'

'Not's I saw.'

But of course they didn't. The thought chilled my bones.

If they'd taken Simon for treason, a warrant would be unnecessary. He might already be dead.

'We had a bit of a struggle, we did,' Will went on, 'with two of 'em having to hold me back. I got a beating, 's you can see.'

'Where did they take him?' I asked. 'Marshalsea?'

He shook his head. 'Newgate, was what they said.'

Fresh shoes, a quick supper on my feet. It was well past curfew. I bought my way across the bridge.

Newgate. Tom Tugg, roused from sleep, had wrapped himself in a surcoat when informed of my arrival, and now stood yawning at the gatehouse door.

'What is this, Tugg?' I demanded. 'Treason?'

He looked at me strangely. 'You know the rub, Gower. Imagining and purposing falsely and traitorously t'destroy the Royal Person of the king, and therewith t'destroy his Realm.'

'I can quote the Statute of Treasons as well as you. But what are the charges? Is there a writ you can show me, something more specific?'

Tugg gave a slow shrug. 'I am a jailer, not a judge.'

'Yes, but—' I stopped pressing him, realizing I would get nowhere with pleas alone. I reached for my purse. 'How much will it take, Tugg?'

'Take?'

'To see my son.'

The keeper stepped back, his head shaking. 'None a' your shillings now, Gower, not a king's ransom for a mote a' time with a traitor.'

'It's counterfeiting, Tugg, not exactly an attack on His Highness's person. I'll credit you a full pound.'

Tugg frowned at me, intrigued – but ignoring the offer. 'Heard nothing about counterfeiting, Gower.'

I instantly realized my mistake – an inexcusable one, for

I'd just revealed to the keeper of Newgate prison the secret crime that could still hang Simon at Tyburn, and exposed my own role in covering up the evidence. Trying to recover from my error, I made a more exorbitant offer. 'Ten nobles, Tugg.'

He stared at me, now looking worried for my sanity, then plucked the heavy purse out of my palm. 'That'll do.'

'Good. Now take me to my son.' I tried to push past him.

Tugg wedged himself into the opening. A guard stepped up behind him. 'Can't.'

'What are you talking about?'

'He's not here.'

'*What*? You told me—'

'I told you nothing. You're the one bellowing about treason, counterfeiting, your son. Newgate hasn't swallowed a new morsel since last week.'

I stared, and it struck me almost violently how far my poise and skill had plummeted over the last weeks. And how pathetic it must have appeared that John Gower, who fashioned himself the great trafficker in men's secrets, had freely handed three of his own to the keeper of Newgate. Then Tugg slammed the door in my face, leaving me to imagine the worst. Flaying, whipping, a cruel surgeon with a dull knife. With these and other tortures pressing my thoughts, I walked home through a city dark with night, knowing my son was somewhere in its foul grip.

THIRTY-SIX

Spitalfields, outside Bishopsgate

The three of them stood in the May drizzle as Agnes's grave was carved in the earth. The strikes of shovel in soil were comforting in their way, though the digger's glossing didn't help. 'Pull a skull out the pit every day, it seems,' he said during one of his breaks. 'Reckon half of hell be filled with Spitalfields souls.'

Eleanor, shivering, could sense them there, waiting for the resurrection, when God would call them up, so the preachers said, when all the decayed flesh and old bones would rejoin their souls like some meat puppet in heaven.

They owed their presence at Agnes's burial to Joan Rugg. In the commotion following the murder, Eleanor and Millicent had slipped out of the Aldgate neighbourhood and back to the Bishop before the questions started, avoiding the gathering of the jury and the coroner's inquest. A beadle recognized Agnes as one of Joan's crew and, after summoning the bawd to the inquest, released the body for a pauper's burial at the Spitalfields, where Joan's cuz, Sam Varney, worked as under-digger. Joan sent word to Bess about the timing, and the three of them came across that morning. They bound Agnes in a rough shroud and loaded her on to the digger's cart for the haul out to the burial yard.

As the hole deepened they gathered bluebells from the far corners of the churchyard and carried them to the edge of the pit, with stems of thyme to give Agnes safe passage to the world beyond, and some separation from the other bodies in the partially exposed pit. The gravedigger made quick work of lining the floor, the bluebell stems in the direction of her feet, the thyme a cushion for her head. Finally he coaxed his nag around to the top of the grave and pulled Agnes out by her feet, sending her shrouded form through the air. It landed on the bluebells with a muted finality. He shovelled dirt on top of her. Soon she was gone.

Bess Waller fell to the ground, smudging her dress in the morbid soil. 'Oh, the beautiful little dear! Oh, the most precious body what ever lived!'

Eleanor, silent in her own desolation, watched Millicent. Her face was blank, though Eleanor could feel her fury at her mother as a living thing.

'Stop it, Bess,' Millicent finally said. 'Just stop it.'

Bess's voice hitched. 'Stop it, you say?'

'Your sorrow is *feigned*,' Millicent said, the last word shot at her mother as an arrow of contempt. 'Where was your concern for this "most precious body" when Ag was a girl? Your "beautiful little dear", her arse split open by half the friars of London.' Millicent's voice shook with hatred. 'Agnes was nothing to you but pennies for her queynt.'

Bess pushed herself off the ground. The digger paused in his shovelling.

'Was you who killed her.' Bess shook a finger. 'You who took the book away to sell to Pinchbeak's man, leaving her in those rooms with nothing to bargain for her life. And for what? Bag of lead plugs, and a cold grave in the Spitalfields.

So don't you talk to *me* about concern for my Agnes. By St Agnes herself, don't you say a word. You're the one put her in the ground.'

Millicent raised a hand, then turned away, clutched her stomach, and vomited on the soil. All her reserve left her then, her face losing its frozen pride in a bare moment. Eleanor stepped forward, but Millicent waved her off, shaking her head wildly, retching between words.

'She be – she be right, an't she? Bess Waller be as – be as right as the cursed – cursed rain, don't she? I killed me Agnes, right as if I bladed her meself.'

Eleanor stared at her in wonder. From the refined diction of a knight's courtesan Millicent's speech had lowered itself to the rough patter of the stews. She sounds like me now, Eleanor thought; no, like Agnes.

'That's not true, Mil,' she said, but Millicent backed away, arms held before her face. She fled from the churchyard and disappeared beyond a distant garden.

Bess Waller turned back to the grave, ignoring her. After a final look at the soil covering Agnes, Eleanor made her way out of the Spitalfields yard. All her thoughts were on Gerald, now her one intimate in all the world.

She went through the city walls at Bishopsgate, then westward, to the Shambles. To her left were slaughterstalls once the largest in London, now diminished by Parliament and the city, though still redolent with mingled breaths of shit and death, halved cows hooked four to a beam, gutters spattered with new blood aglisten in the full sun. A few sheep, cows, and goats occupied the far stalls, while the walls of the abattoir were lined with the knives and cleavers for killing time.

Finally she reached the church. St Nicholas Shambles, the stenchiest in all London, and the only one that was ever hers. Her parents had been steadfast parishioners all their lives, and their parents, and probably theirs for all she knew. Eleanor knew its crumbling stairs, its skewed porch, its plain rood screen like she knew her own teeth. After their mother's death she and Gerald had come every day for alms, along with the rest of the parish's poor, until the parson realized they were orphans and turned them over to the city.

Inside the church was silent, the air familiar despite her long absence from its damp and smell. Her brother stepped from a dark recess near one of the side chapels. He'd lost a bit of his sneer, and let Eleanor grasp his arm and lead him to a bench near the west door.

'That fellow from the Guildhall you sent around,' Gerald began. 'Grimes didn't like it much, when he got wind of the transfer, and all the questions.'

'Grimes killed him, then?'

'Not Grimes.' He looked off. She grabbed his chin, turned him toward her.

'Who then?'

He shrugged. 'Don't know their names. They're the ones that bring the priest around and spread coin. The priest that has them all convinced it's God's will that the butchers of Southwark lead the new Rising, reading to them all from a prophecy, he calls it. Their destiny it is, to save all England with their flaying knives! Then I hear them in Grimes's house, talking about Tewburn. He learned something, Tewburn did, something about the plot. Heard them saying he has to go or he'll bring them all down. So they killed him. And now they're all set to kill the king, kill King Richard! And they have a day set, too. They're to do it on—'

'Dunstan's Day,' she finished for him.

He looked at her, his eyes wide. 'How'd you know that, Eleanor?'

She whispered it. '*On day of Saint Dunstan shall Death have his doom.*'

297

He swallowed, and she told him about the book, from the murder on the Moorfields to the deaths of James Tewburn and Agnes Fonteyn.

'Same as the parson says, and Grimes believes it,' said Gerald. 'It's all true, then. There *is* a prophecy.'

She gazed into the far end of the nave, through the gloom beyond the screen. 'A prophecy, a plot, a pickle. Who knows? What I do know is, a maudlyn and a butcher's boy don't have any business meddling with a king's death. This be far above us, Gerald.' She took his hand. 'When you go back to Grimes you can't let on that you know anything, you hear? Play it humble, like you're his ass or dog got smacked into obeying. Do anything he says. Meanwhile I'll figure it out from this end. If we want to come out of all this with our heads, and the king with his, we best find someone with sway. Some real weight.'

'Father Edmund?' Gerald asked, referring to the old parson of St Nicholas.

'Not him,' said Eleanor, who had already discarded the thought. Though kind, Father Edmund was elderly and frail, and the parson of the poorest parish in London could hardly command the needed attention in royal circles. She looked at her brother. 'But I know just the man.'

THIRTY-SEVEN

Bankside, west of Southwark

The days following my return from Oxford were some of the darkest of my life – as dark, in many ways, as that bleak time around the deaths of my children. Simon, seized in the night, facing torture and who knew what else, if he even remained alive. My greatest friendship, threatened with a treasonous book and a dead girl. Three murders, none of them comprehensible, yet all related in a way I could not yet see. I had lost, too, the trust and goodwill of Ralph Strode, and of other powerful men of the city and the court. I could only imagine the whispers in the Guildhall, at Westminster, in the parvis at St Paul's, at the inns and the Temple, the sneers of derision from the likes of Sir Stephen Weldon and Thomas Pinchbeak. *Gower's finally got his due*, they would say; *serves him right, too, after the way he's built his fortune and his name*. Though terrified for Simon, for the realm, and for myself, I felt frozen with indecision, and moved through each hour in an almost gluttonous torpor, feeding only on my desire for self-preservation.

On the first Sunday I roused myself early, intending to

listen to the dawn office. Instead, without thinking, I made my way past the docks and on to the broad river path running west from Southwark. Soon I had left London far behind, passing Westminster on the far shore, skirting the great houses along the banks, walking as I hadn't in years, from village to village, sometimes on the high road with the horses and hackneys, then along the narrower way by the river, among sheep and cows taking water. For hours I ignored my hunger, the pains in my legs and feet, and it was well past midday when I looked ahead and realized I had come as far as Staines Bridge, a river crossing easily twenty miles from London. The stone marker was there on the bank, leaving me stunned at how far I had walked, and walked alone, despite the dangers. The keeper at the inn gave me a heavy lamb sop with bread and a cheese. The food did nothing to revive my spirits. I thought of borrowing a horse for the return, thought twice, then set off on foot as the parish bell tolled for None.

Several hours later, as I neared the ferry at Putney under the last afternoon glare, the storm clouds gathering behind me made their first distant rumblings. I had expected to find the quay nearly empty, as it had been that morning. Instead a large company of infantry filled the road above the embarkation point, visibly anxious to secure passage to Fulham and the highway to London before the coming storm. The ferry stood thirty feet out, but the ferrymen and his helpers would not bring it to shore. The unexplained delay was causing a growing resentment among the soldiers, several clearly drunk. Conscripts, I guessed, commoners without a knight or squire among them. Not the sort of armed crowd a lightly guarded ferryman would normally put off.

'Haul it in, Linton!' one of them called out, crashing his worn shield against a companion's.

'Bring her to, you wastrel!'

'Want a boot to the neck, ferryman?'

The situation was growing uglier by the minute, and I kept my distance. Many of these conscripted garrisons were no better than loose gangs of highwaymen. I could smell the days of travel on these men, the crusted stink of a forced march. One of the rougher men approached a boy sitting on a post.

'See here, Linton!' the man called across the water, unsheathing a knife. 'Tasty-looking son you have here. Shall we cook him up for our supper, have victualling from his flesh?' The boy leaned away, terror in his eyes.

'Let him go, now!' Linton called from the water. His servants started arguing among themselves. Within moments the quay and the vessel had erupted in a loud melee. Swords were drawn, knives unsheathed.

Then, out of nowhere, a trumpet, and a call ahead: 'The king's guard! Make way for the king's guard!'

King Richard's chief herald, a clarion voice I would have recognized anywhere. There was a general shuffle as the rough crowd parted to allow the chargers through. Three knights looked down from their slowing mounts on to the double ranks of soldiers, all wearing neutral expressions as they obediently made way for better men.

Cavalry and infantry, the eternal hierarchy of war, and now it had likely saved a life. The advance guard approached the quay and called out to the ferryman, whose boy was already helping his father ready the ropes for the vessel's arrival on the shore, explaining the delay. The ferryman had been waiting for these members of King Richard's household, and had been unwilling to bear the infantrymen across the river for fear of incurring their wrath.

The situation was still tense, however, and I was about to call out for their protection of the boy – and myself – when the clatter of more hooves sounded from the high road. Eight more knights, riding two abreast, and between them King

Richard and Bolingbroke, his cousin and Lancaster's son. Every man went to his knees, doffed his hat or helmet.

'All hail the king!' one of them called out.

'All hail the king!' came the echo.

As he passed through, King Richard slowed his mount long enough to speak small words of encouragement, of the sort I had heard him deliver on other occasions to high and low alike. Bolingbroke wore a bored look, bemused, as if sharing his father's disdain for any relations of noble and commoner beyond the barely necessary.

I knelt in an outer rank, my dress separating me from the crowd of infantry, though I wasn't expecting to be noticed. I caught the king's eye, assuming he would pass without a second look, though I also recalled his probing gaze at Westminster a few weeks before.

He pulled his charger to a stop. 'Why, is that John Gower?'

'It is, Your Highness,' I said, hiding my reluctance. The crowd parted to allow the king full view of his hailed subject.

'Come forward,' Richard commanded me. I went to the horse's side, my nose at the level of the king's waist. Richard dismounted, signalling to Bolingbroke to do the same. He handed off his reins. 'Walk along with us,' the king said. I obeyed, though not without fear for my head. Richard's behaviour had grown increasingly erratic by all accounts, and I worried that he would draw on me in his barge just as he had on Braybrooke not three months before. Did he know anything about my involvement in the search for the book, or about the seizure of Simon? The horses were led on and lashed at the ferry's bow. 'You'll cross with us, Gower?'

'I would be delighted, Your Highness, if it's not too much of an imposition.'

'Hardly! I tire of my cousin's dismal company.'

Bolingbroke forced a smile. 'We could use some sharper wit to get us over the river. These knights are a grim lot.'

Richard stepped on to the ferry, looking back at the infantry. 'Unfortunate to make these men wait.'

I followed him on to the shallow vessel. 'They are eager to cross before the storm, Your Highness.'

Richard looked at the low clouds now settling to the west. 'You are far from home, Gower, and on foot. You live in London?'

'In Southwark, Your Highness.'

'Southwark – well! So we'll be taking you *out* of your way, then,' he chuckled. The ferry cast off; the knights standing forward gathered into a loose cluster, listening to Bolingbroke as he regaled them in his vivacious way. For a while, as the shouts and work of the crew got us moving, I watched the king observe his cousin, his emotions unreadable. For the Duke of Lancaster the lack of a crown had seemed always a burden, as if he were weighed down by the continual failure of ambition. For his son this lack seemed a relief, an easing of expectation, perhaps, that gave him confidence in his high status without the desire or need to move beyond it. As a result, young Henry was more natural in front of a crowd than Gaunt, able to speak with older knights and gentlemen with an ease and grace that eluded his father. Richard, who shared Lancaster's reserve, seemed to perceive this freer quality in Bolingbroke. I had often wondered whether the king wished he were more like his cousin.

There was a moment then, as the ferry reached the middle of the wide waterway, when I nearly told the king everything. Years afterwards I would look back on that river crossing with some regret, for speaking up might have forestalled all that would follow. Perhaps the king already knew everything there was to know about the prophecies, I reasoned then; on the other hand, he might be ignorant of the whole affair, and saying something to him would elevate the matter far above where it now stood. Richard and Gaunt were already at one another's

303

throats; who was I to insert myself into this running quarrel? So I said nothing, whether out of fear or self-doubt or lack of confidence in the young king's wisdom I don't know. How to present a king with the prophecy of his own death?

King Richard looked across the water. 'And what are you composing these days, Gower, in your mind or on parchment?'

I stumbled a bit, mentioning my notion of a romance of sorts, though a moralized one, then sought to deflect the question on to him. 'What sort of work would please you, Your Highness?'

King Richard shrugged. 'I find biblical stories tedious. I do like Ovid, at least the chunks of him I've read. And modern stories that make us question ourselves, our motivations and character.'

'Question ourselves, Your Highness?'

'Think of the tale of Sir Lancelot *en la charrette*,' the king said, warming to the popular story. 'Smitten with Guinevere, on a quest to rescue her from her abductor, Lancelot finds himself on foot. He's on the road, fully armed, hardly able to walk – and horseless. Suddenly a cart comes by, a humble cart, driven along by a dwarf. Lancelot begs a ride. Now he's a knight in a cart, entering a city as if a traitor, or a murderer. But Lancelot loves Guinevere so severely that he'd do anything to keep on task, including enduring the humiliation of himself in front of an entire city. The story is about the extreme condition of love, teaching us the consequences of following its commands too blindly, and without regard for our reputation.'

'Quite right, Your Highness,' I said, impressed with the young king's skills as an interpreter. 'Lancelot embodies the danger of excessive love.'

'Perhaps,' the king said, tilting his head. 'But do you know the detail of that story I like most, Gower?'

'What is that, Your Highness?'

'Do you recall the moment when the dwarf, driving the cart, invites Gawain to join Lancelot?'

I confessed that I did not.

'The dwarf invites him into the cart,' Richard continued. 'And when he does, he says to him, 'If you are as much your own enemy as is this humiliated knight, sitting here in my cart, why, climb on in, and I shall take you along.' Gawain refuses, of course, for as he knows very well, it would be the height of dishonour for a knight to exchange his charger for a mere cart.

'Yet Lancelot has already done it. He has climbed into the humble cart, put himself in a base position while Gawain stays proudly out of it, disdaining the thought. But what if Gawain *had* joined Lancelot, as the dwarf asked him to? What if he had made a different choice, gone in a different direction than what his pride told him was right? And what if we, in turn, followed his example? "Are you Sir Lancelot, or are you Sir Gawain?" the poet seems to ask. Will you abase yourself for the sake of something vitally important to you? Or will you stand aside like Gawain, loftily removed from the squalor, even as a greater man climbs within, risking it all?'

I nodded. 'I see, Your Highness. The choices of the characters mirror our own choices.'

'Exactly,' he said, his young face brightening. 'The best stories, it seems to me, are those that force us to ask the most difficult questions of ourselves. They want to be mined for these questions, even as they want our soul to be mined for its will, in the way a priest mines it at confession. The poet is asking us to become our own confessors.'

'Well said, Your Highness.'

The king looked off the stern, then back again, regarding me closely. 'Though in the end, I think, the best story is

305

always the simplest one. For your next work, Gower, I hope you will craft such a tale. Write it for me, your sovereign. Make it a confession, whether of a lover or a saint I don't much care. We need more confession in the realm, don't you think? More disclosure. More truth.' His eyes shone with a righteous lustre, and a shudder moved over my limbs. I braced myself, once again almost spilling it all and appealing for Simon's release, then the moment passed, and the king moved forward to speak with his cousin.

The river lapped at the ferry like the tongues of a thousand eager dogs. We were nearing Fulham Palace, the great house of Bishop Robert Braybrooke in the gardens of which I had learned of the existence of the *De Mortibus*. What a distance I have travelled in these weeks, I thought. Since that first meeting with Chaucer I had been mired in complexity: conniving gossips at court, arcane prophecies of kings' deaths, an unused library at Oxford. Yet what if this story, as the king had put it, were a simpler one? If Chaucer himself were to write this story, I mused, where would it go, and what would be its ending?

Before the Fulham wharf I had begun my bow to the king when he grasped my arm. 'Will I see you at Wykeham's feast?'

'How is that, sire?'

He hailed a page. 'Be sure Master John Gower here is on the bishop's list for the feast on St Dunstan's Day. On my name.'

'Yes, sire,' the page said with a bow.

It caught me from the flank, as if a predator stalking me all day along the river had finally pounced. I almost shouted in the king's face, so violent was my reaction. 'Thank you, Your Highness,' I managed to say.

'At my cousin's urging, I am trying to calm the wrath between my uncle and the prelates who despise him,' he said, appearing not to notice my discomfiture. 'All those bishops

306

and archbishops Lancaster has mortally offended over the years. I am doing my best to gentle the roiled waters separating our factions, but the Bishop of Winchester is a difficult man. A poet's presence is a calming one on such occasions, Gower. Minstrels of the page, as I think of you and your scribbling ilk. And since you are a Southwark man you may easily step right over to Winchester Palace and join our company. Your friend Geoffrey Chaucer will also be there, at my request.'

'Again, sire, I thank you for your courtesy,' I said. 'I shall be happy to attend.'

'I'm delighted to hear it,' said the king. A gentle impact, ropes pulled to, the clank of metal on tack and stomps of hooves as knights led their mounts to the quay and up to the high road in the direction of Westminster and London. I waved off the offer of a horse. The storm had blown over, and though dusk approached I would easily make it on foot to the gates by sunset, then home on a wherry.

Bolingbroke gave his horse a final turn back toward the river, waiting for his cousin with the rear guard behind him. Four knights, still against the sky. The king spurred the charger ahead, the guard falling in behind. 'Until St Dunstan's Day, then,' King Richard called back to me.

As the company receded into the distance, I puzzled over the whole exchange, my pulse calming as I began the walk toward Westminster. Since reading the book in Oxford I had known when King Richard was to meet his fate by the terms of the prophecy. *On day of Saint Dunstan shall Death have his doom.* Now, thanks to the king, I knew where the assassination was to take place.

> *By bank of a bishop shall butchers abide . . .*
> *In palace of prelate with pearls all appointed.*

The 'bank of a bishop': the precincts of Winchester Palace, the Southwark home of William Wykeham, Bishop of Winchester, one of the great prelates in the realm. On the Thames adjacent to St Mary Overey, the palace was as familiar to me as St Paul's or Westminster, even more so: the priory and the palace shared the same span of wharfage, and Wykeham's episcopal offices at the palace had long served as the administrative hub of Southwark.

I thought it through. *Pearls all appointed*. The phrase had to refer to the oyster-and-pearl reliefs that Wykeham had commissioned during a past expansion of the great hall. The Blessed Virgin is like unto an oyster, he would say in his pretentious homilies: the Christ child is the precious pearl of her womb, created miraculously within, as a pearl within its shell. Matching his treasure to his theology, the bishop had commissioned a team of masons – led by Mark Blythe, still imprisoned at Ludgate – to craft stone chains of oyster and pearl along the inner walls of the hall. The carvings had been duplicated by Blythe and others on the palace's main outer wall facing New Rents, lined with subtle reliefs in the same pattern, mortared to the wall's uppermost span on either side of the gate. The *De Mortibus* even predicted the very moment of the attempt on the king's life: the killers would spring forth 'at *spiritus* sung' – a phrase that had to be a reference to 'Ave Dunstane, praesulum', a popular carol proper to St Dunstan's feast day.

King Richard's death, then, was to take place at Wykeham's palace, during the episcopal feast on Dunstan's Day, at the procession preceding Mass. The prophecy put the plot squarely on Gaunt's shoulders, identifying 'long castle' as the traitor casting out the *cor*: deposing the king. Yet who was the 'kingmaker', and who precisely would attempt the murder of Richard? How would it happen? Who were these 'butchers', and what role would the cards – the Prince of Plums, the Half-ten of Hawks – play in the unfolding of the plot?

In the wherry the story of Lancelot came to me, in the form of King Richard's memories of Arthurian tales. My mind resounded with the questions he had posed on the ferry. Are you loyal to those you love, loyal to the point of humiliation? Or are you feckless in your love, unwilling to risk the shame that lies in blatant self-sacrifice? Are you Lancelot, or are you Gawain?

Neither, I told myself with a creeping sense of my own blindness – yet knowing the answer was almost within my grasp. You are, in fact, the dwarf.

✠ ✠ ✠

In the service of Sir John Hawkwood, the knight settled with his daughter into a life as stable as any she had known since childhood. In those years, as now, Hawkwood shifted his alliances like a ram changes mates – by summer he might be found fighting for Florence, by fall for Milan, in winter for the pope, in spring for the anti-pope. Despite all the political turbulence around them, though, the girl was provided for by her father in every way.

The knight chose a new wife, a kind woman from Hawkwood's homeland who took her in hand and reshaped her from the wild rodent she had become into a lady fit for an earl's table. Where this girl's father had taught her mannish things, her stepmother instructed her in the domestic graces of femininity: the correct way to do her devotions, the virtues of the wardrobe, the proper running of a household. She hired a tutor, as the wealthier families do, to instruct her stepdaughter in the reading and writing of Latin and the vulgar tongues, especially her own.

Her stepmother took particular pride in the girl's skills with the needle. You are a natural embroideress, she told the younger woman. Your handiwork will yield things of great beauty, perhaps help win you a husband.

One of the most artful items crafted by the girl – a budding young lady of sixteen now – was a needlework depiction of her most vivid and horrendous memory. She started it the very morning her father told her the news: Prince Edward of England, her mother's ravisher and the father of her brother, had met his end. A sickness, it was said, of mind and body both.

The tidings of the prince's death brought back images of her mother, brutalized by an honoured guest. Of the prince, in all his naked cruelty. Of his brother the Duke of Lancaster, saving her life and her mother's with a blade held to the prince's throat.

With this last scene newly alive in her mind, she resolved to embroider it. Two lords, clad in simple tunics and hose, their arms

310

pointed out on shields poised above their heads, details of livery and falconry added as she pleased: three ostrich feathers around the prince's shield, five hawks around the duke's. She used the false hood of an old priest's silk cope as her base. Already bordered with ornate vines, leaves, and flowers embroidered by a more skilful hand, the cope made the perfect ground for the play of her memory. When she had finished her work, she snipped away the embroidered square and loosely pinned it to a large tapestry of a merchant's festival at the Tribunale, hanging in her father's gallery. There it remained for years, a constant reminder of the cruel lusts of men, and the nature of true nobility.

Such reminders were useful in Ser Giovanni's circles. Hawkwood had a reputation as a singularly brutal man. There were numerous stories of his cruelty. Some shrivel the ears.

Two of his men, having sacked an abbey, stood arguing over the flesh of a young nun found cowering in the dormitory. The matter was about to come to blows when Hawkwood strode up and demanded an explanation.

'She is mine,' said one, 'and I shall have her.'

'Nay, I shall have her,' said the other.

Hawkwood drew his sword. 'You will each have half.' He cut the nun in two, leaving her body divided on the tiles.

Such stories put the lie to chivalry, a myth she had seen violated so many times she could scarcely credit anyone still believed in it. Even her father, so noble in her sight, turned a blind eye to Hawkwood's ways. 'War is war,' he would say after hearing of some new atrocity. Hers was a world defined by men and their means, vicious spirals of brutality in which the flesh of a woman was utterly expendable, as cheap as pigshit on a paver.

She had suitors, of course. Though none of them interested her, her father pushed her toward a match. A gentleman of London, as her stepmother described the smooth young man. Suitable in every way.

He was a minor clerk in Hawkwood's chancery. Il Critto, they called him, a sobriquet reflecting his facility with numbers and ciphers. He served the great condottiero as a cryptographer, he boastingly confided to her when they met, dedicated to unravelling secret codes of all kinds, whether the signals of an approaching army or the rhythms of a lady's batting eyes.

Il Critto was young, handsome, quite obviously brilliant. She liked him enough at first, and the more time he spent in her father's house, seeking her company in the gallery, the closer she came to accepting the inevitability of a married life. He was tormented with love for her, or so he claimed.

Smitten. Tortured. Goaded. Martyred. Oppressed. Not a wordsmith like you, I am afraid, though the poor man tried.

Yet there was about him a certain blankness, some quality of sincerity or directness that seemed to be lacking, no matter how earnestly he spoke, and that caused her to question inwardly the wisdom of the desired union.

Nevertheless, he spoke well, and flattered her father with gifts and kind words. It is likely she would have been betrothed to him within a month's time — had not her world changed in an instant.

PART THREE

Half-ten of Hawks

Day viii before Ides of May to Nones of June, 8
Richard II
(8 May–5 June 1385)

THIRTY-EIGHT

Priory of St Leonard's Bromley

To save our king.

The words of Agnes rang in Millicent's ears as she stood before the gate, the abbey's door to the secular world. A bored-looking porter leaned on the walls. These were now gap-toothed in places, collapsed into piles of rubble. Millicent had heard about floods doing some damage to St Leonard's properties, though she had had no real comprehension of the extent of the devastation. Several dykes along the Lea were collapsed, as were a few of the lesser structures on the outer grounds. The malting shack still stood, and the woodhouse, though the big barn's thatched roof was sinking in places. A pair of carpenters were at work up by the old manor house, their labours desultory, as if done in their sleep – an attitude shared by two men in the near field leading skinanchors of fuel, brought from woods that had receded a shocking distance from the walls. It seemed half the forest of Essex had been denuded, still another sign of how much had changed since Millicent's departure in the arms of Sir Humphrey ap-Roger.

315

She slipped a coin to the surprised porter and passed through the priory's main gate, each structure and passage laden with memories. The porch of the Lady Chapel, where the nuns performed the mystery play on Innocents' Day solely to themselves. The narrow cloister, through which the Mass priest, chaplain, and acolytes would pass on their way to the common room, bearing small ale past the mincing sisters. The scriptorium, where Millicent had acquired the gift of reading over long months with Isabel, now prioress – the nun whose withering attention she would soon endure.

'Millicent?'

She turned. Sister Heda stared in bewilderment. Millicent embraced the nun. Beneath its wimple the narrow disc of Heda's face possessed the same sweet clarity she remembered, if lined with passing years, and the abbey's recent troubles. Millicent pulled her around the corner of the dormitory. 'Where is the prioress today, Heda?'

'The prioress?' Heda's eyes widened still further. 'You wish to see the Reverend Mother?'

'Right away, my dear.'

'She is in her chambers today,' said Heda. 'The bishop has a visitation scheduled for next week. I've been appointed cellaress, you know, and there being so few of us now and it being so close there seems little we can do, so . . .' She looked around in near despair. St Leonard's was in no state for one of the occasional rounds of official visits from its presiding bishop, Robert Braybrooke of London. Heda and her fellow officers of the house would be hard-pressed to make the place presentable in the coming days.

'Will you lead me there, Heda?' Millicent pleaded. 'I won't be stopped if you guide me.'

Heda hesitated, eyes shifting toward the gate. Then the nun silently turned and led her straight past the refectory, where the day's loaves lay stacked on the tables between

316

meals. Left through the kitchen passage, redolent with river eel. Another left across the herbal, its springtime offerings of sage, thyme, and dill. Down a gentle stair into a low, cold building of riverstone. The chapterhouse, the heart of St Leonard's, with voussoirs of banded fleurs-de-lis tracing high arcs along the vaulted entryway. The chamber was empty at that hour, though it would soon fill with the rustle of habits and the singing of Tierce.

Outside the prioress's private apartments stood a young novice. Millicent didn't know the girl, though her face was vaguely familiar. The girl started at the sight of an unknown laywoman in St Leonard's inner sanctum. Heda gave the novice Millicent's name and requested an audience.

'Your business with the prioress?' The novice's voice, like her face, betrayed nothing.

'She must see me,' Millicent said. 'It's a matter of grave importance for Bromley, and for the realm.'

The girl's smile was – bemused? Cruel? Just throw me to the she-wolf, was Millicent's impatient thought.

The novice held up a finger, then pushed open the door to the prioress's parlour. Heda backed away, her brow showing a single worried line beneath her habit, then disappeared around the corner. Millicent heard a few mumbles. A piercing *Who?* The outraged ejaculations of a voice she knew all too well. The novice returned, pale-faced, saying nothing as she held the door.

The prioress's parlour was a lushly furnished space with three glazed windows, a writing desk, and a rug of black-dyed wool thrown over paving tiles bearing the Syward arms. Dame Isabel Syward, the Prioress of St Leonard's Bromley, gazed down from her raised chair with an air of taut disdain. Millicent lowered herself, remaining still until the leader saw fit to speak.

'You have—' Isabel's voice was gravelly with bile. 'You have come home at last, my dearest daughter.'

317

Millicent looked up in surprise, but the prioress's expression belied her welcoming words.

'And what a glorious homecoming it is,' Isabel continued. 'Perhaps you've reconsidered the wicked ways that led to your expulsion. Perhaps you've decided to be grateful for the gifts this house gave you. Food, shelter, rescue from a life of raw swyving, how to rap your Ave Maria on your knuckles. And reading. Oh! I taught you myself, didn't I? Every letter, holding your hand as your fingertips traced patterns in the letterbook. For hours, for weeks, for *three years*, Millicent, I taught you how to read, how to think, how to pray, how to *live*.'

The prioress put a hand to her mouth and sat back, seeming shocked at her own outburst. There was a glistening in the corners of the great woman's eyes. She wiped them and went on.

'Yet you threw it all away. And for what? A fat old January! At least you could have fallen for a squire, strong of arm and stiff of cock. Now *that* would have been understandable, given our sisters something worthy to aspire to, an actual challenge. Instead, what do you do? Why, you settle for the first easy target that comes along, making *yourself* easy in the process, then *off* you go, abandoning the community that opened itself to you. Now you expect the same openness from Bromley? You think you can simply show up, demand an audience with the prioress, get a handout? *Bah!*'

The prioress spat. Millicent lay crumpled on the floor, stilled with the truth of all the woman had said to her, and with wrenching sorrow at the loss of this place from her life.

She squeezed her eyes shut. What could she say that might rein in Isabel's contempt, at least long enough for her to appeal for the help she sought? 'Reverend Mother,' she began, 'if you please—'

'But I know you, Millicent Fonteyn.' Isabel's voice was

flat now, devoid of passion. 'I know you to be the most calculating, self-interested woman in all England, a woman who would spare no thought to betraying friend and family alike. It is simply who you are, my dear.'

Millicent thought of Agnes. The prioress could not know the horrible accuracy of her judgment.

'So I suppose you would not have the spine to show yourself here if you didn't have good reason, and I suppose I am bound to hear it. "A matter of grave importance for Bromley, and for the realm." How grand. Tell us. Then get out.'

Millicent left nothing out, and when she was done the prioress studied her with an intensity she remembered. 'I'm very sorry about your sister, Millicent,' she said with lowered voice. 'Such a loss is difficult, even in these times when we lose so many to war and pestilence. To know that your own greed murdered her – that doubles the guilt, and triples the pain. May Agnes be at rest in God's hands, her sins washed away in the waters of purgation.'

'Thank you, Reverend Mother. Your words are kind.'

Isabel stood with a sigh. She walked to the window looking up to the manor house. 'I have heard of this book from other sources in recent weeks. It is the talk of our order. The bishop has made inquiries about it to the houses in his diocese. A burnable book, Braybrooke calls it. The timing could not be worse, with Pope Urban's delegation set to arrive from Rome before Trinity Sunday.' She turned, her look incredulous. 'Yet you, Millicent Fonteyn, of all people, have read this book?'

'I have, Prioress. Several times.' *Trinity Sunday. Pope Urban.* Millicent thought, with a fleeting confusion, of her sister's death, and the words she had scribbled in coal inside the book. *The crochet . . . father, son, and holy ghost . . . city's blade . . . doovay leebro.* Why were these phrases coming to her now? She had assumed that Agnes, in her own throes, was echoing the last words of the girl in the Moorfields, the couplet thrown into the night sky while Agnes watched from the shrubbery. For weeks she had dismissed Agnes's recounting of the doomed girl's dying utterance. The book and the cloth: these could be sold, after all, while words were just words, and there seemed little reason to credit the girl's final call as anything more than a cry of dread as the hammer fell. Yet now she caught herself wondering if there was something to these words after all, even if Agnes herself had never discovered their meaning. The Holy Trinity, a city's blade – but what was it?

'This house is in enough peril already,' the prioress was saying. 'Our fortunes the property of the manor, our income shrunk to two hundred marks in the year. We've been forced to enclose the park, and lost a thousand acres in Dagenham. And here you are, slinking back like one of King Edward's dogs, with this news. I'd be within my rights to have you cast in the brew cellar, and the key thrown in the Lea. If our celleress hadn't lost the damned key,' she muttered.

'I would have thought,' Millicent began, 'that the Reverend Mother's close relation to the crown—'

'Oh, yes, of course. We've had the corpse of Elizabeth of Hainault, old King Edward's sister-in-law, mouldering in our chapel for ten years. Why, we could sell it for relics! Why hadn't I thought of that? St Leonard's piss is liquid gold!' Her hands dropped to her sides. 'I'm afraid we're no more protected from the threat of ruination than the shrinking forest around us.'

'Prioress—'

'Show me the cloth.'

Millicent reached within her skirts and pulled out the folded embroidery. Isabel spread it in her lap. She ran her fingers along the sides, where the thistleflowers, hawks, plums, and swords were arrayed in numbered sets. She stroked the heraldry arrayed against the king's arms.

'You say Pinchbeak has the book?'

'I handed it to Robert Dawson, his man. Pinchbeak wasn't there.'

The prioress put a slender finger to her lips. 'So we have this book of prophecies, one of them auguring the death of our king and pointing a finger at his uncle. We have the cloth, identifying the chief conspirator beyond doubt as Lancaster. And we have mere days until the feast of St Dunstan.'

'Yes, Reverend Mother.' Millicent watched the prioress's eyes, felt the shrewd calculations taking place behind them.

'I'm told you've been living up Cornhull.'

'Yes, Prioress.'

'I assume you've kept up your embroidery, then, given the neighbourhood.'

'Well, I can't say that I—'

'An orphrey of fine needlework is what we need, and the most ingenious we have ever made.' She stretched the cloth to its full width. 'It must be identical in every respect to this vivid sample, with one difference – well, two.' She pointed to the coat of arms emblazoned on the figure attacking the boy king. 'Do you see these colours, just here?'

The Duke of Lancaster's. They were nearly identical to the king's, the only difference being the ermine label above. 'Yes, Prioress.'

Isabel squinted at it. 'Hand me that glass.' The prioress pointed to a low table in the corner. Millicent walked over and lifted a triangular magnifying glass, set in a bone frame with a wooden handle below. Isabel took it from her and scrutinized the cloth further.

'The brick stitch around the border is remarkable, as is the infilled foliage. And the waffling is superior, must have taken weeks. *Look* at that work. The ground is Italian, or I'm a pregnant goat. But in the middle, the figures of the duke and the king are – well, they're nicely done, but their quality doesn't come close to what I am seeing in the base.

And these smaller emblems – the thistleflowers and hawks and so on – wouldn't pass a seamstress's eye in Cornhull, let alone at court.'

Millicent came to the prioress's side, catching a faint waft of rosy perfume from the older woman's neck. Not all luxuries had been abandoned in Bromley, it seemed. She leaned over the prioress's shoulder and peered through the glass at the cloth. She saw immediately what Isabel's expert eye had discerned. At the edges of the cloth the stitching was tight and uniform, the product of a practised embroideress working slowly and patiently to embellish the borders with an elaborate pattern of vines and flowers. The figures of Lancaster and King Richard, as well as their arms, had been pointed into the cloth in an entirely different style. Looser stitches, higher loops. Skilful and not incompetent, not by a long stretch, but – *youthful* was the word that came to her mind. Finally, the figures of thistleflowers, hawks, swords, and plums surrounding the central figures had been done hastily, with inferior threads and with no regard for the surrounding ground. Three hands, then, working at different times, with different materials, and with varying degrees of competence.

The prioress leaned back. 'This cloth is clearly a fake,' she said, 'cooked up to point a finger at the duke. Besides, Lancaster wouldn't come near a book of the sort you describe. The man eats self-preservation for supper. So who would create such a thing to wrap around a manuscript of prophecies, implicating him as a conspirator against the king?'

Isabel stared at the wall for a moment, then shook her head. 'Well of course. Who else?' She took up the cloth, picked at some threads. 'This work is too tight to unravel without damaging the ground. You, Millicent, will create a new shield for this fellow here, with new arms altogether. In the first quarter, we must have a silver mullet borne upon a field gules.'

Millicent's eyes widened. 'Do you mean—'

'I do.' The prioress's eyes sparkled, and she allowed Millicent the slightest of smiles before returning her attention to the cloth. 'The other must be similarly altered, though with different arms. Here, parti per fesse gule, and on the chief of the second there must be – ah, what is it?'

'A demi-lion, rampant of the field,' Millicent said, remembering the shield. A tournament two years before, she on Sir Humphrey's arm in the stands, the Earl of Oxford mounted below.

'Exactly. Now.' Isabel clapped her hands three times, summoning the young nun from the other side of the door. 'Bring us thread of silver, gold, azure – all of it. We haven't a moment to spare.'

Soon Millicent found herself in her old place at Isabel's feet, frame and needle in her hands. Following the prioress's instructions, she pinned out a portion of the pattern within the smooth frame: the demi-lion, a complex figure to execute, though Millicent felt confident she could complete it in good time, at least as well as the earlier embroideress had pointed in the arms of Gaunt. The pull of the needle, the occasional click of the thimble against the frame: though her fingers soon ached with the unfamiliar labour, it was a good ache.

'Reverend Mother?' she said at one point, tentatively.

'You may speak, Millicent.'

Her given name from the prioress's lips: a balm over a forgotten wound. 'How can we know this will work?'

Isabel gave her a bland stare. 'There is a great conspiracy in the land to slay our king, my child. We can be sure of nothing. But we must do what we can to foil the plot. To bring this cloth before the king on St Dunstan's Day, and from a credible source, we must put it in the hands of someone in the inmost circles at court. Someone of unassailable standing.'

'Your relations?'

The prioress snorted. 'The concubine of the king's second

substeward has stronger connections in the court than my relations these days. No, I have in mind one of our dear sisters. Just there.' She nodded toward the door. 'Margaret is her name. She's properly a nun of Barking, but we've taken her in for a few months given the unpleasantness between the king and his uncle. Abbess Matilde wants her to disappear for a while, at least until after the bishop's round of visitations.' Barking, the much greater house several miles to the east, would often impose on St Leonard's for 'gifts' of space and provision, taking undue advantage of Bromley's diminished numbers and extra dormitory space.

The girl, no more than fourteen, stood out of earshot in the half-opened doorway, her head pointed demurely to the floor.

'I don't understand, Reverend Mother,' said Millicent.

'Her mother has an intimate connection to John of Gaunt,' said Isabel.

Her mother. 'The Infanta?' It was a guess. Millicent knew the young woman had looked familiar, though the face of Gaunt's Castilian duchess didn't seem a match.

The prioress glanced up. Blinked. 'Hardly. She's Margaret Swynford, daughter of the late Hugh Swynford. And her mother is Katherine, Lancaster's whore.'

THIRTY-NINE

Church of St Lawrence Jewry

Edgar Rykener joined the small knot of beggars gathered at the foot of the St Lawrence steps. Some gave him unfriendly glances, taking him for an interloper who would diminish their proper share of charity. He ignored them; the wait wouldn't be long. Master Strode was to appear at the first stroke of the Sext bells, he'd been assured at the Guildhall. The common serjeant likes to take a walk around the ward, one of his clerks had said, before returning for his midday meal with the mayor.

The St Lawrence bell struck, Mary Magdalene soon followed, then Bassishaw, the three parishes competing for the proper ringing of the hour. Still no Strode. Edgar thought nothing of the delay at first, yet as the minutes wore on his concern mounted, until finally he pushed himself off the wall and stepped up on to the porch.

The interior was nearly silent, a heavy wheeze the only discernible sound. It came from one of the side chapels, a half-lit space with shuttered windows and several rows of old seats wedged askew against the walls. Ralph Strode sat on one of them, a silent mound of concern. Even in the dim light Edgar could see his face was ashen. His wide chin sat propped on his knuckles, robed elbows on his knees. The man could have been one of the painted statues, but for the whistley breaths from his guts.

'Master Strode,' said Edgar, his voice a small thunderclap.

Strode's opening eyes caught the glare of the lone candle on the chapel altar. No other movement. Finally he half-turned, his brow bent in a distant frown. A slow nod. 'Edgar, is it?'

'Yes, Master Strode.'

'Came about your brother a few weeks back.' He seemed mildly pleased that he had remembered.

'Yes, sir. James – Master Tewburn was a great help.'

'Tewburn.' Strode shook his head. 'Senseless. A senseless loss of a good young man.'

'Yes, Master Strode. I'm sorry he had to go and die, sir.'

Strode's gaze found him in the gloom. 'You heard, then?'

Edgar nodded, casting about for what to say.

'For my life I can't figure out what is happening in London,' he said. 'Factions moving in stealth through the streets, with their feints and counter-feints. Young men being plucked off the lanes, tossed off the bridge, throats slit in churchyards, dragged from their homes and thrown in nameless pits, all for baseless suspicions from above. London is being torn apart at the seams, and despite my office I am feeling powerless to stop it.'

Edgar took a deep breath, then said, 'It was I found his body.'

His eyes widened. 'Tewburn's?'

'Aye, sir.'

'It was you who alerted the constables, then?'

'Not – no, sir.' Strode was staring at him. 'I found him the day before the coroner's men took him from St Pancras.'

He sat forward. 'Yet you let his body lie there for another day?'

'We had us a time, you see, to meet in the churchyard, and—'

'Tewburn was at St Pancras to meet *you*?' Strode clapped his knees, fixing him with the fiercest stare. 'Whatever for?'

'Master Tewburn said he'd have some news for me about getting Gerald a wardship in London. Said he'd tell me that night when we met. But the justices over there, in the manors—'

'Guildable Manor.'

'Master Tewburn says they were giving him all kinds of grief just to find out how to transfer Gerald's wardship from Grimes's shop. And Gerald says the butchers are stirring up bigger trouble in Southwark. Got a priest riling them up, with Grimes taking the part of Wat Tyler, and the other butchers—'

'*The butchers*. My God.' It was as if the common serjeant had been struck with a seizure of the heart. The large man came to his feet with a surprising agility. He turned to the side, and with his body facing the chapel altar whispered a portion of verse.

> '*By bank of a bishop shall butchers abide,*
> *To nest, by God's name, with knives in hand,*
> *Then springen in service at spiritus sung.*'

Edgar gasped. The last time he'd heard these lines they'd come from the mouth of Millicent Fonteyn, who'd read them from the very book Agnes took from the doomed girl in the Moorfields. Now here was Ralph Strode, common serjeant of London, speaking the same verse.

He had to press him. Strode was staring off toward the upper nave, a haunted slackness to his face. 'That verse, sir. You think it's Grimes and his men set to kill King Richard?'

327

He barked a laugh. 'It's not what *we* think that matters. It's what others can be *made* to think. The perfection of art is to conceal art, so Quintilian tells us.'

'Sir?'

'We have two sets of butchers before our eyes.' He stooped, hands on his broad thighs. 'Butchers in this prophetic verse, and the butchers of Southwark – and one dead clerk. I am not a believer in coincidence, Edgar, not by a far sight. You say you talked with Tewburn about your brother, yes?'

'A few times, sir, he was very helpful, always—'

'Wait.' Strode grasped Edgar's shoulders, his eyes wide. 'What did you say?'

'That Master Tewburn was ever so helpf—'

'Before that. About the snatch of verse I recited.'

'Oh . . . yes. If you thought Grimes and his men were to be the butchers to kill the king.'

Strode's stare was deep and cruel, as if a hand were reaching out from his eyes, down into Edgar's bowels. 'And how did you know?'

'Sir?'

Strode's grip tightened on his shoulders. 'How could you possibly have known those three lines referred to the slaying of King Richard?'

His jaw loosened. 'Well, I – I suppose with the bishop, and the knives, and all that, it just seemed—'

'Don't lie to me, boy.' Strode shook him. 'You've heard someone else speak those lines, haven't you?'

'Please, Mast—'

'What do you know about these prophecies, about the book?'

His hands squeezed harder. Edgar flinched with the pain. Could he trust him, after all, this great man of London, so many spheres above his own?

Edgar left nothing out. The Moorfields, the murder,

328

Millicent, the man with the hooked scar on Gropecunt Lane, the death of Agnes. He even told him about the couplings with Tewburn, and his life of swerving – all of it. Strode breathed deeply when he was done, his lips sucking and blowing the stale air of St Lawrence. The common serjeant's face was calm now, his eyes agleam with a certainty Edgar wished he could share.

'Will the king die, Master Strode?' he asked, and looked into that confident gaze.

'It's not the king we need to worry about,' said Strode. 'No, Edgar – or is it Eleanor?'

He shrugged. 'As you wish, sir.'

A smile, tentative but serene, played on Ralph Strode's generous lips. 'No, Eleanor, I'm afraid we have a smaller life to save.'

FORTY

San Donato a Torre, near Florence

Jacopo da Pietrasanta stood at the door, clutching the letter. Scarlett watched with some amusement as Hawkwood's chancellor worked up the nerve to speak. 'Sire,' he finally said.

'What is it?' said Hawkwood, focused on the game.

'An urgent message, Ser Giovanni. From your brother-in-law.'

'Lodo?'

'Carlo, sire,' said Pietrasanta.

Hawkwood took Scarlett's four. 'Read it.'

Scarlett looked at his lord. With the coming departure for England Hawkwood had grown increasingly impatient with his Italian functionaries, even Pietrasanta, and it was all he could do at times to control his sharpness when addressing them.

The chancellor cleared his throat. '*We send this to inform you that in Milan the hateful count Giangaleazzo Visconti has unrightfully seized our beloved and magnificent lord Bernabò Visconti, as well as our beloved brother Lodovico.*

*We are holding here at the fortress in Crema, and we have
the castle at Porta Romana under our protection. We urge
you to gather your garrisons and march to our comfort
and defence in Milan. You will be amply rewarded for your
effort. The time has come, Giovanni Acuto, to prove your
mettle.'*

Hawkwood made him read it again, and when he had
finished his lips curled up into a sneer. 'He's taunting me,
the hammy little shit.'

Pietrasanta flinched at the epithet. Scarlett knew what the
man was thinking. The Visconti are the most powerful and
ruthless clan in Italy, more than a match for this northern
roughneck. Who is he to hurl such insults at *la famiglia
lombarda principali*? 'How would you like to respond, Ser
Giovanni?'

Hawkwood shrugged. 'We're in no position to respond,
Jacopo.'

'Ser Giovanni?'

'I am in Florence. Our brigades are massed in Bologna.
Bologna still owes us, what, twenty thousand, thirty? What
does Carlo expect, that I'll pull up stakes and hoof it up to
Milan at his bidding? It could take weeks, months, even, to
prepare for such a relief effort.'

'What should we tell Ser Carlo in the meantime, Ser
Giovanni?' Pietrasanta was working hard to keep his voice
measured, Scarlett could tell.

'Write nothing for now.'

'Ser—' Pietrasanta began.

'There is no hurry, Jacopo.' Hawkwood turned on his
chancellor, his eyes grown cold. 'This is a family squabble,
nothing more. We'll bide our time.'

There was a heavy pause as Pietrasanta absorbed the
condottiero's decision. Hawkwood's chancellor had no idea
what his master was planning, nor the bearing of these

plans on his own future. Within a few weeks the dirty wars of the Visconti would be only a memory to the man they had both served for so many years. And Pietrasanta would be out of a job.

'Very well, sire.' Pietrasanta turned to exit, pushing past a young man entering from behind him. Desilio's boy, sent up from the *villetta*.

'What is it?' Scarlett asked him.

'Master Desilio requests your presences, good sirs,' said the breathless youth.

'Oh?' Hawkwood's eyebrows arched up, and he turned to Scarlett with an intrigued grin. They walked together to one of the *villette*, the line of small cottages in a line down the hill from the main house. The grapevines reached from the path up the sweeping rise to the south, and the late afternoon had settled into a mellow glow. My last season in Italy, Scarlett thought, whispering a quiet prayer.

In the *villetta* they found Desilio wedged among several piles of books on a trestle table, which was covered with scribbled papers arrayed in an unpatterned mess around the quire. The scholar's eyes gleamed with excitement as he stood, though he maintained a respectful silence until Hawkwood asked him to speak.

'I have broken the first cipher, Ser Giovanni, and will soon break the second.'

'Is that so?' said Hawkwood, his gaze shifting between Desilio and the table. 'Sit, please, and explain what you've found.'

Desilio took his chair, Scarlett and Hawkwood each to one side.

'The key was the first cipher. Without it everything else in the quire means nothing. It took a bit of thought and effort, but I was able to decipher these first pages without difficulty once I realized what was before me.'

Scarlett peered over his shoulder. 'And what is it?'

332

Desilio waited a moment, letting the curiosity build. 'Sardinian,' he finally whispered.

'*Sardinian*?'

'Yes. Nothing complicated or encoded, just Sardinian. He used it as the first of his ciphers.'

'So you read the language yourself, Maestro Desilio?' Hawkwood asked.

'Hardly,' the logician scoffed. 'I asked around among your men, and one of them knew another who was from that island. I read him the first few sentences, as well as I was able—'

'You *what*?' Hawkwood exploded, his hand poised to strike.

Scarlett put a hand on his arm. Desilio was wagging his beard. 'Nothing to worry about, I assure you, Ser Giovanni. The ciphers mean nothing in isolation. The man had no idea why I was even pulling him in here.'

Scarlett felt Hawkwood relax, and took it upon himself to move the conversation along, reaching over Desilio's shoulder to turn the page. 'What about here, and here?' He pointed to the script on the facing folio. The alphabet was Roman, the hand legible, but the words themselves were clearly nonsense, full of letters bunched seemingly at random, and what looked like extra vowels and consonants, such as an X within a circle.

'It's an extraordinary thing,' Desilio said, a touch of pride in his voice as he looked up at them. 'He was inventing a *lingua ignota*, as I've heard such things called.'

'A new language,' Hawkwood murmured.

'It's rudimentary, of course, without declined nouns or conjugated verbs, and the tenses are rather primitive. But a few hundred words is all one needs to put together fairly sophisticated messages.'

'But how would the recipient know the meaning?'

Desilio smiled. 'A glossary, owned by both parties, translating each word back into Italian. Or any other language. The only way to decipher the code without such a glossary would be through an analysis of letters and their frequency, but for that to work you'd have to have a much larger sample of the language than the mere four pages here.'

'So then,' Scarlett said, confused, 'how were you able to decipher the unknown language?'

Desilio rubbed his palms. 'It all begins with the Sardinian, the simplest of the ciphers. It's merely another language, and anyone who knows it can crack the code, which I've now done with the help of your man. And as I've discovered in the process, the Sardinian is in effect the glossary to the *lingua ignota*. The Sardinian, that is, provides the key to the next cipher.'

'Explain yourself,' said Hawkwood.

'Certainly, Ser Giovanni. Look here, at the beginning of the first column. It reads, "Word seventy-nine is *míntza*" – and *míntza* is Sardinian for "spring". The next sentence reads "The twelfth word is *bidduri*" – Sardinian for "hemlock". Once I had all of this translated I was stymied. The seventy-ninth word of what? What twelfth word is he talking about? Then I realized what your cryptographer was doing here. What he's telling us is that word seventy-nine of the secret language – *the next cipher in the quire* – is "spring". And word twelve is "hemlock". And so on and so forth. And now, by translating the *lingua ignota* as the key, I believe I am opening the lock to the *next* code, which follows in the quire. The Sardinian unlocks the secret language. The secret language unlocks the numbers. Do you see?'

Hawkwood nodded, all admiration. 'Indeed I do, Master Desilio. You are Theseus in a labyrinth of sorts, with each cipher a length of rope guiding you to the next corner, and the next solution.'

'A perceptive analogy, Ser Giovanni. I should have the solution to the subsequent code worked out as soon as I have transcribed and recombined the *lingua ignota*.'

'And what is this next cipher?' Scarlett asked him.

Desilio turned back to the manuscript, showing them the next three pages, filled with scribbled numbers stacked in equations and scattered along lines, shapes, and angles. Once again they meant nothing to Scarlett.

'The next one is numerical, drawing on the mathematics of Master Gersonides,' said Desilio. 'A Jew, and an astronomer of moderate renown. I believe your cryptographer was constructing a cipher based on some of Gersonides' more arcane calculations. Extraction of square roots, binomial coefficients, that sort of thing.'

Hawkwood laughed lightly, slapped him on the back. 'Ah yes. Binomial coefficients. I eat them with my rabbit.'

'It sounds more complicated than it is,' Desilio said modestly. 'This mathematics is several generations old, nothing I cannot untangle. A few more days, Ser Giovanni, and I should be ready to tackle the final cipher.'

'And this final cipher? Do you have an inkling as to its solution?'

'Not yet, sire, though I am confident I'll get there.' He thumbed through the booklet's last few pages and set his finger in the middle of one of them. 'Your cryptographer organized the last cipher around four discrete images, arranged in different combinations across these pages. Here is what looks like a falcon, perhaps. This one is clearly a sword, the next a flower – a spindly one, like a thistle. And here we have a grape, if I'm not mistaken.'

'A plum,' said Hawkwood, his voice suddenly taut. 'It's a plum.'

'And the bird is a hawk,' said Scarlett, seeing it at the same instant. Hawks, thistleflowers, plums, and swords.

The four suits of Hawkwood's cards, written in neat rows and columns across the last four pages of the quire in small groups of two – each group, Scarlett suspected, a letter or a word. The phrases came back to him, like pinpricks along his arms. *At Prince of Plums shall prelate oppose . . . By Half-ten of Hawks might shender be shown . . .*

He should have seen it during his own scrutiny of the manuscript, yet these symbols had blended in with all the other mysterious writing in the quire, and he hadn't taken the time to examine them in their own right before extracting Desilio from the *studium*. How differently all this might have turned out, Scarlett would think later, if he had.

Hawkwood, who always carried a deck of cards slung in a purse, removed them and spread the painted ovals out on the table as they explained to the scholar what the two of them had noticed. Desilio nodded eagerly, getting it right away, and promising to let them know as soon as he had untangled the mathematical cipher and turned to the cards.

'I am entrusting you with my favourite deck, Maestro Desilio,' Hawkwood said as they prepared to leave him there. 'Treat it well.'

'I shall, Ser Giovanni.'

As they turned into the lower gardens Scarlett repressed a shiver. Hawkwood knew him too well to let it pass.

'What is it, Adam?'

'Think about it, John,' he began. 'A book that just happens to survive a deliberate burning in the *villetta*, yet with enough of its pages intact to allow the ciphers to be broken. The first cipher is simply a translation into Sardinian – a tongue Il Critto could have heard spoken in the streets of Florence more than once. It would have been a simple matter to hire a Sardinian man and have him translate the words he needed. The next cipher, Desilio tells us, relies on mathematics that's years, maybe decades old, presumably solvable by anyone with university training. And the final cipher? The only way to break the encryption is with your own cards, John. Doesn't all of this feel too convenient somehow – too easy?'

'Well, I suppose one could—'

'It almost seems as if . . .' Scarlett paused on the garden path, a hand to his mouth.

'Say it, Adam.'

'As if he *wanted* us to find the damned book. Find his book, and break his ciphers.'

'To what purpose?' said Hawkwood, intrigued, though not as troubled as Scarlett wanted him to be.

'Betrayal?' The first word that came to him.

'Or information,' Hawkwood rejoined, his gaze on a distant hill. 'Something he wanted to tell us before he left, and this was his only way.'

'If that's the case, why not simply speak to us in person?' Scarlett said. 'He had an audience in the hall the day before his departure. Why the need for secrecy, when he could have spoken privately while seeking your permission for his trip?'

'Well,' said Hawkwood, taking Scarlett's arm and moving on toward the main house, 'if Il Critto wanted us to break his ciphers, he wanted it for a reason. And I, for one, am determined to nose it out, wherever it takes us.' The *condottiero* gave Scarlett's arm a squeeze. 'Let Desilio continue his work, Adam. All we are after is the truth.'

The truth. Scarlett pondered this weak notion as he resumed his day's tasks. England seemed as far away as ever, and the more he thought over the content of the half-scorched quire, the more he convinced himself that the breaking of the final code would be the last thing in Sir John Hawkwood's interests, or his own. The truth, he sensed with a warming fear, would prove a devastating lie.

FORTY-ONE

Aldgate

On the fourth morning after Simon was taken, I crossed London Bridge at first light and walked once more to Aldgate. From the landing before Chaucer's door I looked far down into the still silence of a London dawn, experiencing the everyday smells and sights – a baker's wife airing a tray of cakes, a smith assaying his coals – with the kind of acuity that comes only with true clarity of purpose. It was time to confront my darkest suspicions.

Chaucer's face was always hard to read. That morning it might have been written in the script of the Moors. He greeted me in the front room. Sparse furnishings, dust-filled cloths on the wall, short shelves of tarnished plate and silver placed at irregular intervals around the interior. The room spoke of Philippa's long absence from the Newgate house. Chaucer had chosen a troubled frown to frame his opening words. 'Simon is missing, I understand.'

'Who told you?'

'That hardly matters.' Chaucer pulled a chair around for

me. 'What matters is his safety, and his return.' His ready knowledge of Simon's peril only made me more furious, though I was determined to show nothing.

'Did you know this would happen, that Simon would be taken?'

He pushed a second chair beneath him and sat, gesturing for me to do the same. 'I worried it might come to this,' he admitted.

'The counterfeiting?'

He shifted on his chair. 'Not that. It's the other matter, I fear.'

'The other matter.' I looked at him blankly.

'Our matter, John.'

I frowned. 'Surely you can't mean—'

'The book.'

'Why? Is there a connection between Simon's abduction and the prophecies?'

'I suspect so, though I have no proof.'

I took the twin chair, maintaining my composure as this sank in. 'I need to know more about the book, Geoffrey. I need to know it now.'

He looked away. In the silence that followed I took Clanvowe's manuscript from my bag and set it on the octagonal table between us. Chaucer stared at it for a moment, then picked it up and leafed through. He grimaced, set it down. 'Clanvowe?'

I nodded.

'I recognized the hand.'

'So did Strode.'

'Though a different hand wrote the book you've been seeking.'

'Whose?'

'It's – complicated, John.'

'So you've known all along.'

'Not entirely.'

'You knew the content of the *De Mortibus* down to the last prophecy.'

'Well—'

'I'll wager you have the thing by rote.'

'Not quite.'

'Yet you sent me chasing after it without bothering to tell me anything.'

'John—'

'And now my son has been taken, probably murdered like Tewburn, or poor Symkok. Will they come for me next, Chaucer?'

'Please, John—'

'And all for a small favour, as you called it. A little thing, John. You'll help me, won't you, John? Help me avoid all that unpleasantness with Swynford, will you, John? And there sat John, didn't he, like a schoolboy waiting for the whip. So deeply in your debt that he couldn't refuse you, not if his life – his *son's* life – depended on it.'

'Simon was—'

'You think because you saved it once his life is now yours to throw away?'

'I couldn't tell you because—'

'Because my ignorance was amusing to you?'

'Because—'

'Because I'm your mouse, a little creature you can tease and claw till it dies?'

'Because—'

'Because you assume that John Gower—'

'*Because I wrote the damn thing, John!*'

At last. I let his words linger. 'Say it again.'

He looked at me, eyes watering. '*Liber de Mortibus Regum Anglorum*. The book is as much my invention as the book of Duchess Blanche, or the *Parliament of Fowls*.'

I sat back, a cold rage running through my veins. Then my joints relaxed, my vision starring as I stood and moved away from him. I honestly did not think he would admit it. Now that he had, I realized how keenly I had wanted it not to be true.

'John—'

'Go to hell, Chaucer.'

'John, as your friend—'

'You are no friend. You are a curse.'

'—as your friend, John, I beg you to see all this from my angle.' From behind me I heard him rise, his shoes crackling the rushes. 'There are constraints on my position. My wife is Swynford's sister. To have revealed my hand in the composition of this work . . . it's difficult to imagine the disaster that might have befallen the duke and his family.'

'And *my* family, Geoffrey?' I said faintly, still turned away. 'Why didn't you trust me with this information in the first place? Did you think I'd betray you to Westminster? You know me better than that.'

'As well as you know me, John.' I turned. Chaucer almost cringed; there were still things he wasn't saying.

'What about this Lollius, then? What was his role in writing the prophecies?'

Chaucer lifted a vase from a nearby shelf, wiping at the dusty brass. 'Lollius is also my invention. A Latinist of real distinction, and his stories are only now being translated into English. He's the *auctor* of what will be my own great work someday, a romance of Troilus.'

'Simon is missing, Chaucer,' I spat. 'Perhaps you might worry about your precious poetry some other time.'

He set down the vase, looking perplexed by his own narcissism.

'And the Lollius of Horace, the poet I chased through Oxford?'

'No relation,' he said. 'Though certainly an inspiration. To blame it all on Horace's Lollius, an unknown poet from ancient Rome? I couldn't pass it up.'

'But to write a poem prophesying the death of our king? You can't be ignorant of the treason statutes, Geoffrey. How many times have you heard them read aloud on the street? To compass or even *imagine* the death of our king: treason pure and plain. You *know* this. I cannot imagine what might have motivated you to write this sort of thing. And "long castle"? You used the same wording in your book for Duchess Blanche. You might as well have signed the damned thing!'

Chaucer was tapping his foot. 'But I didn't – ah, what can I tell you, John, that you won't discover for yourself soon enough?'

'There's *more*?'

'I wrote the *De Mortibus* in Tuscany, John. In Hawkwood's company, during that visit last year. It was a jest, an amusement that took me a few mornings. I never intended it to circulate. But then it went missing.'

'Tuscany.' My skin prickled into gooseflesh. 'Simon knew you'd written it, then.'

He nodded.

'Did he read it?'

'Oh, he read it quite carefully, I should think.'

So Simon knew the *De Mortibus*, had known of it all this time. There was something in Chaucer's tone, though, that bothered me. 'Are you suggesting Simon stole it from you, brought the manuscript with him from Italy?'

He looked at his shoes, a gesture I took then as a sign of shame. Despite his newfound forthrightness, he was still deceiving me, protecting me from knowledge he feared would destroy me. 'The timing doesn't work. It's true that those who took Simon must have made a connection between the book, his service with Hawkwood, and his return to England.

343

But the *De Mortibus* came to London weeks before Simon's arrival.'

'Suggesting what?'

Chaucer's eyes clouded. 'Suggesting there are other forces at work here, John. Larger forces, with motives far from poetical.'

'Isn't there a simple solution?' I said. 'You wrote the prophecies, after all. You can prove it, for the original manuscript is in your hand. And you have the good will of the duke. Why can't we go to him and lay bare what you've done?'

'Impossible.'

'Why?'

'It's gone too far.'

'How so?'

'Well, for one thing, there are already multiple copies circulating. This one you've brought me is in Clanvowe's hand. I assume there are others. Who would believe I wrote it, even if I *were* to confess?'

'So you'll let another man be quartered for your own vanity?'

'It's not so simple.' Chaucer stepped close to me. 'The knowledge of this book reaches deep into Richard's faction. Some of the most powerful men in the realm are arrayed against Lancaster. Warwick, Arundel, Oxford, Buckingham, who knows how many others, all of them convinced that the thirteenth prophecy will shatter the duke's faction, pull the king away from his uncle. If it's known that the *De Mortibus* was written by Geoffrey Chaucer, betraying the king's affinity on the duke's behalf, why – that would be just the wedge the earls need to drive apart Lancaster and the king, breaking an already fragile truce between Richard and Gaunt. Imagine it: Chaucer and Clanvowe, scribbling seditious prophecies at the behest of the recently deceased John

344

Wycliffe and his chief supporter, the Duke of Lancaster. A scandal of the highest order.'

'So it all comes down to politics? Factions and alliances, title and power, government and gossip.'

Chaucer waved a hand. 'Easy for you to say, John. You're a man without a faction – the one fact about you everyone knows. The reason you were chosen for this task was precisely your neutrality. Your ability to do all your dirty work regardless of faction.'

'I "was chosen"? As if the passive voice somehow excuses *your* choice of me as your tool?'

'Oh, you weren't my choice.'

I froze. 'Then whose?'

Chaucer's eyes closed.

'I am sick of your petty secrets. Who suggested to you that I be sent on this fool's errand?'

Chaucer puffed his cheeks, looked at the ceiling. 'Strode.'

Of course. 'And how long has Ralph known that you wrote the prophecies?'

'Since my return from Italy, the week before our meeting at Monksblood's. It was Ralph who convinced me I needed to recover the book. He believed it was already too late to confess I wrote it, which I was prepared to do. We needed your help, your skills. But then, when Simon returned, it was felt that you were too compromised. That you were both in danger.'

I thought again of my trip to Oxford, that earnest conversation with Strode about the allure of false propositions. Strode had been tantalizing me, then, with his *own* false proposition, encouraging my trip to Oxford, even going so far as to write a letter to Angervyle's keeper to help me find a book he knew I would never discover in the bishop's collection. The only factors he had not controlled were my meeting with Clanvowe and the knight's copy of the prophecies.

'Strode was protecting you,' said Chaucer. 'Getting you

345

out of town when things were at their hottest. He continues to protect you, and me as well.'

'*Protect* me? From what? I don't need protection, Geoffrey. My *son* needs protection. He's the one suffering for my sake, as we stand here jawing about your ridiculous prophecies.' I felt short of breath.

'We all need protection,' Chaucer gently said, risking a hand on my back. Despite myself I did not knock it away. 'Don't you see? The book is an axe at our necks. I wrote it in Italy. Simon read it there, and he's missing. You are Simon's father, and you have a copy of the *De Mortibus* yourself. You received it from Clanvowe while dining with Purvey, Wycliffe's closest disciple. Barely four hundreds lines of my doggerel, and they threaten us all.'

'And King Richard.'

'And King Richard,' he agreed.

'Who is behind all this, Chaucer?'

'Hawkwood.' A blood-soaked name. 'I believe he's plotting a return to England. He wants to ensure his legacy, win a greater title for his descendants. Rather than retiring happily to Essex, though, he plans to destabilize the realm by implicating Lancaster in this plot against the king. Hawkwood has Oxford in his pocket, you see. His ties to the de Veres go back two genera-tions, and that's a family that would do anything to heighten its status. Weldon is the go-between. He's now Oxford's man, but for years he served Hawkwood in the White Company. He led the massacre at Cesena, the slaughter of an entire town.'

I thought of the scar on Weldon's chin, the butchery of which the man had long seemed capable. 'And now Weldon is doing everything he can to see the plot to its completion.'

'It's why Simon was seized, I believe, because he's associ-ated with Hawkwood, and knows his plans.'

'As do you, Geoffrey.'

'Even Strode isn't safe,' he continued. 'The only thing to

346

do now is to recover my copy, hunt down any others, and hope for the best. Unless—'

I looked at him. 'Unless?'

'Unless we can find the cloth.'

'What cloth?'

'An ornate piece of work, embroidered with the livery of Gaunt, the alleged conspirator, raising a sword against King Richard. It travelled with the book from Italy.'

'Who made it?'

He looked away and breathed deeply. 'It fits the *De Mortibus* as a glove fits a hand,' he said, ignoring my question. 'From Strode's inquiries we know that the book has been separated from the cloth. Whoever puts the book with the cloth, then—'

'Will destroy the realm.'

'Or save it,' he said. Then he actually smiled. 'There's one final wrinkle.'

'Why am I not surprised?'

'I have it from Strode that the book was brought into the city by maudlyns.'

'*Maudlyns?*' A stir of the absurd.

'Apparently some whore got ahold of it just as I was asking you to find it for me. You'll remember the girl's murder, outside the city walls—'

'In the Moorfields,' I said.

'They sold the book, or tried to. Strode doesn't know who paid them for it. He's trying even now to find out, asking all kinds of questions. The cloth, on the other hand, has not been seen.'

'So they still have it.'

'Presumably.'

I thought about this. 'And I suppose there's no one more suited, in Strode's opinion and yours, to extracting this cloth from the maudlyns of our city than one John Gower.'

'Well, if it's any comfort, you may be the only one looking for it.'

'Where should I begin?'

'Gropecunt Lane, I imagine. Or Southwark. Perhaps Rose Alley, in your own neighbourhood.'

'And how does one go about prying cloth from maudlyns, in your expert opinion?'

Chaucer turned to me, his brow a world-weary arch. 'Drag a sack of silver through the stews and there's no telling what you might find.'

He said it lightly, provoking me with a familiar humour that obscured those deeper truths he still had not revealed.

✤ ✤ ✤

You will remember, my soul, that Dante Alighieri, the great poet of Florence, first saw Beatrice at a feast. He was only nine at the time, as was she, yet even then the arrows of Amor penetrated him deeply, inspiring wild thrums and tremblings and pulsations in his heart despite its tender age.

Our young lady was fully a woman when she first saw her love, though the effects on her soul were no less childish, no less urgent for her greater maturity.

It was an autumn evening on the feast of St Luke, just after the procession of the physicians along the square before San Simpliciano. The last company had passed by, the raucous shouts of the children following in their wake, the oily whiff of torches in the air. As the final cluster of drunk doctors walked past she looked across the open space to the opposite rank of spectators – and there he was, in the smoky light: a fair-haired man, twenty years her elder, she guessed, broad of chest, long of leg, a face that brightened the air as if some new Apollo had deigned to troll the streets of Florence.

The man spared her no glance, turning from the procession and walking along the edge of the crowd.

She saw him again the next week, at the Broletto, pausing at a tinker's table while she examined silks. That day he wore a loose shirt of thin wool, a rough thing hardly fit for a clerk. As she passed behind him she glanced at his hands, those long fingers stained with gall. A man given to writing, despite his unslouched back and clear-eyed gaze at everything around him. He smelled of balsam, of honey mixed with ale.

How she pined for him! How she ached to feel his touch, to guide his blotchy fingers in making of her very skin his vellum and his books.

Then, as she watched him stroll across the market street, he was stopped and embraced warmly by a man she knew quite well.

Il Critto! They were countrymen, of course, though there were so many Englishmen in Florence that she had not thought to ask her suitor about the one she most desired.

'Who was that old fellow I saw you with at the Broletto?' she casually asked him the next morning. They were in the upper gallery, finally usable after a months-long repair to the flooring, seated on the long bench beneath the Tribunale tapestry. Her stepmother sat with several visitors at a proper distance. Embroidery and gossip.

'An envoy from Westminster, and an intimate friend of my father's,' he said, suspecting nothing. 'He arranged my current position with Hawkwood, in fact. I owe him a great deal.' He was proud of his knowledge of Hawkwood's relations with the English envoy, whom he seemed to admire tremendously. He told her a bit about the man's employment (royal customs official), purpose on the peninsula (some discreet diplomacy), obsession (poetry), and wife (estranged).

With a frown and a strange tilt of his head, he pointed over her shoulder. 'Why, look there! Those are the arms of his greatest supporter.'

She turned, her gaze falling on the old cloth embroidered with the opposed livery of the foreign duke and prince. She felt it: the breath of Fate on her neck. To learn that the man she desired was in favour with the duke who had saved her life so long ago – this was a destined match. Everything else would naturally follow.

So she dropped a hint, a mild suggestion, and the next day *Il Critto* (poor fool, she thought) dutifully brought the older man with him to her father's house.

It was a simple matter to put her ambitions in play. A half-hidden smile here, a dropped kerchief there. The Little Weasel no more, she had developed into a captivating beauty, one of the true gems among the ladies of the Commune. Soon enough his visits became the most longed-for part of her day.

They discovered in one another a mutual love of stories and poems. His verses were artful and urbane, pleasuring some hidden part of her with their depth of knowledge and craft. He whispered, too, from some of his more lecherous lays, comparing his desire to a written map of the world, himself to a cold fish marinated in the spicy sauce of her favour. She became an avid listener to this Narcissus of the North, his impenetrable self-regard only warming her further.

The ambassador wrote his poems not on wax but in little books, parchment quires folded within a worn cover of faded leather. Each time he filled one of these booklets with his notes and drafts he would remove it from its cover and place a new quire within. He wrote constantly, rejecting nine out of ten of his own crafted lines. She marvelled at how one man could waste so many words.

Her own stories she spun from the tales of the Moors remembered from her mother. She was his Sherazade, filling her accounts with flying horses and evil viziers, moaning ghouls and poisoned fountains. The only tale she never told him was the story of her life.

One of their favourite entertainments was trading in riddles. Enigmas, he called them, word puzzles in which simple truths are disguised and things are never what they seem. He would slip them to her on torn lengths of waste paper, and she would have to guess their solution before his next appearance.

Some were trivial, riddles about roofless houses and eggs, or chairs and silent goats.

Others were obscene, written to raise a blush on her fair skin.

I am a long rod swinging by a man's leg. He likes to shove me into familiar holes. Who am I? No, not that. A key.

Between two curved legs I quiver, a twist of eager flesh, singing sweetly when fingered. Who am I? No, not that. A harpstring.

The one that most provoked her was an enigma of the moon. He

351

slipped it to her on the second Sunday in Advent, during a procession outside San Lorenzo.

> Whisper the middle of a moon,
> Think the wheel of a wagon,
> Trace the beginning of a king,
>   And mine own shall be yours.

For a full week she puzzled over its meaning, parsing each syllable, looking for that hidden kernel. And on the eighth night, as she slept, a wagon wheel spinning in her dreams—

—she awoke, and she had it. A wheel? The letter O. The 'beginning of a king'? 'King' is 'rex' in Latin. The letter R. And the 'middle of a moon'? A half-moon, of course. The letter C.

'Cor.' Latin for 'heart'. And mine yours, she silently promised him as she drifted back to sleep, and my flesh as well.

Stories, riddles, sin: her father and stepmother were hardly pleased. Florence was starting to whisper, and consorting with this Englishman would only sully her reputation. Il Critto is the son of a landed gentryman, her stepmother scolded her, an upper esquire. This man you favour is merely an esquire en service, with no lands or rents to his name – and married!

Il Critto, too, took notice of her growing attachment to the older man, coming around less frequently and casting dark looks on the two of them from afar. She ignored them all.

Though she recognized the older man's poetical genius (as, indeed, what living man or woman could not? you are surely thinking), some of his making struck her as facile and unserious. She coyly told him so, infuriating and delighting him at once. He told her of his plan for a greater work, a collection of tales in the manner of Boccaccio.

'Though this work, unlike the Decameron, shall be framed not with pestilence but with pilgrimage,' he said. 'The pilgrims shall

all tell their own tales as they travel from city to town. Two stories each on the journey out, two on the way home. The narrator will be a pilgrim as well, his feeble talents serving to convince us that the whole compilation bears the ring of truth.'

She taunted him: 'Your readers must be gullible indeed, to fall for such poetical tricks.'

He waved a hand. 'In this land poets are considered akin to prophets. Look at Florence's own Dante, writing of a journey to Hell and back, telling us plainly it is all a lie even as he inks his tercets at his desk. And yet the people credit him as a true visitor to the underworld! Readers will believe anything they are told to believe.'

She looked at him, a provocation in her gaze. 'And you would be the new Dante? Spouting visions and prophecies with the ease of a sibyl?'

'Prophecy is a game like any other, no more complex than our exchanges of riddles and enigmas,' he said. 'Show me a lunatic with a quill and I will show you a prophet.'

'Prove it,' she said.

'I shall rise to your impertinent challenge,' he vowed, and began a work that promised to redeem his talents in her eyes, and win her to his bed. 'It shall be a book of kings,' he told her. 'A book of kings, and their deaths. Once I have completed it, you must quite me with a work of your own. For then it will be your turn to write for the gullible.'

Less than a week had passed when, on a bright winter morning, the ambassador appeared at her door.

'The work is done,' he told her, pleased with himself. He pulled out his current booklet, which he had filled to the last folio with a rough copy of his creation. 'Take me within, muse, and I shall read it to you.'

Just then his young rival appeared at the end of the street. Il Critto's eyes darkened as he strode forward, his jaw a hard knot of envy. But her love put a kindly arm around the younger man's shoulders and drew him into her father's house, as if nothing was amiss. The three of them went up to the gallery, and it was there that she heard the prophecies.

As her lover recited his tuneful lines, she listened with a thrilled amusement to these beguiling prognostications of royal deaths. How he laughed over his own audacity! The work was an amusement to him, its mortal prophecies cast in the gentle light of his wit.

He had even thought to include an actual game in his prophecies: the thistleflowers, hawks, swords, and plums painted on the oval playing cards he often brought with him to her father's house. Yet to anyone else hearing the work, these prophecies would appear genuine, the true products of some latter-day Jeremiah foretelling the deaths of twelve kings, from poor King William to the late King Edward.

Il Critto laughed with them, his boyish grin easing their concerns that—

Ah, but I must drop the pretence of story, my heart. As I think back on that fateful morning, all I see now are Il Critto's owl eyes gazing over my shoulder at the cloth, those mole's ears resounding with your baleful verse. The eyes and ears of Simon Gower, a serpent coiled in envy and plotting his revenge.

FORTY-TWO

Gropecunt Lane

Years ago, soon after the deaths of my elder children, I once followed the Bishop of Ely up Soper Lane, watched him hand a few coins to a maudlyn, and waited as he disappeared into a stall. I confronted him that same afternoon with the evidence of his sin: a copy of the whore's confession, purchased from a clerk at Guildhall after her arranged arrest. For a pound it can all be forgotten, I said. The archbishop won't have to know.

I'll never forget the look he gave me, half scornful, half amused as he leaned against a column in the west end of St Paul's. Know what, Gower? That I just swyved his favourite whore?

What I learned that day was that episcopal visitations with whores were not only not off-limits but commonplace. Unusable. I never again bothered with maudlyns.

So despite my easy familiarity with the underside of London, I felt a bit awkward as I stood at the foot of Gropecunt Lane that afternoon, wondering how it all worked. I did not have to speculate for long. Fewer than five steps into the lane I was confronted by an aggressive young woman who stepped from the shadows of a horsestall. 'Fancy a bit, good sir?' Her hair, unhooded and wild, swept from her brow in a tempestuous wave. Her eye sockets had been blackened with coal or pitch: a Gorgon, her cheeks painted in a red shade rubbed into pink circles. I shook my head tightly and walked on.

Several more maudlyns accosted me on my way up the lane, chirping of their smooth skin, their fair breasts, their shapely buttocks, ripe for you, sir, ripe for you. Near the end of the lane one final woman stepped forward. Her hair had a reddish sheen and she was small, delicate. She put her arms around me, pushing her lithe form against mine. 'I've a young body for your use, good sir,' she said. 'Youngest you'll find on this stretch, sure.'

I gently removed myself. 'Fourpence to talk.'

'Talk?' She pulled away. 'Want to talk to me that way, do you? Price be the same, though.'

'Not that kind of talk. I need to ask some questions.'

'Like them constables?'

'I'm not an arm of the law. Not even a finger.'

She squinted up at me, scrutinizing my intentions. 'You'll want me bawd,' she said softly, putting a hand on my chest, and I felt in the lingering pressure a gentle warning as she hurried down toward St Pancras. She returned with a large, triple-chinned woman wearing a dun dress of shapeless wool and a hat covered in embroidered flowers, all faded with the years.

'This be Joan Rugg, sir.'

I nodded my thanks, then half-bowed to the bawd. 'Mistress Rugg.'

She beamed. 'Your first time on Gropecunt Lane?'

'It is,' I admitted, strangely abashed, as if I should have been expected to possess more experience of whoring.

'Well,' she huffed. 'We're a mite careful up this way with strangers.'

'I understand.'

'Your purpose?'

'I seek a young woman.'

'Queynt?'

'Questions. It will be worth her while to meet with me.' I jangled my purse.

Joan Rugg eyed it. 'What sort of questions?'

I took a risk; time was short. 'Questions about a book. And a cloth.'

Her eyes narrowed into doughy crescents. 'We're not much for books up this way.'

'I don't imagine you are,' I said, watching her. 'Though this book is a special case.'

She considered this. 'You're not the only one asking questions about such matters.'

'Oh?' I said, acting surprised.

'We've had constables, beadles, brigands of a sort.' She was boasting about it. 'Busted us up something good, shut us down for a bit – though the well be full again already, appetites of cock being what they are.'

'Your maudlyns are in danger, Mistress Rugg.'

She put a hand to her chins. 'You puts me in mind of Master Gartner, good sir, the great lover of me youth. Been departed this earth these many year, though not a bell tolls without his face comes to my imagining. Knew the ways of queynt, Master Gartner did. Played me jolly body like a sautrie, and the pole on him would do Gawain's charger proud.'

She took my stunned silence as an invitation to continue.

'It was Master Gartner purchased me this hat by Haberdasher's Hall.' Fingering it. 'Bands of silk, leather for the brim, the most curious flowers here, and here' – her wide

357

arms rose together as she pointed at the faded buds – 'and all for his ladylove. This hat, for all its beauty, Master Gartner says, be the unworthy gloss of your own beauty, Joan Rugg. Let it ever rest upon your fair head as testament of our cherishing. Let it have humble place there, Joan Rugg, its role ever to shade thy fair skin from the ravages of sun and rain. And ever there it has sat, good sir, nigh on twenty year, and there it will sit even to me grave.'

She stared off in a silent reverie that I ended with a gentle cough. The bawd snapped her head around and saw the quarter noble between my fingers. She snatched it. 'Didn't tell them any of it, nor did my girls breathe a word.'

'Tell them what?'

'But I suppose I'll tell you who might tell you who has it. Or tell you who might tell you who might tell you who has it, as the case might be.'

Patiently I said, 'And who would that be?'

'Bess Waller,' she whispered. 'Queen whore of Southwark. Sign of the Pricking Bishop, Rose Alley.'

Rose Alley. The Bishop of Winchester's liberties, up the bankside from St Mary Overey. Joan Rugg had named a bawdy house not a hundred steps from my own front door.

I arrived within the hour to find the narrow lane nearly deserted. Grateful for the lack of idle eyes, I approached the Pricking Bishop and gave a nod to the old woman seated in the low stone entryway. Her skin, pitted with pox and age, twisted into a quizzical frown when I announced myself.

'Gower, flower, hour, power – your name makes no differ-ence to me,' she wheezed. 'Now, coin? That'll open St Cath's ear, sure as a morning stiffie opens her legs.'

I tossed her a groat then stepped into an empty front room, the only furnishings a low table swirled with old candle wax, a rough bench against the far wall. A narrow door gave on to the next room, where a young woman wearing only a shift lay on a pallet, snoring loudly. Despite the open window the space reeked of couplings. The maudlyn's eyes fluttered open, then narrowed as she put on an alluring smile and, keeping her gaze locked on to mine, rolled on to her back and raised her shift.

I looked away. 'Cover yourself.'

'As you please,' she said, coming to her knees. 'Most like to start right off, but I don't mind the wait.'

'Is your proprietress about?' I asked.

'Eh?'

'Bess Waller?'

She fixed me with a cold stare, then got to her feet and put her head out the window. '*Besswaller!*' One animal-like burst of sound, then another: '*Gen'manforyou!*' With that she stalked out of the room, leaving me alone. I paced the width of the chamber, trying to ignore my surroundings.

'Sir.'

I turned. In the doorway stood a woman of uncommon beauty despite her age. Her hair fell loosely about her shoulders in ringlets that clung to a long neck rising from a yellow dress. This was faded, austere, but shaped closely to her slim form.

'Mistress Waller?'

'The same.' A sharp, inquisitive voice; no need for niceties here.

'I've come to make a purchase from you.' I held out a purse.

She looked at it with some irritation, then back at me. 'Want a girl to carry along, take home to bed? That's not my trade, sir, not been these five year. The law of the bishop's stews makes plain: swyving permitted in his houses only, not yours.'

'It's not flesh I'm after. It's a cloth.'

She started, tried to hide it. Turning away, she went to the window and laid her hand on the sill. 'Yet you come here unarmed.' She gave me a wistful smile. 'Joan Rugg sent you, I'll be bound.' Her voice had dulled, tinged with sorrow.

'She did.'

'All my slits been chased from this house on account of that damned book. Constables, king's men – St Loy knows what they were.'

'A cloth?' I prompted. She said nothing, and still looked suspicious. 'We're fellow parishioners, Mistress Waller. I let a house from St Mary Overey, and have for some ten years.' Though I had never seen the bawd at the priory, parish identity is nearly as strong as blood. We are neighbours, I was telling her; you can trust me.

She sighed. 'You'll be wanting my daughter.'

'Your daughter.'

'Millicent,' she said. 'Millicent Fonteyn. Got herself in a muck of trouble, she did, and my Ag as well. My younger. Buried her in Spitalfields, poor little maudlyn as she was.' Her eyes teared.

I waited a suitable interval. 'Was your daughter the woman slain in the Moorfields this March?'

She shook her head. 'But Ag's the one saw that girl die, sure as light from lamps.'

I recalled the barristers' play at Temple Hall: the wig, the paint, the furore of the serjeants. 'Where is Millicent now?'

'Not up Cornhull, that's sure.'

I shook the purse. 'Where is she?'

She looked down at the purse, then into my eyes. She exhaled. 'St Leonard's Bromley.' Bess Waller turned and departed the chamber, leaving the purse in my hand.

FORTY-THREE

St Leonard's Bromley

In the parlour Millicent sat at the prioress's feet, watching John Gower. A tall man, quiet but confident, handsome if somewhat gaunt, with a neatly trimmed beard and a peculiar cast to his aquamarine eyes. These were piercing yet somehow clouded and he blinked frequently at times, as if warding off a troublesome gnat. Millicent had heard the name before, a whisper of disapproval from Sir Humphrey ap-Roger in one of his frequent fits of pique at the vagaries of courtly politics. She could tell Gower was troubled, or else hadn't slept in weeks. Dark crescents smeared beneath those curious eyes, his spine a tired arc. Yet he seemed to have the trust of the prioress.

With her work obscured by Isabel's robes, Millicent listened as the two of them discussed it all. The book, the prophecies, a futile search at Oxford, the fate of his missing son. It was amazing, what he said. For during the same span of weeks in which she had sought to sell the book, this man had been searching urgently for it, and would have been happy to part with a great sum to procure it – yet Millicent had never crossed paths with him, nor even heard of his existence. Now here they were at St Leonard's Bromley, neither in possession of the manuscript, yet both intent on forestalling the threat to King Richard this evil work embodied.

'You haven't seen the book yourself?' Isabel asked him.

'Not the original,' he replied. 'Though I have read the *De Mortibus* in a copy.'

'And you believe we have this book here at Bromley?'

'No, Reverend Mother. Not the book.'

'You've come about the cloth, then.'

'I was told by a certain – well, a certain procuress of my acquaintance—'

'A *procuress*, Gower?'

'—a bawd of Rose Alley—'

'A *bawd*?'

'—by a bawd of Rose Alley—'

'Not of your *warm* acquaintance, I should hope.'

'I only met her yesterday.'

'And she told you what?'

'That I should ask after her daughter, Millicent. That I would find her here, at St Leonard's.'

'And what is the significance of this cloth, Master Gower?'

'I have been told that it is embroidered with the livery of the supposed conspirators against King Richard. That it reveals their identity without question.'

'So this cloth must be revealed, to preserve the life of the king against his would-be assassins?'

Gower hesitated. 'Or be destroyed. This entire affair, I believe, is a fabrication, an attempt to make an innocent lord appear guilty of the worst crime imaginable.'

'Oxford's doing, of course.'

Gower stared at her. 'How—'

'Oh, you're not the only one with good sources, Gower.' She cast a sidelong look at Millicent.

'Yes, Reverend Mother.' He cleared his throat, blinked those eyes. 'In any case, the feast of St Dunstan is in a week. The king will appear at a great feast at the Bishop of Winchester's palace. The details of the prophecy suggest the attempt on Richard will happen there.'

'When, precisely?'

'The prophecy maintains that the assassin will spring forth "at spiritus sung". I believe this refers to a processional proper to that day. Evidently the attempt on Richard's life will take place during its performance. At "Prince of Plums", so the prophecy reads.'

'A curious phrase, Prince of Plums.'

'I believe it refers to a game of cards.'

'Cards.'

'Playing cards, Prioress. They're all the rage at court. Swynford herself owns a deck, and is known for inventing new games. The plums, thistleflowers, hawks, and swords are suits – with cards ranging from one to nine in each suit, and face cards ordered as princes, dukes, queens, and kings.'

Seven of Swords, Millicent thought with a thrill, finally understanding the strange symbols positioned around the centre of the cloth.

'So then.' She tightened her habit, spreading the material tautly across her knees. 'It all comes down to the cloth.'

'The cloth is the key to the book. If we can—'

'We have it.'

A pause. 'I suspected as much, Prioress.'

'Allow me to present Millicent Fonteyn, one of our laysisters. She brought the cloth here several days ago. Millicent, explain how it came to you.'

Millicent stood and Gower raised his chin, watching as she haltingly began her account. She watched his face in turn, noting the flickers in his eyes, the changes in his colour as he heard her story. He interrupted her to ask questions, probe the details, and it was in those moments of heightened attention that his eyes remained open and unblinking. He was taken with her intricate memory of the prophecies, which seemed to match his own knowledge. When she had finished she bowed her head and waited.

Isabel said, 'Show him the cloth.'

Millicent reached for her work.

'The other one.'

She turned to Isabel's great chair and lifted the original cloth from the back. She held it out for Gower's inspection, seeing through his eyes the violent scene of treason limned in thread of so many hues: the boyish face of a crowned prince or king, his brows knit together, his mouth opened in a cry of surprise; the long knife pointed at his heart; the bearded face of the attacker, scowling as he aimed the weapon at the royal breast; the heraldry of England's greatest magnate, poised against the royal livery of his victim.

Gower slowly shook his head. 'Lancaster, of course. The obvious suspect.'

'Quite,' said Isabel. 'The cloth is clearly an attempt to incriminate Gaunt, to make him seem the prophesied slayer of his nephew.'

'Though—'

'I don't believe it for a minute, of course, and neither do you. Yet what we believe is hardly at issue. What our flighty young king can be made to believe? That is another matter.'

'The cloth must remain hidden, Reverend Mother. If anyone puts this with the book there will be no mercy for Lancaster.'

Isabel turned. 'Millicent, show Master Gower your work.'

'Yes, Prioress.' Millicent stooped and gathered up her embroidery: a shield and badge, crafted in the style of the cloth, and nearly ready for careful boring into the original.

Gower stared, his high brow lined in thought. As Millicent

watched, the creases grew shallower, his skin smoother, until his lean face took on an almost beatific smile. Finally he looked up, his hand on his stomach, and laughed the laugh of a man unused to merriment. A crazed and joyous sound.

When he recovered, Gower looked at the prioress, his sobriety returned. 'How will you get the altered cloth into the right hands?'

'Millicent will pass it to Lady Katherine Swynford just before the feast,' said Isabel. She explained the abbey's connection to Gaunt's mistress. 'Lady Katherine will be expecting the cloth, and we'll depend on her to reveal it at the right moment.'

Gower shook his head. 'With respect, Reverend Mother, I don't believe relying on Swynford is wise.'

Isabel was unused to being contradicted, especially in her own parlour. 'You have a better idea?'

A slender finger to his chin. 'I have in mind an unusual alliance, Reverend Mother. An alliance that only the direst threat to the realm could create.'

The prioress tilted her head. 'Tell me, Gower.'

FORTY-FOUR

St Mary Overey

Southwark suffered the vigil of St Dunstan beneath a soaking spring rain, the clouds low and close, the house damp with cold as I spent a day alone at my writing desk. Scribbles, pen trials, some scattered rhymes in French and English were the extent of my accomplishment, distracted as I was. I drank far too much wine at supper, also taken alone, and retired early with an ache in my head and a tightness in my gut, fearful of what the feast day would bring.

Though the fear, I discovered, was not as acute as the ignorance. Having gone through most of adulthood in firm control of nearly every aspect of my life, it was jarring to anticipate an event of such magnitude that was entirely out of my hands. No one to threaten or bribe; no whispered scandal to use; no idea whether my son lived or suffered; no certainty about whether the entire course of events over the last weeks had been anything more than a phantom.

That night, sunk in a deep slumber, I saw a tower on a hill, and below it a field stretching to the horizon. On the field were hundreds of ploughmen, toiling silently in unison, digging in the soil, though for what wasn't clear. All they turned up was rock, heavy stones they would shove to the side before going back to their holes for more. The ploughmen worked for what felt like hours, days, weeks. Then, like a scythe cutting through a lawn, sleep overcame them all simultaneously, and they fell to the ground.

It was only then that I realized I was one of them. My hands were filthy with the muck of the field, my back an aching quarter moon, my joints exhausted and worn after a fruitless search for the unknown.

At one point in my dream I had the distinct sense of an obscure figure hovering over me. I could not make out any features, as a luminous arc shone from behind. An angel? Its touch was warm, its breath moist on my skin. It spoke. *I am sorry, Father. Sorrier than you will ever know.* An urgent whisper, a gentle hand on my cheek.

I woke with a start, drenched in fear, my heart fluttering beneath my ribs. No one there. Or was that—? A presence I knew. The smell of my son.

Simon. There, in the doorway, backing out. 'I – I am sorry, Father,' he murmured, seemingly to himself. 'Forgive me, Father. You must forgive me. So – so sorry—'

I came fully awake only to see him turn and stumble forward into the gallery. I called after him but his footsteps were already on the back stairs, clomping down to the rear garden. The slam of a door. I threw open the shutters. He was in the priory sideyard, awash with silver beneath a newly cloudless sky, making diagonally for the high street. I called out again but he ignored me. He ran with a limp, a new injury, his hand clutching a dark bundle against his side.

I lit a candle and walked through the house, sensing his traces in every room. An overturned chair, a table set at an unfamiliar angle against the hall wall.

I immediately saw why. High on the western face of the hall

367

hung the Gower arms, the colours and crest of my father and his father, embossed on an oaken shield that had once hung in our family seat. The shield had been torn from the wall and now hung by one corner, exposing a small recess gouged from wattle and daub between the timbers. I stood on the table and reached into the hole, feeling only the rough boards on the house's street side. The hole was just the right size to hide a large purse, a box of gems, perhaps a silver cross.

Or a book.

FORTY-FIVE

New Rents, before Winchester Palace

The poor of Southwark could smell out a feast from a league's distance, and here they were, all shapes, sizes, and ages, crowding Eleanor's way, though also masking her from anyone who might be watching for her. Closest to the palace's great outer gate stood the usual clutch of old gossips, making a din that competed with the hoarse shouts of the men ranked behind.

'First and third argent? That's Buckingham, sure.'

'And there's Warwick's dragons, I'll be bound.'

'Ah, Lady Anne!'

Earls and bishops, knights and squires, even the untitled were recognized and named as they rode through the gates and into the palace grounds. Most slowed to hand out coins or purses, some more liberally than others.

Midway through this procession of gentry there arrived an armed man on horseback whose appearance raised a less welcoming note from the crowd. A knight, Eleanor saw: lean, tall on his horse. She couldn't see his face from that angle.

He turned his head. Eleanor gasped. From his lip to the

lower part of his chin a wide scar traced a crescent, the only flaw on his ruddy skin. With a thrum of fear, Eleanor recognized him: the man from Gropecunt Lane, the man she felt certain had killed poor James Tewburn. Sir Stephen, the night watchers had called him.

With her own face hidden, chin at her chest, Eleanor leaned over to the bonneted woman to her left. 'Who's that, the knight just there?'

'Sir Stephen Weldon,' she replied with a look of disgust. 'Most generous man in England, gifted my purse with an entire farthing last of Wykeham's feasts. He'd pinch a dead babe's face for the coin in its eyes.' Eleanor watched Weldon carefully as he made his way through the guarded gate.

She looked down the high street, along the market rows, waiting for Gerald and thinking about the meaning of Weldon's presence at the feast. Eventually, through a gap in the crowd, she spotted the butchers making their way up New Rents. As Gerald had told her, the bishop didn't like too many fires going at once on the grounds, least when the king was to be present. So twenty lambs and six piglets would be spitted by Wykeham's cooks in a shallow firepit along Cutter Lane, to be carted to the palace for carving, and now here they were. Ten butchers and apprentices processed with the cooked flesh, guarded by bishop's men on either side to keep the hands of the poor off the tender meat, which wafted a delicious scent throughout the market. Grimes himself was in the lead, a pompous air about him, full of his own status as the unofficial leader of the guildless Southwark meaters. Eleanor saw the wild look in his eyes as he fingered the two large knives strapped to his side. Gerald walked at the rear of the bunch, loping after the last cart as it drew toward the smaller postern a ways up from the gate.

Eleanor dashed to the far side of the street past the fish-wives' tables, the custard-mongers and bakers along the drainage. After a careful look in both directions, she stepped forward and grasped Gerald's arm as Grimes disappeared through the postern.

Gerald looked at her, surprised. 'Not a place for you to be, Ed—Eleanor,' he murmured beneath the market din. 'Not today, at all rates.'

'Nor you, Gerald,' she whispered, pressing his arm. 'It's all known to the bishop's men.'

The third butcher and his apprentice wheeled the second handcart through the postern.

'What's known?'

The third cart was stuck, a wheel wedged between two stones. Three of the men worked to free it. 'Give a hand, Rykener,' grumbled one of them, seeing Gerald idling with a woman.

'All of it,' she said. 'Who, how, when.'

He looked at her as he backed toward the postern, a shade of doubt in his eyes. She stepped toward him, chin out as she breathed a last warning into his ear. 'And they're *ready* for it, Gerald. You have to get out of this somehow, prophecy and Grimes be damned. Disappear, while you can.'

'What's the hold-up, boys?' Grimes, his greasy face reappearing at the postern. His eyes darkened when he saw Eleanor. 'Get that swervin' ganymede outta my boy's way,' he said to one of the guards. He pulled Gerald inside the walls.

A guard pushed her roughly from the cart, now freed and rolling forward. The bell of St Mary Overey shuddered above them. The guard started closing the door from within. As she backed away from the postern Eleanor caught a last glimpse of her brother's face, a wan circle of fear.

FORTY-SIX

Winchester Palace

Luke Hodge had served William Wykeham as chief steward for nearly twenty years, rising to a position of quiet prominence in the official life of Southwark. Our early acquaintance had involved a sensitive matter regarding Hodge's daughter that had left him breathless with gratitude. Despite the pre-feast frenzy, the bishop's steward was glad to invite me within the palace's service gate to observe the final preparations.

As the first arrivals streamed through the gates the inner gardens and hall were abustle, the large staff garlanding shrubs and trees, setting tables with servingware and glass, arranging chairs. On the lawn a large tent was being raised, and in the hall, where the wide doors sat open to the inner court, I noted tables set up in the northeast corner for games and amusements. On the dais the bishop's high table beneath the baldachin was arrayed with serving dishes and a ship of salt-pot and cutlery. A dozen ewers stood in a line along the south wall.

I found an inconspicuous spot by the outer passage to the bishop's kitchens, massive chambers filled with smoke, yells, the clatter of roasting pans and utensils. A company of butchers arrived with spitted lambs, which they flung on boards and proceeded to carve with a determined energy, flashing knives glistening with grease, competing with the bishop's own cooks as they loaded the results on to large platters held by the servers. As I watched them at their work I started to notice several of the men trading peculiar looks, as if sharing an unspoken secret among themselves. Others were pale in the face as they carved, and I wondered for a moment if they might be ill. Then one of the butchers, a large, beefy man who seemed to be the leader, started to move among the others, patting their backs, speaking softly into their ears, getting grim nods in return, though one young man, perhaps his apprentice, received a hard smack to the ear, and an order to get to it.

By bank of a bishop shall butchers abide.

The line came to me with the force of a hard sneeze. *Butchers.* A metaphor, I had thought, signifying a clutch of armed men primed to attack the king during the feast. Yet what more efficient, more sinister plan could one hatch than to enlist a company of butchers, already armed to the teeth, in the slaying of a royal? The lower trades of Southwark had acted notoriously during the rising, none more so than the butchers. What if the butchers named in the prophecy as Richard's killers were not soldiers or knights after all but . . . just butchers?

I moved quickly out to the kitchen yard, where Hodge stood on a tree stump and addressed a crowd of servants. 'The hour before the king's arrival there will be games and amusements in the hall,' he called out. 'Beers, wines, bird tarts. Aim here is to refresh the ladies' cups as often as possible.'

A few gruff laughs.

'Upon the arrival of His Highness the company will

proceed to the gardens. Then Mass for St Dunstan, with the bishop presiding. Craddock, the mass pavilion?'

A man to the steward's left visibly winced. 'Cracked post, sir.' He held up his axe. 'But we felled us that small elm before the gates at sunrise—'

'Yes, I heard you at it – as did the lord bishop.'

'Ah!' the man said to scattered chuckles. 'So his worship'll know we got it down, then. Tent'll be upright sooner than a cock at a maud's mouth.'

'Glad to hear it. The bishop's pulpit?'

'Already in place, carted out last night.'

This went on until the steward had ticked most of the way through his list, then he clapped his hands. 'A word more.' Hodge straightened himself, spreading a wise smile to all corners. 'We are to have an additional guest or twenty at our feast this day. With the bishop's consent, His Most Indisputably Charming, His Most Esteemed, Generous, and His Most Faultless and Unimpeachable, His Most Excessively Irreproachable Excellency the Duke of Lancaster will be present for the festivities.'

A low murmur from the servants, some calls of scorn. Wykeham and Lancaster despised each other, a sentiment shared throughout the factions of the two magnates, from the lowliest stableboy to the uppermost baron. The domestic servants gathered here would be especially keen in their bitterness toward Gaunt, whose notorious contempt for the commons flavoured every mention of the duke among the city's servingmen.

'I'm told that His Highness King Richard wishes to put an end to the enduring hostilities between our households,' Hodge continued. 'His esteemed uncle, his most trusted bishop – these men should be allies, not enemies. And for today, at least, they shall.'

'Bah!' came a call from the crowd's edges. Hodge shrugged.

'Look to your work. It's not your pounds paying for the puddings.'

'Just our backs,' someone muttered.

Hodge dismissed them all after a few words with the head cook. I followed him into the hall, where he wiped out a silver soup basin as I approached him. 'Gower!' he said, looking up. 'Settling in for a long day?'

I hesitated. 'Keep a hard eye on those butchers, Hodge.'

He looked at me strangely. 'Why's that?'

Challenging me, as if he knew already what to expect. Taken aback, I stumbled a bit, then said, 'Keep an eye on them, will you?'

A thin smile. 'Already am, Gower. Already am.' He left me there, feeling rather foolish, and only slightly reassured.

In the lower lawn the accoutrements of the bishop's Mass had been arranged at the east end of the pavilion. Most notable was Winchester's moveable pulpit, an ornately crafted thing of polished wood with ivory inlays that had been carted out to elevate the bishop above the congregation for his St Dunstan's sermon. I stopped in front of it. In addition to Wykeham's arms, two chevrons sable between three roses gules, the front panel had been carved with the same pearl-and-oyster pattern visible on the stonework above the hall. *In palace of prelate with pearls all appointed*. I stared at the woodwork. Even here, at the site of the bishop's holy Mass for St Dunstan, the signs of King Richard's death.

FORTY-SEVEN

Pepper Alley, Southwark

Millicent waited in the noontime shadows not far from the southern end of the bridge. Southwark was too small a town by far, and though she hadn't swyved on this side of the river in years, there were still men about who knew her face. She edged a slight way down the lane to get a better view up the high street. The alley met the broad thoroughfare at a fork, where a knot of hucksters peddled to passers-by going in both directions.

She soon spotted a grand company coming smartly up from the Thames, their jennets colourfully flounced for the occasion, the commoners parting at their approach. The younger of them ran alongside the horses, shouting for pennies. There were both lords and ladies but mostly ladies, perhaps twenty of them, veiled and bound for the palace and the Dunstan's Day feast. As the company passed the mouth of Pepper Alley two of the horses split off, with several guards falling in behind them. The guards wheeled round and allowed the two ladies to proceed up the alley about fifty feet, where they reined in their horses and pulled up their veils.

The powdered tip of a fine nose, then the face of Katherine Swynford. Millicent had seen this nose only once before, during a mayor's show on Cat Street when she had stood proudly at Sir Humphrey ap-Roger's side, her knight pointing out the array of gentry in the crowd, though Millicent would have recognized it anywhere. Swynford wore a dress of silk brocade in white and blue, trimmed in furs of pured miniver dusting her fine neck.

'You're the prioress's girl?' Swynford said, her voice hard. Her companion gazed up at the tenements. The women looked strikingly alike.

'Yes, my lady,' Millicent said.

'My daughter tells me to trust the Reverend Mother.'

'Yes, my lady.'

'I agree,' said the other lady.

With a gloved finger, Swynford flicked a fly off her knee. 'Lancaster won't do a thing, of course,' she said to her companion. 'He doesn't credit for a minute that Richard would actually fall for this – this prophecy. Believe me, I considered telling him everything. But what would be the point?' She raised her chin. 'King Richard. Ugh! Staring off into space, making up little fantasies to amuse himself. As I've told John a hundred times, if that brat once gets it into his head that you're out to depose him, why – that's the end of the game, and we're all quartered for our troubles.'

'Surely, though,' said Millicent, hesitantly, 'the duke will not suspect your involvement, my lady. Won't you be handing the cloth off to the Countess of Kent before the feast?' This had been John Gower's suggestion, which the prioress had approved during his visit.

'It is more complicated than that, I'm afraid,' Swynford sighed. 'I have been asked for a round of Prince of Plums. By the Earl of Oxford himself.'

At Prince of Plums shall prelate oppose. The first line of the prophecy rang in Millicent's ears.

'Prince of Plums?' said Swynford's companion.

'Cards, Philippa,' said Swynford. 'It's a game of cards.'

The second woman was Philippa Chaucer, Millicent realized as the prophecy's words continued to echo in her mind. Swynford's sister, and the wife of a minor official in customs, though everyone knew the man was a long-time favourite with Gaunt. 'Why would you possibly front yourself in such a way?' she asked her sister. 'And at Oxford's bidding? What are you thinking, Katherine?'

'He approached me last week, all charm and baby fat. You know how the earl can be.'

Philippa turned away, her eyes closed.

'Everyone is speaking of this feast as a chance to make peace between Oxford and Lancaster, and Lancaster and the king,' she said, pleading her case. 'A moment of reconciliation, as the bishop is casting it, to unite us all before the renewal of the inevitable hostilities with France. Oxford believes the gesture will mean something to Duke John. That showing the duke's mistress in a favourable light may be met in kind, perhaps with a preferment by King Richard, or, I don't know—'

'Garter robes?' said Philippa.

Swynford ignored the jab. 'The chancellor has asked me to arrange the cards so that the game ends a certain way. In any case, the prioress assures me all is in hand. But if my duke suspects I'm part of this what will he do with me?'

'What Lancaster always does with you,' said Philippa, with a sad smile. 'Ignore you during the feast, make you leave by yourself, then order you to his bed once he's returned to the Savoy. He won't let a little prophecy get in the way of his prick.'

'This is different, Philippa. If there's to be an attempt on the king's life today—'

'Don't be indecisive, Katherine,' said Philippa. 'John is the great lover of your life, you have nothing to fear from him. It's Oxford who should terrify you.'

Swynford's thin brows knit in a deep frown. 'The earl is the king's favourite, and the king is the king. I just hope Prioress Isabel hasn't gone weak in the head.'

Philippa waved away a fly. Swynford looked down at Millicent, then extended a hand. 'Give it to me.'

Millicent handed up the cloth, folded into a neat roll and bound with a thong. As Swynford wordlessly turned her horse the animal's tail thwacked Millicent's cheeks. She stepped back right into a stopped gutter. Lifting her shoe out of the muck, she watched as the small company moved back up the alley, the guards falling in before and behind the mounted women. Soon they were gone.

Until a few weeks ago she would have given a painted fingernail for an audience with Katherine Swynford, even in such a miserable spot as Pepper Alley. Yet now she found herself longing instead for the simplicity of St Leonard's Bromley, where the food was plain and the dress plainer, the sisters quiet and, for the most part, kind. She shook her head, thinking of Agnes. What is happening to me? she wondered, not for the last time.

FORTY-EIGHT

Winchester Palace

The Bishop of London and the Duke of Lancaster sat on the dais, deep in discussion, both looking uncomfortably tense. The hall's long central tables were already set for the feast to follow Mass, the plate and glass filling the great chamber with a lustrous glow. At the west end the company had arranged itself around several trestle tables angled out to make room for games. Four men played dice off in the far corner, two went at Nine Men's Morris on a specially carved bench, and the remainder toyed at chess or engaged in idle conversation nearby.

There was a loud clap. Oxford had mounted a table. His hood, lined with ermine, was caught back from his hair in a way that framed a bashful smile. 'Good friends,' he called out to the company, 'I give you Lady Katherine Swynford.'

Oxford held out a hand. With a light step that I could only admire given the circumstances, Swynford joined the earl on the table. A smile as modest as she could manage warmed her face.

'Your ears, if you please.' Her voice was steady, though to me she seemed ill at ease.

On the dais Lancaster and Winchester had stopped talking, the bishop aghast at the sight of the duke's mistress calling for attention in his own hall. Gaunt wore that embarrassed but carnal smile he tended to show whenever he and Swynford appeared together in public. Oxford, I realized, had made a shrewd calculation: by recognizing Lancaster's mistress in this way he was granting her a certain unspoken status among the higher aristocracy, mimicking Lancaster's own habit of leading Swynford's horse on occasion. A friendly gesture on its face, in the conciliatory spirit of the day.

'For our amusement before the Mass,' Swynford said, 'we will have a game.'

'What game, Lady Katherine?' someone called from a bench.

'Prince of Plums.'

There were whispers as the guests decided whether to go along or turn away with courtly indifference.

'And the rules of this game, Lady Katherine?' the same voice inquired. It was Thomas Pinchbeak, the serjeant-at-law, lending his respectability to Swynford's provocation. It worked: she now had everyone's attention.

'There are seventy-four unique cards in this deck. Seventy-four guests will each take one card, and only one,' she said, her voice buoyed by Pinchbeak's approval – arranged, I felt certain, by Oxford. 'He must keep it with him all through our day, from the king's arrival through the feast after Mass. The single rule of the game is this: you may not look at your card, nor will I as I hand them out. Only at the departure of our king will each guest's card be revealed.'

'Let me take the first card, Lady Katherine,' said Pinchbeak, rising from the Morris bench and hobbling over. She handed him down a card, gave the second to Oxford, then the other guests formed a line, none of them wanting to be left out now that the serjeant-at-law and the earl were in. I secured a place in the line and watched the distribution. Once the cards were nearly gone Swynford, with a brazen disregard for propriety, approached the dais. In the silence she handed a card up to the bishop, who took it from her as if it were a live river rat to be held by the tail. Lancaster was more gracious, actually standing, bowing to his consort, and taking the card from her hand.

I looked from the dais to the far wall, across a sea of two hundred eager faces. One of the men in this great chamber carried the Five of Hawks, the fateful card named in the prophecy, though how Swynford's game would turn out was anyone's guess. With a studied indifference, I strolled out the buttery door and into the foreyard, where I stopped below a high wall that separated this small plot of grass from the kitchen gardens beyond. After a glance back over my shoulder, I discreetly removed my card, my eyes closed as I held it at my waist. Holding my breath, I looked.

Seven of Thistles.

I tucked the card away, strangely relieved. When I turned again, my aim to make my way back into the hall, a peculiar sight froze me in place. Through a long aperture formed by a rose arbour and the forked branches of a pear tree, I saw Ralph Strode, standing at the buttery door. From a distance of nearly eighty yards he was watching me across the lawn, dark pouches framing his sunken eyes, his hair lifted by the May breeze, his mouth a rigid line set in the great plane of his face. I raised a half smile, gave the common serjeant a nod. Yet Strode simply stared, a look of cold appraisal that I took as a silent intimation of my own blindness.

❖

Grimes's shop and yard on Cutter Lane were empty, as she knew they would be. Eleanor peered over the streetside fence, spying exactly what she had hoped to find: a row of clothes drying on the line. She vaulted the fence, took what she needed, and stripped off her dress, bunching it into her bag for later. She pulled on a pair of breeches and a one-piece shirt of the sort favoured by the butchers. An old pair of slaughter boots, found in the corner of the first barn, completed the outfit, though as Edgar left the yard he grabbed a stained apron from a hook and wrapped it around his middle. He roughed up his hair, put on a cap, smeared a bit of ash on his cheeks and brow, then left the butcher's precinct the way he had come, heading for the palace, and Gerald's fate.

FORTY-NINE

Winchester Palace

The thickening crowd flowed toward the gate facing New Rents. The palace yards were festooned with banners showing innumerable colours, England's heraldry on full display for the coming of King Richard. Winchester's gateyard was normally ankle-deep in muck and dung from the bishop's stables, and often it could be difficult to tell that the area was paved. Now the stones at my feet practically glistened, as if Wykeham had sent his entire household out for a week with brushes and vinegar. Even the scent was invigorating, with fresh juniper and rosemary underfoot. Over it all loomed Mark Blythe's pearl-and-oyster reliefs, tracing a pattern that summoned one of the clearest lines in the prophecy. *In palace of prelate with pearls appointed.* By the next bell, I brooded, King Richard could be dead.

I fell in place beside Thomas Pinchbeak, who was speaking earnestly to Sir Howard Payne. I listened in for a while, an interested smile fixed on my face, then moved to a spot off the gateyard's pavement to await the king's arrival from the hunting lodges at Easthampstead, feeling alone. The sky had darkened, hints of another May shower in the air. The moist breeze deadened voices, casting a clammy pall over the hushed conversations preceding the royal entrance.

Katherine Swynford, with Philippa at her side, took a position in the rearmost echelon of ladies; no cruel whispers that day, as the duchess was absent. In the faces of those closest to the gate – Wykeham, Gaunt, Oxford, Joan of Kent – I read a dark foreboding, as all seemed to be exchanging glances of secret knowledge and hidden intent. To my mind the entire assemblage felt taut, as if a bowstring had been pulled back to its limit, the archer's fingers on the verge of release.

If an attack on the king came, it would take place soon after his arrival. The bishop and his company were to greet the king and his court inside the palace's great gate. Together the two companies, the episcopal and the royal, would make their way to the pavilion to hear Mass. The singing of the processional hymn would begin upon the commingling of the companies, and conclude before the introit.

From outside the walls came the loud blasts of trumpets, the call of the chief herald, the roar of the Southwark commons. Hinges groaned, heads turned. Through the wide opening on to New Rents the royals appeared on foot, having dismounted before the gate. The king's guard had already clustered around Richard in a tight circle. Wykeham's own guards formed a solid line marching forward. The gate closed behind them.

The greeting was swift and simple. King Richard entered the palace grounds and came to a stop before Wykeham. The two exchanged bows, then the king took the bishop's hand and kissed his ring. Palm in palm, the two turned for the gardens as their retinues fell in behind them. With that the processional to St Dunstan began, the first stanza intoned by the Austin canons of St Mary Overey as the melody filled the courtyard.

Ave Dunstane, praesulum
Sidus decusque splendidum,
Lux vera gentis Anglicae,
Et ad Deum dux praevie.

The singing continued as the two companies turned to process to Mass. Those who knew the tune or words joined in with singing or humming, though in those agonizing moments I forced myself to keep my attention solely on the king.

Now the second stanza. My mind Englished the lines as I followed the king's progress. *In you do we place our trust, in your sight do we lift up our hands . . .* The crowd of guests started filling in behind as the magnates processed past the foreyard. I mouthed the next line, appropriate to the occasion: *Mucrone gentis barbarae*, 'the sword of a barbarous race'. I thought of Dunstan's famed role in prophesying the Danish invasions, of King Richard's present role in the holding off of France. As in the *De Mortibus* itself, past and present here collided with the force of a hurled stone on a palace wall.

I positioned myself at the front right edge of the crowd. Here my view of the central group was now somewhat obstructed. Looking around, I saw behind me the lip of an old, disused well, long since filled in. I stepped up on the stones. The extra height gave me a clear view of the king.

Richard and Wykeham had reached the entrance to the hall, which was standing open. The uppermost members of the company positioned themselves in a wide arc around the two magnates. Oxford stood just steps from the king. Behind him walked Sir Stephen Weldon, his palm on his swordhilt.

They turned at the passage to the kitchens, heading for the pavilion and Mass. All appeared well. No attack seemed to be forming, no apparent threats to the king that I could see. Would all this worry, all the trouble of these last months, be for nothing? I realized I had been holding my breath since the song's previous stanza. I started to exhale—

A flash of metal, in the darkened passage. *The butchers*. I looked around, but no one else seemed to have noticed the movement. I realized why: thanks to the well's stone lip, I alone stood at that particular angle to that corner of the passage.

Now the hymn's final verse, which extolled Dunstan's role in bringing hope, peace, and light to the world.

Per Te Pater spes unica . . .

Movement in the kitchen passage. Yes, the butchers, huddled in a bunch, assembled to rush the king. I was sure of it now, even from forty feet away. I looked around in a panic.

The voices of the Overey canons broke into harmony as they descanted on the second line.

Per Te Proles pax unica . . .

I stared in a cold horror even as my ears rang with the hopeful line. The butchers of Southwark were massed less than twenty feet from King Richard. Their leader was in front. He held a cleaver in one hand, a long knife in the other. Ten butchers at least, bristling with blades. Despite the king's guard how safe could Richard be?

'Your Highness!' I called out weakly over the din of the hymn, attracting annoyed looks from those nearby.

With no regard for propriety or my own fate, I started to push through the ranks, my gaze still fixed on the kitchen passage. The butchers crept forward in the shadows, still unnoticed by the crowd, all attention on the king. I pushed someone aside. 'What in—' Thomas Pinchbeak fell back as I passed, tripping over his stick.

Now an arm, and a leg – did no one else see them?

'Your Highness!' I was almost there. One of Richard's rear guards saw me coming. He reached for his sword.

The canons descanted the third line. I pushed toward the frontmost ranks, pointing madly back at the passage.

'Your Highness!' I yelled. I was shoved aside, by whom I would never know, and fell against a pavilion post.

> *Et Spiritus Lux—*
> *Spiritus!*

'Richard!' I cried as I came to my feet.

The singing stopped. Heads turned, including the king's.

'*For the commons!*' With a hoarse chorus of shouts the shadows came to life, and the butchers flew as one from the kitchen passage, twenty blades raised for the attack. For an awful moment all I saw was a tangle of arms bristling with blades, some grotesquely spiked machine of war hurtling toward the king. There was glee on their faces, a righteous madness bellowing from their opened mouths.

There was a scream. Wykeham leapt backwards. King Richard froze before his assailants.

Then, with a swift rush of air, the sky fell. A cascade of arrows took the butchers in their backs, necks, and chests. The entire group collapsed in place, most of them past agony before they hit the ground. I looked up. Royal archers, at least twenty of them, lined the inner roof on three sides, new arrows already notched.

I gaped at the spectacle. The butchers were dead or dying, pools of new blood glistening on the stone. A pile of corpses. Richard had been safe the entire time.

FIFTY

Winchester Palace

Edgar Rykener saw the shower of arrows before he saw his brother. At first he assumed Gerald was among the attackers, and the sight of his death was like an arrow in his own neck, so sudden and violent it was. Then he looked at the kitchen passage and saw Gerald's face, pale in the shadows. His eyes were wide, registering his boyish shock at what his fellow butchers had done. Edgar's heart soared. Gerald turned and fled.

As the crowd started to react to the attack Edgar dodged around a privet hedge and sprinted for the kitchen gate. Gerald was just disappearing through a second passageway toward the west courtyard. Edgar followed him as the shouts spread in their wake. The courtyard was deserted aside from an old horse and an empty wagon. Gerald sprinted across the space and dodged left at the wagon, angling for the west tower.

'Gerald!' Edgar called ahead before his brother disappeared. Gerald hesitated, turned.

'Edgar! What the—'

Gerald ran up to the next landing. It gave on to a poorly lit chamber above the bishop's lower gallery. He turned toward Edgar, kicking up dust.

Edgar embraced him, loving him for his defiance of Grimes, and felt his brother's hesitation before he returned the hug. 'He's gone now, Gerald. Grimes can't hurt you now.'

Gerald was trembling. 'Now I'll only be hanged,' he murmured.

Edgar didn't doubt it. He looked around, casting for a plan. The space was filled with old rugs and broken furniture, muffling the urgent shouts from below. 'Wykeham's probably rounding up all the kitchen folks as we stand here, seeing if others are part of it,' he said. 'You have to get out of the palace, and right soon.'

'How—how?'

Edgar looked at him in the darkness, asking himself the same question. Then he had it. From his side bag he removed the bundle of clothes and thrust them into Gerald's arms. Gerald looked down. He spread out the dress, then let out a cruel laugh.

'Oh, so now *I'm* to be the swerver?'

Edgar glared at him. 'You've a better thought?'

Gerald hesitated.

'It's the only way, Gerald,' said Edgar. 'Otherwise you're like to be caught and killed this very hour. Now, *put it on.*'

Reluctantly, Gerald eased himself out of his rough breeches, tunic, and apron then pulled the dress over his head. He tugged and smoothed until the garment, a one-piece woollen affair full of patches and stitching, sat more or less right.

Edgar stepped back and appraised him in the half light. He wet his fingertips to wipe some grime off his brother's cheeks, then teased the strands of hair pushing out of the plain coif he had tied around Gerald's head. His brother's voice hadn't yet cracked despite his age, no whiskers on him, and his thin-soled shoes could pass for a scullery maid's. He figured it would all do for the purpose. He walked to the top of the stairs and listened. Voices, two or three men approaching the tower. He turned back and pulled on Gerald's arm.

'Straight for the postern, Gerald. Then the Pricking Bishop on Rose Alley.' He handed him a few coins. 'Give these to that old sheath on the steps, and wait for me inside.'

Gerald looked at him, and Edgar wanted to laugh despite the danger. He put a hand to the back of his brother's head and pushed it down. 'Eyes to the ground and you'll be fine.'

Halfway down the stairs Edgar gave his brother a gentle push. Gerald didn't look back, but as he entered the west yard Edgar watched him through a narrow aperture along the tower wall. Gerald passed two guards but neither spared a glance for the ragged servingwoman coming from the tower. More guards in the yard now, searching out conspirators.

Now for his own escape. Edgar looked down at the courtyard, forming an idea. The horse-drawn cart was one of many in Southwark that doubled as a pageant wagon at festival time. Though the wagon itself was empty and wouldn't do, its undercarriage was obscured by the frayed cloths hanging over each side. He had to get to that wagon.

He waited for the last guard to disappear into one of the surrounding buildings. When he was gone Edgar climbed on to the stone sill, threw his legs over, hung for a moment, and dropped, meeting the courtyard pavers with a painful impact. He stood, ankles still sound. He darted for the wagon and slid beneath the cloths. Wedging himself between the clouts, he took his weight off his arms and tested the fit. It would work. He waited patiently, his mind on Gerald, until the cartman returned to the courtyard. After a word with the guards, he took the horse's reins. Edgar felt a lurch. The cart moved slowly toward the palace's back gate.

FIFTY-ONE

Winchester Palace

The king's guard had encircled Richard, swords drawn. The crowd, moments ago riven with cries of fright, had quieted itself to a low murmur. Most were huddled in small knots, watching ghoulishly as it became known that the danger had passed and a pile of bodies lay on the ground, and a search was on for any remaining conspirators. Hodge ordered the corpses hauled off, a swift task involving several handcarts and a dozen servants. Others brought out buckets of water and washed the blood off the pavers. The bishop spoke to the king, and it seemed the procession would continue to Mass when a loud voice filled the air.

'Your Highness,' said Robert de Vere, in a voice that carried through the assemblage.

'What is it, Oxford?' The king looked unsteady, sickened.

'With your leave, sire, I wish to speak.' The king nodded. The earl approached Richard with his right arm raised. He took a slow circle around the front of the pavilion, displaying something for all of us to see. 'Your eyes and ears, please,' he called out. The earl's hand clutched a book. A thin volume, with a simple, unembossed binding, and no clasps.

'What's the meaning of this, Oxford?' the king demanded.

'We have been preparing for this day with grim resolve, Your Highness,' said Oxford. 'In this book lies the key to this attempt on your life. The book is called the *Liber de Mortibus Regum Anglorum*. In our tongue, "The Book of the Deaths of English Kings".' The title sent a thrill through the guests. 'The work's author is named Lollius. A writer of ancient lineage, inking these prophecies during the reign of King William.'

Things had moved so quickly between the king's entrance and the death of the butchers that I had had little time to gather my thoughts. My first reaction to what had just happened was to assume that the plan to kill the king, whoever its instigator, had been thwarted, the prophecy proven false by a hail of arrows. Richard, after all, was alive and unharmed.

Yet now, with the disconcerting sight of the book in Oxford's hands, I was forced to wait as the ingenious machinery of the plot unfolded before my weak eyes. After so many weeks of ignorance I mistrusted my own reactions, and felt at the mercy of the many forces around me – beginning with the intimidating presence of Robert de Vere.

'Who was this Lollius?' asked the king. 'Was he an Englishman?'

'Little is known of him, Your Highness.' Oxford hesitated. 'Though his works are in favour with the followers of John Wycliffe.'

'Preposterous!' thundered John of Gaunt, who had been standing silent since the attack. 'Wycliffe's dissent was a theological one, Your Highness, not a political one.'

Oxford gave the duke a withering look. 'It is known that a copy of this work was made by Sir John Clanvowe, and that it has been circulated among Wycliffe's followers.' His cold eyes found me in the crowd. 'There are copies of this book being handed around in their conventicles, Your Highness.'

'You lie, Oxford,' Gaunt taunted him.

'Silence, Lancaster!' King Richard barked, causing a stir of frightened awe among the assembly. Despite their private disagreements, no one had ever seen the king dress down his uncle in public. This whole affair had just taken a dangerous new direction. I felt sick.

Gaunt stared in disbelief at his newly assertive nephew. King Richard turned to Oxford. 'Continue, Oxford.'

'As you wish, Your Highness,' said Oxford with a puerile sneer at Gaunt. 'We have recovered this book through the devices of Master Thomas Pinchbeak, appointed serjeant-at-law by good King Edward.'

'It is true, Your Highness.' Pinchbeak, having risen from his tumble, stepped forward and knelt gingerly before the king. King Richard looked at the powerful lawman: his leg lame from war, his back bent with compensation of his injury, the serjeant's stripes on his arm. Here was an unimpeachable source confirming Oxford's claims, a serjeant-at-law, appointed by patent of Richard himself.

'What is in these prophecies, Oxford?' asked the king. 'Tell us.'

'Certainly,' said Oxford. 'The prophecies, Your Highness, foretell the deaths of thirteen kings, beginning with the great William, Norman conqueror of the Saxons. Their deaths are related in detail and with an accuracy that matches the accounts set forth in our chronicles.' He went on to give several examples from the *De Mortibus*, all of them by now intimately familiar to me.

I watched the king's reaction to the earl's masterful discoursing. Richard was trying to remain impassive, though he was clearly affected by what he heard. By the time Oxford reached the death of the late King Edward, the crowd, I could tell, had been swayed. All that remained was for Oxford to convince the king that the final prophecy had been foiled.

'Yet it is the thirteenth prophecy, Your Highness, that most concerns us today.' Oxford's voice found a pitch that matched the insidious content of the matter. 'For in this final prophecy, your own death is shadowed forth in lines that leave little doubt concerning the day, place, and manner of the plot.'

'Read it, Robert,' Richard ordered, feigning a confidence belied by the deep blush that shot up his cheeks. Behind him, Bolingbroke looked similarly stricken.

The earl intoned the final prophecy:

> 'At Prince of Plums shall prelate oppose
> A faun of three feathers with flaunting of fur,
> Long castle will collar and cast out the core,
> His reign to fall ruin, mors regis to roar.
> By bank of a bishop shall butchers abide,
> To nest, by God's name, with knives in hand,
> Then springen in service at spiritus sung.
> In palace of prelate with pearls all appointed,
> By kingmaker's cunning a king to unking,
> A magnate whose majesty mingles with mort.
> By Half-ten of Hawks might shender be shown.'

Oxford looked up at the king as he recited the final line.

> 'On day of Saint Dunstan shall Death have his doom.'

The crowd erupted. During the reading of the prophecy more of the king's personal guard had stepped forward. Twenty powerful soldiers now surrounded the company of magnates, their intention to apprehend – and, I feared, likely to slay without thought – anyone named as a conspirator. I wondered how many of them were truly the king's men, and what portion fed from Oxford's trough.

King Richard, regaining some of his composure, stood straight, a hand at his belt. 'Unravel this prophecy for us, Oxford,' he commanded.

'Yes, Your Highness.' Oxford looked around. 'I have consulted with men of Cambridge and Oxford, sire. Our wisest masters of theology. They have glossed this ancient prophecy, explaining its words, its symbols. I shall interpret it for you in turn, word for word – beginning with the "prelate", a great man of the realm who opposes the "faun of three feathers".'

'Three feathers,' King Richard repeated, slowly nodding. 'My father's crest?'

'The very same,' Oxford said with a brisk nod. 'Everyone knows the legend of your father at the Battle of Crécy, the ostrich feather seized from the crown of King John. You are the faun, sire, the offspring of Prince Edward.'

'What about this "flaunting of fur"?'

Oxford gave an exaggerated shrug. 'Like the three feathers, it must refer to heraldry. That part of a lord's livery consisting of animal fur.' He looked up and cast a meaningful glance over at Gaunt. 'Points of ermine, would be my best guess.'

The king slowly turned his head, staring at the band of ermine points on Gaunt's collar. Lancaster looked at Oxford with a searing hatred.

'Go on,' rattled the king.

'The next lines are clearer,' Vere continued. 'A "long castle" will collar and cast out the core. The core is the *cor*, Latin for "heart". You are the White Hart, Your Highness, to be cast out and your reign to "fall ruin". The Latin phrase *mors regis*, "death of a king", suggests that the deposition will come at the expense of your life.'

The king had gone pale.

'The prophecy even tells us the time, place, and manner of your death, Your Highness. The place: "by bank of a bishop", in the "palace of prelate with pearls all appointed". And here we all are, gathered at the palace of the Bishop of Winchester on the banks of the Thames, with these fine carvings of pearls adorning the walls above our heads.' He spread his right hand, drawing all eyes up to Blythe's ornate pearl carvings.

'And the time,' said Oxford. 'We knew all along that the attack would take place on Dunstan's Day. Yet the prophecy is more specific than that. Our killers are to spring forth "in service" – during the Mass procession, Your Highness – "at *Spiritus* sung": in other words, at the singing of the word *spiritus*, a word which appears in the final verse of the processional proper to this day. And so it was: at the very moment this word was sung, your would-be assassins sprang forth to attack you.'

'Yes,' said King Richard, nodding weakly in the face of Oxford's relentless explication.

'And finally,' said the earl without a pause, 'we come to the killers themselves, and their weapons. Here the *De Mortibus* reads as follows: "By bank of a bishop shall butchers abide", with "knives in hand".' Oxford waved a hand toward the spot where the butchers had met their deaths, bloodied on the ground. 'You've seen our butchers, Your Highness. You've seen their knives.'

Finally, with a slow turn, he pointed to John of Gaunt. 'And here we have our "kingmaker", this cunning conspirator intent on seizing your crown – in the words of the prophecy, a magnate whose majesty mingles with *mort*. Your death, sire, and the death of England. Had we not discovered this conspiracy you would be dead, Your Highness. I give you the man thinly disguised in the prophecy as "long castle" – none other than your treacherous uncle, the Duke of Lancaster.'

398

John of Gaunt had few friends at Winchester Palace that day. The lawn and pavilion were shot through with an uneasy silence, as all present shared a common thought: What was to prevent the king's men from slaying Lancaster on the spot? With an assassination attempt foiled and the evidence of his uncle's guilt in hand, what would prevent King Richard from ordering his uncle's execution on the palace grounds? Such an order would be perfectly justified before all these witnesses – in fact, I reasoned, it would be much safer to kill Gaunt now rather than wait for a legal proceeding, which would give the forces loyal to Lancaster time and opportunity to redress Oxford's lethal accusation against the powerful duke.

King Richard looked from his uncle to Oxford to his guard, struggling within himself. I closed my eyes, waiting.

'Pray stay your hand, sire.'

A woman's voice, shattering the silence. I opened my eyes, and through the clearing blur saw that the speaker was Joan of Kent, mother of King Richard. The king turned with visible relief toward the countess as she stepped forward from the edge of the crowd.

'What is it, Countess?' he said in a quavering voice.

'Our Lord the Earl of Oxford has given us a remarkable performance,' said Joan with a tight smile. 'Why, he's almost convinced me that my husband's brother is behind this attempt on your life today. That it was Lancaster's hand guiding the men who nearly killed my son. Oxford's account is convincing, and you are right to take this dark prophecy with the utmost seriousness.'

She looked around and raised her voice. 'Yet there is one additional piece to this strange puzzle. As Lord Oxford knows very well, this book of prophecies has travelled from abroad wrapped in a cloth, a piece of embroidery fitted to the manuscript like a glove to a hand.'

Oxford looked delighted to have an unexpected ally. 'Your

noble mother is correct, Your Highness. The book and the cloth have travelled together. The cloth went missing and hasn't been recovered.'

'The cloth has been found,' said Joan of Kent. Murmurs of surprise, and she held it bunched up above her head. Oxford looked at the embroidery like a dog at a cutlet. 'The cloth came to me, Your Highness, by the hand of the Mother Superior of St Leonard's Bromley, Prioress Isabel, who was brought the cloth by one of her former laysisters. It reveals with no room for doubt the identity of the agent behind this conspiracy.' She paused for effect. 'May I unfurl the cloth, Your Highness?'

'Please, Countess,' said Richard, almost pathetically grateful to have his moment of decision deferred.

'And with your consent, Lord Oxford?' The earl responded with a courtly nod.

With a flick of her shapely wrist, Joan snapped the cloth open. I craned my neck and smiled at the result of Millicent Fonteyn's handiwork. Where Lancaster's heraldry had once been embroidered into the cloth, there now appeared the arms of Robert de Vere, Earl of Oxford, emblazoned on a mounted knight, his sword thrust in the breast of an unarmed king bearing Richard's colours. A perfect substitution, and I found myself in a state of awe at the ingenuity of Bromley – and pleased that I had suggested the countess rather than Swynford as the agent of its revealing.

After the appropriate exclamations, everyone started speculating wildly. King Richard looked from his mother to the earl. 'What do you say to this, Oxford?' he demanded.

'This—' sputtered Oxford, as word and sight of the cloth spread quickly through the crowd, 'this is absurd, Your Highness! An outrage of the highest order!'

'Who could disagree?' Joan of Kent said. 'This cloth throws the whole of the prophecy into doubt, Your Highness. Many would say your close friendship with the Earl of Oxford renders the man half a king already, so the "kingmaker" could just as well point to him. And heaven knows that this "flaunting of fur", supposedly Lancaster's ermine points, could as easily refer to Robert de Vere, who ladies about wrapped in his fur-lined hood!'

There was scattered laughter as Oxford's hand went to his hood, lined in fox.

The countess was not finished. 'God Himself knows how deeply I have despised my late husband's brother.' Lancaster said nothing. Joan approached her son and took his hand. 'But he loves you, Richard, as does his son.' A brief glance at Bolingbroke. 'You are the duke's liege lord, and he is your most loyal subject of all.'

Joan dropped the king's hand and looked around, matching Oxford's flourishes and volume with her steadiness and grace. 'The Duke of Lancaster has had many opportunities to take your life since your coronation, Your Highness. How often have you hunted together in Knaresburgh Forest, when a stray arrow might have taken you in the back? Instead he has protected you, Richard: from enemies, from slander, from treason. All of this while others conspire against you.'

'No, Your Highness!' Oxford protested. 'I beg you, sire, don't believe these words from your mother's false mo—' He caught himself before voicing the irrevocable insult, then straightened his back. 'The Countess of Kent has been fooled. This cloth is a false replica, Your Highness.'

'There are many false replicas in your kingdom,' said Joan to her son. 'False loyalties, false friends.' She looked at Oxford. 'And false lords.'

Oxford shook his head. 'The original embroidery is emblazoned with the arms of Lancaster, I swear it.'

'You have seen it, Robert?' the king demanded.

'Yes, Your Highness, though before it went missing.'

'Then why didn't you bring it to me earlier, along with this book, and tell me about this whole plot?' Richard sounded almost petulant; I winced for him.

Oxford hesitated. 'It was thought better to wait, Your Highness – to gauge the seriousness of the conspiracy, and allow us to reveal the perpetrators. As I believe we now have.'

'Indeed,' said Joan of Kent, her meaning lost on no one.

The earl's eyes brightened. 'There is one final token mentioned in the prophecy, Your Highness. One final sign of your betrayer.'

'And what is that, Oxford?' said the king, starting to lose patience.

'The Prince of Plums,' he said. 'The prophecy begins "At Prince of Plums" – a phrase everyone here will understand. Right now, Your Highness, we are in the middle of a game called Prince of Plums. Seventy-four of us, on our persons, carry a card from Lady Katherine Swynford's deck, a card to be revealed at some point during the feast.'

A number of the guests started patting themselves. Oxford raised a hand. 'Halt!' he shouted. 'Do not touch your card, under pain of seizure.' The guards spun round, warning the assembly against disobeying Oxford's orders. It was then that I realized what the earl had done. Somehow he had connived Swynford, Lancaster's mistress, into leading the guests in the card game – never revealing that its purpose would be to condemn the father of her children. I could only imagine what Oxford might have promised Gaunt's unknowing concubine in return. The Order of the Garter, perhaps?

'Each of the guests has been given one of the unique cards from Lady Katherine's stack, to carry on his person until the feast is done. According to the prophecy, your would-be killer will be known by the "Half-ten of Hawks". Whoever bears the Five of Hawks, then, is the agent behind this murderous plot.'

402

King Richard raised his chin. 'Hold your cards aloft, my good people,' he called to the crowd. 'We shall test the truth of Oxford's claim.' Numerous hands dug into pockets and folds, and soon dozens of cards were held overhead. Those without cards looked on in visible fear. Anything, it seemed, could happen now.

'Who holds the Five of Hawks?' Oxford demanded. He surveyed the elevated cards, walking about the crowd before coming to a position before Gaunt. The duke had not obeyed the king's orders. Instead he was staring with contempt at his card, which he held at waist height. 'Show us your card, Lancaster,' Oxford said to him.

Gaunt slowly turned his card toward the king and the earl. The Five of Hawks.

Oxford whirled toward the king. 'Do you see, Your Highness? "By Half-ten of Hawks might shender be shown." Lancaster's guilt is now beyond doubt.'

The king stared at the card in his uncle's hand, then slowly raised his eyes to meet the duke's.

'Now show us your card, Robert,' Gaunt said into the silence.

Robert de Vere scoffed.

'Yes, my Lord Oxford,' said Joan of Kent softly, looking intently at the earl. 'Show us your card.'

Vere shrugged and reached within his coat, pulling out a card without looking at it. The king stepped forward and took it from him.

King Richard looked down at the card. He audibly gasped. 'The Five of Hawks! Identical to Lancaster's card!'

As the gathering cooed astonishment I looked for Swynford, who had melted into the crowd behind the altar. Then I found her, standing between Ralph Strode and the Baron de la Pole. She had covered her mouth with a gloved hand, and I realized what she had done. Oxford must have requested the game of

403

Prince of Plums from her well in advance of the feast, presenting it as an entertaining diversion and assuming she would go along with his plan to slip the Five of Hawks to her lover. But Swynford, as I knew from that appointment at La Neyte, possessed two identical decks, and an agility with the cards that would have made it an easy matter to place an extra Five of Hawks into the deck and slip it to Oxford. I was glad to see the familiar twinkle of amusement in her eye, and I wondered who had come up with the ingenious contrivance. Strode, I suspected, or perhaps the chancellor himself, each standing to one side of Lancaster's mistress as the spectacle unfolded.

'Again – again, Your Highness,' Oxford stammered, 'there has been a substitution of some kind, another attempt to deceive you. There is only one of each card in Lady Katherine's deck. The Duke of Lancaster has drawn the Five of Hawks, as we have all seen. That two Fives of Hawks have appeared in this game is—'

'A mysterious circumstance indeed, Your Highness,' said Lancaster quietly. 'Lady Katherine distributed the cards before your arrival. The Bishop of Winchester himself took one of them. He is no friend of mine, as you well know. But he will attest that there were no substitutions or trickery of any sort.'

King Richard looked at Wykeham, who said simply, 'His Lordship the Duke of Lancaster speaks the truth, Your Highness.'

The king stepped into the circle formed by his uncle, his mother, the earl, and the bishop. He looked small and wan. 'So here we are, then,' he said, spreading a sad look around the assemblage. 'The prophecy tells me that my uncle the Duke of Lancaster has betrayed me.' The king stared up at Gaunt. Lancaster's chin lifted; he would not meet his nephew's gaze. Richard then approached Oxford, who looked at him with a mix of deference and defiance. 'And yet this cloth, revealed to me by my own mother, suggests that another faction wishes me dead.' He placed a hand on Oxford's cheek. 'That Robert de Vere – friend, companion, loyal knight and earl – that it is you, Robert, who plots against me. Can it be true?'

'Of course not, Your Highness,' said Oxford hastily. 'The very thought is—'

'And yet if I am to credit these cards' – Richard held up the two fives – 'both of you want me gone, and soon.' The young king sighed, his shoulders sagging with the burden of indecision. 'So then. Whom should I believe? What is the solution to this awful dilemma?'

No one spoke as Richard weighed the consequences of all we had seen that day. The king's palm rested on the hilt of his sword, which, I feared, would be drawn at any moment and pointed at the man he decided was the guilty one. The moment stretched: the weightiest choice of King Richard's reign, an irrevocable decision that would alter the future in unimaginable ways. Whatever the king decided, whichever way he went, there would be heavy conflict, possibly all-out civil war. Richard's question hung in the air until a familiar voice sounded from the edge of the crowd.

'It is France, Your Highness.' One hundred heads swivelled toward the voice. It belonged to the Baron de la Pole, the Lord Chancellor.

'What's that?' The king peered through the throng. 'Who has spoken?'

At the far side of the pavilion the guests parted. The chancellor stepped into the tightened circle and took a knee before the king. Richard waved away his guard and bid the baron to stand. 'Explain yourself, Lord Chancellor.'

De la Pole came to his full, commanding height, dwarfing the king in stature and maturity. The baron had stood by King Edward's side for many years, a long history of dispassionate service to the realm evident in his bearing and the respect he was accorded by all. I remembered our last exchange, just outside St Lawrence Jewry, and wondered what he knew. 'Your Highness, we have learned that this book came into the realm through the agency of King Charles, aided by the Scots.'

Murmurs of concern. 'You're quite sure, Lord Chancellor?' asked the king.

'Indeed we are, Your Highness.' He held up a document. 'We have intercepted an encrypted dispatch, bought off a messenger in the service of Burgundy. As you know, sire, the truce has recently expired, and the French are eager to renew hostilities. According to this dispatch, which we managed to decipher only yesterday, the admiral of France is to set sail from Sluys with a thousand lances, bound for Dunbar. The book and the cloth are part of a larger plot to destabilize the realm in advance of an invasion, as was the clumsy attack by the butchers of Southwark, cooked up by a Scottish priest in the pay of the French. Our archers were prepared for the attack, of course. Lord Oxford informed me of the prophecy nearly a week ago, and your royal life was never in jeopardy, though we had to let it go forward to test the reliability of our information. Now we know it is solid. This is good news, Your Highness.'

The King gaped. 'So you're saying all of this was the work of Charles? Who brought the book here, and who managed to deceive so many?'

'French spies, Your Highness, perhaps a whole nest of them.' I heard quite a few gasps as the assembly absorbed the news. The chancellor let them die down. 'Circulating copies of these foul prophecies, passing around cloths, trying to turn our highest noblemen against one another.' Here he paused again to bow to the duke and the earl, then did the same to the countess. 'If your lordships and your ladyship

406

will pardon the expression, you have been played by the French. We all have, Your Highness. And they nearly succeeded in their aim.' The baron stared down Oxford, who looked about to protest but thought better of it.

When the noise had subsided, the king addressed his subjects in a voice cracking giddily with relief. 'Thanks be to God we have learned the source of this plot, and that through your good offices, Lord Chancellor, we have aborted it. A prophecy of my death, written as a poem and seeming to point a finger at no less than John of Gaunt, the Duke of Lancaster.' He laid a hand on his uncle's arm. 'A beautiful cloth, embroidered with the heraldry of one of the realm's greatest lords, Robert de Vere, the Earl of Oxford, tilting at his sovereign.' Another hand on Oxford's shoulder. 'And a game of cards incriminating both of you at once.' He hesitated for a moment, perhaps seeing a weakness in the chancellor's story, then deciding, like the rest of the assembly, to gloss over it in the interests of peace. 'Now it appears that we have been deceived, and by our common foe. Let us put it all behind us, and move forward in harmony, if we can.'

A wave of relief swept through the crowd.

'One last word, Your Highness,' said the chancellor, his voice stern but guarded.

'By all means, Baron,' said King Richard.

'I would appeal to the loyalty of this assembly in asking for discretion. It is imperative that no one speak of what has been heard and seen here today. Should word of this intercepted dispatch get to the French, they would know of our penetration of their networks, and our position would be greatly compromised.'

'Well spoken, Lord Chancellor,' said the king, nodding boyishly. 'By my command no one present may record or speak of what has happened here today. Your silence will be the test of your loyalty, to me and to this realm.'

Watching the effect of all this I marvelled at the chancellor's disingenuous appeal for circumspection. The servants were already whispering, and soon every detail of the exchange would cover London as rumours of Dido swyving Aeneas blanketed Carthage. It was the *performance* of discretion that counted, the useful fiction that we were all somehow privy to the clandestine workings of the military. The aristocracy has always loved such insider talk of espionage and coming war, and Michael de la Pole played to this fancy like a master.

'Uncle,' said Richard to Gaunt, 'take the arm of the Earl of Oxford.' With a reluctance lost on no one, though also with a visible relief, John of Gaunt and Robert de Vere joined arms and faced Richard. 'And now,' the king continued, 'if the Lord Bishop of Winchester will permit it, our Mass shall continue.'

The disordered crowd became an orderly congregation, the women finding their places to the rear of the assemblage. When the Mass was concluded I spent a while looking around the grounds for Chaucer, wanting to ask him the dozen questions rattling through my mind, though he was nowhere to be found. In the hall Wykeham sat alone on the dais, his guests of honour absent, a scowl and a napkined lip accompanying his every sip of wine. Though the feast was only beginning, it seemed that nearly everyone of importance had left the palace grounds: Lancaster, Swynford, Joan of Kent—

Though not Oxford. He had remained in the central courtyard and was leaning against one of the large posts holding up the pavilion, staring off into the distance with the copy of the *De Mortibus* still clutched in his hands. I approached him and waited until he turned to me.

'Give me the book, your lordship,' I murmured.

His lip curled. 'Why would I possibly do such a thing, Gower?'

'I know everything there is to know,' I lied, though fairly confident in my speculations. 'Hawkwood, Sir Stephen, the origin of the prophecies.'

He flinched. 'Who would believe *you*, of all people?'

'Belief is beside the point, my lord,' I said tiredly. 'Written proof? That is another matter.'

His eyes widened for a moment, then settled back into their familiar disdain. 'Your tricks don't intimidate me, Gower. You have nothing.'

I waited before I spoke, giving him a long moment to squirm. 'Are you quite sure, my lord? Simon is a thorough young man. You don't think he tracked Weldon's comings and goings, or thought to leave behind a record of some kind, perhaps a document or two in Sir Stephen's hand – or yours? I can show them to you, if you'd like.'

The earl shifted on his feet. I held his eyes, watching as the weakness I had always sensed in this man crept slowly over his features. Finally he looked away, then down at the manuscript still in his hands, this book that had caused so much anguish, sought by half a kingdom and now seemingly worthless. The earl appeared to realize this as he gave a slight shrug and handed me the volume. I stuffed it in my bag.

'You have made a wise decision, your lordship.' I gave him a slight bow, allowing him to save face in case of any onlookers. 'We shouldn't need to speak of this again.'

He waved me off as he turned, calling angrily for his page and making for the main gates. The Earl of Oxford was still young, though his back was stooped as he walked away from me, his stride unconfident and self-conscious. This magnate would end the day a lesser man.

I was about to turn for the stable gate and home when I saw a movement to the earl's right. From the far side of the grange Sir Stephen Weldon emerged and stood in front of Oxford with his hands upraised, blocking his way. The two of them exchanged words. They were too far away to make anything out, but it was clear the knight was speaking angrily, even defiantly, to his lord, whose slouch now indicated the extent of his humiliation before the king. Oxford raised his fingers to his face, pinched his nose, wagged a hand. Not dismissing Weldon, I thought; it looked rather like a gesture of acquiescence.

Weldon spun on his heel and strode off, heading for the postern door farther down the wall. The earl watched him for a moment, then turned slowly back. I did nothing to conceal myself as I came into his line of vision. He looked unfazed by the evidence of my eavesdropping, which Weldon had not observed. The earl gave me a long look, then tilted his head slightly in the direction of the postern before turning for the main gate.

Weldon had already disappeared through the low door on to New Rents, though the earl's message seemed clear enough. It would be in my interest to follow him, Oxford was telling me, wherever it led. I stood there for a moment, exhausted, wanting nothing more than a drink and a rest. Then, with a growing unease, I turned for the postern and the streets of Southwark.

FIFTY-TWO

New Rents, Southwark

An attack on the king?

In the midst of Mass.

But who done the thing?

And where can we find him to give our thanks?

Or a 'Better luck next time!'

Or a 'Richard? Why not Lancaster?'

None of that talk, now. Enough treason in the bishop's liberties to go around.

Who done it, then?

Fishmonger, what I heard.

No, a butcher.

Butcher?

Whole scare of them, led by that cutter Grimes.

Ah! No surprise there.

Millicent hardly noticed the postern opening to her left, rapt as she was by the news being shouted about at the gate. The man who stepped through noticed her not at all, and until he passed she gave him no more than a glance, assuming that anyone exiting Winchester Palace by that door would be a servant on an errand. As he walked past Millicent saw his lower face, though his eyes were shadowed beneath a knight's hood. A scar traced a crescent-shaped path from his lip to the turn of his chin. Millicent knew that scar.

It came to her, finally. A hooked scar, white against sun-darkened skin. The ward watch, Eleanor said, had identified him as 'Sir Stephen' – and now she recalled his surname. He was Sir Stephen Weldon, a longtime member of Sir John Hawkwood's company, and a knight of Oxford's household. Sir Humphrey had pointed him out to her at a tournament, making an acerbic comment on the Italian style of his arms and raiment. 'Rides like a Visconti,' he'd said with disdain. 'Scarred like one, too.' Weldon was a badged man, sporting Oxford's livery proudly around his collar, and his own on the back of his surcoat. Quarterly or and gules, and there, in the first quarter, a mullet argent: the silver star of the Veres, plain as the moon.

Yet even as she watched his back recede down New Rents she heard another voice in her head. *It's the crochet. His face.* Some of her sister's last words, gasped from a bleeding mouth. Now she understood them. Sir Stephen Weldon, the man with the hook on his face.

The killer of Agnes.

Without thinking Millicent followed him down the alley beside the Overey churchyard and on to the crowded high street past the fishwives and the pillory. He jogged left on Pepper Alley, then into a narrower lane that led toward the mills on the river side of the palace wall. Millicent kept a safe distance, though never once did Weldon glance behind him.

As they neared the bankside she slowed her steps. Weldon's route had traced a full circle. He was now climbing a short but rough stairway built into the near embankment. He disappeared over the top. She took the steps slowly, stretching to peer over the dyke and down to the river. Just as she reached the uppermost step, she caught a glimpse of him on the near side of the wharf, keying open a low door set into the embankment. With his foot the knight dragged a small stone to the opening, wedging the door open before disappearing within.

She descended the moist stair to the embankment and realized where he had gone: into the underpassage below the great chamber and almonry of Winchester Palace, where the bishop had his stores of drink delivered directly from the water. From this cellar the palace's river doors opened to the wharfage through a series of covered channels and ramps carved into the Thames bankside. Silently she pulled open the door, keeping the stone in place, and followed the knight into the dank passageway. She had been here before, though not since her childhood, when the palace environs had been a favourite destination for games of hide-and-tag with her many companions in the liberties. The cold river air felt distantly familiar, the splash of dripping water from the vaults summoning old memories as she walked away from the river and toward the palace undercroft. She heard voices.

'The garrison is encamped at Dartford, Sir Stephen, by the abbey mill, awaiting your orders.'

'There's been a change in plans.'

'A change in plans?'

'The men will need to stay in place for now.'

'For how long?'

There was a pause. Millicent edged around one of the great buttresses ascending to the undercroft's roof and beyond. She peered around and down a short stair into a wider chamber perhaps three feet below, awash in pale light from an opened trapdoor above. Weldon paced the chamber's width, giving orders to a nuncius wearing the king's colours.

'Next Friday is the feast of St Augustine, no?' the knight finally said, turning away with a hand to his mouth.

413

'And the third Ember Day.'

'They're to come up that day and camp at Mile End, on the green. Their orders will come Trinity morning, likely by Tierce. Then it's up Aldgate Street as planned.'

'Anything else, Sir Stephen?'

'That's it for now. Keep me posted.'

'Yes, Sir Stephen.'

The man ducked through a low doorway. Millicent watched as the knight took a few slow turns around the dank chamber, one hand on his scarred chin, the other cupping his elbow. She thought about what she had heard, putting it together with the prophecies and the failed attempt on the king's life. It sounded as if Weldon had been planning to bring troops up from Dartford in the aftermath of the planned assassination. Who knew what else he had in store. She turned for the river door.

She slipped. She quickly recovered her footing, but not before a small fragment of stone, dislodged by her shoe, tumbled down the stairs. Weldon's head spun round. Frozen in terror, Millicent hesitated long enough for him to meet her gaze. His eyes widened, then narrowed in recognition. She knew that cold stare.

Rose Alley. Weldon had been the leader of the riders, the man challenged by St Cath at the porch of the Pricking Bishop. Looking for Millicent, and the book.

Millicent shot up the stairs. Through the door, over the dyke, down Pepper Alley. She looked back. Weldon was just making the turn.

She ducked between two tanners' stalls on the upper end. Rows of stretched hides gave some cover. An open door, at the end of the second yard. She sprinted through it. A tavern. Low ceiling, small crowd around a far table, the air sour with ale. She stepped from bench to bench and knocked several down on her way out, slowing Weldon a fraction.

He stumbled, cursed. She heard his boots on the tables. The street door was also open.

The bankside again. She hesitated. Right, to the high street and the bridge? Or left, and into the stews? She went left.

The right decision, she knew as she sprinted past the mills. On the wide high street the knight would have had the advantage of speed. Here, among the dense and disconnected clusters of shops, houses, tenements, shacks, barns, yards and pens making up the bishop's liberties, she had the advantage of memory.

For though the neighbourhood had undergone many changes in the last ten years, it was all so familiar. Every corner, every turn, every gap between buildings came back to her. Narrow passageways appeared right where she expected to find them. Through the twists and turns of the liberties she ran, the very air before her seeming to shape itself into the form of a child leading her on. She was not alone.

The little girl ran wildly before her, golden hair in tangled streams. Dodging barrels, cornering barns, leaping ditches. *This way, Millie! Faster, Millie!* She never slowed as she led Millicent through the twisted byways of the stews. *I will catch you, Agnes, I will catch you!* The Southwark breeze chilled the tears on her face, as the unmapped warren of the liberties became an elaborate labyrinth through which only this little girl knew the way. Finally, nearing the mills again, the girl slowed. Turning back, her face shrouded in a blinding pool of light, she rose from the soil like a dove lifted by the wind.

With no breath left in her, Millicent squatted at the corner of a pighouse facing the eastern edge of the larger millpond, the phantasm still burning her eyes. She looked behind her. No Weldon.

Loud voices on Rose Alley, a woman's angry shout. Millicent peered around the corner of the low structure.

Weldon stood at the door of the Pricking Bishop, having it out with St Cath. His head started to turn.

Millicent hurdled the fence. Squatting beside a great sow, clutching her dress tightly against the muck, she watched through the slats as Weldon looked down the narrow lane to the millpond. The deliberate sweep of his scarred chin, the jewelled scabbard at his side, the devilish gleam of his eyes: all these Millicent took in as she humbled herself with these Southwark pigs. The Overey bell rang None. The knight turned and struck St Cath with the flat of his sword. She collapsed against the doorway. Weldon spun on his heel and entered the Pricking Bishop.

Millicent hesitated, every part of her wanting to spring out and flee across the bridge, leaving Weldon to do what he wished. She thought of her mother, this woman who had never given her more than a bed to swyve on for her own profit. And why should I give her anything more in return? Then she thought of Prioress Isabel, and how the holy woman would answer this question. Finally she thought of Agnes, her sister's generous, selfless spirit, and it was then that she knew what must be done.

Millicent closed her eyes, said a prayer, and hopped back over the fence. With her fists clenched at her sides she strode down Rose Alley, wondering how on earth she might save her mother's life.

St Cath still lay on the stone, though she looked to be breathing. Millicent edged through the door and stood listening. She moved toward the rear of the building and heard the knight's heavy footsteps above, as he stomped around the upper floors, raising screams of terror from the maudlyns, a few indignant shouts from their unlucky jakes.

'Millicent.' She peered through the gloom. Bess Waller stood at the kitchen door, beckoning her forward. 'In here, girl,' she whispered.

Millicent dashed forward and had almost reached the kitchen when she tripped on the corner of a pallet. With a crash she fell into a deal table against the wall, knocking a brass ewer on to the floor. The *clang* resounded throughout the Bishop. The sound of the knight's boots above ceased, then began again with a renewed vigour as he crashed down the side stairs.

'Quickly,' said Bess Waller, pulling Millicent from the floor. In the kitchen the cellar door lay open to the stairs. It was all Millicent could do to stay on her feet as her mother pushed her toward the gaping hole in the floor. Once below she scurried down the steps. Her feet met the dirt floor. She looked back and caught a last glimpse of Bess Waller's face as the door slammed shut above, sealing her in darkness.

FIFTY-THREE

New Rents

Weldon was gone by the time I exited the palace through the postern and reached the market. I stepped up on a half-barrel and peered in both directions. Nothing. The knight had disappeared, absorbed into the thick crowd. A clutch of five street urchins were plucking at my hose, begging for coin. About to swat them away, I thought better of it and stepped off the half-barrel, reached into my purse, and knelt down, a handful of pennies clutched in my palm.

'One for each of you.' Three boys and two girls, their faces grimed in that way only a young Southwark face can be grimed, though they all seemed eager to earn despite the squalor. 'And another if you'll find someone for me.'

'Who, sir?'

'Who?'

'Who?'

'Who's it to find, good sir?'

'Man or woman, *I'll* find them, that's sure,' said the smallest of them, a girl of five or six.

'You know Sir Stephen Weldon?'

A few tentative nods, but the little girl shook her head truthfully.

'A knight with a curved scar, just here?' I traced it on her small chin.

'Hook on his face, bright as the moon!' crowed the little girl.

Nods all around. 'We know him, sir!'

'Find him for me, then,' I said. 'He left by the postern a little while ago. He can't have got far. First one back gets two pence.'

They sprinted off, getting underfoot of the merchants, pushing around the corners, spreading like a dropped sack of grain. It wasn't long before the first of them, the little girl, returned. Out of breath, she steadied herself on my leg then looked up in triumph.

'Saw him, sir, saw him I did.'

I knelt in the dirt. 'And where did you see him, my dear?'

'Past the millpond,' she said, 'on that Rose Alley. Going into the Pricking Bishop for a swyve, looked like.'

After paying the girl off I headed west past the Overey churchyard and toward the stews. Skirting the millpond I dodged a pighouse and entered Rose Alley. Few residents were about, all drawn to the palace, and no one looked my way as I walked beneath the low awnings and haphazard upper extensions lining the narrow lane. I was halfway up when I saw a figure leaning over a prostrate woman before the front door. Not Weldon, but a much younger man, slight, almost feminine. The old woman gave a gentle moan as he leaned her against the house's outer wall. He stroked her hair then turned for the door, which was unlatched and partially open. He turned, we locked eyes, then he disappeared into the Bishop. After peering up and down the lane I jogged to the house and followed him within.

❖

Edgar heard the shouts from the back of the house, which he approached through the same front room he'd crossed weeks ago, before taking the book. Reaching the kitchen door, he pressed his ear against the rough wood surface.

A man's voice. '. . . in the rancid stews of Southwark. Home of women and fish.'

Then Bess Waller: 'Get you gone from here, sir, there'll be no—'

'Where is she?' A few mumbles, then: 'So she *is* here, you lying whore.'

'No – no, sire, she's not, I'd swear it on—'

'On what?'

'On the blood of Mary, and the Maudlyn, and—'

'And your own?'

'Sire?'

'Or perhaps on the blood of your daughter. Not the one I've just chased through the stews, but the younger one. That pretty little thing over by Aldgate.'

Silence. Edgar closed his eyes, the sight of Agnes's body coming back to him with a wave of sadness. Then a groan of metal, a clap of wood, a shout.

'Leave her be!' Millicent's voice.

'Ah!' shouted the man. 'So *that's* where you were hiding, you snooping slut.'

Edgar pictured the kitchen. Bess Waller must have hidden Millicent in the cellar—the same dark space in which Edgar had trapped the bawd while searching for the book.

'You're the devil.' Millicent this time, her voice low with fury. Edgar braced himself against the door.

'Millicent, is it?' the man hissed. 'Former consort of the great Sir Humphrey ap-Roger, Humphrey the fat, Humphrey the codger, hmm? Your blood, perhaps?'

'Not her blood, false knight.' Bess's voice had steeled. 'Not Millicent's blood. I'll not have her harmed. Though this is

Southwark there be laws in the bishop's liberties, and you're bound by them well as I. You leave her be.'

Edgar heard the swipe of the knight's sword. 'I'll leave neither of you be.' Another swipe, a splinter of glass.

'*No.*'

Edgar had heard enough. He looked about for a weapon of some kind. He pictured Weldon's short sword drawn, the point at Millicent's throat. His hand brushed a heavy candlestick. It would have to do. Calming himself with a deep breath, he grasped the latch.

A hand squeezed his arm. He turned in fright, ready to swing. *Gerald*. His brother had removed the dress and stood in his breeches, bare-chested and thin, though butcher's muscles were already outlined on his arms and torso. A knife was still at his belt.

'There another way in?' he asked. 'Through the alley, p'raps?'

Edgar thought about it, recalling his search through the kitchen. 'The walls be eight, nine feet deep on the wharf side. Door's bolted.' There had been so much flooding on this side of the Bishop's Wild that high berms had been built between the river and the lanes and alleys up from the shore, leaving the embankment vulnerable to severe erosion in the event of the river's swelling. 'There's a high window in there, you can get to it from the back. But you'd have to climb—'

He was already gone. Edgar watched his back for a moment, then turned to the kitchen door and pushed it open.

✣

The door swung wide. Millicent saw Edgar Rykener, in butcher's raiment and brandishing a candlestick. At his entrance Weldon spun and swiped the blade in an arc close to Edgar's face. With one step Edgar sprang toward Bess and Millicent. Now he stood with them, the candlestick held in front, the three of them huddled against the kitchen wall.

The high windows beneath the eaves, fully covered in parchment during the winter but now partially open to the air, let in enough light to catch the glint along the blade's embossed fullers. The same shafts brought out the scar on Weldon's chin, the jagged crescent Millicent couldn't help comparing even in her fear to the hooks aligned above the hearth. She imagined being impaled on them, suspended before the knight's seething eyes, hooked iron in her brains.

She glanced sidelong at the garden door.

'Don't think of it,' said Weldon. 'I'll cut you before you reach the bolt.' He moved to the side. Pushed a table and a heavy cutting board against the door, blocking any hope of escape. He took a step toward them, waving his blade. Another step.

Millicent shrank back. Edgar raised the candlestick. He gave it a feeble swing. Weldon dodged it. With one slash Weldon sliced Edgar's hand. He dropped the candlestick. Millicent picked it up, then swung it through the air as hard as she could. The knight dodged this blow, too, with a deft step to the side. He raised his blade and plunged it into Bess Waller's chest.

Millicent screamed, then the inner door to the kitchen was filled with the faces of Bess's girls, drawn by the commotion. The moment stretched, and Millicent would always remember the three things that followed it. The first was a tearing sound from above, as the rolled parchment fell away and a figure leapt from the upper window. He landed on the knight's sword shoulder, disarming him with the force of the impact. The second was the rush of the maudlyns, five Southwark whores descending on the knight. The third was the aquamarine eyes of John Gower, the gentleman from St Leonard's. Now he was here, in her mother's kitchen. His features were the last thing she saw as her vision darkened and Bess Waller died in her arms.

✤

I have witnessed many deaths. Hangings, quarterings, drownings, knifings on the Southwark streets. Once I watched at a tournament as a knight of the king's chamber was decapitated by a lance, his blood arcing toward the stands, his head falling to the earth with a gruesome finality as hundreds of England's highest of birth held their stomachs.

Yet nothing had quite prepared me for the grim work of these Southwark maudlyns as they swarmed toward Sir Stephen Weldon, covering him like a hill of ants meeting a honeyed bun. They gouged his eyes, bit his ears, pummelled his neck and his stomach. They stretched his arms and legs to their full length, tore off his clothing, and wrote their fury on his bare skin. They killed him with their fingers, their fists, their feet. They killed him with their teeth and their nails. The way his body was tossed among them they might have been a pack of dogs at a hart. I could almost feel sorry for Weldon, despite the private satisfaction I took in his death.

'Enough!' I shouted into the dim light. 'Enough!'

The fury slowed. The young man who had leapt from the window crawled toward the far wall, moaning with the pain of a broken leg. He made it to the side of the slight man I had seen on Rose Alley. The two embraced. Beside them was Millicent Fonteyn, the laysister from Bromley, holding her mother's outstretched body in her arms. The maudlyns circled their dead bawd, pawing at her bloody neck and chest. I stared at them, wondering at their peculiar courage.

A wheeze from the floor. I looked down with amazement at Weldon. Incredibly, the knight was alive, though clearly moments from his last breath. I knelt beside him, shielding his broken frame from view of the maudlyns, who were still crowded around their dead bawd.

He looked at me, blankly at first, then his sole remaining eye flashed recognition as the ragged edges of his lips lifted into a thin, cruel smile. 'Hawks,' he croaked, his windpipe nearly crushed. 'Hawks always strike twice, Gower.'

'What's that you say?' I hissed, shaking him, wondering what secrets would die with this man, wishing I could buy them all. I slapped his face. 'Who are the hawks, Weldon? When will they strike?'

'Always twice,' he said, then his eyes froze in death, the meaning of his final words lost in the slaked howling of the whores.

The fingers throb, the eyes weaken, the bent back aches. I have scraped these words throughout this long winter night, all the while picturing you in Rome, venturing out from the abitato to walk with the sheep among the ruins, clearing your fine head after a day of subterfuge at the papal curia.

Such pleasant thoughts must now be pushed aside, and this sad tale brought to an end.

❖

Simon Gower, no fool, had been watching us most carefully: our subtle looks, our secretive gestures, the wanton press of skin on skin as we made our greetings. He sensed the rising heat between us, our swelling need.

Jealousy is as fierce as the grave, the Song of Solomon teaches us, fuel of the truest fire and the fiercest flames.

It started, it must have started, with the cloth. My piece of youthful handiwork had hung in the gallery for over ten years, embroidered with the livery of Wales and Lancaster, both sons of old King Edward. The only distinction between their heraldry was in the labels: three points argent on Prince Edward's, three points ermine on Lancaster's.

As I recollect it now it seems so obvious, yet so darkly ingenious at the same time. With the death of Prince Edward, the royal arms passed to his son, then a child but now the king, who retained his father's label of three points argent. In every respect King Richard's arms match King Edward's. To anyone viewing the cloth in our day, the duke would appear to be attacking not Prince Edward, but King Richard.

Ermine against argent. Duke against king. Once a scene of noble rescue embroidered by a lost girl, the cloth now showed a spectacle of royal murder.

If the cloth inspired Simon Gower's betrayal, it was his envy of you, my heart, that guided his pen. 'Why, if Geoffrey Chaucer can fool his readers with counterfeited prophecies, so can I!'

But how did he do it? Let your thoughts take you back just four weeks, the day before your company's departure to Rome. You will remember your distress one morning at my father's house. 'My little book has gone missing from my rooms on the Via dei Calzaiuoli,' you whispered to me, your hand pushing through your thick hair. 'The quire is gone, and with it the prophecies I wrote for you.'

Yet your anguish seemed too great for such a trifle. Yes, you had written me an amusing poem, but its loss would hardly merit the fear I read on your face. There was more to this book, I suspected, something in it other than your clever prognostications.

It was Simon, of course, who stole your little book – stole it, copied it, then augmented your work with a poetical prophecy of his own. A thirteenth prophecy, added to your twelve, bringing the book's dark matter into the present time.

The victim?

England's young king.

The chief conspirator?

The king's uncle. The duke who saved my mother's life, and my own.

In the prophecy Lancaster is marked by his livery and his name, both disguised as they were in another poem you once shared with me. You called it an elegy, and you wrote it for the duke himself, on the death of his first wife. I can still recall the line, the company riding toward 'a long castle with white walls' as they pursue a white hart.

Lancaster, the White Hart: here again Il Critto chose carefully. His prophecy imputes the regicide to this same 'long castle,' a magnate and kingmaker whose identity the verses barely conceal. Still less do they disguise the alleged victim, young Richard, whose badge bears the white hart.

Nor do they obscure the identity of the author, despite your amusing effort to credit the work to your invented Lollius. Anyone familiar with your Book of the Duchess would easily detect your handiwork.

This, I believe, was Simon's hope. A master of deception, he used old parchment and disguised his hand to make the book take on greater antiquity. He then decorated the margins with plain

426

but skilful drawings of the thistleflowers, plums, hawks, and swords that answered to the playing cards evoked in the prophecies.

Now it needed a final touch. Simon paid me a last visit on Epiphany Sunday, soon after your departure for Rome. Gone was the cavilling bitterness he had shown while the two of you were tilting for my attention. Instead he was all smiles and warmth. He expressed regret for his earlier behaviour, and we parted on the most pleasant terms.

The sole purpose of his visit, I know now, was to pilfer the cloth. He must have unpinned it from the tapestry while my attention was diverted, stuffed it away even as he lisped his pleasantries. It was then an easy matter to commission the embroidery of those simple shapes from Hawkwood's playing cards: plums, thistleflowers, hawks, and swords, surrounding the royal livery, tying the cloth inextricably to the book.

Now all that remained was to get the book into the hands of his master. 'By kingmaker's cunning a king to unking.' Simon wrote that line for Hawkwood. He knew this man, his grandiose designs, his thirst for new legitimacy in his homeland. To imagine himself as the kingmaker would feed his ambition and stoke his pride.

Yet to present the book directly to the great condottiero would have been unwise. Hawkwood is known to be changeable, and he might well have suspected a trap. So Simon arranged to have the prophecies made known to Hawkwood, dangled in front of the man like a riverbug before a pike.

Hawkwood, as Il Critto knew he would, bit.

You are asking yourself how I know all of this, by what means I gleaned this foul grain. There is a man in Hawkwood's inner circle, another Englishman. His name is Adam Scarlett. Though he has a less turbulent soul than his master's, his name is as respected as Hawkwood's, and nearly as feared.

Two evenings ago, a week after Simon's departure for England, Scarlett came to see my father. I heard their voices and walked over

427

to the far north corner of the gallery, where there is a squint down to the hall below. He was asking about Simon.

'Il Critto spent much time in this house,' said Scarlett. 'Tell me all you know about him.'

My father replied that he knew nothing of Simon's doings beyond the failed courtship of his daughter. Why, what else was there to know?

'Master Gower's departure was somewhat – abrupt,' Scarlett explained. 'Ser Giovanni sees no cause for concern in the matter. I am sure he is correct. But I am a thorough man.'

They went on like this for a while, as Scarlett plumbed my father's mind but found nothing. Then he asked a final question. 'Did Il Critto ever mention a book?'

'A book?'

Scarlett described the work to my father, explaining how it would abet Hawkwood's larger aims – aims for which we are all labouring, as he put it – and every word he spoke was a poisoned dart shot from his lips.

Prophecies.

The Duke of Lancaster.

The Earl of Oxford.

Sir Stephen Weldon.

St Dunstan's Day.

Treason.

Execution.

Rome.

France.

It was as if the thousand pieces of a shattered window reassembled themselves in an instant, and I saw it before me, in all its grim totality. Hawkwood, Scarlett, Simon, even my father: all of them in cruel confederation, striving for destruction. An intricate plot to destroy a duke, a king – an entire realm.

I dashed to the gallery. The cloth was gone. On the bench below the tapestry I saw Il Critto, or rather my memory of him. His eyes wide as he gaped at the cloth, his long limbs coiled tensely as he gazed with jealousy on our swelling love. I knew everything, and the knowledge boiled me with terror. For your life, for the life of the duke, for the blood of all England.

Now it is clear what must be done. Simon has been gone for over a week. Your prophetic book precedes him, augmented with his final prophecy and even now making its way overland to London, by the Rhineland roads. When you return to Florence in another fortnight, you shall find only these parchments waiting for you, sealed with my ring, and a very wet kiss – the only kiss you will receive for many months. For by then your bitter orange shall be gone.

Worry not for her safety, my poetical prince. There is still something of La Comadrejita in her, after all. She knows how to steal, how to stab, how to darn a gentleman's hose, wash a lord's pot, peel an earl's root. How to ask for a meal in a dozen tongues, yet garb herself as a peasant. How to barter like a tradesman's wife, yet mewl like a lady of the court. How to slit a man's throat. I dare say her life has equipped her for such a journey better than most.

She will act alone, her quest to find the book herself and prevent the fulfilment of Hawkwood's true aims. To find the book – or die trying. A long journey to England, then, by land and by sea. And when she finds the book, when this accursed volume is in her hands at last, she will burn it to finest ash.

I leave you with one last enigma, my only heart, in the spirit of our games of love and verse. May it goad and prick your mind as you follow our course to England.

> Though faun escape the falcon's claws
> and crochet cut its snare,
> When father, son, and ghost we sing,
> of city's blade beware.

I shall gloss it for you when our lips finally touch and the danger is well past, though I suspect you will have puzzled it out for yourself by then.

Until that blessed moment, I remain yours most faithfully—

Written at the Via dei Calzaiuoli,
by the Misericordia,
the Thursday next after Epiphany Sunday,
by Seguina d'Orange

✤ ✤ ✤

FIFTY-FOUR

St Mary Overey, Southwark

On the third day following the deaths of Sir Stephen Weldon and the butchers, as I dozed in the back garden, Will Cooper appeared at my side. 'Master Chaucer for you, sir.'

We drank small ale beneath the arbour, with the heavy scent of thirsty roses filling the air. Our talk was amiable, though he sensed my reserve. He would hardly meet my eyes, and he fidgeted on his chair.

'What's tickling your thoughts, Geoffrey?' I finally asked, wanting to get to it.

Chaucer let out a breath. 'I have been avoiding this conversation, frankly.'

'I should think so,' I replied indifferently, though over the following hours this indifference would yield by turns to wonder, then outrage, then gnawing doubt.

He started with his arrival in Italy, and his introduction to Seguina d'Orange. Simon had been courting her and was obviously in love, yet she used him to meet Chaucer. They developed a quick intimacy and a ready attraction, meeting frequently as they moved among the English residents of Florence.

'When you are newly in town, of course, everyone wants to hear about doings at Westminster,' Chaucer said. 'The king's new wife, the buzz around Lancaster and the rivalries for the crown. Seguina's stepmother was an Englishwoman – a Londoner, in fact, the widow of one of Hawkwood's men. She had books and books of English romances, and Seguina herself spoke our language like a native. Her interest seemed only natural.'

He stared off over the priory walls, the line of his lips unbending. I stared at him in turn, wondering why I felt surprised at yet another example of Chaucer's baffling selfishness. A married man attempting to seduce a young woman nearly betrothed to the son of his closest friend.

'Seguina was a great story-teller,' he went on. 'The two of us swapped tales and enigmas like children trade river stones. Hers were fantastical, full of beasts and magic, caliphs and flying carpets, boiling oil, thieves visiting at night.'

'And the prophecies?'

'It started as a wager, really, a bit of a dare. I'll write a new work, I told her. Not my usual fare. Something darker, but tuned to the ears of the gullible. When I finished it I planned to read it to her. I showed up at her father's house, the draft in hand, quite pleased with myself.' He turned to me. 'Simon was there that morning, John. Come to pay a call, he said. Seguina invited him in, and together they listened to the prophecies as I read them aloud in the gallery.' Chaucer was measuring his words, trying to soften a coming blow. 'I suppose it was then that Simon saw his chance.'

'His chance? What are you talking about?'

He swallowed drily, his slender neck bobbing with the effort. 'A few weeks before my return to England I had to make a long-scheduled trip to Rome. I would be gone a month, perhaps more, before returning to Florence. The day

432

before my departure, as I was packing my things, I realized it was missing.'

'What?'

'My little book.'

My little book. Chaucer's phrase for the leathern bifold he kept with him at all times, replacing the inner quire as needed. I recalled our meeting at the customhouse, the new red cover such a surprising replacement for the hand-worn skin he had carried for so many years.

Nothing here made sense. 'So you lose a book in Florence, and you ask me to find it in London?'

'Hardly,' he said, still hesitating. 'The book you were looking for was a copy of my own, made by . . . it was – it was Simon who stole my book—'

'As I suspected.'

'—who stole my book, copied out the *De Mortibus* word for word, line for line, and then—'

He stopped, a hand at his mouth as he looked sidelong at me.

'Then what, Geoffrey?'

'Then he added a final prophecy of his own.'

My vision blackened entirely, though only for a moment, and afterwards I felt a clarifying and melancholy sadness. Simon's involvement explained so much, and about everything. His return to England, his eagerness to mingle with the chancellor and official Westminster, that peculiar scene with Chaucer at Windsor. It was as if a piece of gauze had been torn suddenly from my lame and weakened eyes, even as a new weight settled around my heart. I wondered if anything Simon had said to me, anything at all, were true: his longing for home, his desire for a new intimacy with his father, his need to hear of Sarah's last days. All of it feigned?

'Simon wrote the thirteenth prophecy,' was all I could say.

'Out of spite, and simple jealousy,' said Chaucer. 'The jilted

433

lover, revenging himself on the man who stole his lady's heart. One of the oldest stories there is, though in this case augmented by a reckless disregard for all the other lives affected, even the safety of the realm. With my little book in hand he would have indisputable proof that I was involved in the *De Mortibus*, along with a host of other information he could peddle back in Westminster.'

'Information?'

'That quire was dangerous, true, but not only because of the prophecies, which, you must remember, I still regarded as nothing at the time. The book, you see, had all my jottings about what I had learned of Hawkwood's plans over my months in Italy. Troop movements, financing through bankers in Venice, plans for garrisoning and travel. While Simon was copying the prophecies he saw what was in front of him, and recognized it for what it was.'

'So why didn't you tell me all this earlier, Geoffrey? When we first spoke about it, or that day in the customhouse? Think of the time and trouble you might have spared me, and yourself.'

'Well, in my defence, I was almost as ignorant as you when we met at Monksblood's. I had suspected Simon of lifting my book but had no proof, nor even certain knowledge that he had returned to England. Then, once he showed himself, it became . . . personal, I suppose. I could see that you were taken with him, that the two of you were starting to reconcile after so many years.' He stopped, closing his eyes. 'And I have only just confirmed that Simon wrote the final prophecy.'

There was a large rose bush climbing an old trellis on the priory edge of the garden. My eyes had fixed on one stem heavy with newly opened buds, and as Chaucer pressed on I watched spots swimming in a field of cloying pink.

'It was Simon's peculiar mind that conjured the details that made the thing so damned convincing,' he said, as much to himself as to me. 'Wykeham has always had a feast on St Dunstan's Day, and Simon used to speak with such admiration about those pearls. You would show them to him when he was young, while Mark Blythe was carving them over the gates.'

Sunday strolls along the palace walls, admiring looks up at the reliefs. I recalled my visit to Newgate so many weeks ago, the feel of the mason's hands, rough with his labour. And of course the heraldry, the bit about the 'pearls all appointed', even the word *spiritus* from the processional, which Simon would have remembered from his years as a boy chorister.

'He made a fair copy of the prophecies, including his new verse, but used old parchment, masking the whole thing as an ancient manuscript written in the days of King William. He also drew thistleflowers, hawks, plums, and swords along the borders, to correspond to the symbols I had written into the prophecies.'

'From the cards,' I said, making another connection.

'Hawkwood had given me several decks as a gift my last time in Italy. I gave one of the decks to Swynford, simply as an amusement. But that was years ago, well before any of this. As for the verse, all that letter rhythm and so on?' He smiled, almost bashfully. 'I was amusing myself by writing in the rough style of other makers, like this William Langland or the poet of the green knight. *Rum, ram, ruf*, that dross. It was a simple thing to mimic, or misinterpret, as the case may be.' He hesitated. 'As was the heraldry on the cloth.'

'Not Simon's work, surely?'

The smile faded. 'Seguina's.'

'Peculiar,' I said, trying to make this piece fit. 'Why would Seguina participate in Simon's plan?'

'The cloth had nothing to do with the prophecies, not originally. Seguina had embroidered a cloth years before with the arms of Prince Edward and the Duke of Lancaster.'

'And Edward's arms passed to his son, now our king.'

'Precisely.'

'But how on earth did Seguina come to embroider the arms of Gaunt and Prince Edward?' The question, I would now learn, at the centre of it all.

Chaucer looked at me, his eyes lined with a sadness that, for as long as he lived, would never entirely disappear. Over the following hours, as afternoon turned to dusk and dusk to evening, I listened to the saddest story I had ever heard. A story of Castile and Aragon, of Spain and Italy, of Moors and Christians. A story of two Spanish brothers, Pedro the Cruel and Henry of Trastámara, divided against themselves in war, and of Pedro's English allies: Prince Edward, eldest son of King Edward, and his brother, John of Gaunt, fighting on his behalf in Spain.

Yet most of all it was the story of a young woman. A daughter, a sister, a witness, a survivor, a beautiful girl who had seen her mother raped, her brother die, her noble father humiliated into the life of a mercenary. From the Castilian marches she had made her way to Lombardy and Milan, where her father hired himself and his men out to the great English *condottiero*. There, still a child, she learned to get by in the many languages spoken by Hawkwood's mercenary mélange: French, Italian, English, a smattering of Moorish, even Hebrew, all added to her native Castilian tongue. As she grew into a young woman, she learned to defend herself with fist, tooth, and knife, though she was saved from a life of savagery by her stepmother, a London gentlewoman living among the small English communities in Milan, then Florence. A skilful embroideress, her stepmother taught her this and other arts of womanhood: how to dress and care for her body, how to gesture and stand, how to feign interest in the conversation of men. She might be a lady herself someday, her stepmother told her, and it's best to be prepared. Yet through it all Seguina d'Orange never forgot the scene of her mother's violation, nor the English duke who had saved both their lives.

From the oratory came the distant drone of the office, the voices of the Austin canons carrying through the churchyard.

'Prince Edward, then,' I said into the cooling night. 'Edward was—'

'Her mother's ravisher. Picture our good Prince Edward, heir to the English throne, abiding with Lancaster in Castile, waiting for Pedro the Cruel to pay his war debts. He never did. So Edward took it upon himself to extract them from the countryside and its people on his way back to Aquitaine. He was already falling ill, you know, and there were hints of concern about his mind. He'd learned his tactics from Pedro, and from his own long experience in the wars. He taught his men in turn to burn and rape their way through the land. He took what he wanted.'

'Prince Edward,' I whispered, my memories of the man already distant and opaque.

'The blackest prince who ever lived,' said Chaucer. 'They descended on the marches after the war, when her father was still absent, cleaning up with Pedro. She remembered the arms of her mother's rapist and her own saviour—'

'Gaunt.'

'—and pointed both of them into the cloth. When Simon saw it in her gallery it fired a connection in his mind with the prophecies I was reading them. The rest you already know.'

'Hawkwood must have been singing like a lark,' I said. 'Just as he's plotting a return to England, this falls into his lap, and gives him a covert means to get Lancaster out of the way.'

'I would put nothing past Hawkwood.' Chaucer sounded almost admiring of the man. 'He wears loyalty like a snake wears skin.'

'And Oxford?'

'Hawkwood's family has deep connections to the de Veres going back generations. John de Vere, the seventh earl, fought with Hawkwood's father in France.' He sighed. 'It was an ingenious plan, and might well have worked. Put the English king and his uncle at one another's throats, and bring down the House of Lancaster months before your own arrival with the French. Hawkwood values friendship and loyalty only when it suits his own purposes.'

I looked askance at him, incredulous at his lack of self-knowledge. He caught my glance and visibly winced.

'I know, I know. But put yourself in my place, John. You come home after a long absence, terrified for your lover, only to hear lines of your own poetry being whispered at court, along with rumours of a seditious prophecy on the death of King Richard. I suspected Simon was involved but had no idea how. That's why I had to meet with you as soon as I returned from Italy, and that's why I set you on the trail. I needed to find out what Simon knew, and where all of this was coming from.'

I recalled Chaucer's early suspicions at Monksblood's, testing my knowledge, more curious than concerned – then his shock when I confronted him at the customhouse.

'And I know you, John,' he continued, picking at a snag in his hose. 'Once you learned the nature of this book you would stop at nothing until you had it. What I didn't know, of course, was that there were two books all along.'

'Three, actually,' I said, thinking of Clanvowe's copy, now stowed with Oxford's manuscript in the wall of my house.

'And more, for all we know, given how quickly everyone seemed to be quoting from it.'

'Even Braybrooke's friars.'

'Yes. And it was Oxford, I gather, who started the ingenious rumours of interest in the prophecies among Wycliffe's followers. Then the book itself, with the cloth, was planted at La Neyte, and its contents hinted to a number of hermits in Gaunt's dependency, one of whom let it slip to me. The intention was to have it "discovered" at La Neyte by the king's guard, and Lancaster hauled away for conspiring treason well before St Dunstan's Day. The butchers, the card game, Oxford's speech at the bishop's palace – that all came later, once the book went missing.'

I frowned. 'So who stole the book from La Neyte?'

Chaucer said nothing, the moist curves of his eyes reflecting the low moon.

'Seguina d'Orange,' I said at last, as the chill of certainty swept my limbs. 'She was the girl murdered on the Moorfields.'

'She has to be one of the most resourceful women who has ever lived,' he said, his eyes flashing with admiration. 'When I learned she had left Florence I discovered that she used my contacts from the wool trade to arrange passage on a ship from Pisa, with a company of Genoese bankers bound for England. When she came to London, her aim was to find the book and the cloth. She had met Weldon in Florence and knew he was the go-between to Oxford. Once in London she must have followed him, learned the location of the book, recovered it, and fled with it through the city—'

'Pursued by Weldon—'

'Who caught her in the Moorfields—'

'After she handed the book to a maudlyn,' I said, filling in what he didn't know. I told him the rest: about Millicent Fonteyn, the murder of Bess Waller, the death of Sir Stephen Weldon. It was the knight's violent death that brought us back to Seguina's.

'That's how I see it.'

'But why?' I said. 'What motivated her to make such an impossible journey to England? Was it – was it merely love,

439

a desire to protect Geoffrey Chaucer, her adulterous suitor, from bodily harm?'

'I think not,' Chaucer said wryly. 'That sort of sacrifice would have been predictable. Seguina was too great a woman for such a thing. Love was part of her motivation, I suppose. But remember, her life and her mother's had been saved by Lancaster – and it was Lancaster whose life she came here to save. I was incidental in the end. She wrote me a long letter explaining it all, then ordered a servant to deliver it to me upon my return from Rome.' He absently patted his breast. 'A story, really, and one for the ages.'

I looked at him, then guessed. 'You never found it.'

'Her servant would have been terrified of being found out by one of Hawkwood's men. I went to visit Seguina when I returned, only to learn she had left Florence a week before, ostensibly to visit a cousin of her mother's. I distinctly recall the servant meeting me at the door, taking my bag while I waited for an audience with Seguina's father. The servant hid the letter in my bag, assuming I would find it in the folds of my little book. This one, in fact, which I had commissioned from a leatherworker in Rome.'

He tossed it to me, and I examined the construction. Aside from the colour and feel of the leather, it was an identical bifold to his old one, with matching vertical pockets on each inner cover, allowing the first and last folios of each new quire to be tucked inside. 'I found her letter two days ago. The morning after you confronted me at my Aldgate house, in fact. I was switching out quires, and there it was. The letter confirmed everything I had suspected but never knew – including Simon's authorship of the thirteenth prophecy.'

I thought for a moment. 'So you had Seguina's letter with you that day at Monksblood's?'

'But without knowing it.'

'Extraordinary.' I handed back his book, moved and shaken

by the knowledge that Chaucer had just shared. The entire story of the last several months, carried on my old friend's person the entire time.

'When did Simon tell you of his involvement?' I asked him.

'At the St George's morrow feast at Windsor. That was the first time I had seen him since Florence, and he both admitted to stealing the book and confirmed Seguina's presence in England, though he swore he knew nothing about the last prophecy. Seguina had been dead for weeks by that point, and I was furious at him for all he had done – but also terrified of the implications. I thought he might well have killed her himself.'

'Was that you at the river inn that night, after the Garter feast?' A dog's bark, and Simon pissing from the landing, lying about his trip to the privy after that whispered encounter in the courtyard.

He looked confused.

'Simon told me he and Seguina were betrothed, you know,' I said quickly.

A bitter laugh. 'Another lie. A way of finding out if you knew anything about her.'

'Which I did not.' I recalled the look on Philippa Chaucer's face, the flash in Katherine Swynford's eyes at the mention of Seguina d'Orange. 'But Philippa did.'

'I'm not surprised,' he said. 'I wrote a ballade on her name, before I knew she had died. "To Seguina, My Orange, Wherever She May Dwell." Scribbled it on a scrap of banker's paper in our household account book. Philippa saw it when she was at our Aldgate house, and knew I had taken a lover in Italy.' He shook his head. 'Stupid, I know, to leave something like that lying around. But there it is.'

I smiled at him. 'You're remarkably careless with your poetry, Chaucer. And always have been.'

He spread his hands, then leaned forward and placed his

441

hands on my knees. 'You know, John, despite everything, Simon could have betrayed me so easily once he was back in England with my first little book. Why, he could have taken it to Robert de Vere and proved that I wrote the prophecies even while trading on everything else he knew. No one would have noticed that the last prophecy wasn't there. My draft was just a draft, after all, scratched in my hand. For all anyone else knew I was in league with Lancaster against the king.'

It was a good point, though I still had many doubts. I found myself sifting every word and gesture, going back over every hurried meal and whisper of cloth, looking for the missed seed of Simon's mendacity.

Chaucer read my thoughts. 'Simon is confused, John. Brilliant and confused. He has been for years, despite that cock's face he wears. But confusion isn't a sin. What matters most is love. And Simon, for all his faults, loves you deeply.'

I let Chaucer's unmerited confidence hang in the priory air.

'There's one part I still don't understand,' he said. I tensed. 'At the end of her account Seguina left me an enigma, a puzzle of the sort we often invented for one another.' He pulled the letter out of his breast pocket and read it aloud.

> *'Though faun escape the falcon's claws*
> *and crochet cut its snare,*
> *When father, son, and ghost we sing,*
> *of city's blade beware.'*

He looked at me as he put the letter away. 'Have you heard this riddle, John, or read it yourself?'

'No,' I lied, recalling where I had seen those very words.

'A crochet, a city's blade. A bit threatening, wouldn't you say? Do you know what it means?'

'No,' I said, this time speaking the truth. *Hawks always*

strike twice. Weldon's final words sounded again in my mind, the latest inkling of something missed. I said nothing to Chaucer. He had done enough, and I had no further patience for his manipulations. I felt almost gratified by his ignorance. For there had been something weak about his whole story, a subtle sense that his account was incomplete. That it failed to comprehend the full complexity of the aims motivating those he thought he knew best: Hawkwood and Weldon, Seguina and Simon. Especially Simon.

He was looking at me, waiting for some wisdom. I shrugged, covering my agitation. 'Likely just a lover's riddle. The butcher's blades did no harm, after all, and the king is alive. That's the important thing, I should think.'

There seemed nothing more to say. By the time Chaucer stretched and yawned I felt utterly drained, despite my inner turmoil at hearing Seguina's riddle. There was a twinge in my back. 'We are becoming old men, Geoffrey.'

He barked a laugh over the orchard as we rose. 'Old age is relative, John. It's writing that keeps us young. Or so I hope this summer will prove.'

Not for the first time I found myself wishing I saw my making as Chaucer experienced his. The man aged backwards, it seemed, accumulating youth with each fresh scratch of ink. For me every line of poetry is another grey hair, a defeat as much as a victory.

'So what will you write?' I said to his back, willing him to leave. I had a suspicion to confirm. He preceded me through the kitchen, the darkened lower gallery, the hall. We lingered outside my door, soft moonlight playing on the priory lane. 'This pilgrimage conceit, the miller and prioress and so on?'

His hand went to his chest again, and there was a whisper of parchment on his thumb. 'That comes later, after more thought. For now I have in mind the story of Cressida, told in that book of Boccaccio I gave to you. An old tragedy of

443

war, and impossible love.' His dark eyes caught the flicker of the lanterns up by the gate. 'And a remarkable woman who learns to survive in the cruellest of worlds.' With that we parted, and Chaucer moved through the Southwark darkness, his lover's story still pressed to his heart.

FIFTY-FIVE

St Mary Overey

Ember Days. Penance and prayer, self-denial in all things, the mind focused on our faults and our tenuous hopes of salvation, so the priests instruct us. Chaucer swears that fasting clears the head like nothing else. Perfect for poets, he says, though his own abstinence is notoriously light. While Sarah was a pious observer of this Embers ritual, I tend to ignore it, as I do so many of the Church's more ascetic dogmas. I felt that week that I would have starved myself for a glimmer of discernment.

Over seven days had passed since Dunstan's Day. The maudlyns had carried the corpse out of the Pricking Bishop that same night and abandoned it to the animals of Winchester's Wild. The king, the duke, and the earl had reached a tentative reconciliation, and in the aftermath of the palace affair it seemed that things had moved on. The king was resolved on a military expedition to the Scottish border, Gaunt was rumoured to be plotting his return to Castile with the help of Lisbon, and the Earl of Oxford had left London for Hall Place, the de Vere family manor at Earls

Colne. A papal delegation from Rome was to arrive before Trinity Sunday, and the court had bigger things to think about than an expired prophecy.

The Friday after Pentecost found me in my study, wondering once more what I had missed. Weldon's dying words – *Hawks always strike twice* – carried a threat that would not leave my thoughts.

On the desk were the two copies of *De Mortibus Regum Anglorum* now in my possession. I knew every folio of Sir John Clanvowe's manuscript, written out in his neat, restrained hand, as I had studied it with great care in those weeks leading up to St Dunstan's Day. The copy in Simon's hand, the manuscript that had travelled from Italy and that I had taken from Robert de Vere, was different. The texts themselves were nearly identical, a few scribal errors here and there all that distinguished Clanvowe's text from the version he had copied from the more ornate manuscript. While Clanvowe's book was plain and undecorated, the margins of the Italian copy were decorated with the same four emblems found on Swynford's cards. Thistleflowers, hawks, swords, and plums, arrayed in an ascending pattern: one of each embellishing the first prophecy, two of each the second, and so on.

Yet there was something more. Seguina's couplet, composed in the common metre of the lays of Robin Hood or Sir Thopas, and scrawled beneath the last line of the final prophecy. I had dismissed the enigma's importance when Chaucer read it to me from her letter, had even lied to him about seeing it previously. Though I had read those scribbled lines after taking the manuscript from Oxford at Winchester Palace, once the dreadful events of St Dunstan's Day were past I had given them little thought. Yet to learn that the enigma had emerged from the mind of the woman at the middle of all this changed everything.

That very night I had rushed inside after Chaucer's departure, opened the manuscript, and puzzled over the riddle's meaning, as I had done every day since. The lines were written not in Simon's neat hand, but in a thin and spidery script, scratched on the parchment with a charcoal nub and already fading.

> *Though faun escape the falcon's claws and crochet*
> *   cut its snare,*
> *When father, son, and ghost we sing, of city's blade*
> *   beware.*

The lines seemed meant to recast the imagery from the thirteenth prophecy while adding something darker to the mix. The 'faun', of course, was King Richard, and the 'crochet' had to be Sir Stephen Weldon, whose scar resembled nothing so much as a fishing hook. The falcon was surely Sir John Hawkwood, and the meaning of 'father, son, and ghost' seemed clear enough: the Holy Trinity. What continued to defeat me in this extra fragment of verse was the ominous evocation of the 'city's blade', which could refer to practically anyone in a city as large as London.

And who had written Seguina's peculiar couplet in the book? Perhaps Seguina herself, as she fled with the book from La Neyte, though it was hard to imagine her pausing to scribble a riddle in a manuscript while being pursued from Westminster and into the Moorfields. The lines did not appear in Clanvowe's copy, yet they carried a threat all the more ominous for their very uniqueness. Making a decision, I packed the two volumes in my bag and left the house.

✣

Westminster. In the great hall Sir Michael de la Pole was holding forth inside the priest's porch. When he saw me he gave a subtle nod, finished his business, then ushered me into his chambers. I spoke with the Lord Chancellor for over an hour, revealing nearly all I knew, even Simon's authorship of the thirteenth prophecy, though somehow he had already been made aware of that unpleasant fact. I showed him both books as well, making sure he understood the full implications of what I was telling him.

'You're saying there is to be a second attack on the king, then,' said the chancellor, sounding sceptical.

'Yes, my lord.' I repeated Sir Stephen Weldon's final words at the Pricking Bishop. '"Hawks always strike twice," he said. "Always twice." We all saw the first attack at Winchester's palace, how that turned out. And now the king's guard is down. I believe Seguina's lines are telling us the second attack is to come on Trinity Sunday.' I paused. 'Tomorrow, my lord.'

The chancellor still looked unconvinced. 'How can we know for certain that—'

'The thirteenth prophecy, the butchers, all of that – it was smoke,' I said, the words tumbling out of my mouth. 'Hawkwood's ruse, meant to turn suspicion on Lancaster, have him eliminated. And it nearly worked. But Lancaster was just the glaze on the bun. The real target is the king.'

'And you're basing all of this on this girl's two lines of doggerel? This chicken-scratch in your manuscript?'

'Not *my* manuscript, Lord Chancellor. This is the book from which Lord Oxford himself read on Dunstan's Day. The book we have all been tracking down for months.'

He gave me a strange look. 'Are you quite sure, Gower?'

'My lord?'

'You're quite sure this is the book we've all been looking for?'

He could see the confusion on my face. With a studied calm, the baron stood, walked to a book chest against the wall of his chamber, and fussed with the lock. He removed a small volume, no thicker than a short quire and covered in a skin of plain and weathered black. It looked familiar.

Back at his desk he opened it and spun it around. I recognized the hand immediately as Chaucer's. The quire was a messy jumble, the margins covered in notes and drawings: tables, columns of figures, sketches, maps. I had struggled with Chaucer's shorthand before, and though I could make out little of his notation, I saw immediately that half of the quire was taken up with the *De Mortibus*. There was only one difference between this copy and the two on the chancellor's desk, I saw as I paged through to the end – a rather major difference.

The thirteenth prophecy was missing. Chaucer, then, had told me the truth. He had not written the prophecy of Richard's death.

'Three books,' I said, looking up.

'The one in your hands now is the original,' he said. 'Chaucer's draft, written in Florence, and covered with his notes and observations. Then came this one.' He tapped Oxford's copy, the book in my son's hand. 'Simon, when he wrote it, added the thirteenth prophecy.'

'Which Sir John copied along with the rest,' I said, indicating Clanvowe's manuscript.

'Though *before* your mysterious couplet was added. Otherwise Clanvowe would surely have copied that as well.'

I nodded absently. 'But how did you get Chaucer's original, my lord? Who gave it to you?'

A long pause. 'Your son.'

Of course. I thought of Simon waking me that night at Overey, the hole in my house's wall. It made a strange kind of sense, though the chancellor's subsequent account would leave me cold.

'As you know, Gower, King Richard made Sir John

Hawkwood his ambassador to Rome just after the Rising,' he began. 'Not the most courtly envoy in the world, but Italy is a privy. We needed a strong presence there, a man flexible in his alliances. Hawkwood fit the bill like no one else. And he's one of us. An Englishman, yet with no ambition in his homeland.'

He settled his hands on his stomach. 'Or so we thought. As we discovered about three years ago, Hawkwood has been buying up land and properties near his family seat. Nothing too substantial. Perhaps his wife was pregnant, and he was thinking about his legacy, was our thought. It happens. But then he started purchasing properties in other places. London, for one – a house here, a block of tenements there – as well as Essex. Gosfield, Sible Hedingham. It became clear that Hawkwood didn't want to simply retire. He wanted to come back here as a powerful man. Not just titled but garrisoned, it seemed. We tried to keep an eye on him from afar, but he was growing increasingly erratic. Envoys and letters were not enough.'

'You needed a spy,' I said.

'We wanted a man in Hawkwood's chancery, someone gifted with ciphers and scripts, who could tell us from abroad what he was up to, and get us the information we needed in a form we could trust. A forger, a cryptographer, a natural spy. We chose Simon.'

I frowned. 'You *chose* him? And how soon after his arrival in Florence was this?'

The baron looked chagrined. 'You don't understand, Gower. We sent him to Florence.'

'You *sent* him?' It hit me. 'What about the counterfeiting, the death of that man on the wharfage? Simon killed him. Chaucer cleaned it all up. That's why Simon went into Hawkwood's service in the first place.'

He gave a modest shrug. 'A charade, every bit of it. My

450

man More set it up. The ward constable who was killed –
and not by Simon, if that's any comfort – was an informant
working for the French, lured to the wool wharf with the
promise of an exchange. The watchmen were ours, paid from
the royal treasury. It was a simple matter to get them swearing
up and down they had watched a struggle and an accidental
death at Simon's hands.'

'But Chaucer—'

'Chaucer had to be convinced it was all legitimate. That
Simon had to leave London, and quickly, with the taint of
scandal following him.'

I gaped at him.

'You have to see it our way,' he said, leaning forward.
'Chaucer and Hawkwood go back twenty, twenty-five years,
since before Geoffrey was taken prisoner at Retters. It was
Hawkwood who negotiated Chaucer's release on behalf of
King Edward, you know, along with the others. After that
they were together in Spain, France, Italy – getting up to
God knows what. You've heard the stories.'

I admitted I had. Most of them I didn't believe, though
the few that seemed credible could curdle milk. 'So you
exploited Chaucer's long friendship with the man to get
Simon placed down there,' I said. 'Then why did you send
Chaucer back last year? Wasn't that something of a risk,
given the circumstances?'

He grimaced. 'We needed to get a message to Simon, but
couldn't risk having Hawkwood capture one of our messengers.
So we sent Chaucer down there at the head of a diplomatic
company, ostensibly to see about the wool.'

'Wool?'

'Nothing more complicated than that – nor more crucial
to His Highness's treasury.'

'Wool, the goddess of the merchants,' I murmured, recalling
one of my own French lines.

'Our greatest export,' said the chancellor, 'and the Genoese the only foreign shippers allowed to bypass Calais. Thousands of sacks a year from Southampton to Italy. Tens, maybe hundreds of thousands of pounds. We're always stepping in to sniff around for smuggling and evasion. Chaucer has been controller of the wool custom for some time, and he was only too happy to make a discreet trip south for a few months, get him away from Philippa. "We need some feathers smoothed," he was told.'

'He contacted Simon on your behalf, then, while in Tuscany?'

The baron scoffed. 'Hardly. We slipped one of our own men into his entourage.'

'Who?'

His look told me I didn't need to know. 'Simon got our message, did what we asked him to do. What he did next, though – copy Chaucer's book, pen a treasonous prophecy? That was all Simon, I'm afraid.'

He avoided my gaze, and I felt a sting of remorse, knowing what he must have been thinking. His father's son, apples falling close to trees. Everything I thought I knew about Simon had proved mistaken, as if my own son were a distant stranger, or one of Mandeville's monsters, a three-headed beast perched on the edge of the world. From a counterfeiting traitor to a loyal spy for the realm to a forger and cryptographer for a mercenary, in the space of a few days.

The chancellor looked at me, not unkindly. 'To be around a man like Hawkwood for that long, it has to rub off on you.' Thinking this would comfort me. 'Chaucer's company returned from Italy in early March. Simon had already been here for weeks, though without showing himself to anyone, including you.' I nodded vaguely, remembering Simon's appearance at St Mary Overey – exhausted after the long road from Italy, he had told me. 'Once I learned your son was back in London my intention was to bring him in, hold

452

his feet to the fire. Make him tell us why he had left Florence without warning us.'

'When did you know he had returned?'

'You'll recall our chance meeting on Cat Street, that day you were searching out Strode's clerk. Ralph himself had just told me Simon was back.'

Strode had been feigning ignorance that day about Simon's return, then. Yet another deception. 'You covered well, my lord.'

He waved it off. 'When Simon came in that same week he told me he had simply left Hawkwood's service a few months before. That he hadn't bothered writing in advance of his return but had done everything we asked of him, and more. Then he was overheard having a heated conversation with Chaucer during the Garter morrow feast out at Windsor, telling him he planned to sell his little book to the highest bidder, get him strung up for his treachery. It was only then that we began to suspect Simon's connection to these prophecies.'

'Was that one of Oxford's men, then, at the river inn?' This was the question that had confused Chaucer during our last conversation.

'No. It was my man More. He and Simon had arranged a meeting during the feast, supposedly in order for Simon to hand over the book and reveal everything he knew. They met in the courtyard. But Simon demanded money – lots of it – and claimed to have offered the book to the Earl of Oxford, with Sir Stephen Weldon acting as agent. I couldn't let that happen. Simon was speaking too freely about it all. I worried that the whole thing would explode in our faces. So, once More reported back to me, we decided to bring Simon in, press him harder this time.'

'Then he was taken.'

'Weldon got to him first. Plucked him right out of your

house before your return from Oxford. Took him God knows where.'

'How did he escape?'

'Don't know. Don't know that he did escape, or that he was even under duress. But it was clear that Simon had been lying through his teeth, both to our man in Florence, to me at Westminster, probably to Hawkwood and Oxford as well. He's been playing us all against each other, and where his loyalties lie is anyone's guess. Chaucer confirmed as much.'

'I thought Chaucer was ignorant of it all.' Until he discovered Seguina's letter, at least – the one part of the whole story I had kept to myself.

'Of Simon's role, yes. But he learned more than he wanted to about Hawkwood. It seems Chaucer was digging around in some Genoese shipping manifests, tracking sacks of English wool, when he discovered a large number of commissions from Hawkwood for transport of troops this upcoming summer. It gave him a glimmer of Hawkwood's plans. He never confronted Sir John about it.'

I considered this. 'Chaucer knows more than anyone what the man is capable of, I suppose. Hawkwood would torture his own leg if it was holding out on him.'

'Our man's dispatch reached us a week before his return, though none of us made the connection with the prophecies and Hawkwood's plot against Gaunt until much later. Only Simon knew all of that.' He looked at the three books, still opened on his desk. 'Now you're suggesting the king himself is the real target after all.'

'I believe so, my lord.'

'I'll admit the timing is – harrowing. France knows Richard is weak. The Scottish border needs defending. Word is King Richard will march up there this summer, leaving London and Westminster vulnerable.' He puffed his cheeks. 'You have to admire Hawkwood's audacity. Circulate a prophecy incriminating Lancaster, get him hanged, then go for the king. Once they're both out of the picture, swoop in and help install a new sovereign.'

'A kingmaker indeed,' I said, thinking of that line from the thirteenth prophecy, and marvelling at the cold ingenuity of Simon's poetry. I thought of Hawkwood in Florence, still believing all of this was unfolding hundreds of leagues to the north.

Then the chancellor dropped his last surprise. 'Though we won't have to worry about Hawkwood supporting an invasion, whatever happens after the truce expires.'

'My lord?'

'Simon left a little gift for Hawkwood a few days before his departure from Florence. An encrypted message, accusing one of his closest men of betraying his greater ambitions to us all along.'

'What man?'

'Adam Scarlett is his name. Hawkwood's chief lieutenant. A number of months ago we intercepted a rather shocking letter from Scarlett to one of his associates in Paris, boasting of Hawkwood's plans to join forces with the French following the truce. Simon was instructed to find some way of scuttling Hawkwood's plans. In the process, he believes, he will have turned the *condottiero* against his most loyal man.'

'I see,' I said, and I finally did. 'So that was the true purpose of last Autumn's diplomatic mission to Italy. Chaucer's mission.'

'Yes, though again, Chaucer was kept ignorant of Hawkwood's plans until he discovered them on his own. In any case, Simon believes the device he created will convince Hawkwood of Scarlett's disloyalty, and that its discovery will stem any further militant plans on Sir John's part toward England.'

I was incredulous. 'So Simon, despite all he's done, will stay in Hawkwood's good graces.'

'And in ours, to a point,' said the baron, with another of his pragmatic shrugs. 'Our business now must be the king.'

I thought for a moment, trying to push aside all the chancellor had told me in order to focus on the plot at hand. 'Can the festivities be cancelled, or abbreviated in some way? What if the cardinal were to process with the archbishop only rather than with the king and his retinue? I imagine you could come up with an excuse for the royal absence.'

He shook his head emphatically. 'Richard won't hear of it. He regards the abbey as his personal shrine, the embodiment of his invulnerability. You know the places his mind is taking him these days. By now he's convinced himself his survival on St Dunstan's Day was a miracle. That it was God's hand that shot the butchers.'

I pointed up. 'An angel's, perhaps?'

He scoffed. 'God, an angel, royal archers – all the same to His Highness. In any case, halting the procession and Mass is out of the question. We've just got through that whole Dunstan's Day business. If Mars himself were to come hurtling at the king I couldn't get him to change course.'

'I understand, my lord,' I said. The chancellor had higher men to please.

He leaned forward, his face lined with concern. 'St Dunstan's Day was one thing. The attempt took place in the Bishop of Winchester's courtyard, a site easily contained and with a few hundred in attendance. But Westminster, between the abbey and the palace yard? With three or four *thousand* in the crowd – and our assassin any one of them, any *hundred* of them? That's another matter entirely.'

I agreed.

He stood, pacing the floor on the far side of his desk. 'We

need to know where this originated, Gower. Does this last snatch of verse refer to a native plot, another bit of deception by Oxford and Weldon? And "city's blade" – what could that possibly mean? Are the mayor's men involved, the Guildhall? But that's unthinkable.'

He looked a bit desperate. I had never seen him in such a state. He said, 'The cardinal's delegation arrives from Windsor this evening, and the Mass is set for Sext tomorrow. We need more time. Or the answer to this damned riddle.'

I looked down at the book in question, still opened to the final prophecy and the scribbled verse. I thought of the manuscript's recent history. Where it had been, who had held it, stolen it, read from it, peddled it. As the chancellor had pointed out, the final couplet had to have been written into the book after Clanvowe copied from it – which meant what?

I felt a twinge of something. 'There may be another way, my lord.'

✣

The next morning I was at the gates of St Leonard's Bromley at first light, though I had to linger by the almonry until the Prime office had concluded before I could be escorted into the prioress's apartments. Coals glowed on the small hearth, despite the rising heat outside. Eventually Prioress Isabel bustled in from the chapterhouse. The sight of me brought her up short. 'What is it?'

I told her, as quickly as I could, then she sent for Millicent Fonteyn. There was a sober cast to the young woman's face when she entered the parlour. Darkened eyes, nearly expressionless below the close-fitting bonnet worn by the order's laysisters. As I recalled from my prior visit, she was an extraordinary beauty, though I could see what a toll the deaths of her mother and sister had taken.

Wasting no time, I removed the book from my bag and opened

it to the final prophecy. I turned it toward her and pointed to the peculiar couplet. 'Did you write these lines, madam?'

Her deep-set eyes widened at the sight of the page. She looked at the prioress, then at me. 'I did.'

'And why did you not tell me this before, when you showed me the cloth?' Not accusatory, but prodding.

'I confess I did not think it was important, Master Gower. With the prophecy of the butchers, the cloth, all the talk in the streets . . . these lines seemed a small nothing.'

'I understand why you might have regarded the verse as insignificant, in the light of everything else.' Nodding kindly, hoping to spur her memory. 'Where did you read these lines?'

She shook her head, the loose curls at her nape tossed by her vehemence. 'I never read them, sir. I only heard them, spoken by my sister.'

'Agnes,' I said, recalling the name, and her mother's sorrow. 'The one killed by Sir Stephen Weldon, up near Aldgate?'

'Aye, sir.'

'When I was here before St Dunstan's Day you told me your sister witnessed the murder in the Moorfields, yes?'

She blinked twice. 'She did, sir.'

'Is that where she heard these lines, on the Moorfields?' She nodded.

'Tell me about it now.'

'The woman was kneeling in the dirt, Agnes said, right in the clearing. The fire was going out. He asked her some questions. She didn't answer them, or Agnes didn't think she did. But she couldn't understand a word they were saying. Then he raised his hammer. That's when she screamed it.'

'Screamed what?'

'The verse, sir. The verse I wrote in the book. Agnes swore it was intended for her, that the girl knew she was still there. She couldn't get it out of her head. For weeks she repeated

458

it, kept blurting it out at the oddest times. She felt sure it meant something, though to my mind we had enough trouble with the prophecies in the book, and they sounded like a minstrel's lines, and what could be the importance of that? I wrote them there on that final leaf, just to calm her down.' Millicent paused for a well-deserved breath.

Something about her account was odd. I closed my eyes, thought it all through, then looked at her again. 'You said the man was questioning the girl, but Agnes couldn't understand a word. And yet she understood this verse well enough to repeat it to *you* days later. How do you explain the discrepancy?'

She stared at me, confused, then her face relaxed into a sad smile. 'Pardon, Master Gower, I thought that part was clear. They weren't speaking English, you see.'

'French, then?'

'No, Agnes would have said. She'd had enough Calais jakes to ear out French, that's sure.'

'What tongue, then? Did she catch any snatches of it, any words that stood out?'

She thought for a moment, her brow knit. I felt my heart sink. Then her face brightened. 'Indeed she did, Master Gower. *Doovay leebro.*'

'*Doovay leebro?*' Something shifted inside me. 'You're sure?'

'*Doovay leebro*, is what Agnes said.' Feverish nods. '*Doovay leebro, doovay leebro*, like he was singing to her. Sounded like a lullaby, is what she said, and he kept at it until he killed her. *Doovay leebro.*'

Doovay leebro. And then, with a calm astonishment, I knew. 'Where is the cheese?' I whispered. The knowledge balanced me.

'Where is the *cheese?*' the prioress barked, her voice an incredulous smear. 'What on earth are you prattling about, Gower?'

'*Dov'è il formaggio?*' I said, the question a delicious taste on my tongue. The talgar at Monksblood's, a snatch of Italian, a girl killed for a book.

Millicent Fonteyn stared at me in a kind of rapt confusion. My vision, too, had a clarity it only rarely achieved, and she was in that moment the most beautiful thing I had ever seen. I could have kissed her; I could have kissed the prioress for that matter. Instead I bowed and took my leave, the life of King Richard hanging on the speed of my horse.

FIFTY-SIX

Westminster

Even if one avoids London altogether the ride from Stratford-at-Bowe to the city of Westminster is a hard and circuitous one, and as I splashed across the Lea it struck me that I might not make it in time for the procession, set to start shortly before Sext and the Mass of the day. Pushing the thought aside, I approached London on the Mile End Road at a swift gallop. Going through town, however direct the route, would slow me down considerably, so I branched off well before Aldgate and circled the city from afar, with the Moorfields to my left and the tower of Bethlem barely visible over a few low trees.

I came into Westminster from the west and posted my horse well up Orchard Street, going the rest of the way on foot at a jog, dodging around the crowds moving to the palace yard. The announcement of the papal delegation had stirred Westminster, London, even Southwark, hundreds of citizens boating up and walking over for a glimpse of the foreign officials. The crowd thickened as I neared the palace, then slowed as dozens crammed through the last feet of the lane.

The wide expanse between the palace yard and the abbey was a churning sea, a great plain of bobbing heads, lifted caps, shouts and cheers. The whole area had been cleared of hucksters and peddlers, all but a few of the fires extinguished. It appeared that the king and the cardinal had not yet left the palace, where a private service was being held in the St Stephen's upper chapel, though judging from the anticipation in the air the procession would begin at any moment.

The chancellor would be in his chambers off the hall. He avoided processions like the pestilence. My work, he would always say, is best done out of view, a sentiment I shared.

Two doors, then the lesser hall and the chancellor's rooms. My face must have registered my fear, for when he saw it, Sir Michael de la Pole, usually cool, stood at once. With him was Edward More, his secretary and fixer, a man I had dealt with many times. Broad-chested, commanding, with a head and beard of shining white, More had a reputation for ruthless partisanship and calm under pressure. 'What?' the chancellor demanded.

'It's Hawkwood,' I said breathlessly, my words barely a wheeze. 'He has a man, in the papal delegation.'

'How do you know this, Gower?'

'There's no time to explain, my lord.' A deep breath, holding my side. 'But believe me, my information is good.'

'Who is he, Gower?' More asked.

'We'll know him when we see him, I suspect. A trained assassin. Hawkwood wouldn't take any chances with a middling knife. One of the cardinal's guards, would be my guess.'

The chancellor went to a position by the outer door of his chambers, ducking his head to look out to the palace yard. 'We can't stop the procession. They just left the palace. We're too late.'

'Then we catch them,' said More, belting on his short sword. 'Even if it takes us to the abbey altar, we catch them.'

462

'Very well,' said the chancellor, arming himself as well. I followed them out of his chambers and across the hall, which was nearly empty as the procession got going from the palace. De la Pole summoned a clutch of pursuivants idling on the west porch, and we all sped together from the hall toward the royal procession, now making its slow way through the palace yard to meet the crowd still pouring in through the abbey gates, overwhelming the guards at the gatehouse.

As I saw immediately, the king and cardinal were on foot rather than mounted, as they would have been on the longer processions from the Tower, and it was nearly impossible to see them over the masses between their position and ours. The crowd was at least twenty ranks thick, all elbows and indignation as everyone fought for position. With the chancellor, Edward More, and the pursuivants we were ten men strong, though against so many moving hundreds we could hardly hope to force our way through. The noise was deafening, too, and our shouts could not be heard over the din. The pursuivants headed straight into the crowd, angling toward the king's position. I bobbed along behind the outermost rank of spectators, taking short leaps into the air, feeling useless, attempting to get a glimpse of the principals and those clustered around them.

I stopped for a moment and took in the scene from afar, imagining myself atop the Wardrobe Tower at the far corner of the yard, or the bell tower opposite, and picturing the next few minutes in my mind. I reasoned that the attack, when it came, would happen before the abbey's west entrance, where the procession would bottleneck to move through the great doors. If I could get well ahead of the principals I would have a better angle on any potential attacker, though it wasn't clear to me what I could do about it. I pushed my way toward the abbey and gave two boys a shilling apiece to give up their spot on a column base.

I was now elevated two feet above the yard, but that was enough. Pockets of commotion everywhere, hard to tell what represented danger and what did not. I saw More. He was leading the chancellor and the small wedge of pursuivants toward the rearmost line of the procession. His focus was on the cardinal's guards, a rank of ten Italian soldiers, dressed for the occasion in livery and flounce, with banners and flags held above as they marched. The guard had accompanied the prelate all the way from Rome. Despite the procession's gaudiness these were seasoned, well-armed men. Any one of them would be capable of assassinating the king without a thought.

Yet even the closest of them was nearly forty feet from Richard. It would take a great effort to clear the distance, especially with the royal rearguard positioned where they were. For the first time since leaving Bromley I felt a twinge of doubt.

My gaze moved forward, along the intermediate ranks between the cardinal's guard and the principals. Most of them were clergy, separated by order and office. In the rear walked monks of the abbey, a dozen of them in two close ranks. Next came the friars, six Franciscans and a lone Dominican, the seven of them forming a single rank. Before the friars marched five bishops: Wykeham, Braybrooke, William Courtenay the Archbishop of Canterbury, and two Italians, all of them grand with their caps and mitres in various bright hues.

In front of them, forming one rank behind Richard and the cardinal, walked the king's guard. Twelve hardened knights, a squat rectangle around the royal person and the papal delegate. Their heads swivelled at every step, looking for threats. My eyes swept back again, over the lines of clerics, back to the cardinal's guard, then forward once more, looking for something, anything that might indicate—

There. A face, standing out against the others. A friar. One of the Italian Franciscans – no, the Dominican, his black robe stark against the grey favoured by the other order. The balance of the clerics – canons, monks, friars, and bishops alike – had pious, beatific looks on their faces, all pretending not to be enjoying themselves as the citizens of Westminster and London showered the company with spring flowers and words of praise.

The Dominican was different. His features hard, his frame lean, his stance taut as he walked, coiled, ready to spring. His eyes two slits of malice, measuring distances, reckoning angles. The ripple of his robes, loosely cinctured, obscured his hands, which seemed at the moment to be tucked behind him as he walked.

The procession was nearing the abbey door. The frontmost rank of guards would soon start to slow. I looked for More and the chancellor. The pursuivants were still too far away. I looked back at the friar. He was making his move. A flash of steel, and his knife was out, held against his chest, partially obscured by his hands. No one near him had noticed.

'*The friar!*' I shouted into the deafening roar, waving from my position at the column. '*More, More! It's the friar!*' The Dominican, oblivious of my shouted warnings, started to move, pushing gently through the row of bishops in front of him.

'*The friar!*' I shouted again. More didn't hear me either. I might as well have been screaming into a bucket sunk in the sea. But just as I had that thought the chancellor looked up at the abbey door and saw me pointing wildly. He pulled on the sleeve of the pursuivant immediately ahead of him. They both gaped at me. On an impulse I clasped my hands together, bowed my head in mock prayer, and pointed urgently to the cluster of friars pressed against the king's guard, which had now slowed to a near crawl. The abbot of Westminster prepared to welcome the king and cardinal at the abbey door, less than twenty feet in front of King Richard.

I mock-prayed again, pulled on an imaginary hood. The chancellor's eyes widened. He understood. *A friar*, I saw him mouth to the nearest pursuivants.

With a surge of forgotten strength the aged Lord Chancellor pushed ahead, taking Edward More and two pursuivants with him. They were fifteen feet from the friar, twelve, eight. Then, with a snake-like precision, the Dominican, sensing movement behind him, leapt forward, slashing at the necks of the king's guard, intent on his target. But one of the guards had heard More's and the chancellor's shouts. His sword was out. It slashed at the friar in a protective arc. The friar ducked, and it took another swipe to halt his lethal progress toward the king. Two of the chancellor's pursuivants had finally reached the spot. There was a brief but furious melee, arms and swords and knives flying about.

It ended quickly. By the time the king and the cardinal bothered to glance over their shoulders the threat had been neutralized, the friar sliced to a bleeding mess. The principals exchanged a few words with the abbot, received the blessings, and pressed forward through the doors, the seemingly minor nuisance behind them. Only the bishops looked somewhat flustered. Braybrooke, two ranks behind the king, gave me a dark look, which I returned with a low bow and a hidden smile.

The crowd surged against the abbey's west façade, all craning for a last glimpse of the king. The pursuivants dragged the friar against the tide of the commons, and few bothered to glance at them. Soon they had him hoisted on their shoulders, a trail of blood spattering the pavers in their wake. Walking behind the chancellor, Edward More turned to look back at me from the abbey's northwest corner. He gave me a small nod. The pursuivants, with the dying assassin, disappeared. More followed them.

Two groats to the abbey guard got me into the nave, where I watched the procession conclude before the altar. All was calm, disconcertingly normal after the madness outside. St Peter's nave glistened, gem-like, the clerestory windows casting mottled sun on a large crowd of nobles and clerics of all orders finding their places. The grand service began, an elaborate introit in five voices echoing to the vaults.

Not feeling prayerful I decided not to stay for Mass, angling instead up the nave and into the south transept along the narrow passage past the chapterhouse. There I paused for a moment before a painting of St Thomas I had always loved. Not St Thomas Becket, nor St Thomas Aquinas the philosopher, but St Thomas the Apostle. The great doubter, his unbelief perpetually etched in his face at that precise moment before he touches Jesus's side: his gaze cast down, his finger bent over his savior's open wound. This Thomas, I think, has always been my favourite occupant of the canon of saints. The patron saint of doubt and suspicion, of verifiable information, in whatever form it comes.

FIFTY-SEVEN

Priory of St Leonard's Bromley

'Prioress Isabel has asked me to remain at St Leonard's,' Millicent Fonteyn said to Eleanor Rykener. The sky was clear that afternoon, awash in a blue deeper than any in Millicent's memory. They sat in the small herb garden off the almonry, a promise of summer in the piney waft of rosemary from behind the bench. 'Says she'll take me in again as a laysister.'

Eleanor had begged a slab of tar from a ditcher along the walls. She had her shoe off, patching the leather. 'Will you stay, do you suppose?'

Millicent nodded. 'Not a sole doubt in my mind. Though maybe one small regret.'

'What's that?' Eleanor rubbed dirt over the tar, smoothing the patch with her palm.

Millicent smiled, thinking of John Gower. Widowed, tall, rich. 'Can I live my life without the touch of another man?'

Eleanor snorted. 'I'm touched by another man six, seven times a day. Can't say it's much to miss.'

'I suppose not,' said Millicent with a sigh. 'Though I'll miss my figs.'

'No figs at St Leonard's?'

'No figs, no money, no men.'

Eleanor slipped her shoe on. 'Nothing wrong with going figless, Millicent. Nor penniless, nor even cockless.'

'Millicent the Cockless,' she mused. 'I like it. And as Agnes used to goad me, I've always wanted a title.'

'Agnes,' said Eleanor wistfully.

Millicent regarded Eleanor Rykener with a stab of shame. Millicent had spent just a few years in her mother's service at the Bishop before seizing the opportunity to flee to St Leonard's and a new life. Eleanor Rykener had lived nearly ten years now on her stomach, enduring the gropes of monks, squires, and franklins, and all without a trace of the bitter self-pity that Millicent spoke like a second tongue.

She thought of the saints, that litany of suffering women whose works and lives the nuns of St Leonard's would intone in their offices. Of St Margaret, swallowed by the dragon, then standing triumphantly on its back. Of St Cecilia, her virtue threatened by a Roman despot, suffering three sword-strokes to her neck. Of the Blessed Maudlyn herself, lifted by Jesu from the bowels of the swyve. And here was Eleanor Rykener, enduring more trials of the flesh than all these sainted women put together. Yet no one would think to write Eleanor's life for an Austin canon to include in the *legendum*. No one would compose St Edgar Rykener a hymn, nor sing a collect in praise of St Eleanor the Swerver.

She had a sudden thought. 'Would you take up other work, do you suppose, if the opportunity came?'

Eleanor waved away a fly. Shrugged. 'Seems God suited me for swyving. There's not another line of work would let me be true to my mannish side, least that I can tell.' She smiled sadly. 'Imagine I'll keep with it till Gerald reaches his majority. Then we'll see.'

The next day Millicent visited the prioress in her apartments. All was arranged with a few words to Isabel.

'Your timing is propitious, Millicent,' the prioress told her. 'Bromley has received a generous endowment, in the neighbourhood of twenty pounds.'

'Twenty pounds?' Millicent marvelled at the sum. 'Who established this endowment, Reverend Mother?'

'Our benefactor has asked not to be named, though I can tell you he's a Southwark man. But the funds are not given freely.' She said this with a trace of disapproval. 'The endowment's terms are quite clear. It is to be employed in perpetuity for the benefit of the maudlyns of Southwark and London, with Bromley required to come to their aid and succour whenever possible. So it won't be difficult to budget ten shill a year for your Eleanor Rykener. Scullery work?'

Millicent nodded, delighted with the prioress's response. 'Or the animals, Reverend Mother. Whichever you think best.'

'She'll be your charge, Millicent, not mine,' said the prioress. 'But don't let me catch you running a flock of whores out of the gatehouse.' She went back to her book.

'No, Reverend Mother,' said Millicent with a hidden smile. She started to back out of the parlour.

'And, Millicent?'

She looked up. 'Yes, Reverend Mother?'

'Will Tewes, our yeoman cook, grows old,' said the prioress, her gaze still on the page. 'He's in need of a cutter, a young man good with a knife. See that one is found for him.'

470

FIFTY-EIGHT

San Donato a Torre

A knock at his opened door, then a boy's voice. 'Ser Giovanni invites you to dine with him, Master Scarlett.'

Adam Scarlett, annoyed at the interruption, turned from his desk with a frown. Not even a page at the door, but a boy from the villa's kitchens. He sighed, set down his pen, and closed the ledger. He followed the boy from his rooms and through the labyrinth of low hedges leading to the side door.

In the hall Hawkwood was bent over the central table, concentrating on a mess of papers. Two of his dogs, hunting hounds, all nose and tongue, were curled around his feet. The closer one licked Scarlett's hand as he sat.

A servant set a goblet of wine between them and a thick soup at Scarlett's place. At Hawkwood's inviting gesture he sipped contentedly until the *condottiero* looked up and joined him in the meal. Scarlett told him the news of the day – another letter from Carlo Visconti, a herd of poached sheep lost in transit from near Poggibonsi. Hawkwood nodded at the right places, asked a few questions; all seemed perfectly normal. Yet Scarlett could sense a certain tension in the air.

There was a stiffness to Hawkwood's manner, a formality he rarely saw in the man when they were alone.

Finally Hawkwood leaned back, sighed, and put a hand on Scarlett's arm. 'Desilio has broken the final cipher,' he said, a note of longing in his voice.

Scarlett felt a leap of hope, though Hawkwood quickly dashed it. The *condottiero* lifted the topmost paper and read, his gravelled voice weighing the deciphered message with a heavy finality.

My Lord, know by this that our earlier suspicions are confirmed. John Hawkwood, false knight and traitor to the crown, plots against His Highness's rule. His brigades will sail from Spezia no later than the Feast of St Edmund, to join the French fleet off Sluys. Five thousand spears, with a thousand from Hawkwood, four from France. The coastal garrisons must be reinforced, the forts heavily manned, the artillery strengthened, and with all deliberate speed.

As Hawkwood recited the missive Scarlett felt his shoulders sink, all his fears realized. 'We are done, then. Betrayed, and by that snivelling runt.'

'So it seems,' said Hawkwood, patting Scarlett's arm. Scarlett grasped his master's hand, feeling the surge of disappointment through the rough skin.

They finished their meal in silence, the air heavy with regret and stifled ambition. When the service was cleared Hawkwood took a final swallow of wine, wiped his lips, and handed the goblet to Scarlett, who sipped once, then again – and his hand stopped in midair as three of Hawkwood's roughest men entered the hall from the direction of the main gallery. They positioned themselves in a shallow triangle around Scarlett's chair and stood, silent, as Hawkwood brought out his cards.

472

'My lord?' Scarlett said, hating the sudden fear in his voice.

'I'm learning, you know,' said the mercenary, placing down a first card. 'I've got my own set of signals now. "When I wipe my lips, enter the hall and surround the disloyal sack of shit." Not as sophisticated as Il Critto, perhaps, but it seems to work. And no need for a cipher.'

Scarlett said nothing, though his breathing grew shallower with each card Hawkwood arrayed on the table.

'Desilio came to me yesterday.' Another card. 'His face was pale, his hand shaking as he talked me through every step of the final code.' Four more cards, all face up. 'I was impatient at first, but he insisted that I work out the solution myself.' The third row complete. 'And he was right, for I would never have believed what I read had I not sifted through those pages myself, transcribed every letter in my own hand at his instruction. It wasn't difficult, really.' The last two cards, face up before Scarlett's hands.

From a bag at his side Hawkwood took out the scorched quire and went on, as if instructing a schoolboy in grammar. 'Each grouping of cards is a letter, you see. Start at the end and the beginning of the deck, excluding the trumps and taking the first and last cards as the letter A.' He pointed to the first pair he'd arranged. 'The second and the penultimate are B, the third and the antepenultimate C, and so on until you've exhausted the cards and the alphabet. Then you start over, with the second and the penultimate cards standing for A this time, the third and the antepenultimate for B – I won't go on. The suits must be ranked, of course, and it can get quite confusing if you forget which sequence you're on. There are as many as five different pairs standing for the letter S in this message alone. But Desilio took me through it, and eventually I was able to work out the message I've just read you.'

'I see,' said Scarlett, his uneasiness growing.

'What I didn't read you, though, was the last little bit. Do you mind if I do so now?'

'As you wish, Sir John,' said Scarlett stiffly, dreading to hear what came next. One of the dogs moved at his feet, nosing for a hand.

Hawkwood read.

To ensure its delivery to your hands, and to guard against the seizure of a messenger, we have sent this same information by land and by sea. Trust you in the truth of this, for Hawkwood himself has revealed all. Written at San Donato a Torre, by Firenze, the feast of Sts Perpetua and Felicitas, by your humble servant Adam Scarlett.

At the final words Hawkwood nodded up at his men, who descended on Scarlett as he sat frozen in his chair. He hardly noticed as his arms were thrust across the table, his wrists pinned in place by much stronger hands, his thumbs splayed to the sides as his palms were pressed against the wood's cool surface.

Hawkwood stood, took a heavy knife from one of the men, and brought it down on Scarlett's right thumb. Scarlett screamed, his legs quivering beneath him.

Yet even as his hand sang with an almost exquisite pain, his continuing screams now muffled by an oily cloth clamped over his mouth, he heard a sound that transcended agony. The crunch of bone, his bone, in the mouth of a dog.

At Hawkwood's signal the man behind him forced his head to the side, his eyes widening in terror as he watched the hound chew and spit, chew and spit, lick, then lip, then chew and spit again, the shards of his thumb now a moist bolus on the floor. Another flash of Hawkwood's knife, and the second dog had his treat. The men pressed vinegared cloths on Scarlett's fresh stubs, strumming his nerves even as they stanched the blood and kept him from passing out.

'Every lying finger, Adam,' said Hawkwood, his voice a calm promise of misery to come. 'Then every false toe. Then each treasonous ball, then your traitorous cock. After that – well, after that we'll heal you up and get to work on your face.'

Scarlett closed his eyes, knowing it was useless to protest his loyalty to this man he would never have thought to betray. He was on the north downs, on Detling Hill after a walk from Maidstone. He had promised himself he would return there once back in England, and that his death, when it came, would not be in vain. So much for promises, and salvation.

'We'll keep you alive as long as we can, Adam Scarlett,' said Hawkwood. 'I wouldn't want you to miss a moment of the feast.'

FIFTY-NINE

St Paul's

On St Boniface's day, the fifth of June, I arranged an appointment at St Paul's with the bailiff of the Aldermen's Court. Nothing important, merely a glimpse at a recent deposition I had been wanting to see. But I suspected the chancellor would be at the cathedral that morning, and that he would be summoning me sooner or later in any case. While speaking with the bailiff I stood at a spot in the north transept by the passage to Minor Canons, where the baron would see me as he passed.

It did not take long. Once the bailiff had left I leaned on the doorway, composing a pair of couplets in my mind, until I felt a presence behind me.

'How did you do it, Gower?' I turned to see the baron, framed against the crossing. I bowed. 'How did you know?'

'They were speaking in Italian, my lord,' I said as we walked toward the less crowded south transept, our voices low. 'That night on the Moorfields. Weldon was interrogating her in Italian. That was the first clue.'

'So . . .?'

'So London had nothing to do with the "city's blade". The girl was being questioned about the book, but she knew more. And that's what she revealed with her final words – in English, so that the maudlyn, Agnes Fonteyn, would understand and remember them. Weldon spent years with Hawkwood, and his Italian was as good as Chaucer's. He knew what he was doing. Recovering the book was crucial to keeping everyone focused on these elaborate prophecies and ignorant of Hawkwood's more direct plot against the king. The Trinity plot, like the book, originated with him.'

'"City's blade",' the chancellor mused. 'A city in Italy, then?'

'Florence, most obviously, though that wasn't quite it.' We had reached the opening to the chapel of St Katherine, empty but for a sole worshipper kneeling at the altar of Mary and Martha. 'But once Agnes's sister told me they were speaking Italian on the Moorfields it all came to me. London is to an Englishman what Rome is to an Italian: the principal city. After that it was a simple matter of translation. In Latin, the possessive of "city", *urbs*, is *urbis*.' I paused. 'She was making a pun, my lord.'

'The blade of Urban,' said the chancellor with a rueful smile.

'Pope Urban's blade,' I finished. And there it was, I explained. *When father, son, and ghost we sing, of city's blade beware*. The assassin – the true assassin of King Richard, not the bumbling company of butchers riled up by Weldon and Oxford and their skulking priest for St Dunstan's Day – would be a member of the papal delegation, scheduled to process with the king at the abbey on the morning of Trinity Sunday.

'The man was a professional and seasoned killer,' the baron said. 'Bernabò Visconti's deadliest knife, or so he claimed before we broke his neck. Planted by Hawkwood in the papal delegation. Had he not been stopped the king would surely be dead, taken with a blade in the ribs before his closest guard could blink.'

I silently wondered whether Oxford, in the thick of the plot against Gaunt, had known about the planned attempt on the king, despite the close friendship between the two young men. Weldon surely had, though this ugly knowledge had died with him. The foiled assassination would remain known only to a few, I observed, and lost to history.

'Just as well,' the chancellor said with an air of tired discretion. 'Though I do wish I could have met the girl, this Seguina d'Orange. Geoffrey Chaucer hardly deserved such a woman's love.'

'It wasn't all about his clever book in the end, my lord, let alone about him,' I said, speaking thoughts I had been mulling for days. 'There was a greater purpose to her sacrifice than saving the skin of a London poet.'

'That's why Seguina d'Orange came to England, then,' the baron mused. 'Not only to save Lancaster, or Chaucer, nor even to find the book, as important as that was.'

I peered into the chapel, at a high wall scorched with years of pious smoke. 'King Richard was the brother of her dead brother, and thus her own sibling, after a fashion. But he was also the son of her mother's ravisher – and yet she came here in part to save his life.'

'And she did it, didn't she, with her last words,' he said, his voice a soft coil of wonder.

'Though only just.' The close call before the abbey was still fresh in my mind.

'I was there, you know,' said the baron quietly.

'My lord?'

'The battle at Nájera, with Prince Edward and Lancaster, all those years ago.'

'You were in Edward's household,' I recalled, prompting a nod. 'During the Castile campaign for Pedro.'

'I wouldn't have been with them at that woman's castle. I was with the Gascon encampment at Burgos during those weeks. But I remember Edward's illness after the battle, the fevers and the raging, this sense that the man was . . . detaching from himself, that his mind had bent somehow. Everyone agreed afterwards that Spain was the sad beginning of a long end for the prince. Seguina's mother wasn't the first woman he brutalized in those years, nor the last.'

We stood for a while longer, listening to the hurried murmurs of a priest from one of the chantries before the south porch. I think we both sensed a circle closing, though the machinations that had brought us here were clearly the beginning of something much larger. I thought of Hawkwood, spinning his sticky webs in Tuscany. Of Simon, fled for who knew where. Of Sarah, who had died knowing nothing of her son's chosen profession; a minor blessing.

'So what next?' I eventually asked him. 'Will you return the favour, have Hawkwood snipped?'

The chancellor let out a sigh, a slow wind of realism. 'We need Hawkwood, Gower, even more than Hawkwood needs England. I see a long war ahead of us. There's no reason to go stirring the pot over an unfortunate incident easily got past. This is how it works in the end. We pardon our second-worst enemies, make treaties with our former slaughterers. Overlook treason to win a battle.'

I told him I understood. He would get no objections from John Gower for choosing political expediency over moral purity. 'And Simon?' I asked neutrally. 'Will you pursue him further?'

'I will leave that in your hands.' He gave me a baronial look. 'The realm owes you a great debt, Gower. God knows your talents can create some peculiar twists. In this case, though, they've won the day.'

There was a rather uncomfortable pause. I knew what the

479

chancellor expected me to say. He stood there, waiting for my demands. The Exchequer's books, a bishop's house on the Strand. Even a knighting by the king was not out of the question.

I surprised myself by not asking for a single shilling.

❖

The next morning, after one of the soundest sleeps of my life, I left the priory grounds on foot, crossing the bridge and walking beneath the outer arches of the St Thomas Chapel as the first glimmer of sun broke through low morning clouds. Once on the north bank I descended to the wharfage and the offices of the wool custom. Chaucer, so a clerk at the customhouse told me, was out of town. A difficulty at Hythe, rumours of illegal wool.

The clerk stepped out for a moment, giving me the opportunity to take a glimpse at Chaucer's desk. On it sat a small quire, weighted open to a page nearly empty of content: pen trials, a few doodles, some couplets. I leaned over and read.

> *Befell that in that season, on a day,*
> *In Southwark at the Tabard as I lay*
> *Ready to ride forth on my pilgrimage*
> *To Canterbury with full devout courage,*
> *At night was come into that hostelry*
> *Well nine and twenty in a company*
> *Of sundry folk, by adventure fallen*
> *In fellowship, and pilgrims were they all,*
> *That toward Canterbury would ride.*

I had to read the lines again. *In Southwark?* Chaucer was a London man, through and through, and as far as I knew had never gone on pilgrimage to Becket's shrine, or anywhere else, for that matter. If he travelled to Canterbury it would be for business or pleasure, not for faith. False prophecies, false pilgrimages: all the same to my slippery friend.

Outside the customhouse I stood on the wharfage, watching the slow, careful movement of the Goose as it craned a pile of wool from the dock. On the decks of the trading vessels workers toiled at the crates and barrels of goods brought to London from around the earth, from the looms of Lyon, the vineyards of Alsace and Tuscany, the olive groves of al-Andalus, and there, on the river's edge of London, with the low bulk of Southwark rising before me, with the dense span of the bridge against the sky, I felt the unboundedness of it all. A history I would never fully understand had passed me by, these great machinations linking Florence, London, the marches of Aragon and Castile – and the narrow lanes of Southwark, and a dead woman on the moor.

We live in an immense world, whole universes of taste and touch and scent, of voices commingling in the light, and dying away with the common dread that stands at every man's door. Yet we perceive and remember this world only as it creates those single fragments of experience: moments of everyday kindness, or self-sacrificing love, or unthinkable brutality. I angled my face to the sun and blinked away a spot, then another, these dark blemishes floating in my sight, mottling my vision, more of them by the day. Yet behind and beyond them I could imagine, for a moment, the holy sheen of Sarah's skin, the faces of our children, the intricate gloss of some forgotten book, and I thought how simple it should be, to know and cherish the proper objects of our lives.

On the near end of the bridge I bought a bird pie. The pigeon was bad, I realized after the first bite – though thankfully before swallowing. I spat it out. I thought about returning to the pieman's booth though I would have to push back through the crowd, which had thickened with the unwelcome intrusion of aristocracy. A lower knight, mounted and shouting

481

for space, passing over from the bankside. Then the catcalls, some trash dropped from the houses above, a few small missiles thrown, all done with that urban mix of defiance and cheer, the common resonance of this angry city I bafflingly loved.

It came to me then, the source of Chaucer's folly. A hostelry at night, a diverse company of pilgrims, a tale of fellowship and adventure, all beginning at the Tabard, of all places. A book for England's sake: stories within stories, and the stuff of life, encompassed by the one great story we all must share yet none of us will ever get to read. At the foot of the bridge I stumbled on a loose paver but recovered my footing as a flock of starlings whorled above, as the way widened into the teeming breadth of Southwark, like a narrow river finding the sea.

A Note to the Reader

One of the strange pleasures of writing *A Burnable Book* has been the discovery and partial correction of my own ignorance about much of medieval life. After half a career spent studying and teaching the literature of the Middle Ages, it came as a rude awakening to realize I couldn't answer a simple question posed by my younger son: 'Did they have forks?' (Yes, Malcolm, after a fashion, though not many of them, and mostly for serving, not eating.) Though I have drawn on many of the same sorts of sources I regularly consult in my academic work, fiction requires a more eclectic approach to research guided by the idiosyncrasies of story and character. As often as I have read around in the latest scholarship on aristocratic politics during the reign of Richard II, I have found myself consulting the work of nineteenth-century antiquarians on gutters and drainage in the Southwark stews.

I hope this note will guide readers in following up on any aspects of the historical setting that interest them, as well as help answer questions about the specific choices I have made in depicting a medieval world so familiar yet so foreign to our own. Readers will find occasional posts about setting and sources on my blog, *www.burnablebooks.*

com, and I am happy to receive queries and corrections as they arise.

John Gower's London was three cities, not one, and much of its life and culture was shaped by the distinctive character of the two smaller suburbs lying outside the walled city itself (and beyond its jurisdiction). The history of London, Southwark, and Westminster in the decades following the Black Death has been the subject of considerable scholarship in recent years that has helped me flesh out the bones of a story set in a richly complex milieu. The works of urban history I have consulted most frequently include Caroline Barron's *London in the Later Middle Ages*, a magisterial study of the medieval city, its institutions, and its diverse population; Sheila Lindenbaum's numerous articles on everything from urban festivals to aristocratic tournaments; Robert Shepherd's *Westminster: A Biography*, with its rich appreciation for the historical contours and character of the royal city; Martha Carlin's *Medieval Southwark*, a thorough guide to the intricacies of life and politics in the small suburb across the bridge, where bishops and butchers, tanners and taverners lived side by side and elbowed for room; Barbara Hanawalt's *Growing Up in Medieval London*, with its inspiring recreations of individual lives of the young; the myth-busting scholarship of Judith Bennett, Marjorie McIntosh, Cordelia Beattie, Kim Phillips, and others on the lives, careers, and literacies of medieval singlewomen; the work of urban archaeologists on Winchester Palace, the customhouse near Billingsgate, and other medieval sites; and Frank Rexroth's *Deviance and Power in Late Medieval London*, a field guide of sorts to the underworld of urban grime and petty crime that surrounded Gower, Chaucer, and the other city-dwellers populating this story. I have also benefited from new work by Linne Mooney and Estelle Stubbs on the scribal culture of the London Guildhall, home to an urban bureaucracy that included the likes of

Ralph Strode and Adam Pinkhurst – the latter, perhaps, Geoffrey Chaucer's most notable scribe. (The map included at the beginning of the book is based in part on the map of late-medieval London included in Mooney and Stubbs' *Scribes and the City*, enhanced by the renderings in Carlin's *Medieval Southwark* and the wonderfully detailed maps created for the third volume of the British Atlas of Historic Towns.)

Other bureaucracies are also part of the story told in *A Burnable Book*, particularly the legal profession emerging during these years and the peculiar educational system that trained its members. The origins of the Inns of Court in the final decades of the fourteenth century are shrouded in obscurity. While the Inner and Middle Temples were organized well before 1385, the earliest written records from any of the four inns come from the 1420s; the exact nature of legal education and barrister culture in the fourteenth century is thus a matter of pure speculation (hence the raucous spectacle performed by the apprentices at Temple Hall, invented for this book). We do know something about the various personnel who defined the changing profession. The character of Thomas Pinchbeak, serjeant-at-law, is based on a real member of the Order of the Coif. The history of the order has been treated in great depth by J.H. Baker, whose many works have helped define the study of medieval English law and its institutions.

As one of my early readers helped me see, *A Burnable Book* is in part a story of town–crown conflict, with the novel's largely London-based narrative playing out against the political crisis that more broadly defined this period of English history. The year 1385 was a pivotal one for the nation's aristocratic classes, with the expiration in May of a truce with France, Scottish incursions along the northern border, and rising tensions between the uppermost factions in the realm. Just months after the events portrayed here,

King Richard would create a number of new dukedoms and earldoms: John of Gaunt's brothers would become dukes, Michael de la Pole the Earl of Suffolk, and Robert de Vere the Duke of Ireland. While the machinations of magnates are only a small part of this story, they are an important backdrop to the intrigue surrounding the book sought by Gower and others, and a domestic counterpart to equally pressing international affairs. Here I am indebted to studies of Richard II's reign by Nigel Saul, Chris Given-Wilson, Michael Bennett, and Anthony Goodman; to Jonathan Sumption's stirring history of the Hundred Years War, particularly his comments on the importance of spies; to biographies of the mercenary Sir John Hawkwood by William Caferro and Stephen Cooper; to Paul Strohm's many studies of literary culture and court politics; to books by W.H. Ormrod and Stephanie Trigg on the Order of the Garter; and to Alison Weir's *Mistress of the Monarchy*, a luminous re-evaluation of Katherine Swynford. The genealogical tables at the front are intended to bring out the close relationships between the upper English aristocracy and its foreign counterparts, including the crown of Castile and the Visconti of Milan.

The character of Eleanor/Edgar Rykener was inspired by an extraordinary document discovered by Sheila Lindenbaum in the Corporation of London Records Office. The document, subsequently transcribed and translated by David Lorenzo Boyd and Ruth Mazo Karras, was published in the first volume of the *Gay and Lesbian Quarterly* as 'The Interrogation of a Male Transvestite Prostitute in Fourteenth-Century London'. The work of Ruth Karras on medieval prostitution and the lives of those who practised it has been immensely helpful to me in imagining the denizens and cultures of Gropecunt Lane and Rose Alley, as has Carolyn Dinshaw's scholarship on medieval sexualities and gender.

Though the labours of modern scholars are an invaluable

resource to any writer of historical fiction, they are no substitute for the primary sources in which medieval people speak to us in something like their own voices. I have consulted a wealth of sources attesting to the lives of the women and men of this era, always with an eye for unusual details. Coroners' rolls and bishops' registers, law cases and legal moots, memorandum books and conduct manuals: in these documents can be found the makings of countless medieval life stories whose contours appear only dimly to our modern eyes. Sources such as parish registers and household accounts have furnished given names and surnames (some of which I have altered for literary effect), while probate inventories, wills, and household account books show us glimpses of the objects, commodities, and habits that shaped the material world of late-medieval England. Readers wanting a taste of medieval London's documentary record for themselves might enjoy paging through the hundreds of examples collected and translated in Henry Thomas Riley's *Memorials of London and London Life in the XIIIth, XIVth, and XVth Centuries* or the *Liber Albus*, an immense compilation of rules and customs relating to city governance compiled in the early fifteenth century (both are freely available online). For a general guide to daily life and customs in the period, readers can do no better than Ian Mortimer's *Time Traveller's Guide to Medieval England*.

I have also consulted the writings of monastic and lay chroniclers of these fascinating years. The Westminster Chronicle details the tensions between John of Gaunt and King Richard over the first half of 1385, as well as contemporaneous events in Italy surrounding the Visconti and Sir John Hawkwood. The metrical chronicle of the Chandos Herald recounts the 1367 campaign of Edward the Black Prince in Castile and Aragon in the months surrounding the Battle of Nájera, providing the tragic background to the story of Seguina d'Orange.

The literature of medieval England, my own scholarly specialty, has been a constant source of reference, dialogue, and slang; readers familiar with the writings of Chaucer, Gower, William Langland, and others will find allusions and borrowings on nearly every page. The prophecies of the *De Mortibus Regum Anglorum* are modelled on the alliterative long lines of Langland and the Pearl poet. In addition to literary texts, innumerable historical and documentary sources are excerpted in the *Middle English Dictionary* and its compendium. As I always advise my students, the *MED* is far superior to the *OED* for anyone interested in early English wordings, first usages, and forms of address. (As the *MED* demonstrates, for example, words and phrases such as 'my lord' and 'sire' were ubiquitous in the period and used even within the household, despite the common assumption that they were reserved for aristocrats and kings.)

Finally, John Gower. Despite his prolific career, his adept use of three distinctive literary languages, and his featured role in Shakespeare's *Pericles*, Gower has always suffered by comparison to his more illustrious contemporary, Geoffrey Chaucer. Yet the two poets were close and perhaps life-long friends. We know about this friendship from several documentary sources, including one granting Gower power of attorney for the duration of Chaucer's 1378 trip to Italy (the later trip imagined here is my own invention). There are also several moments in which the two poets speak to one another within the lines of their verse. One of these, an apostrophe addressed by Chaucer to 'Moral Gower' near the end of *Troilus and Criseyde*, has largely shaped the critical perception of Gower's character.

The protagonist of *A Burnable Book* is a more . . . let's say *compromised* Gower. In exploring the darker sides of his character, his family, and his friendships, I have been guided above all by the poet's own writing: by the bleak, even nihilistic tone one often finds him adopting toward the many subjects he treats.

For particular details of Gower's life and circumstances (including the encounter along the Thames with King Richard, based on the highly stylized account in the *Confessio Amantis*), I have relied on the scholarship of Robert F. Yeager, Derek Pearsall, Candace Barrington, John M. Bowers, Andrew Galloway, Jonathan Hsy, and Diane Watt, whose work sparked some of my initial thinking about the poet's shadier side. If the John Gower imagined here strikes specialists as untenable or overdone, I hope they will attribute this in part to the poet's own sense of our collective estrangement from the ever-changing world around us. As Gower puts it near the end of his greatest work, 'I know not how the world is went.'

Acknowledgments

G.K. Chesteron once called Geoffrey Chaucer a 'poet of gratitude,' a writer 'positively full of warm acknowledgment'. Of all the poet's qualities, this is perhaps the easiest to imitate. Over the years I have accumulated many debts to friends, colleagues, and correspondents who have leant support of various kinds, from careful readings to open ears and ready pints. They include Linda Blackford, Carol Blount, Heather Blurton, Andrew Cole, Edward Dusinberre, Mark Edmundson, Katherine Eggert, Dyan Elliott, David Gies, Jennifer Hershey, Jen Jahner, William Kuskin, Jana Mathews, Deborah McGrady, Christian McMillen, Howard Morhaim, John Parker, John Pepper, Caroline Preston, Patrick Pritchett, Myra Seaman, Lisa Russ Spaar, Emily Steiner, Beth Sutherland, John Stevenson, Michael Suarez, Christopher Tilghman, Cynthia Wall, and Mark Winokur. Paul Fox, chairman of the Heraldry Society, advised me on some of the finer points of royal heraldry in the Edwardian and Ricardian age. Amy Appleford shared her knowledge of burial practices for the poor of London. Paul Strohm, formerly the J.R.R. Tolkien Professor of Medieval Studies at Oxford and an endless reserve of knowledge about medieval London and its culture, read the manuscript in an early draft and made numerous suggestions about setting, chronology, and historical detail. Andrew Galloway and Claire Waters read the book meticulously and with careful attention to details of idiom and language.

As a teacher of medieval culture I am also indebted to the scholars whose formative teaching exposed me to the wonders of the medieval world—its history, its books, its literature, its music, its theology, and its art. Thanks to Teodolinda Barolini, Christopher Baswell, Marvin Becker, Caroline Walker Bynum, Rita Copeland, Consuelo Dutschke, Joan Ferrante, Carmela Franklin, Barbara Hanawalt, Robert Hanning, Ron Martinez, Linda Neagley, Susan Noakes, and David Wallace.

The editorial teams at HarperCollins (UK) and William Morrow (US) have shepherded this book through the complex and exciting process from contract to publication. I am deeply indebted to Julia Wisdom and Rachel Kahan, who acquired A *Burnable Book* and saw it through revisions and production, for their wisdom, support, and patience. Thanks also go to Emad Akhtar, Ben Bruton, Trish Daly, Jaime Frost, Tavia Kowalchuk, Ashley Marudas, Rachel Meyers, Anne O'Brien, Aja Pollock, and Kate Stephenson.

My marvelous agent, Helen Heller, plucked a manuscript out of her slush pile and took a chance on an unproven writer of turgid academic prose. She read multiple drafts of this book with her unique blend of patience and severity. Her support, dedication, and pep talks have meant the world to me (as have her unflinching critiques).

My parents, Sheila and Harry Holsinger, deserve endless gratitude for the selfless support they have given me over a lifetime; as do Carol Holsinger, Eric Holsinger, and Anna Jullien, my siblings, for their constancy and love; Betsy and

Bob Brickhouse, my in-laws, for their warm friendship and encouragement; Campbell and Malcolm, my sons, for all the joy, energy, and soccer; and Anna Brickhouse, for love, brilliance—everything.

John Gower returns in…

THE INVENTION OF FIRE

London, 1385. Young King Richard II faces the double threat of a French invasion and growing unrest amongst his barons – and now there's evil afoot in the City. Sixteen corpses have been discovered in a sewer, their wounds like none seen before. One thing is clear: whoever threw the bodies there knew they would be found – and was powerful enough not to care.

Enter John Gower, poet, intellectual, and trader of secrets. Against the backdrop of medieval London with its grand palaces and churches, dark alleys and mean backstreets, Gower pursues his dangerous quarry. Seeking insights from his friend Geoffrey Chaucer and using his network of contacts, Gower comes to the shocking belief that the men have been killed by a new and deadly weapon of war.

Known as 'the handgonne', it will put untold power into the hands of whoever perfects its design. But who has commissioned this weapon? A man who will stop at nothing to achieve his secret goal…

Coming in January 2015